A STRANGER'S EMBRACE

Condemned as a witch, sensuous, strong-willed Linness of Sauvage bravely faces her doom—until a gallant knight comes to her aid and rescues her from the flames. But after a night of magnificent passion, her dashing champion vanishes. And Linness must escape the still-pursuing mob by posing as a nobleman's betrothed.

A KISS IN THE NIGHT

Banished from the realm for his heroic deed, Paxton Gaillard Chamberlain is haunted by the memory of the exquisite enchantress who claimed his heart on that rapturous, unforgettable eve. Now fate has called him home, where his beloved Linness dwells in the house of his powerful, despised brother—closer than Paxton dared to dream, yet more forbidden than ever . . . forcing the handsome knight to risk all in the sacred cause of a love magically destined and gloriously true.

Other Avon Romantic Treasures by
Jennifer Horsman

VIRGIN STAR
WITH ONE LOOK

*If You've Enjoyed This Book,
Be Sure to Read These Other*
AVON ROMANTIC TREASURES

COMANCHE RAIN *by Genell Dellin*
MY LORD CONQUEROR *by Samantha James*
ONCE UPON A KISS *by Tanya Anne Crosby*
PROMISE ME *by Kathleen Harrington*
SHAWNEE MOON *by Judith E. French*

Coming Soon

TIMESWEPT BRIDE *by Eugenia Riley*

JENNIFER HORSMAN

A KISS IN THE NIGHT

An Avon Romantic Treasure

AVON BOOKS ◆ NEW YORK

A KISS IN THE NIGHT is an original publication of Avon Books. This work has never before appeared in book form. This work is a novel. While inspired by a true event, neither the story nor the characters should be construed as real.

AVON BOOKS
A division of
The Hearst Corporation
1350 Avenue of the Americas
New York, New York 10019

First Avon Books Printing: July 1995

AVON TRADEMARK REG. U.S. PAT. OFF. AND IN OTHER COUNTRIES, MARCA REGISTRADA, HECHO EN U.S.A.

Printed in the U.S.A.

RA 10 9 8 7 6 5 4 3 2 1

Chapter 1

France, 1513

Three ropes bound Linness of Sauvage to the pole, one at her shoulders, one at her waist, and one at her feet. The kindling sticks formed a small mountain below her.

She looked across the courtyard to see Bishop comte de Berry. The man, with his one hideously white blind eye, stared up to the heavens. A crimson cap covered his balding head, matching the long rich robes that draped his stocky frame, all of the finery splashed with mud now and pressed against his frame by a goodly breeze. His hands held the parchment where the edict was writ. She and two others had been condemned by the ecclesiastic court to burn at the stake. A half dozen priests and monks followed behind him. Two of the brown-robed monks held torches, while one held the torture-saving noose.

They had all witnessed her short trial.

"How did you know Mistress Franz's third child was breeched?"

"I am a seer. I have the sight."

1

"From Satan! The Bible says—"

"Nay." She shook her head, horrified at the charge. " 'Tis from heaven. I have seen angels and heaven. Like our Lord Christ, I only help the poor and common folk—"

"For avarice!"

She lied, "Only what folks can pay!"

"Deceit and treachery . . ."

The girl was possessed. . . .

Linness stared at the noose. If you confessed your crime and begged for God's forgiveness, they would snap your neck before the flames licked at your skin. She dropped her head to the small mountain of kindling sticks at her feet before lifting her gaze to heaven.

Save me, Mary, I am not strong!

Twice as many knights as priests followed behind the imperial man. They were knights of the bishop's guard, the Jesuit priests, here to fight the advancing menace of the archpriest once and for all. More knights manned the feeble battlements that surrounded the abbey walls. The village of Sauvage beyond the walls was burning bright. Thick smoke filled the air as the people wailed against this senseless loss. The outlawed army— made up of fifty demons wearing men's skins— had demanded the bishop's coffers and treasures, or promised death to everyone and everything with a heart. The foolish bishop had refused. He had sent word to faraway Gaillard, and Rouergue, begging the lords of these places for knights to fight the archpriest who had terrified the French countryside for two years now and had eluded even the royal knights of Francis, the king of France.

As he waited for these knights he thought to pacify the peasants and God by a sacrifice of the burning of the unfaithful in return for His mercy. Fingers had then quickly turned to her, fingers had always pointed at her.

The common folks fanned in a perfect half circle behind the priests and knights. Some shouted curses up at the condemned. Others cried hysterically that the world had ended and the apocalypse had begun, while most of the poor chanted prayers that begged for salvation.

Outside the wooden stakes of the abbey walls, black smoke poured from the burning village nestled along the hillside and billowed into the sky above. The outlawed brigandine army shot flaming arrows over the battlements. They were close. Screams sounded in the distance. A baby wailed furiously, trying to escape the safety of her mother's arms as she knelt in prayer. The smell of fire filled the creatures with fear: The hounds bayed angrily, tugging at their ropes in the kennel, horses neighed and kicked helplessly, and the pigs, with their eerily humanlike screams, called out from the pen. Two goats raced across the courtyard, searching for an exit.

The bishop and his priests stood before the old woman first. She, too, was tied to the pole, kindling sticks piled beneath her bare feet. The gray hair formed a perfect halo about her head; her old, dark eyes were blank and unseeing with the ignorance of the truly mad. Unaware of what was happening to her, she smiled down at the audience of priests, who appeared as black and brown silhouettes against the gray sky. She nodded at the familiar faces among them, mumbling bits and pieces of the rosary that she remembered.

Linness knew the old woman well; everyone in the Sauvage valley knew her. Old mad Mistress Grilldue. She had been born in the year Mercury crossed Venus in the twelfth month, an auspicious sign borne out by her sixty-odd years of a rich life, but one fated to end in violence. The many times Linness had told the old woman's fortune, she had never told of the tragic death she had foreseen. She had never mentioned the ropes or the flames. And what bitter irony that she never saw herself in this picture.

Long ago, when Mistress Grilldue had been in the first blush of her beauty, she had caught the eye of the late Charles de St. Pol, a minor land baron of Sauvage. She had given him a cherished daughter and he had given her a sturdy stone house on the hillside and all the land to the river. Her grief, upon witnessing her daughter's death, was too great to fit in her heart; it spilled into her mind and had made her go mad. The poor, witless common folks were easy prey for the church's voracious appetite for land. After convening for less than five minutes, the court decided her madness was demonic possession and her punishment was death at the stake.

Linness had shaken her head when she heard how the bishop had proclaimed that if the church rid the Sauvage valley of the unfaithful, God would send an avenging army of righteous knights to reach them in time and beat back the outlawed army at the abbey gates. Such a foolish old cock! she had thought. Prancing about in his fine crimson robes, screeching about the devil and damnation with nary a word about heaven and hope and our dear Mother Mary . . .

Yet now the old woman's eyes, feverish from the light of the fire, focused on the bishop's crimson robes as he called up to her, "Do you renounce your pact with Satan and accept Christ as your Lord and Master, and Savior of all sinners?"

The old woman looked to the darkening sky and coughed.

The bishop repeated the words as if it were a question of deafness. "Do you . . ."

The crowd shifted nervously, waiting for her "aye." A terrified, squawking chicken flew into the midst of the people. A shuffle ensued as they attempted to shoo away the bird. A man grabbed it and snapped its neck.

Linness felt it as if it were the snap of her own slender bones. As if she had suddenly woken in a nightmare played in the light of day. Her heart pounded wildly against this destiny.

She did not want to die! She was too young! She wanted to live!

In her mind's eye she saw the life she had yet to live. She was unmarried still, a virgin. She had never felt a man's lips on her mouth or his flesh in her womb. She had never seen her child's face or felt a mother's love. A hundred as yet unlived events came to her: She had never worn silk, walked in Notre Dame, tasted an orange, played a harp, or sat at a royal feast. . . .

Linness watched in horror as the bishop motioned to the priest who held the deadly torch. The priest dropped the torch to the sticks. Red flames washed up the pile of sticks. "Mistress Grilldue! Mistress, please to God! Look at me!"

The old woman's weary eyes turned to Linness and found something familiar in those silvery depths. "Say aye!" Linness cried to her. "Aye!"

Mistress Grilldue suddenly gasped in fright as the flames consumed the mountain of wood beneath her feet, and leapt up toward the pole. Her weathered gray head pressed back against the pole in alarm. Her eyes went wild with panic.

"Merciful Mother Mary, save her!" Linness screamed again, "Say aye!"

Shocked, as if waking from a long sleep, the old woman nodded, and in a weak whisper at last said, "Aye . . ."

Relief swept through the crowd; nearly everyone dropped to the knees with praise to God. The bishop motioned to the priest holding the noose at the end of a long pole, who slipped the rope around the old woman's head. A guard stepped forward and laid hands on the pole. The two men jerked the noose upwards and the old body convulsed at the instant painless death.

Linness collapsed with relief.

From over the wall, a flaming arrow landed on the stables and set the thatched roof on fire. People screamed in terror before three men rushed into the burning building to free the trapped animals. Two dogs and a horse raced out. Then another hound raced out with yelps and whimpers as two more horses followed. A line of men and women formed to pass buckets from the well. The nearby fence of the pigpen also caught flames and a kitchen servant rushed round to open the gate for the crying pigs, which rushed screaming into the courtyard.

A great crash came from outside. For the first time fear showed on the bishop's face. He stared ahead at the burning body of the old woman, as if he realized that the burnt bodies would not be enough to save the abbey.

The gates would have to be opened soon. The outlawed army would sweep inside and slaughter everyone and everything. Horses might be spared if the men could stop their blood madness. Most often they couldn't. The bishop's head would be the prize.

But the bishop was going to serve his own blood-lust first. He looked at his second victim, turning his blind eye away from the face of his death in order to see another's. The old Jew, known as Saul, was the finest boot maker in the whole valley. Linness knew him well, too. He was in his fifties, with short, curly hair, still black, unmarked by gray, giving him a much younger appearance. His beard touched his naked chest. Only a loincloth covered his thin frame. Red welts from the lash of a whip marked his chest. He did not mind renouncing his faith, for he had done so many times before to save his life, but the court had had to torture him repeatedly to get his confession of collusion with Satan.

She and Saul had been friends since she was twelve, shortly after she had settled here at the Sauvage valley. She had sought his skill for her first pair of lady's slippers. A red pair, the fashionable kind with the toes curled up in a loop. How she had loved those slippers. He had made them, then laughed at her foolishness when she bemoaned the fact that they made her large feet look even larger. They had often broken bread together after that. He was a simple, good, and kind man who had suffered enough in his life, God knew. Enough. His wife, his sister, and a brother-in-law had died on

the stake after being indicted by the Spanish In-
quisition. And he had fled to the safer shores of
France. Only to finally face the same death here
now.

Anger suddenly overwhelmed her fear.

Merciful Mother, stop this madman!

"As God is my witness," she began, but stopped
as the stable roof collapsed. Flames shot up thirty
feet from the burning stables.

"Open the gates!"

The shout came from a man in the water line.
Fire licked the sides of the building as the walls
began to collapse. The man dropped the bucket and
fell to his knees, shouting, "We are doomed!"

Screams sounded from all round. More people
dropped to their knees. Guards turned to the gate
and back to the bishop, awaiting his orders. The
fire leaped to the stone wall of the abbey keep,
scorching it. Red sparks flew about in the breeze,
landing at last on the roof of the gatehouse.

" 'Tis the Armageddon come at last!"

"The Antichrist is among us!"

The bishop ignored the pandemonium, the pleas,
everything but his purpose. Linness cried at the sad
resignation on Saul's face as the bishop commanded him to renounce his God and religion in
the name of all that was holy. Saul did, nodding
with a loud "Aye!"

Linness squeezed her eyes shut as the noose
slipped over his head and his neck was snapped.

"Mother Mary . . . who art . . . in heaven . . ." She
gasped each word as hot tears fell down her cheeks,
brought from the sting of smoke. She could not
breathe. For one wild moment she thought she was
on fire already. She fought furiously with her binds.

"Save me! Oh, please save me! I am too young to die, too filled with life yet. I want to live to know a man and bear his child! Oh, please let me live to have a child! I promise to use my sight for profit no more; as long as I shall live, I shall use it only to serve God. This I swear!"

A strange tingling shot through her limbs. She opened her eyes to see the noose in front of her face. She shook her head frantically, sending the long plait of dark hair swinging wildly over her breasts. She cast her gaze to Saul, hanging lifelessly from the pole as flames spread up and over him. The air filled with the sick scent of burnt flesh. She cried out as Saul disappeared in the smoke.

"Do you renounce your pact with Satan and accept Jesus Christ as Savior—"

She knew the words. "Aye! Aye! With all my heart!"

The priest moved the noose to her head and she screamed, "No! No!" She shook her head in terror, the movement tearing the strap that held her tunic in place. "Please! I do not want to die! For mercy's sake! I'll take each moment more of life given by the torture of the flames! Let me burn alive!"

The bishop gasped, drew back slightly as if slapped. The other priests genuflected to ward off this certain sign that the devil spoke through the girl. Holding tight to the torch, the wide-eyed priest stared hard at the Bishop, awaiting his signal to ignite the wood beneath her. The bishop stared at the girl. Her tunic had slipped to her small waist, revealing the untouched white skin of her heaving bosom, her arresting, beautiful face twisted with the agony of these last moments.

The Bishop's eyes narrowed with outrage. He

shot a glance at the priest and nodded. The priest lowered the torch. Firelight changed her silver eyes to red as she stared at the flames that would bring her death.

"Mother Mary, Mother Mary, Mother Mary!"

A tingling sensation shot through her limbs again. The fire grew, smoke streaming up the column and filling her chest. Tears poured from her closed eyes in protest.

There came another great crash and the gates opened at last. Mounted knights and foot soldiers rushed into the keep. The Gaillard army the bishop had sent for clashed viciously with the last throng of the archpriest's army. With screams and shouts, the bishop and his priests rushed away from the flames to the castle keep. Thundering horses' hooves clamored into the courtyard, more and more. The clang of swords sounded weak against the hungry ravishment of the fire. She couldn't see through the smoke. Gray and black clouds formed a swift-moving stream that shot right up to her face. She coughed and coughed, until she collapsed, her chest convulsing in desperation for the mercy of air.

A spark caught her hair and she screamed as it touched her tunic. No sound issued from her choked and scorched lungs.

Lord Paxton Gaillard Chamberlain sent his sword across the foot soldier's thighs, disarming him but leaving him mercifully alive when he turned back to see the girl through the smoke. Like a nightmare, he saw a young, half-naked girl bound to a pole and set on fire. His heart trembled violently as he forced his warhorse into the burning logs beneath her bare feet. Horse's hooves crashed over burning wood. A sword sliced through the air and she was suddenly falling, falling into burning embers. A strong arm circled her waist and for one wild moment she imagined she flew up to heaven again. She was thrown stomach side down over a warhorse and she held onto the horn with all her strength, coughing, choking, her eyes burning with smoke.

Her rescuer swung his sword in a wide arc, connecting to the metal of another sword, to send it flying through the air. From the corner of her eye she watched him thrust the sword through the edge of another knight's metal chest plate and withdraw it bloodied, leaving the knight screaming as he dropped to the ground.

His black-gloved hand came to the slender arch of her back. A tingling shot up her spine. An arrow hit the rider's chest, bouncing off his metal plates, slipping over her legs and to the ground.

She remembered little after that. Ashes and smoke swirled about her. The world turned vicious with the sound of screams, the furious clang of swords, the terrified neighs and thunder of hooves as the rider slew four men in his way. Curses and screams sounded in a symphony of terror. Within minutes the stables, pigpen, and kitchen were in smoldering ruins. Blood splattered across his horse and hit her legs. She squeezed her eyes tight.

From seemingly far away she heard the man who held her shout, "These fires smell of the foul deeds and our holy church. Hang the culprits from the battlements!"

"Aye, my lord!"

"Ready the remaining ranks. Send out half in search of my brother's wife. The other half goes to chase the retreating army! Let no one escape!"

He turned his horse through the gates and suddenly there was fresh air in her lungs, the sweetest mercy shot straight from heaven. She coughed and sputtered and coughed some more. The thick leather saddle massaged her midsection hard while the gallop of the warhorse slammed her against the saddle so that she couldn't think to understand what was happening. She couldn't think past the purest joy of drawing sweet air into her body.

Blue summer sky rose overhead. Soft white clouds scattered against the blue, oblivious to the march of human folly below. The horse headed to the wooded foothills behind the burning village. Trees began to appear, spruce and beech with long silver trunks and spiky tops. More and more brambles grew in bright green clumps, and in places these bushes reached over six feet. Green beds of undergrowth crowded beneath the shade of the very thickest part of the forest. The sound of running water filled the warm air.

The knight stopped his horse. He swung down and turned to help Linness. Too late. She was sliding off the horse already. Her feet touched the ground. Her silver eyes searched the familiar surroundings, as if to determine for a fact she was still on earth. When this miracle was perceived and felt, it washed her in an emotional ebullience so swift, so powerful, as to be a kind of madness.

She dropped to her knees laughing and crying. She kissed the green earth ten times before she lifted her lovely eyes to the heavens as she thanked Mary over and over.

Then she started dancing.

She leaped up with the words, "I'm alive! I'm

alive!'' She turned in fast circles, laughing and crying. "I'm alive!"

Paxton's dark blue eyes watched the girl dance like a Gypsy in firelight. His heart still thundered violently, pumping the battle rage hard and fast through his tall, muscled frame. His broad chest heaved with the girl's own thirst for fresh air. He had not slept, eaten, or drunk for two days as he led his Gaillard knights in chase of the outlaws terrorizing the countryside. Now, in the aftermath of battle and for the first time in his warring life, he felt it. The battle lust.

The girl's very same madness filled him; the madness brought by having faced the certainty of death a dozen times, only to find now, quite unexpectedly, he was suddenly very much alive. And the need to celebrate this miracle came in an explosion of desire.

An explosion that caught his breath and nearly knocked him over as hot blood engorged his groin and tightened each second he watched this strange and magical wood creature fly across the forest floor. With her arms spread wide, her head tilted, her mysterious cloudy eyes filled with the joy of the living.

Her loosened hair, singed at the ends, fell in a stream of dark ringlets down her back. Her comely face was flushed and smudged with ash, her eyes lit with madness and joy. She wore only the odd tunic of a condemned woman and the cloth hung about her small waist, down to her bare knees. Her legs were long, slim, and pale. Her bare breasts, dear Lord, were full and ripe, more tempting than heaven, brushed by the streams of her dark hair.

He removed first his blood-soaked gloves, then

he began unlacing his heavy leather jerkin and the heavier haubert underneath. For the first time in his life he wished to God for a page or squire. He could not get his clothes off fast enough. She looked wild and mad and more beautiful than any maid he had ever seen. His hands trembled with his need to touch her, to cup the softness of her breast, to lay her down to the soft moss of the bank and part her thighs.

Linness felt Mary's blessing cascading over her like a stream of warm tingling caresses. She closed her eyes and held perfectly still, wiping at her wet cheeks, overwhelmed with gratitude. She was alive. . . .

The strange stillness and whispers of the forest came to her in a sudden heightening of senses. She heard the running stream, the slow plod of the warhorse moving to it, the rustle of the leaves overhead. A merlin called out in flight above. She listened to the little noises of footsteps, soft fringed wingbeats, her own pounding heart and deep breaths. Then she perceived his labored breaths.

She opened her eyes as her arms came over herself to protect her modesty. The knight stood a dozen paces away. The orange sun was setting behind him, casting him in a majestic glow. He stood unusually tall for a man, taller than any man she had seen before. Like all warriors, tightly corded muscles encased his towering frame and his bronze skin displayed more battle scars than stars set in the distant Milky Way. Red cuts and bruises were laid over these. His hair was light brown, streaked by the sun, and the only soft thing about him. His was not a handsome face, but she was struck by the compelling lure of its unnatural strength: his square-cut, too large chin, his hawkish nose and wide lips, thick brows that darted like wings over his black, widely spaced eyes. Absolutely black eyes. His bare chest had a mat of curly dark hair. His heavy clothes lay in a pile behind him: the leather metal-plated jerkin and chain mail, boots, helmet, and gloves. None of it mattered. Nothing mattered but the idea that presented itself to her.

In a whisper of wonder, she said, "Mary sent you."

The words were tossed up in the still air. She was unsure if he heard her. She was unsure if he was real. . . .

The idea disappeared as her gaze riveted to the mound of his raised manhood beneath his breeches. He was enormous; he would kill her. She started to shake her head in protest that rose from her virgin's fear.

"Aye," was all he said. All he had to say.

She froze, watching with widening eyes as he stepped towards her. *Mary sent him, Mary sent him,* she told herself over and over to keep herself still and give herself courage as he came to stand in front of her. He towered above her, a good foot taller, maybe more—and she was considered tall for a woman. She stared into his eyes, dark blue eyes, but appearing as black orbs reflecting her own pale and frightened face. Her senses filled with his scent made of fire and blood.

Her sight did not often come so forcefully.

It was like an opening into a kaleidoscope made of images drawn from his memories. First she saw him practicing the warring arts as a boy, then mounting his warhorse as a man. She saw the mangled bodies of his slain—and they were many. He

was discussing wine vats with an old man he
loved, a man with blue eyes that had lost their
shine but none of their wisdom. She saw him staring in wonder at fields of vines. She saw him studying books and paper by candlelight. Then he was
kneeling at the altar as he married a lady clad in
yellow velvet. She saw the woman's death and felt
his grief. There came to her mind a beautiful castle
surrounded by farmland and vineyards, and she
felt his love for this place. He was nursing a sick
hound that he loved, then helping children climb a
ladder to the hayloft where they swung from a rope
he had made. He joked and teased his peasant cottars and made them laugh. He was singing as he
bathed.

The string of images lasted a minute, no more,
and yet she now saw the shadow of a man who
loomed large over his life. A darkness that always
hung around him. This shadow was like a cold,
bitter wind he had to fight constantly against. This
shadow man was his brother.

He felt the intimate probe of her eyes. Silvery,
catlike, startling eyes. Beauty was considered
blond, blue-eyed, dainty like a wildflower. She was
the opposite. A steamy-eyed witch-child, sculpted
with flesh and bone, made of earth and wind and
fire.

He felt a stab of raw desire as he stood there
staring down. "Will you fight me, witch-child?"

The question was asked with incongruent gentleness. For a moment she lost herself to the compelling
lilt of his voice, French, aristocratic, deep, as his callused hands came to her slender shoulders. The
touch of the large hands went through her like a
shock. She drew a sharp breath, her eyes darting over

his face with confusion. She closed her eyes a moment, and struggled to find her courage.

She shook her head. Yet she asked, "Would it matter?"

A serious question. She saw him search his conscience, and what he said next made her know he was heaven-sent. "Aye, it would matter." His hands caressed the sculpted muscle of her slim back, and he leaned over to breathe deeply. The scent of lilacs and smoke was in the dark hair. "I would not want to hurt you. I don't think I could, and yet, my sweet temptress, and yet . . ."

He never finished. He swung her up in the air as if she were made of straw, and carried her to a mossy bank near the stream. Bracing her back with his arm, he lowered her against the green backdrop and came partially over her.

The press of their bodies brought on a jolt that left them both speechless. He closed his eyes, struggling up through the sweet assault on his senses. Raw, hot sensations washed over them, so many millennia removed from the Abbey of Sauvage, the ravages of the flames, or the bloodied battle fought and won there. So many millennia removed from anything on earth.

She stared up in astonishment, waiting for him to explain this magic. Excitement rushed through her veins like a potent fuel, pumped by her pounding heart and quick breaths. He brought her hands above her head and held them there with one of his own. She struggled to get enough air, and each intake of breath riveted her consciousness to the naked muscle and heat against her, the press of her breasts against his bare chest, his hard shaft against her side, his thigh pressed between hers.

His breath came hard and fast, too. His hair fell in a riot of curls around his handsome face. For a moment she thought he struggled with the same astonishment, but no, his pause was a desperate measure to catch the wild race of his desire. His struggle only grew as he drank the sight of her dark hair spread over the moss, studied the bewitching eyes and the beckoning of her parted lips, and felt the thrust of her breasts against his chest, a sudden flood of heat as she shifted beneath his weight.

She felt a tingling rush along the nerves of her arms and a tightening in the tips of her breasts, a hot swelling deep inside. She went very still as he watched her. Her shock was so virginal, he asked huskily as his lips grazed hers, "You handle like a virgin, my witch-child. Tell me you're not."

The question made her panic. She closed her eyes and tried to shake her head.

"Are you?" he asked again as he let his lips graze her mouth, gently biting her lower lip. Their breath mingled, and he closed his eyes, lost in the incredible sweetness of her scent. "Or were you sent by the heavens as an undeserved reward for my questionable service?"

She gasped with the shivers this caused. "Aye," she said in a whisper, "I was sent to you just as you were to me. You saved my life and I owe it to you now." She intended no melodrama; she meant every word. "I surrender my will; this humble gift is yours."

He ignored the questions posed by the girl's perfect courtly French. He did not want to know who she was or how she came to be condemned by the church. He didn't want to know anything, not the alchemy that changed brass to gold, nor the rhyme or reason of the rotations of the heavenly bodies. He wanted only to sink his flesh in the sweet mercy of hers. . . .

Desire had changed her features; her pale skin colored with heated anticipation, and he knew her pulse raced as fast as his. He forgot the question, forgot everything but the demanding immediacy of their joining. He brought his mouth down hard.

All panic exploded in a fiery burst as the kiss molded his lips to hers with a barely restrained force. Yet the lingering trace of his violence melted the instant he felt the exquisite softness of her mouth. One taste and it changed. He groaned deep in his throat as he brought her head back farther to drink deeper.

The hunger of his passion swept into her body and through her veins, more real, more urgent, than the blood flowing there. She felt the intrusion of his tongue and suffered the briefest moment of confusion and fear, until his tongue slid with tantalizing slowness over hers. She couldn't think or breathe or know anything past the enticing tease of his kiss, a feeling of melting into a shimmering pool of heat and need.

His warm, callused hand swept over her shoulder and pulled off the remaining strap of her tunic as he breathed deeply of her scent. "My God, you are soft. . . ." Cool air grazed her skin before his hand slid with unconcealed impatience over her shoulder and side to cup the high, full breast. She gasped as his large, warm palm soothed and stroked, massaging erotically, while catching her tiny gasps in his lips as he kissed her again. The slow thud of her heart dropped to her loins and made her arch her back as she tore her mouth from his with an anguished cry.

He caught the sound in his mouth. "You taste like the heavens, sweeter than life itself. I am lost, my witch-child. Lost . . ."

She opened her eyes with a question, only to find his attention driven by a force far beyond words or vision. His touch felt like warm licks of fire, feeding trembling shivers through her, soothing them, yet only to spark them anew. 'Twas a madness she could never have imagined before and she closed her eyes, dazed by the serums heating up in her body that made her want to writhe and squirm and cling to him. His warm lips began teasing her, beneath her ear and along her neck. Chills rushed from the spot, gathering below in a hot knot of sensation.

His firm lips came to her bare breasts. The shock of it went through her like a lightning bolt and she tensed with the unexpectedness of this action. He laved the swell until he reached the tip, circling it with a building swirl of wetness. He drew softly, then more swiftly, before moving on to the next waiting orb. Shivers exploded in rushes between her legs and she gasped for air as though her lungs were starving. She instinctively arched her back and her breasts rose to fit tighter against his lips.

A millennium had passed before he could think of anything but the ferocious need to bury his sex in this bewitching wild creature. His flesh trembled with the feel of her small body yielding, then tensing, then yielding again as he answered her cries and brought his mouth back to hers with a kiss that brushed his soul.

He lifted her thin skirt. He twisted, then turned

her undergarments until he finally ripped them from her. His hand fitted over her flat stomach, then lower....

The hot, tight ball in her loins seemed to leap at his touch, and without realizing it, her thighs parted as his warm fingers slipped over her sex. Bursts of pleasure answered the stroke of his hand. She felt her sex swell until she became wild and supple beneath him. She could tell that he could not wait. His hands slid under her buttocks, lifting her. Tingling anticipation rose in quivers, falling, then rising again as his smooth sex slid over hers again. She didn't know she was moaning, until the sound abruptly stopped as she felt a stab of pain.

He stopped instantly and closed his eyes as an unknown pleasure washed over him in hot waves. She was so small and hot and tight. "No, don't move," he said in answer to her fear, opening his eyes to peer into her closed ones. "Look at me, love." She did. "Look at the face of the man you will remember forever. Aye, forever, love. We are joined forever." His warm hand smoothed the hair from her forehead, his touch gentle, atoning. "I have not yet spoken your name, nor you, mine, and yet you will belong to me forever...."

Those words echoed in her mind. *Forever*. She understood the magnitude of them only partially, though she knew it was as certain and unalterable as the sun rising tomorrow. For Mary had sent him. And for a long moment as he held still and unmoving inside her, their gazes locked with a mystical understanding that brushed their souls and bound each to the other *forever*....

Strange dreams visited her as she slept nestled against his huge, warm body on the forest floor.

His male hips fitted tightly against her buttocks, his arm wrapped protectively around her form. She dreamt of those heated tremors, his lips on her neck, gently sucking, teasing. His hand slipped along the dramatic curve of her waist, over her hips and back again before cupping her breasts. She sighed, languidly arching her back to push her breasts into his warm palm. Her nipples grew hard and tight as he gently massaged them, over and over before his hand slipped over her flat stomach to nestle between her legs.

She came full awake. Her nerves went wild. Small pants and gasps escaped her lips as the hot, tight ball grew between her legs. Hotter as she felt the smooth stroke of his sex, the tingling warmth of his breath on her neck as he slipped inside of her. The erotic movement of their entwined bodies grew faster and faster until hot spasms of pleasure washed through her and she felt his huge body stiffen dramatically, and she was sinking, sinking into the darkness of sleep . . .

At first she only dipped below the surface of sleep, skimming along there like a fish in shallow water. She dreamt of the stars above, edged by the uppermost spikes of trees and suspended within the reach of her hand. A breeze rustled through the nightscape, carrying a winged version of Mary, smiling down at her sleeping form. Mary was trying to convey that this man was not sent to her, but that she had been sent to him. She could not reason why this mattered, but then nothing mattered, not heaven nor earth as she swam down deeper and deeper, nuzzling her nose to the sweet-scented earth and into the unending waters.

Lips brushed hers. Heated whispers rose in the

night. "The night has bound us forever. Just as you shall never forget me, I fear that I, too, shall never forget you. . . ." More whispered words, a warm caress. She nuzzled closer to the earth as the warmth left her, "Good-bye, my sweet virgin witch. . . ."

A woman dressed in black appeared before her then. Linness stared in surprise. The woman sat stiffly on a wooden chair surrounded by darkness. Her small, olive-colored hands sat on her lap, and that was all Linness could see of her. She wore a black dress. Black Italian lace covered her dark hair. A veil covered her face.

Time seemed to stop as Linness stared at the mysterious creature dressed in black. She knew without understanding that this mysterious woman was the most important person in her life. She did not know how or why. She struggled to make sense of the strange vision, but it was fading. Gray edged the perimeters of her vision until it strained the center. Then she was gone. . . .

The sun rose and she turned in protest, but the warm pulse of its heat finally roused her from the peaceful slumber. She opened her eyes, staring up into a piece of the blue sky above the treetops. Hunger gnawed at her and yet she felt so warm and blissful, as if she had slept a fortnight.

Dreamily she sat up and looked around her unfamiliar surroundings. The previous day's events came to her in a rush. Her gray eyes flew about the quiet forest floor. He was gone as if he never existed.

As they had lain in each other's arms after the first time he washed her soul with that dark and deep and sweet pleasure, she had asked, "Tell me your name?"

"Paxton . . ."

Paxton. Paxton. Paxton. She sang his name like a spell or incantation—the man who had taught her love on one magical night, who had washed her body in pleasure and carried her soaring through the heavens. *Paxton . . .*

Gone as if he never was, like a cherished memory or a vivid dream, he would live only in her heart and mind now. She tried to tell herself it was enough, one night was enough, but she understood the one night would cost a lifetime of longing. A lifetime . . .

She rose shakily to her feet and she saw her tunic laid across a stone. She moved to it, her silver eyes darting around the forest as if he might reemerge. She bent down and retrieved it, lifting it over her head and straightening it to cover her nakedness. She spent several anxious minutes righting the ripped strap before she saw it.

It was carved on the tree trunk behind the place where she had slept. She slowly approached the spot. A trembling hand reached to follow the lines he had carved.

A single star placed over a heart.

Star-crossed lovers, never to see each other again and yet never to be forgotten. As long as she lived, his would be the face she saw each night as she lay down to sleep, and the face swimming through consciousness in the mystical hours of morning that were neither sleep nor wakefulness.

A small notch had been carved in the tree. A gold necklace hung from it. She slowly picked it up. On the chain hung a ring. A bright emerald stone surrounded by diamonds on a thick gold band. She stared at the gift, more precious than the king's treasure box. It was all she had left of him, all she would ever have of him. The father of her child.

She slipped the necklace around her neck. Then she stood there, tracing the heart beneath the star, over and over, as his words echoed through her soul. "*. . . you will belong to me forever . . .*"

Finally she forced herself away. A new day had started and she had to decide what to do. She could never go back to her village or her home. The church would condemn her again immediately. But where could she go? What could she do? Where would she get shelter for herself and, praise Mary, her child, should she be so blessed?

She needed to see an omen of where she should go and what she should do. Standing very still, she searched the forest for the divine signal. Minutes gathered. Nothing happened.

She sat down. These things, she knew, sometimes took time. There was nothing to be heard but a gentle wind, the soft drone of heather bees, the trill of two skylarks against the trickle of the stream.

A movement in the forest caught her gaze. Sunlight streamed through two tall trees in the forest, their branches reaching up and entwined. A beautiful doe and her fawn walked below the entwined branches.

A good omen if ever there was one!

The enchanting sight was surely meant to assure Mary would be watching over her and guiding what was to happen to her. After all, Mary had saved her from death. Mary had answered her secret wish and sent her Paxton.

She would just start walking. Which way, though?

She looked for another sign. A sparrow lifted

from a tree and headed west. She smiled as she turned toward the west, her gaze still fixed on the little bird. He flew up and back around toward the south.

She stopped. Well, the south was a good direction too. . . .

Chapter 2

$\sim\!\!\!\curvearrowleft\!\!\curvearrowright\!\!\sim$

S unlight glinted from the round towers of the Château Gaillard, sparkling over the wide river that rushed through the valley. The château had been built from a castle's remains, and still showed many elements of the ancient castle. The stone structure rose at the southern end of the township of Gaillard, and Paxton, accompanied by two of his knights, rode at full speed through the outlying village to the gatehouse.

The château was an enormous structure, as large as Notre Dame in Paris and completely enclosed by a deep freshwater moat made by the river at its side. The wide moat circled the outer bailey, which was a three-story stone wall topped by battlements connected by wall walks. Surrounding the château were the domestic buildings: the knights' barracks and servants' building, the stables, piggery, garden, and exercise yard. There was a lesser bailey that enclosed the castle keep, its towers and forebuilding.

The famous Gaillard vineyards stretched up and over the hillsides in every direction. The barley, oat, and wheat fields reached from the north all the way to the valley's end. Thickly forested mountains enclosed the whole. This day was made of blue skies and bright sunlight, and the Gaillard valley, its castle, and the wealth of its rich farmland stole Paxton's breath. The profound beauty of his land would always strike him.

Nay, he thought, not my land. My brother's land. Morgan de Gaillard Chamberlain, his older brother by an absurdly meaningful two minutes. They had shared the space of their mother's womb for nine months, where even then Morgan had tried to squeeze him out; his brother had been born hale and heavy, a goodly weight for a babe, while he had been half his brother's size, frail and sickly and expected to die before the winter months were through. His mother and her ladies saw this at once—and to everyone this seemed to explain his mother's indifference to him and her blind adoration of his brother. And so it had begun, the joining of their two lives. They were like two rams that had locked horns in a battle, only the battle seemed to last forever. Brothers and enemies by turns of heart . . .

The warhorse thundered over the wooden planks that led to the gatehouse. Two guards rushed down the stone steps to greet Paxton, but he continued to stare straight ahead as he crossed over the moat and under the wide stone arch of the entrance keep. His knights galloped behind him. A trumpet sounded, alerting Morgan and his men to his brother's return. As Paxton came through the entrance gate, he first saw John Chamberlain, his uncle and his brother's steward. The older man rushed down the stone steps of the keep to greet him as well.

Paxton drew the horse up sharply, dismounting before the great stallion's legs crashed back to earth. His knights headed straight for the stables. Paxton's black cape billowed behind him as he approached his friend. The gray-haired man's gaze filled with anxiety, so much so that Paxton stopped and asked, "What say you, John?"

" 'Tis bad, Paxton, 'tis very bad. Henry returned just before you. He's in the hall with Morgan now, telling of . . . of lurid deeds that he lays at your feet."

Hands on hips, Paxton demanded, "What deeds be these?"

John met Paxton's level gaze, his arms reaching up to firmly grasp Paxton's muscled biceps, as if needing more of his nephew's attention. "Henry claims you abandoned the battle and carried off a condemned witch to the forest, that he followed you there and came upon your lustful coupling. He says you stayed away half the night, abandoning the search for Lady Belinda to lie with this witch."

Paxton swore softly, viciously.

A curious assortment of half-truths. Nay, he realized with sinking dread. 'Twas no half-truth. He had done just that. Worse, after the magic of the one night with his virgin witch, he would do it all again and again. The entire ride back he could think only of her, his witch-child, and how, as soon as he found the Lady Belinda, he would find the silver-eyed girl and bring her to Gaillard. Even now, he could close his eyes and see her with her strange beautiful eyes, her red mouth, the cascade of her hair, the curves of her slim form, her pants and cries as he filled her. . . .

He had no excuse. There was no explanation.

"Deny it, Paxton!"

Paxton's dark blue eyes seemed to turn black

with his thoughts; his gaze remained steady, unwavering. "I cannot."

Paxton's honesty was a rare thing, John well knew. Rare and presently regrettable. He shook his head in wonder of this ill news. "God's teeth, Paxton, if it be true, Morgan will not forgive you this."

Morgan had spent over two years negotiating the dowry and land acquisition for his marriage to Lady Belinda Saint de Beaumaris, daughter of baron and baroness De Beaumaris of Nancy. Two years. The discussion of the lady's travel plans alone had taken two months, every detail taken into account: the route, the number of knights to accompany the lady, footmen and their livery, the provisions for her serving woman, the inns to be stayed at, which party would pay for the knights' lodging, every detail gone over and worked out to mutual agreement.

Then word had arrived from faraway estates that the so-called archpriest, an outlaw who had been joined by fifty or so men, was relentlessly marching over the land, raping, pillaging, and setting to flame all villages and homes that could not pay his ransom. Paxton had wanted to gather Gaillard's knights and meet the army at once, but Morgan, like most other lords, said, "Nay, 'tis not our problem. Perhaps when they ride farther south..." Morgan's indifference, or what Paxton always saw as cowardice, had infuriated him. It always infuriated him. Then the Bishop comte de Berry's word had arrived and it was realized the Lady Belinda would be crossing this outlawed army's path on her way to Gaillard. The news had alarmed Morgan as nothing else could, and at last he had granted permission to Paxton and their men to ride out to battle the archpriest and rescue the Lady.

Now this lurid tale of a witch and a coupling . . .
He appealed to his uncle for help. "John . . ."

"Morgan swears he cannot forgive you this time.
He imagines you acted with malice of purpose, in
the perverse hope of denying him a wife and heir,
that he will see you banished—"

The great wooden doors above them opened at
that instant.

Morgan appeared on the top step between two
stone lion heads mounted there, the knights Henry
and Clifford behind him. Indeed Morgan's handsome face was filled with fury as he raced down
the steps, cursing Paxton's name.

Though twins, the two men did not look alike.
Paxton's face was arresting and the strength there
almost frightening; like John the Baptist, people always said. His brother was, by consensus, the more
handsome. And despite his auspicious head start at
birth, Morgan was not as tall as Paxton. Whereas
Paxton was built lean and muscular, like the warhorses he loved, Morgan was heavier of bone and
limb. Once as a tailor was fitting them, Paxton had
made everyone laugh by the wry comment, "From
the day we were born and every day since, my
brother has insisted on taking up more space than
me. . . ." His brother had darker hair, too, and dark
eyes. A full beard hid the same dramatic thrust of
square chin, softening Morgan's appearance somewhat, and with a far more modest nose than his
brother's, Morgan's features appeared regular and
more conventional, altogether less dramatic.

"Brother," Paxton started to explain as the two
men faced each other, his blue eyes offering sympathy when he knew it would not be accepted. "We

have not found the lady yet. We crushed the outlaw army and I have half my men searching for the lady, while the other half are chasing the renegades through the forest. I came to get—''

Paxton was utterly unprepared for the hard blow of Morgan's fist. Bent over, he put his hand over his face, trying to gain himself a moment to overcome the shock. Morgan waited the precious minute for Paxton to rise, and when he did, the silence that followed was filled with the weight of understanding.

The two brothers had grown up fighting each other, or rather Paxton had grown up enduring the near daily humiliation of being beaten to a bloody pulp by Morgan. The last time they had taken blows to each other, they were fifteen and both had returned to Gaillard from their individual stretches as squires. Paxton would never forget that day. Morgan had taken one look at him and knew that it would no longer be Paxton who suffered defeat in a physical battle. They were twenty-five now. These ten years had been filled with a lifetime of resentments and grievances, and as Paxton rose to his full height and looked at Morgan, he understood that he had waited for this moment all these years.

With the reflex honed by a hundred battles, Paxton's arm shot up to block Morgan's next blow, while his fist shot to Morgan's stomach. A grunt sounded before Morgan swung again, but Paxton ducked, swung back, and sent Morgan flying to the dirt.

John shouted for them to stop in the name of God and then their mother, but they were far beyond any reason now. As Morgan came to his feet again and lunged toward him, something snapped deep inside Paxton, letting loose all the rage he had suppressed all his life. Blow after blow followed. All too soon Morgan lay on the ground, his arms shielding his head, and still Paxton's fist pummeled his body.

Henry and Clifford leaped to pull Paxton off Morgan, but it was too late. Paxton was crazed. He turned his strength on them, and this saved his brother's life. The near deadly force of his blows dropped first Henry and then Clifford to the ground. Henry did not get up. Clifford lifted partially up, feeling his broken jaw, which would not move, and pain throbbing through his body.

Breathing heavily, Paxton stared in shock at his brother. John was lifting Morgan up in his arms. Morgan's lips were bloodied. He spat out more blood and wiped at his mouth with a trembling hand. One eye was swollen shut, but his other eye searched for and found Paxton several feet away.

He hid none of his hatred as he pronounced the punishment. "The lady will be dead now!" He tried to catch his breath, feeling the dull ache of a broken rib. "And I lay her death at your whoring feet!" He struggled up to stand, needing to face Paxton as he said his last words. "I banish you forevermore from my Gaillard, do you hear me? Banished! By God, if I ever see you here again, I will have your head hung from the battlements! This I swear!"

Paxton heard John and Clifford gasp in shock, and watched as the older man he loved and trusted immediately stepped between them and tried to make Morgan take it back. Morgan pushed him away violently. It was too late. The words had been said.

Banished forevermore . . .

Paxton turned his back to Morgan for the last time.

A sudden grief almost dropped him to his knees. Only the absolute refusal to ever suffer another humiliation at his brother's hands kept each booted foot moving until he reached his waiting horse. He mounted and turned the beast away, not daring to take a last glance at the land, its château, and the people he loved. With his back ramrod-straight, he stared only ahead to the road that led away from Gaillard and into an uncertain future.

"Good riddance, brother mine," Morgan said, his voice rising to cross the distance as if it might possibly reach all of Gaillard. "I want no one to mention his name to me ever again. I have at last finished with my nemesis, my brother, my enemy in this life."

Linness still remembered the night her mother had crept up behind her with a thick wooden staff and struck her hard across her head. She had just turned five. Thunder and lightning had lit the darkened sky. She had been standing in the doorway of their small stone cottage, watching the rain fall in sheets. The river where her *maman* had taught her to swim was rising. Mud had poured from the hilltop behind the cottage, rising halfway to the window and making her mother say, "God have mercy," over and over. A vicious cough kept interrupting the prayer, reducing it over and over to pitiful gasps for breath.

Poor, poor *Maman* . . .

Water from the well had spilled over, making it look like a fountain. It had made a puddle in the front of the house. She remembered her excitement as she thought she could swim in it in the morning, how, if she grabbed a log and made a sail, it would carry her out to the sea where she would at last see Neptune. Her mother had told her the magical stories of Neptune, Zeus, Athena, and all the gods of olden times. She loved these gods very much. They were not like the prickly cruel God of the church, though she must not say this out loud, she knew. Her mother told her, "A body could burn for that heresy. . . ."

She had clapped her hands as the puddle grew deeper and wider still, lapping now at the side of the sheep's water urn and against the old tree trunks. The animals had been brought inside. One of the sheep, Monsieur Henry, named after a king, nudged her hand, where he often found treats, baying when the little girl held out her open hand for inspection. He licked it anyway and she giggled. The chickens had been brought inside, too. They filled the cottage with a musty scent of wet feathers. They cried and *bawk*ed and her mother cried too because the moist air made her cough worse.

Poor, poor *Maman* . . .

She knew it was her mother creeping up behind her because she heard her cough. She started to turn to her and from the corner of her eye had seen her mother holding a staff high over her head. It was the last thing she remembered from this world, because the violent act sent her to another place, into the world of the spirits and the unborn and God.

She beheld heaven.

Infused with a strange and magical light that was benevolence, she understood the light was God. An angel, Mary, spoke to her without words, telling her she was not yet ready to leave the earthly world below, but that her mother would be coming to be with Mary in heaven. But first her mother was to take her to the Benedictine Abbey, where the good sisters would love and cherish her.

She remembered wanting to explain that she didn't want to go to the abbey, that she would very much like to go to the ocean to see Neptune, but there were no words in this place. Then Mary began showering her with love as a warm light cascaded over her and changed her forever.

The contrast between the dream and reality had been startling when she finally opened her eyes again. Her head hurt and her mother hovered over her with a warm cloth. The sun shined through the clouds and the rain had stopped. Her mother coughed blood into a cloth. Once upon a time her mother had been beautiful, but the cough made her look old and haggard.

"Poor, poor *Maman*," Linness said gently. "Mary's taking you to heaven soon. Mary said I must go to the abbey." The silvery eyes widened with sudden hope. "*Maman*, I want to swim. In the big puddle."

"Linness, did you see the blessed Mary?"

"Aye. She was beautiful. I want to swim. . . ."

Her mother had nursed her until she was well enough to make the four-day journey to the abbey. In truth her mother's coughing fits made the journey slow, but Linness was glad for it, for her mother had told her many strange and sad stories that she never forgot. And they were all she had of her.

Her mother had also taught her the story they

would tell the sisters. This story was made of truths and lies, all mixed up, so that first it became a confused jumble in her mind, and then, when they had finally reached the white stone abbey nestled in a valley surrounded by high green hills, Linness believed every word she told the abbess.

Only the richest and most noble families could afford the dowry the church required to accept a child into its many religious orders. The noble families who could afford the hefty fortune usually gave up one and sometimes two children to the church. The child was then educated, taught to read and write and molded to assume a place in the order, be it priest or nun. To have a child accepted was considered one of the greatest blessings. It was known as the easiest and most expedient means of getting to heaven.

Linness's mother was a poor woman, barely etching a meager living from a small plot of land and fingers put to a spindle. God had graced her with an unusually bright, beautiful, and healthy child whom she loved more than life itself. She had known death waited nearby and there was no one with whom she could leave her little girl. She had to somehow get Linness into the abbey as a novitiate before she died. Her desperation had given rise to this far-fetched plot. The blow to her head was to create a convincing bump. She'd tell the sisters her little girl was struck by lightning and lived; that 'twas a miracle they could not ignore. She hoped it was enough to win a place for Linness, and when God Himself aided the effort by taking the child, even momentarily, up to heaven, she knew it would work.

"Lightning struck me here." The little girl

pointed, proud of the bump. Five nuns had already examined it before they had led the little girl down a clean corridor to the wooden door that had a cross hung on it. An older woman, The Abbess Constance, sat inside. She wore a white robe that reminded Linness of Mary. "It shot me up to heaven."

The abbess's eyes widened, and she cast an uncertain gaze to her underling, standing to her side, who crossed herself.

The beautiful silvery eyes sparkled with all the attention; she beamed with pride. "I talked to Mary, who is an angel. God was there too," she added in an afterthought.

Then the little girl's gaze had faltered; she bit her lip. "Part of that is not the truth."

"Oh?" The abbess had inquired. "Which part, my child?"

"Mary did not really talk, 'cause there is no talking." She brightened suddenly with a smile that could affect the most cynical, which the good abbess was not. "It was like thinking-talking." Her beautiful little face changed with sadness, like a capricious shift of wind. "Mary said my *maman* was going to heaven and that I must come here. Mary said you would love and cherish me." She looked at them curiously. "Will you?"

The child would have convinced the pope of the miracle. In their three-hundred-year history the good sisters of the Abbey of Benedictine accepted their first charity novitiate. Still, they didn't know what they were getting into. Little Linness, whose name they had tried to change to Joan, without success, at first appeared so perfectly normal, a bright and charming little girl and nearly everyone's fa-

vorite. The precocious little girl with all those irrepressible questions, who was far happier in the
stables or climbing the green fields for wildflowers
than kneeling at vespers, was cherished and loved
by all.

And so the angel's prophecy came true.

Then one winter day as they rose before dawn,
after washing in preparation for morning prayers,
the good sisters led their four young novices down
the corridor to the galley. Linness turned to Sister
Teresa and said sadly, "Good-bye, Sister Teresa. I
shall miss you. Please say hello to beautiful Mary
and my *maman*."

"What are you talking about, child?"

"Why," she said, smiling, "the angels are coming. You shall fly up to heaven."

Sister Teresa grasped the nature of those words
and dropped into a faint. She never recovered and
she died two days later.

"Linness, how did you know Sister Teresa was
going to heaven?"

"I do not know. . . ."

She gave the same answer after the flood she had
foreseen had come, or when she knew a stranger
was going to arrive, or new orders came from
Rome where the pope lived. She gave the same answer after she saw the baby in Sister Carleta's
womb before there had been any sign. She also innocently revealed the father when Sister Carleta
had refused—Peter, the shepherd boy. She had
seen them rolling in the wildflowers. The abbess
had forced the two lovers to marry, knowing that
becoming the wife of a poor shepherd would be a
just punishment for breaking the holy vows.

By the time Linness was seven she began seeing

visions from people's past. She saw the good abbess herself, crouching behind a trunk in terror as the little girl watched her father beat her mother, and she made the abbess cry when she asked if she was still scared of her mean father. She saw the bishop sleeping in a big bed with an altar boy, and after she told this to the Abbess, and her face turned ashen, she had asked if they could sleep together, too. She knew Sister Marguerite's much-loved sister died the day before the message had come. Sorrow filled her large gray eyes as her thin arms wrapped around the older woman and she told her she was sorry that her sister had died but that she was certain she was happy in heaven. " 'Cause Mary's there and she is as warm and good as sunshine, and Mary loves her more than you . . ."

The abbess herself soon took over Linness's training and she began meeting with little Linness each morning after prayers. The abbess was a wise woman, extremely pious and devout, and little Linness's sight, more than anything, replenished her faith each day. She saw the little girl as holding one of God's graces; a gift to be used in service to God. That the child was sent from heaven, she had no doubt, and yet such a gift would be very harshly scrutinized if it were ever demonstrated to a larger audience. She began coaching the girl in the art of secrecy, her gentle authority and lessons given with tenderness and love.

During the winter of Linness's eleventh year, the abbess died. A simple death of influenza. Linness had not foreseen this tragedy; she would learn that her sight, while uncertain in the best of cases, was unreliable when directed at herself. Her light refused to turn inward. Instead she had developed a keen intuition to compensate, which saved her life.

The new abbess arrived from an abbey in faraway Italy. She was small and dark and spoke an unintelligible French. The new abbess watched the little girl with an unveiled suspicion, which grew instead of diminished as she repeatedly heard the other sisters gushing praise for her gifts and witnessed their unnatural fondness for the girl. Linness knew to be afraid of this new woman; she knew because her intuition made her hands go cold and clammy whenever they shared the same space and she felt the penetrating stare of those dark eyes come to her.

The new abbess sent for the famous bishop, Peter Luce, a man sent to examine all unusual members of the clergy. Linness heard the worried whispers of the sisters that this bishop found Satan lurking beneath every stone, but she took comfort by the addition "If our dear Linness were not so perfectly good and pure, she might be in danger. . . ."

All fear disappeared the day she saw him. For she was still at the age when goodness and a pleasing appearance made one and the same impression. She stared at the red crimson cap over his blond curls, his bright golden eyes and stiff shoulders. He was so handsome! She had been sure he would not hurt her.

Linness still remembered their first meeting. Two sisters had stood on either side and she was comforted by their familiar friendly presence as she knelt to kiss his jeweled hand. He had stared at her beautiful young face. His hand lifted suddenly to his gold crucifix and in a voice suffused with a lifetime of anger that lifted the hairs on the nape of her neck, he said, "How does thy dark presence make my crucifix shake?"

The sisters had gasped and drawn back. Bewildered eyes shot questioningly to his handsome face. "Milord?"

"Take her away. . . ."

The sisters had helped her escape before the trial. With nothing but the clothes on her back, and at the tender age of eleven, she had left the abbey and struck out for the wide world on her own. Just as she was doing now.

For once again she had nothing and no one. Nothing but the memory of a magical night spent with a man named Paxton. A man she would never see again. A man who had forever altered the course of her life . . .

The sunshine fell against Linness's bare arms and legs as she walked through the forest. She felt as if she still walked in a dream made by the warmth of his huge body cradled against hers, his lips on her neck, the hot pleasure of his flesh in her womb.

Oh Lord, how love burns bright and hot!

His name was seared upon her soul, a treasure to keep and cherish and—

"Ouch!" She lifted her foot, where she felt the sharpness of a pebble. She looked down at her bare feet with dismay. She did not even have shoes now, let alone shelter or food. She gathered up her unruly hair, twisting it into an unattractive knot at the nape of her neck. Paris beggars had better rags than she! Ash and dirt were smudged across her legs and arms, and no doubt her face. The late summer days were still warm, but winter would sweep upon the land soon enough.

And dear Mary, if she was with child, whatever

would she do? How could she even present herself in a township looking like this? Perhaps if she bathed and combed through her hair and if she found a shawl, just a shawl . . .

Lost to an unpleasant contemplation of her uncertain fate, she didn't notice the slain bodies at first. She was staring at a fast-moving river, its murmur of running water sounding a pleasant backdrop to the quiet of the forest. The name of the river started with a G, she knew, and it went through the rich vineyards south of here and all the way to the sea. She had to cross this river to the other side, where the road to the Midi lay less than a mile to the north.

The other side.

She first spotted a horse, his great head lowered as he picked at the grass. Behind a cluster of trees, she saw a coach. Her silver eyes darted back and forth until she began to make out the bodies. Five, no, six men and, dear God, yes, a lady!

A slain woman lay on the mossy bank, her green, rich-looking traveling clothes spread in a fan over the brighter moss. Her caul rested several feet away, pointing like a sundial to the sky.

Linness rushed to the water's edge as she called across, "Be anyone still alive? Please to God, answer! Be anyone still alive?"

A chill shot down her spine as she waded in the cold water. It reached her waist and she plunged into its depth. Strong, sure strokes carried her to the opposite side, slightly upstream. Dripping wet, she rushed upon the lady.

A very young lady—she could not be much more than her own ten and five years. A puddle of blood covered her chest. She was deathly pale and frigid cold. With a startled gasp, Linness saw the girl was quite dead. The devils who killed her had chopped off her fingers to get at her jewels.

"Oh, you poor, poor child . . ."

She rushed to a knight and caught her scream when she saw he was decapitated. She slowly approached another to see the same. Within minutes she saw they were all quite dead, mutilated, left for the night creatures to pick at. For a long moment she stared in shock at the gruesome sight, then shut her eyes tight, willing the bile in her throat down and down.

She backed away and fled into the forest. She ran until her lungs burned and her legs gave way. She dropped to her knees on the leaf-covered ground beneath the canopy of trees and with all the fierceness of her faith, she began to pray.

She prayed for their souls' salvation.

Those poor, poor people . . .

Minutes passed, collecting into an hour, and still she prayed. But hunger acts upon meditation, and taken with her exhaustion, the cataclysmic events she had just lived through, made her slip into a deep, dreamlike state. The forest teemed with nesting birds, rabbits' cautious gazes and prickling whiskers, the silent hooves of deer, the sly scurry of a hedgehog, the rustle of leaves and the shifting of light, and all of it faded in front of her. The prayerful meditation produced a miraculous calm that settled over her weary heart. The horror disappeared. She had been given grace in understanding that each member of the slain party, indeed all of life, was received by God in heaven and granted eternal peace. God's unmerited mercy over mankind . . .

She didn't see Mary as much as feel her presence. The question formed in her mind. As Mary's servant, what were her obligations to the slain party? Should she bury the bodies? There were no villages nearby that might offer help, as they had all been torn asunder by the archpriest and the avenging army, but it seemed possible she could drag the bodies to the river and let the water carry them out to the sea. Should she attempt this for mercy's sake?

The vision was swift, lasting no more than a second. She saw men with strong backs lifting the slain bodies into coffins, the coffins lowered to the ground, a humble priest singing their burial mass, and she need not worry over this but for one.

The slain lady. She saw herself dragging her body into the river. . . .

Then, suddenly the slain girl emerged in her mind. She was bending over her trunk, opening it for her. There were no words, but she understood the lady was giving her the things in her trunk, and somehow this offering meant much to this lady.

The kindness overwhelmed Linness; tears sprang to her eyes, and as her heart opened with an outpouring of gratitude, there came a warning. Not a warning but an order, a demand of a favor in return for her trunk, and it was as clear as if she had spoken the words. "Be you kind to my mother as I never was; give that good woman the daughter she never had and take great care with her love. . . ."

And then suddenly Linness awoke from this meditation and found she was staring into the forest. 'Twas so strange, these revelations! She was relieved the bodies would be properly buried. And she assumed the mother was Mary in heaven. She knew well to obey; the slain lady need not have warned her to take care with her love. For she loved Mary with all her heart. And Mary had answered her prayers and sent her the slain woman's trunk, along with a blessing.

She rose shakily to her feet. She turned toward the direction of the river, where the slain bodies lay. She genuflected and drew a deep breath. They were but flesh now; their souls had transcended. They would be buried soon.

She was offered the finery in the trunk.

A gift, she knew, that could save her from starving . . .

She slowly made her way back.

The sun hung in the still afternoon sky. The barest whisper of a breeze blew through the trees. Her senses pricked, she was prepared for the gruesome sight as she stepped through the trees.

All was the same.

She tried hard not to let her gaze rest on the bodies as she neared the coach. She was conscious of the deep silence and stillness that surrounded the dead and of her own deep breaths, the soft steps of her bare feet, the rush of the river behind her.

Only the very wealthy had a coach. She approached it in wonder; she could not help it. She had never seen one up close before. The velvet curtains had been ripped and slashed. The door opened with a creak. Red velvet seats; the girl must have been a very wealthy noblewoman. The slain knights must have been her failed guards.

She carefully lifted up the seat to find a three-foot hand-carved wooden trunk. It was beautiful. She spent several minutes attempting to pull the trunk out from the seat, without success. A metal lock kept it shut. She struggled in vain for several minutes before she realized the lady herself would have had the key on her person.

She turned slowly to the lady, her eyes searching. A gold chain hung about the dead girl's neck.

She approached with great trepidation and a prayer in her mind. She gently lifted it from beneath her bodice to see a lovely diamond cross and the precious gold key. How strange that the madmen did not take it! As if the cross of Christ had been a bad omen for them, one they would not take even for its riches.

"God have mercy..." a tortured voice whispered.

Linness froze in her tracks. A chill raced up her spine. She turned slowly around, her wary gaze searching the area. A gentle breeze rattled the trees, blowing over her hot skin to make her shiver. A rustle came from behind her. She swung toward it. The sound came from the river. She stepped cautiously to the bank, holding perfectly still until she heard it again.

She found the knight lying by the muddy bank in the cattails and hidden by bulrushes. An aging knight, his helmet discarded, his eyes glazed. She knelt at his side.

"Sir, you are alive!"

He tried to focus on the voice but found it difficult. Slipping in and out of consciousness, he felt the lifeblood ebbing from his body. With some effort he perceived the dirty face of a young and comely girl. "Lady Belinda, my God, you are still alive...."

"Nay, I am not her. The lady was slain. I am Linness of Sauvage."

He tried to focus but found the effort taxing.

"Can I help you? Oh, please, where are you injured—"

She gasped as she perceived the blood soaking through his chain mail. He must have a sword wound in his back, for there was no visible opening in the front. He grimaced in pain. "Oh, my poor sir, you must have a back wound—"

"Aye," he said. " 'Tis a bad one. I am not long for this world."

She felt a deep sadness upon witnessing his courage at the hands of death. "What can I do to ease thy discomfort?'

"A cask in my saddlebag hanging on Calihab there. See 'im? He ran away as soon as he unseated me and returned like a beaten dog when he saw it was safe. They never got him. . . ."

She nodded quickly and rose.

Linness slowly approached the horse. Calihab stopped his munching and leveled his small brown eyes on her. She stopped as odd black and white images rose in her mind. She saw the thirty or more horses stampeding toward the riverbank where this lady's small party had hid to escape the advancing army. She felt the poor beast's terror and confusion as his nostril's filled with the scent of blood. She heard the shouts to the Lady Belinda to run. She saw the knight reaching for his sword as two warring men descended on him with flying sabers. She felt the creature's pain and confusion as he watched his knight fall. . . .

She had never got the sight from a creature before. She reached her hand out to stroke his long neck. Calihab nudged her, stomped his foot with a lingering trace of his agitation. "Oh, you poor beast. You were very scared, were you not? 'Tis over now and sadly done. . . ."

She spoke softly to him as she reached in the saddlebag and found the cask. She told Calihab to stay until she returned. The horse, whether he understood or not, began again to munch on his feast of grass.

Linness slipped her arm beneath the old man and raised his head to pour the wine down his throat. He lay back with a sigh and closed his eyes. His pain ebbed away like a slow tide; 'twas almost gone. He took another two drafts.

"What be thy name, good sir?"

He spoke haltingly and slow at first. "I am Jean de Braille, of Nancy. We were escorting the Lady Belinda Saint de Beaumaris to her betrothed, Lord Morgan Chamberlain of Gaillard, when . . . when it happened."

"What befell ye, Sir Jean de Braille?"

He spoke with his eyes closed. "We first ran into the peasants running from the army ahead. We could see the smoke fillin' the sky a couple of miles ahead. We had but six knights and two footmen and we decided to pull off the road and wait—" He grimaced with a sudden sharp pain.

Linness gasped, slipping her arm beneath him to lift his head again for another draft. He swallowed as much as he could. "Ye have a kind soul, girl."

"Not so very good, though," she answered. "I was going to rob your lady's trunk when I heard you cry."

To her astonishment, the man smiled at this confession, his chest heaving with silent laughter.

"God forgive my words, but the lady deserves no better. She was a mean-spirited and spoiled young lady. Nothin' but foul complaints the whole trip—indeed, her whole life. A dark temper. Ye know," he said, smiling, "I do not believe I ever heard her voice level or sweet? Not once. 'Twas always a loud, shrill cackle, worse than a fishmonger's wife." An amused smile lifted on his cracked lips. "We heard that her own good parents celebrated with crackers, cakes, and fireworks the day we left." His laughter died. "I felt sorry for Lord Morgan the moment word came he agreed to have her. We all thought someone ought to have warned him the misery his fine title had bought. . . . I guess now it matters not. . . ."

Linness's brow drew together as she listened to this. She cast her eyes to where the girl lay. "She looked like she was pretty. . . ."

"I've heard that said before, but I never saw it. 'Tis said that a person's soul shines out through their skin. Hers was a too harsh glare that made a man squint." His fine eyes focused suddenly on his benefactress. "You, however . . . you look surrounded in soft candlelight, the kind that fools men into thinking they're starin' at the Virgin beauty. And, why, ye speak like any lady I've known. . . ."

The pool of his blood touched the edge of her tunic.

Jean closed his tired eyes and felt himself sinking deep into the warm mud of the riverbank. The world grew dimmer, then suddenly brighter.

Linness tried to pull him back. "Oh, Sir Jean, shall I remove your mail?"

"Nay, Linness of Sauvage. Go on. Take the poor lady's gowns and any jewels not cut from her fin-

gers." As long as Linness lived, she would never
forget the mystical smile that came over the old
man's face. "Linness of Sauvage, with ye beautiful
gray eyes, ye be more of a lady than Belinda could
ever be. If ye are clever, ye could pretend to be her
and go in her place."

Once said, the idea took sudden importance in
his mind. He opened his eyes to see her more
clearly. He chuckled, coughed even, as he reached
for her hand and squeezed it. "Lord Morgan has
never laid eyes on her before, and while he has seen
a portrait, you have enough of a liking to Belinda
to pull it off. The same long, dark hair and even
features. You look about the same size. God's teeth,
it could work. . . ." He was smiling, delighted by
the idea. "No one, but no one, has ever traveled
between here and Montegrel; least of all the girl's
parents. Her father's sickly, ye know, what with his
gout and all. They think they've seen the last of
their daughter. And with your silver tongue, you
could be a lady. You could be Belinda. You could
land yourself inside the Château Gaillard married
to its lord and master. . . ."

Astonishment changed her face as she took in the
fantastic suggestion. "Me?" she questioned in an
awe-filled whisper. Yet he did not respond. She
anxiously placed a finger over his mouth. Only to
discover his last breath had already left his body.

Hands over her mouth, Linness backed up as her
mind rushed over the incredible suggestion. To
pretend to be a lady! 'Twas fantastic! Preposterous.

True, she was convent-bred and could pass as a
lady with a little finery—she had the tongue and
knew most of the manners, she supposed. She
could read the Scriptures and write in French let-

ters, but still, would not something give her away? She knew nothing about Montegrel or Nancy. She had never heard of these places before. Still, she often thought one place was very much like another. . . .

What if he, this great Lord Morgan de Chamberlain of Gaillard, discovered her incredible deception? Her thin neck would be strung out over the gates, no doubt.

She glanced back over the scene of death, her gaze stopping on Lady Belinda, the vision coming back to her. Mary wanted her to send the lady's body into the river. She had seen thus in a vision.

Merciful heavens.

She rushed to Belinda's side and stared down at the body. It was hard to see past the pale mask of death, but aye, when she managed to force herself to look, there was a resemblance. Nay, not a resemblance but a similarity. They were of an age; Belinda looked a bit shorter but mostly the same size and with even features of face. Her own hair was more russet, streaked by the sun and crinkled, but it was the same length as the lady's.

And really, what would it matter if no one had seen Belinda before?

Linness rushed to the riverbed and, sinking to her knees, she held herself as her mind raced over the whole. If she stripped Belinda and pulled her into the river, the water would carry the body away. No one would ever find more than bones; no one would ever know she died. A rich lady would have a scribe to write letters, and she could smear the signature or sign with a heart, and so she could probably correspond to the lady's parents. Yet, if she said the wrong words to them, or if someone ever traveled to Gaillard from Montegrel . . . doom!

But the good knight had sworn no one ever traveled between Gaillard and Montegrel. She would marry a lord. He would bed her as Paxton had. Her thoughts stopped here.

The idea was not pleasant.

She could close her eyes and pretend she was somewhere else.

Nor was she a virgin now, though she supposed this lord might never know that for sure. She had heard of many virgins who did not bleed on their wedding night, leaving their husbands with an unanswered question the whole of their lives. A man had no sure way of knowing. Thank God for that. Then, too, many men, she had been told, did not really care if the dowry was large enough.

And if she didn't become Lady Belinda, would she not starve anyway? Famine was rife in these times, and right now she had as little to her name as a beggar. How many deaths from want of food had she witnessed in her short life? Twenty, thirty, fifty? At least that many, and since the day she left the convent, she had known too many times how very close she was to suffering the same fate.

These were harsh times indeed for the poor folk. What if her circumstances sunk lower and 'twas not begging she was forced to do to get something to eat? That idea sent her thoughts tumbling dizzily as a memory rose in her mind.

It was the harshest winter. The village crops had been burned the year before and most of the livestock killed by way of necessity for food—leaving the village without milk and eggs from the goats and chickens. During these times she took to searching the forest for roots to boil and eat, anything really to fill an empty stomach. Sometimes she was lucky and managed to find certain rare herbs—pennyroyal, mugwort, camphor—which, if she could find a buyer, she could sometimes sell to get a loaf of bread and a slab of lard.

It had been on one of these searches that she came across a mother and two children. The smell had alerted her first and she approached with trepidation. Their three bodies were huddled together. A sight far more gruesome than the one she looked at now. Their flesh was rotting beneath the tattered rags, black with a trail of ants taking what little the birds had left. No shoes. They had no doubt started out from another village, hoping to find someone or something that could keep the slow death of starvation off long enough to reach the summer months. . . .

The sight was not uncommon. It happened all the time.

A hand went to her abdomen. And what if she should carry Paxton's child? Dear Lord, 'twould be so much worse! And what if she could be this Lady Belinda and never see another day's poverty as long as she lived?

Mary, should I, could I? Is this the fate you meant me to have? Is it possible?

She went very still again, searching for a sign. Never in all her life had she needed a sign more. Anxiously her gaze swept the heavens.

Nothing happened.

The river raged on and her gaze dropped to the ground.

A fat frog leaped near the bulrushes.

That was a sign of sorts!

How she would love to be fat for once in her life,

to eat lots and lots of food whenever she felt hungry. Steaming hot trencher bread full of thick stew! Strawberries and thick cream! Cheese and honey spread over real wheat bread, hot possets and custards. And, oh Lord, she would love to sleep in a featherbed, with a servant to rush about, fetching her all this fine food. She would love to have a trunk full of pretty clothes and a waiting woman to dress her hair! To be rich enough to exercise the virtue of charity! People would say she was a saint, she would be so kind to the poor folks.

Mary would smile on her efforts.

Still, she needed one more sign to be sure. Her gaze lifted to the heavens again.

A sparrow! Sent by Mary! Sparrows always meant the coming of happiness!

The matter was settled. She looked toward the poor Lady Belinda. She knew what she had to do, and she approached the body to take the key. She never saw the swift flight of a hawk, swooping down and snatching the sparrow from the heavens. . . .

Chapter 3

The sun dipped down behind the mountain, slanting the last hour of sunlight across the Gaillard valley. Calihab's steady trot marked the dusty road that wound through miles of vineyards. The leafy green grapevines climbed up row after row of sticks, forming a green sea of crosses. Without exception, the cottars, bending over the fields where they added a mixture of dried fish to the soil for fertilizer, straightened to stare at the lady dressed in blue velvet atop a warhorse. Two boys stopped from their chores to chase after Calihab.

At last the township gate rose ahead; she had finally arrived at her destination. As the neat row of two-story thatched-roof dwellings peeked above the stone gate, Linness stared in wonder. Gaillard. Once Lady Belinda's destiny. Now it was hers.

"Mother Mary, if I am wrong, if you do not mean me to be the Lady Belinda, stop me now. . . ."

She held her breath, half expecting to fall from Calihab or to see an angel blocking the way. She did not. Fear pumped blood through her heart hard and fast. Her limbs went numb. She felt hot and cold and shaky all at once.

Even while the priest had torched the kindling

beneath her feet, she had not known such fear. She managed to remain seated on Calihab for one reason only: Mary had chosen this fate for her, she was sure. Mary had sent her here to Gaillard, where she would present herself as the Lady Belinda to her betrothed, the Lord Morgan de Gaillard Chamberlain.

Her child, the heir lord of Gaillard, would be his in name, yet hers and Paxton's in heart. . . .

If all went well. She must relinquish her doubt, and she would, she truly would, if only it were not so much easier to believe she would be hung by the day's end.

Two main thoroughfares divided the township neatly in four, like a cross viewed from far above. Her gray eyes rested on the château as it rose in ancient splendor at the far end, a vision drawn from the most fanciful notions ever imagined.

Gaillard was much like any other township these days. The land was farmed, the peasants well fed, and with few exceptions, the place had been untouched by war or plague for many years now as Francis, king of France, spent his energies and monies in the infernal Italian campaigns far away. She knew these things; it was talked about among people. The Italian campaigns were an endless series of battles the young king insisted on fighting for no reason anyone knew, wars interrupted by occasional treaties and punctuated by intrigues, mysterious disappearances, and renewed calls for justice. No one alive understood these wars, or if one did, Linness had never grasped the purpose past the young and vain king's insistence that he was the rightful monarch of the provinces of the Kingdom of Naples and the Duchy of Milan—issues easier settled by marriage as far as she was concerned.

Flowers appeared in boxes beneath the windows on the upper levels of merchants' homes, while the wooden shutters were let down on the lower levels from over the windows, making counters that stuck out on the street, from which proprietors sold their wares. The shops were small. Painted signs directed the buyers. There was a pie shop, a bakery, a tailor, barbershop, and sausage store, among many others. Calihab trotted past the stables, where the town's blacksmith worked. Dusk settled over the landscape, and few people darted about in the street as the shops were closing one by one.

The few people remaining, however, all stopped to stare at her. A plump woman with a broom, a butcher carrying two bloodied deer heads, a group of children playing marbles, a hot pie seller closing her shop window, two roofers, another group of women, they all stopped to stare at her. She appeared as a strange and beautiful creature dressed in a blue velvet gown, the matching cloak draped loosely about her waist, as she rode a man's warhorse down the cobblestone street towards Château Gaillard.

The tailor's wife drew back and whispered to her friend, "The lady doth not wear shoes. . . ."

"Who can she be?"

"Look at the gold light falling on that long hair. . . ."

Linness held her head high, staring straight ahead. Calihab, sensing their destination, fought the bit and broke into a less than enthusiastic gallop. His hooves pounded across the wooden bridge over the moat, then they passed through the gatehouse and beneath the arch of the entrance. The horse ran in circles around the courtyard.

This was the first time Linness had ever mounted a horse, and as any first-time rider quickly learns, mastery over the creature does not come effortlessly. Once she drew back on the reins, she had exhausted all means known to her of stopping him. She almost screamed as the galloping jousted her innards like a chambermaid pounding out a rug. Calihab at last sensed this and, tired anyway, he came to a stop as two guards rushed to grab the reins from her small, red and sore hands.

"My lady!" The young man stared aghast at the woman's disheveled appearance as he held the reins. The other guard fitted hands around her small waist and lifted her to the ground. "Who might ye be?"

Her heart banged in her chest. She was aware that this was a determining moment in her destiny, that once she spoke Belinda's name, she could never go back, and she felt her strength gathering and collecting inside. She tilted her head regally—like a highborn lady—and squared her shoulders as she pronounced in her flawless convent-learned French: "I am the Lady Belinda Saint de Beaumaris."

She heard their gasps. She faced their shocked appraisal. She carefully fitted the velvet cape about her waist. The real Lady Belinda had been a slightly smaller woman. No matter how she had pulled and tugged, the gown would not reach to cover her bare feet. To make matters worse, it had barely spanned her bosom. She felt she was one breath away from spilling immodestly from her bodice. No slippers had come close to fitting either—her cursed, too-large feet.

She had selected one dress and the cape and set fire to the rest so no one living could ever find this wardrobe and produce it to condemn her. The ill-fitting gowns might provoke suspicions. She needed the cape to hide this discerning fact, hoping it would shield her until she could secure new garments somehow.

"Sound the trumpet," one of the guards shouted up to the battlements. The other guard quickly led Calihab away toward the stables. "Michaels, milady," the blonde-haired young man said as an introduction with a slight bow. His face was heavily marked by the pox but was otherwise handsome. "Please this way."

Linness, dizzy with this first success, followed him up the stone steps to the castle. They passed by two stone lion heads and through the great wooden doors. Torchlight filled the entrance hall. She stared at the scrumptious carpet beneath her bare feet. She had never before seen an inside carpet to cushion the weary foot as it touched the stone floor, and it was a wonder. The guard spoke rapidly to an approaching servant, who understanding who the lady was, rushed ahead to tell his lordship. "This way, my lady," he said again.

My lady, my lady, my lady...

The title echoed through her mind as they continued down the corridor and finally through the doors of the main hall. Her eyes lifted in awe at the sight that greeted her, at the wealth and opulence of this magnificent room, while the footman approached the table to bring the shocking news to Morgan.

Linness had never been in a baron's hall before, though she had imagined it a hundred times. The room was half the size of a cathedral, its ceiling elevated two stories, maybe more. This grand ceiling had a light-filled center made of stained glass. A bronze candelabra hung from this dome, tiny candles floating in a circle of scented oil. An enormous stone hearth rose on one side of the room, blazing with a fire. A smaller hearth stood opposite it. Wooden squares inlaid with white marble covered the floor, banners of gold and green silk decorated the wall. A handsome wooden screen with doors that must lead to the kitchen and buttery covered the far wall. A hand-carved wooden table sat on the slightly elevated dais, and there three men sat.

The man must be as rich as the king of England. Her knees shook like reeds in the wind, her hands went clammy again. For the three noblemen had risen and stood staring at her across the distance. Then the man who would change her life was coming toward her. She knew at once it was Lord Morgan Gaillard Chamberlain, the lord of the manor. She saw that he stood tall and might even be handsome, if it weren't for the bruises and swelling of his face, and dear Lord, she wondered who would have had the strength and fortitude to strike such a man.

The loose tassels of his gold and black doublet swayed and his metal spurs clanged noisily as he came toward her, making her more scared than a cornered rabbit. His facial disfiguration looked worse the closer he came. He stopped in front of her, staring down with astonishment and something else, something she saw as disbelief.

There was something familiar about him, unnervingly so.

With a gasp, she realized he looked like Paxton.

Morgan watched the lady's lovely, confused eyes search his face. She looked more comely than the miniature he had stared at for two years; it had not, he saw, done the lady's beauty justice, and it was odd how that thought pressed foremost on his mind, and inexplicably overwhelmed the more arresting fact that she was alive. She was alive.

Morgan's amber eyes traveled from the rich dark hair tumbling down her back, to the large gray eyes, straight, narrow nose, and sensuous lips, slightly parted. Her neck was long and slim, like the rest of her. Save for the rapid rise and fall of her full breasts, spilling from a mercilessly tight gown, where his bold gaze lingered.

No, hers was not the delicate fairness that every man hoped for in his wife. Her beauty was something very different. 'Twas the kind that tempted and teased and put in mind thoughts that did not often rest on the mother of your children. 'Twas the kind that made a man's pulse race and his blood heat. . . .

"Lady Belinda?"

She nodded as her face drained of color. It felt like a cruel trick, how he looked like Paxton! Paxton with darker hair and brown eyes and a beard. She didn't understand how it had happened; as if to torment her and make her pay for the charmed life she had stepped into, Mary had made Lord Morgan look like her Paxton. "And you, sir, must be Lord Morgan Gaillard Chamberlain?"

"Aye . . ." For a long, anguished moment as they stood there staring with surprise and shock at the revelation of each other's appearance, she felt so queer, as if cold steel had pierced her tender heart. A warning chill raced up and down her spine, trying to warn her, but of what, she knew not.

Mary, help me. . . .

The moment stretched. The men stared, shifting booted feet restlessly across the marble tiles as they waited for an explanation.

'Twas only nerves, she told herself. She was so frightened! Her gray eyes dropped uncertainly and she swallowed, nervously clasping her hands in the blue velvet folds of her cloak.

Morgan abruptly demanded, "My God, what befell you, milady? Every blessed man I have is out searching for you! We were certain you were dead—"

She drew slightly back at the thunder in his voice. A delicate hand, trembling, lifted to her mouth as if to contain an anguished cry. The fear of discovery, the fear of death, relief to find herself alive—all this brought her panic and tears forth.

"I fear I have lost all my good knights! They were slain like . . . like beasts of toil! These . . . these evildoers swept upon us like a cold gale wind from the very bowels of hell. I had just enough time to run to the woods to hide. I heard their screams. . . ."

No man alive could have resisted the wholly feminine fear put in those eyes, and when her lovely face grew paler still, when she seemed to sway too far back, Morgan stepped to her and caught her up in his arms. "She has fainted!"

John Chamberlain, Morgan's uncle and steward, snapped an order to a startled servant. "Prepare the lady's rooms at once! And for God's sake, someone send for the lady's serving woman . . . the one who came yesterday. What was her name again? Mistress Clair, I believe."

Linness's eyes opened wide. "My serving woman?!"

"Aye," Lord Morgan said, "she will be besotted with joy, no doubt. She thought, she seemed quite certain, you had died in the attack."

Morgan quickly carried Linness from the hall, his men following behind. The servant rushed out to find the matron Clair, calling out as he did so for help.

Linness began praying.

Outside and across the courtyard, Clair sat on the edge of a raised pallet in a small room she shared with four other serving women, blankets drawn around her sagging shoulders. The kind waiting woman of Gaillard had finally left her alone to her relentless tears. She could not stop crying as she relived the terror of yesterday, over and over, as if the next time she viewed it in the recess of her mind, it could change.

'Twas not that she would ever mourn the Lady Belinda's passing, but no one, not the lowest beast in France, deserved to die as that young, foolish girl had. The Lady Belinda would not go, no matter how she had begged and pleaded. She had begged Lady Belinda to run into the bushes with her; she had ordered it first in the girl's father's name, then her dear mother's, and at last she had used God's sacred name as a directive. To no avail.

"What do I have knights for, I ask?" she had snapped back. "I shall not abandon the comfort of my carriage for a band of ruffians! I will not! If my knights are worth half the coin my father pays them, then these thieves shall be slain in blood. I want to watch."

Clair had been horrified by this crowning demonstration of the girl's obstinacy and disagreeable nature. The servants of Montegrel, the Lady Belinda's former home, had always frowned at the child's difficult nature, her constant complaints and extreme vanity, the cruelty of some of her more notorious deeds. "A real queen of Sheba, she thinks she is. . . ." They'd shake their heads more and more often as Lady Belinda grew into womanhood and her faults seemed to increase with every inch of height. Even her dear mother had finally abandoned hope of the girl ever becoming a real lady of worth and charity. Everyone secretly looked forward to her marriage departure, especially the girl's good parents.

The thought of returning to Montegrel to tell them of the tragedy made her wail louder. She could not do it; she just couldn't. Besides, she didn't want to return. She had buried two husbands there, and in these last years of her life she had become increasingly tired of the same scenes and same faces each day, much as she cared for them. She had spent two years preparing to leave, at least two months saying good-bye to people she would not likely ever see again in this life, and it seemed so unfair to have wasted all those tears and fare-thee-wells. Oh Lord, why did this happen?

She remembered the good man Jean riding up to the carriage. "They are upon us! Run for cover, milady! Flee!"

"I will not, I tell you! I will not. . . ."

'Twere the last obstinate words their lady had uttered.

She had decided her duty did not require her to die with the girl for no good reason. So she had run to the river and plunged in, coming out on the other side, where she hid in bulrushes, watching the slaughter. Oh, 'twas too horrifying! All the screams and blood—

She was startled out of this memory by the sudden opening of the door. A young page appeared, his face flushed, his eyes filled with excitement. "Madame," he said, "your lady has just arrived . . . well, I think . . . and ever so alive."

Clair wiped her small, bright blue eyes as if it might clear her ears. "What?"

"Your lady, madame! The Lady Belinda! She has just arrived at the hall and is well!"

"Alive? Ye say Lady Be-Belinda is alive?"

"Aye. She is waiting for ye now."

Clair had never believed in ghosts. Yet, it would seem that this was the only explanation. For she had witnessed the outlaws surround the carriage. With her own eyes, she watched her mistress flee at last and run toward the river. She saw the man ride beside her, raise his terrible sword, and strike her flesh. The girl had fallen at the water's edge, soaking the mossy bank with blood.

"Lord have mercy!"

The young page's face filled with happiness and excitement. The news of the lady offset Paxton's banishment. For Morgan would surely forgive his brother now. Paxton would return and they would have a grand wedding feast. "Please come at once. Do hurry, madame. Milady anxiously awaits ye!"

"Can it be true?" Clair asked while rising, her mind numb with confusion. There must be some mistake. There must. She saw her mistress felled like a young sapling. She saw it with her own eyes!

"Please!"

Clair stepped forward as if in a dream. Shaking her head in disbelief, she followed the young man out to the courtyard and then up the steps of the keep. This couldn't be happening, it just couldn't. He must be taking her to see the corpse!

The idea made her stop, and Michaels turned to her questioningly. Her chubby hands clasped her heart; she was shaking her head again. The older woman had round, manlike jowls that shook as she did so. "Are ye taking me to see her dead body?"

"Nay, good woman," he laughed kindly. "The lady is quite hale. Nary a scratch on her!"

She had never been known for particularly quick wits, she knew, but this was not because she did not have them. She did, but these wits failed her now. For here sat a bigger puzzle, as boggling as the question of how many angels fit on a sewing pin. She could not reason through it.

They continued on up the stairs to the solar chambers, down the hall, and stopped at a wide hand-carved wooden door. Michaels knocked and waited. The door opened and he stepped inside to announce her arrival.

Clair stepped into the room.

Lamps had been lit and a fire blazed in the hearth. Firelight suffused the chambers, with the exception of the window alcove, which remained in dark shadows. Lord Morgan and John Chamberlain stood on either side of an enormous featherbed. Thick blue velvet curtains around the bed were pulled back, offering her an archer's view.

Yet there was no Lady Belinda in that bed.

A young woman lay against the carved headboard, staring at her, with large silver eyes that begged for her silence. For the briefest moment their eyes locked; a message was exchanged. In this same moment, Clair's mind wandered through a labyrinth and then reached a decision.

For firelight lit those eyes a silvery gray, like the color of an owl's wings. They were without exception the most beautiful eyes she had ever seen. She knew instantly, whatever else the lady might or might not be, she did not deserve the death sentence her next words might very well produce.

Which made her say, "Milady, 'tis a miracle!"

And they fell into each other's arms.

"I thought ye dead, milady, I thought ye dead!" These were the words the men heard. Though to the young woman Clair whispered, "Ye better be more clever and quick than the king's tax collectors, because now 'twill be my head as well as yours."

"Don't worry, I am," Linness cried, then realizing what she was saying. "I mean I am not—"

From the start Clair seemed better at the deceit than Linness. She drew back and with red, swollen eyes, she said tearfully, "I saw ye running and a man chasing ye on his steed and I thought he killed ye. I thought my poor poor lady was doomed—"

"I outran him!"

John Chamberlain tried to picture this. "You outran a man on horseback?"

"I . . . I ran into the water and swam away. Yes! The river carried me far downstream. I climbed out and waited almost until nightfall before returning, only to find—Lord have mercy—my knights were slain." Sadness changed her eyes; a gentle hand came to Clair's face. "Poor Jean. I found him alive still and, a-a-and I stayed with him until he died!"

The story impressed the men, Morgan most of all.

Clair cried harder into her kerchief. "Jean was always ye favorite...."

"Oh yes!... he was my favorite," she said, tired already of spinning tales. "Jean was always my favorite."

Morgan did not seem interested in her professed affection for the man.

"Like a father, he was," Clair said between muffled sobs.

"I have already notified my new sergeant at arms," Morgan said. "The bodies shall be recovered soon. Father Gayly will oversee the burial rites," he added, and with an acknowledged nod to Linness, "That is, as soon as you are sufficiently recovered, milady."

"The bodies..." Clair repeated in whispered alarm, shifting her gaze to the young woman. "The bodies will be recovered—"

Linness shook her head slightly, just enough to let the woman know this would not be giving them away. It had been a gruesome task, but she had had to do it. She had first removed the lady's clothing and burned it before she had dragged her body to the water. This had been difficult because, as the swift-moving current had carried the corpse into the pitch-black night, she had realized, with much guilt, that the Lady would not be having a proper burial. And her guilt had hardly been assuaged by the bits and pieces of the girl's life that had come to her; fragmented images as she touched her clothes, tossed them into the fire. The girl had been rather stupid and vain in the way of the most selfish. Still, everyone, no matter what her life, deserved a proper burial.

Thinking of this, Linness said, "My good knights deserve the grandest burial, for sure," and she went on, elegantly spouting a touching speech about their bravery.

As she spoke, Morgan felt the pleasurable tightening of his loins just looking at her. She seemed ignorant of her effect on men, not just him but his uncle, and even young Michaels. And 'twas a most potent effect.

The thought made him almost laugh. He vowed then and there to see any daughter she gave him cloistered and raised in a convent.

"Michaels, fetch a cask of wine," he ordered, startling Linness midsentence with this rude interruption of her high-minded speech.

Morgan took no notice. He was not in the habit of listening to lengthy speeches made by women—this was probably his first. He continued to stare at her, though.

As Michaels started to leave to do his bidding, Morgan added, "And bring me the miniature of Lady Belinda. I believe it rests in the right-hand drawer of my trunk."

A miniature. All thoughts fled Linness's mind. She sat perfectly still, abruptly understanding what it meant to be frozen with fear for the first time in her life. Morgan de Gaillard was going to compare her to a miniature of the Lady Belinda and realize that she was an impostor.

How could she possibly explain the disparity? She waited for a lie that would save her. Waited and waited until she looked to Clair in desperation.

"Oh, aye, the lady's miniature . . ." Clair began

haltingly. " 'Twas a bad time when 'twas painted. Remember, milady?"

"Well . . . I—"

"Why, ye had the influenza. Pretty little Sara sat for the painter most of the time, ye were feeling so poorly."

The woman was a genius!

Linness nodded enthusiastically, and began another long speech about her bout with influenza. Clair added "ayes" and " 'twas terribles" at the proper junctures. Perhaps they were too enthusiastic in this description, for the older man, John, began to look at them both with suspicion—which, curiously, made Linness's voice go higher as she added more details to remove his doubt.

Linness was still discussing the harrowing trial of her illness, noticing how the Lord Morgan never seemed to listen to her words, but instead just stared at her. Stared at her as if she were a criminal and he an executioner. That she was in fact a criminal magnified the effect of his silent gaze. Her voice trailed off just as the door opened to admit a serving woman with a tray of cups and pitcher of wine.

All Morgan gleaned from the lady's lengthy verbosity was that this was her shining fault. She spoke too much. Like all men, he preferred his women, indeed all women, quiet and docile—he would not at all mind if they were struck mute. Why God gave the creatures tongues in the first place would always be a mystery to him; a woman's words were like the air, constantly surrounding a man but never requiring thought, much less notice. Well, no matter. She would learn his preferences soon enough. . . .

Morgan held out his cup as the woman served him first, never once taking his eyes from his betrothed on the bed. He looked as if he might devour her. Her discomfort grew more pronounced as the door opened again and Michaels appeared.

He presented a gold case to Morgan, who opened it and stepped to the fire to look at it better. "Come see this," he said to John, handing him the miniature. "The painter was poor indeed! He managed to capture none of the lady's beauty."

John carried it directly beneath a lamp and stared down, then across to Linness. His gaze bounced back and forth between the two maybe four times before his gaze narrowed and he commented, "I've seen cottar brats draw more convincing portraits in the dirt."

Sudden fear struck Clair as the magnitude of the moment began to dawn on her. "The Baroness Saint de Beaumaris was very upset by the whole. Alas! The poor painter had already departed by then and there was little we could do."

The way Lord Morgan stared! Linness half wondered if he would call her up for her trick and have his guard escort her to the guillotine. His bright amber gaze stayed upon her, lifting only as he drained his cup and returning at once as he approached the bed. He stood over the bed, staring down at her until she looked away. She held perfectly still as it happened.

He reached a callused hand to her bosom, where it lingered, sliding over her cold skin until she gasped. Then he drew the gold chain from her neck and stared down at Paxton's ring. A slow smile curved on his lips. "So you wear my betrothal ring against your heart, milady." He laughed, "I am pleased. Very pleased."

Thoughts raced hard and fast through her head as she tried to make sense of his words. He slowly dropped the precious ring, his fingers sliding down her bodice to drop it back against a heart that hammered furiously.

He thought Paxton's ring was his betrothal ring. How could this be? For the love of Mary, what made Morgan think 'twas his ring?

Her frightened gray eyes darted anxiously over the darkening room as Lord Morgan and his steward withdrew to let her rest, the young page following, too. Only Clair remained, waiting a safe few seconds to speak, while the other servant was introducing herself and telling her how happy she was that she was alive.

Linness hardly heard her as she stared off into the fire that blazed and crackled. With sick horror, she saw that Paxton must have been the Lady Belinda's slayer. She tried to imagine his strong arm raised to slay a woman. She could not. It was not possible, she told herself over and over.

Her sight would have warned her. . . .

It must have been his warring men!

Her tender feelings instantly seized upon this explanation. It was his warring men and not his hand that killed a defenseless lady! Then these butchers had given the ring to Paxton, who in turn had given it to her. Perhaps not even knowing the evil deed from whence it had come. She had to think so, or she'd lose the blessed light that surrounded her unborn child.

The necklace speared her with a tingling warmth. She lifted it up, staring at the jeweled charm.

"Does milady Belinda care for a late supper?"

Linness looked up and smiled at the servant. This heavenly phenomenon sent from Mary, this miracle, was complete. She was Lady Belinda, betrothed to Lord Morgan Gaillard of Chamberlain. Nothing could change that now. Nothing and no one. "Yes, I would." Boldly, with nary a doubt left, she said, "And please call me Linness. I prefer it to my Christian name."

The woman curtsied with a pleased smile and hurriedly rushed from the room. The door closed. She met Clair's bright blue eyes as the woman said, "So 'tis Lady Linness, is it? And who were ye before today?"

"Linness of Sauvage, a humble seer of the past and the future of common folks."

Clair drew back with her shock. "A fortune-teller?!"

"Aye. And my sight tells me you are Clair of Montegrel, serving woman to the deceased Lady Belinda and her mother before her. You have buried one . . . no, two husbands, I see. You are more clever than the next ten people, though few have noticed this. You have a large heart, are quick to laugh, and yes, like me, you are guided by your intuition. 'Twas what saved me. You looked into my soul and you could not condemn me."

Clair's eyes narrowed with suspicion. "Ah, I wager ye say such to everyone. Or nearly such."

A bright twinkle came to Linness's eyes and her smile seemed to light up the room. "Oh no, Clair of Montegrel." Linness laughed, all the tension of the day released with sudden animation as she explained, "When I am telling a fortune and my sight fails me, which often happens, this is what I say,

'You, sir, or madame, have had a life mixed with tragedy and blessings.' They always gasp at the wonder of my powers. I say, 'I see you have many complaints about the trials of your day . . . ' Then they proceed to list these complaints to me. Then I say, 'You do not count the joy and merriment in your life often enough. Right now I see you laughing and with your arms around . . . who is it? I can only see it is a good person, someone you love?' Then they tell me a name, again amazed by how well I have seen into their life. Lastly I add, 'I see that you have lost someone very dear to you.' They nod, of course, and say aye, my mother or my first-born or my sister. Then I say she is calling to me from heaven, and asking me to ease the burden of your sorrows, for they are in bliss and know some-day you will be joining them.''

Her thin brows arched mischievously over her silver eyes. "And then, as they are bowing, as pleased as a well-fed pig, I add the very last.''

"Oh? And what might that be?''

"Five ducats, please.''

Clair threw her red head back and the two women laughed merrily before they reached for each other's arms. A warm friendship sprang be-tween them, born first of necessity but one that each sensed, even then, would grow with mutual love and regard. The feelings grew that first night as Linness began the telling of her remarkable, wholly unbelievable tale. . . .

The heated exchange began as soon as they shut the door on the lady's room. John, steps behind Morgan, said, "This changes everything. I will send out a scout to track down Paxton and tell him to return at once—"

Morgan reached the bottom step and, without turning around, he continued down the corridor to the great hall, his loud voice booming with these words, "You will do no such thing."

"What?" demanded John as he hurried to catch up to him.

"You heard me," he answered.

John rushed in front of him, wanting to see his nephew's face. The torchlight blazed behind Morgan, casting him in darkness and shadows, and yet John could see the determination set in the hard line of his lips. "But the lady is alive!"

"No thanks to my dear brother."

"Wait, Morgan. You banished Paxton because you assumed he had caused the Lady Belinda's death! Now we find, through miracle or fate, she is not only quite well but, by God's grace, she is safe within our very walls. He is absolved of this crime—"

"Is he?" His voice lowered dangerously. "Is it not still true that his famous appetite for whoring took him away from battle?"

John did not point out that Morgan's appetite was every bit as prodigious as Paxton's, more even, for Paxton tended to be extremely selective about his women, whereas Morgan, inexplicably, seemed only to require that the creature be of a low kind. The insult he could not bear, though, was the falsehood that Paxton left the battle before it was through.

Through gritted teeth John said, "The battle was over, I say. And you know well Paxton would never leave his men to battle without him! Why, his battle skill is sung across the country. Even the king has called him to service for the Italian campaign. And thus you well know, Morgan!"

"Bravery," he scoffed. "Even if that is true and the battle over and every last rebel knight slain, my *brave* brother"—he drawled the word with scorn, granting John no measure—"then rode away from the search for my wife. My wife. Even if she is alive now, she might have died, and for no more reason than his prodigious lust! And you want me to forgive him? Nay." He shook his head. "I will not. Never, I say."

John followed Morgan into the great hall, desperate to make Morgan see reason. His personal affection aside, Paxton did not deserve banishment from all that he loved, all that they all loved. Gaillard. Paxton of all men did not deserve it.

Besides, they needed Paxton.

Morgan had always needed Paxton. If for nothing else than Paxton's superior skills with the harvesting of Gaillard's precious grapes. In these last few years his burgeoning knowledge had become invaluable. The first part of Paxton's life had been spent learning the warring arts, but the last years had been spent learning the art of wine making. And learn, he had. For Paxton foresaw the peace the king would bring to France at last, that soon the measure of a man would be what he could make of his land.

For three long years Paxton learned everything there was to know about wine making. He had consulted wineries across France and the Holy Roman Empire, forced Morgan to send scouts abroad in an effort to gather the newest methods and means of wine making, and all the while he read every word written on the subject. In the last few years he implemented the modern method for the cultivation of the soil and planting at Gaillard, brought innovative responses to the annual disasters, learned how to maximize the benefits of a heavy rainfall, built a better wine press, convinced Morgan to purchase the stronger English oak barrels, and most of all, selected the harvest date. Paxton had demonstrated uncanny luck in choosing the harvest date—an all-important day that made a sweet, potent wine or a bitter or tart one, a day that determined wealth or poverty.

Morgan's wealth or poverty . . .

The whole of the township's wealth had been built and maintained by Paxton's careful administration. He could probably still maintain this in Paxton's absense for a year or two, but he was well aware of his age. He could not work so hard forever. Besides, Gaillard would not grow without Paxton's skillful overseeing.

Morgan could never pick a fortuitous harvest date. . . .

The older man sank onto the velvet-lined bench. The complexities of Morgan's and Paxton's love and hatred could fill a book as thick as the Scriptures. Their father had died when the boys were still in swaddling clothes and he always felt it might have been different had that great man lived. Their father might have been able to balance the scales that fate had tipped dramatically in Morgan's favor. For some reason Morgan had owned their good mother's regard. Since the day the twins had been born, she had showered all her motherly love and affection on Morgan. Occasionally she tossed leftover crumbs in Paxton's direction, but it was not enough. Everyone saw that it was not enough.

And everyone, including himself, had tried to make up for it. So in a curious way, Paxton had always had the love of the people. Morgan had everything else. And everything else was all of Gaillard.

As firstborn, Morgan inherited the richest land of the region, its ancient château, the wealth of its vineyards. Paxton had nothing more than his knighthood, and the position he had earned as wine steward. Yet, from their boyhood, it seemed the less Paxton got, the harder he worked. The hard work made him into the most skilled warrior in all of Southern France, perhaps beyond, and now a great master of wine making, a man, unlike his brother, of rare shining character, noble ideas, intelligence, and wit. Paxton was a man whom other men turned to in need, whether that need be a greater crop yield or an easy laugh. Paxton could always see the solution to problems long before others even saw the problem. So Paxton had outshined Morgan. Therein lay their troubles.

Not that Morgan was a bad man; he wasn't.

He just wasn't as good. . . .

"Morgan." John broke the silence, drawing his nephew's gaze to him. "Despite everything that has happened between you and Paxton, he is your brother. I cannot help but believe that beneath it all you still love him, that you always will."

Morgan did not deny it. He turned to the fire in the hearth, and for a long moment, the comment kept him silent. At last he confessed in a softened tone, "Love? Ah, perhaps, Uncle. Perhaps. Yet these brotherly sentiments for Paxton have always come with such a sharp sting." He shook his head. "Grand as it is, Gaillard is not big enough for the both of us. It's never been big enough for the both of us—I do not care how much he has mastered our family's vineyard." His amber eyes found his uncle as he added, "Has it occurred to you that I have done my brother a favor by banishing him from his home? Aye! He has spent his whole life fighting for something he cannot have. And I have finally set him free."

Passionately he continued, "Gaillard is mine by right of my birth. And it will be passed to my sons—by God's grace, that lady will give me a son." The thought pleased him and he suddenly laughed, "And while it would give me enormous pleasure to see my brother look upon my wife and watch his eyes blaze with envy, I do, in fact, keep enough brotherly affection to want to spare him that final straw."

As they stood by the table, Morgan picked up a carafe and splashed wine into his cup, raising it with a toast. "To you, my dear Paxton, wherever fate may lead you. May you find fortune and happiness, may you live long and well. And by God's grace, may I never hear your name again. . . ."

Yet he did hear his brother's name on the eve of his wedding day two weeks later, and from the most unexpected source. After his lady's slain knights had been found and carted in coffins to be buried in the Gaillard graveyard, Belinda—who liked to be called simply Linness—had begged for time to prepare a new wardrobe. Though it was hell waiting for the ceremony, he had relented. The wait was almost over and the idea put him in a fine mood as he made his way up the stairs and to his empty chambers. He waved away Franz, his squire, and began to undress himself.

She watched from the darkened alcove.

He first caught the faintest hint of her perfume. Lilac-scented oils. She had taken to bathing in the river every day, where she applied this oil to her long hair to keep knots out, he had discovered. The faint scent followed her about, teasing him unmercifully and driving him nearly mad at times. He first thought he was imagining it, but no. He looked up and around the room, finding her as she stepped out of the shadows.

"Linness," he said, much surprised as he took in her slender shape draped in a gold and white robe. He saw at once she was frightened of something. Her eyes were wide with anxiety, her face pale, her lips redder because of it. She clasped the folds of the robe tight about her neck, but the long hair fell unrestrained down to her waist. Her countenance made him soften his tone. "What is amiss? 'Tis ill luck to see your betrothed on the eve of a wedding—"

"I had to speak with you."

"Aye." He came to stand by her. His concern mixed with suspicion; he had learned to be wary of a woman's emotions.

Her eyes fixed on his face. "Young Michaels was carting out a trunk today with some other men. A beautiful hand-carved trunk. I saw it and . . . and it put in mind . . . I saw a man. I mean with my sight—"

"Your sight," he repeated with exasperation and amusement both. Already the servants spoke of nothing else but the lady's miraculous "sight."

Though she knew better than to discuss such foolishness with him, apparently she claimed to have gotten the sight after a childhood bump on the head. This had never been mentioned in the marriage contract, and thank God for that. The negotiations would have ceased immediately; the last thing he wanted was a wife with addled wits.

"Michaels told me you have a brother. His name is . . . Paxton." She whispered the unbelievable name with reverence. "Nan and Philippa, my serving women, both said the same. They took me to the Gaillard Bible, where I saw his name written in ink. Michaels said . . . he said that this brother was banished because, because of . . . me."

He stared down at the hot worry in those gray eyes. Was she so tenderhearted that she would worry over a person she had never met?

Aye, he saw. It softened his heart even more.

He turned from her, dismissing the vexing feelings this inane conversation solicited from him. "Milady, you are not to concern yourself with my brother."

"Is it true? Milord, please. Tell me if it can possibly be true."

There was desperation in the question.

"Aye 'tis true. Though you hardly caused the rift, milady. 'Twas there the day we were born. Oh, aye, the war would be interrupted by laughter and jests and sometimes goodwill, but always it was there between us—this darkling feeling of . . . rivalry. He was serving me and Gaillard as wine steward, but he is even better known for the warring arts, and so Paxton was in charge of finding you. Instead he left the search and was discovered . . . well, to be blunt, whoring with some"—he waved his hand in a gesture of disgust—"some condemned witch. The incident could not be excused. I banished him from our home. You are in no way responsible. Now," he ordered, "I am weary of his very name. I will hear it no more."

Linness's mind raced over this explanation. The man who had discovered Paxton with her must not be near or must not reconize her, she realized. Though that was the least of her worries now.

Morgan's thoughts traveled far away as he proceeded to undress in front of the fire. He removed his belt, his heavy mantle, and boots. He poured himself a cup of wine, drained the contents, and poured some more. Then he looked back at her.

She had retreated back into the shadows.

She pressed herself against the cold stone wall. 'Twas impossible to believe. Impossible. 'Twas Morgan who was the shadow over Paxton's life, while she was Paxton's condemned witch. She had begged Morgan to postpone the wedding so she knew for sure 'twas Paxton's child she carried. And so it was.

The jeweled ring burned against her chest. Haltingly she had to know, "This betrothal ring you gave me. Has it been in your family long?"

Morgan never expected a woman's mind to turn in neat circles. So he never wondered at the sudden shift of subjects. "Nay. My mother had them made when we were born."

"Them?"

"Paxton and I. She had matching rings made."

It explained everything, she realized. There were two rings. Morgan's ring must have been lost or stolen with Belinda's things. Paxton had given her his. . . .

Morgan stared into the fire as he thought of the two rings. Paxton still wore his ring on his neck. He had never given it to his first wife.' No doubt because the ring was all Paxton had ever received from their mother, and Paxton had cherished it as a good-luck charm. Paxton did not know the truth about those rings. John had once confessed that his saintly mother had only one ring made at first. For him. Paxton would have been ignored again. But then his father had intervened, and insisted she have two rings made, one for each boy. She had actually argued that Paxton would not live long enough to be betrothed to a lady, that she did not want the expense. John said it was the first time she voiced it out loud, her certainty that Paxton would die, and that their father had been furious to hear it. He ordered two rings made, and made her swear never to speak such in his presence again.

Linness was crying openly now as Mary whispered softly to choose. Choose now before it was too late. She must choose between accepting or abandoning the priceless wealth and security offered to her unborn son, who would be the next lord of Gaillard, master of this grand and beautiful land. She could set off at once in the cold dark of the night, chased by Morgan's entire guard, penniless, destitute, and carrying a child, in a desperate search for a dream.

A dream named Paxton . . .

She would never find this dream. Michaels had said his trunks were being sent to the French court, where he had already gone to assume the lofty responsibility of lord general of the king's guard. The army was marching to Milan. Even if she could make the long journey on foot to that faraway place, before she starved herself or lost her child, it was unknown how long he would be gone. "It might be years," Michaels had said. Years before he returned. Years of a grinding poverty that might once again land her at the stake.

Morgan came to stand in front of her, in the shadows. He gently wiped the tears falling from her closed eyes. He breathed in her sweetness until each breath came faster. A hand came under her chin, drawing her eyes to his face.

She had no choice.

Yet the moment his lips came over her mouth, a darkness descended like a veil over her heart and soul. The darkness was the future. A future draped in the wealth and opulence of a lady's life, and filled with untried love and all the terrible longing that brings.

'Twas a future without dreams. . . .

Chapter 4

Six years later . . .

Just outside of Gaillard, the river wound through the low-lying mountain range where the vineyards at last gave way to the forest. Here cliffs, enormous granite boulders, and towering trees edged and narrowed the swiftly running waterway. Ivy and moss draped the boulders and dripped from overhanging branches of the trees, darkening the landscape and shading the world below in an enchanting emerald green light. Sound, too, traveled in an unusual manner through the earthly corridor, and the distant laughter reached the three riders as they approached Gaillard.

Paxton stopped his horse, stilling the creature's dance as he listened to the sound ricocheting through the valley in an enchanting musical trill. A smile curved his lips. "Do you hear that?" he asked his two knights, Simon and Williams, who had stopped their mounts alongside him. "Someone has braved the frigid spring water, and God's teeth, it sounds like a woman. . . ."

Lord General Paxton de Chamberlain and his two knights had ridden hard from Florence to the

Gaillard valley, a journey that had taken two weeks. At last, they had reached their destination this morning. Paxton meant to plunge into the cold depths of the river and don fresh clothes before presenting himself at the château. Only Morgan was expecting him. He and Morgan had decided to keep the reunion a secret, wanting to surprise their uncle John on his sixtieth birthday.

Paxton could hardly wait to see the old man.

"Aye," Simon said presently, listening as well, but then, guessing Paxton's intention, he looked askance at his friend. "Milord, these frigid waters you speak of, they are not the ones you mean to bathe in? The river that I recall you had described was warm, clean, and inviting?"

"Simon, you old, coddled wretch." Paxton laughed as he turned his horse towards the river and his men followed. "Peace has made you soft. Do not tell me my bravest knight is set to tremble at the thought of a little cold water?"

"Not the thought, milord," Simon explained, "not the thought . . ."

The sun shone bright overhead, shimmering in tiny diamond pinpoints where Linness swam with her young five-year-old son, Jean Luc. Clair, now the boy's overworked nursemaid, watched from the shade of the mossy banks, shivering just from the sight of the two splashing and swimming about. Long ago Linness had ignored the protestations of the entire household and had the boy in the water and swimming even before he took his first steps—and now he swam like a fish. Just like his mother. Lord Morgan never put a stop to it, not then and not now. The man doted on his wife and his boy, spoiling them both. Neither could do any wrong. . . .

The heavy shuffling of horses' hooves sounded behind her and Clair turned to see three riders approaching through the trees. Her bright blue eyes shot back in panic to the water where Linness and Jean Luc swam as naked as the day they were born. "Milady, riders! Milady!"

Too far away, Linness never heard. The rush of river water drowned out all sound.

Clair turned back to assess the three men. She almost screamed. Not just ordinary men, but hardened knights who looked as if they had ridden through battles for days. Like a coward, she backed slowly into the bushes and out of sight in case she needed to run for help.

Home at last.

Paxton's men came up behind him as he looked out over the water and found the source of the enchanting musical laughter echoing over the river. A young woman swam with her boy. Unaware of anyone watching, the woman tossed her boy up with all her strength, laughing as the boy's howl of delight sounded in the air and, knees drawn against his chest, he splashed back into the water. He could not hear the words they shouted to each other, and then the boy started for shore while his mother swam out farther.

"Milord, you look as if you know her," William noticed with a grin.

"Aye." Paxton grinned back as he removed his leather gloves. "My imagination must be playing tricks on me. For she looks very much like a lady I once knew well."

"In the biblical sense, milord?"

"Aye." And Paxton laughed at the memory of the enchanted creature who had so altered the course of his life. Linness. The young silver-eyed virgin witch with the long hair and slim shape, fitted perfectly for a man's dreams. He would always remember Linness.

He had looked for her repeatedly over the years. He had searched everywhere in the first weeks after leaving Gaillard; he had even sent his men to surrounding villages and townships in hopes of finding her, a measure he had tried each time he returned from abroad. To no avail. It was as though she had disappeared from the face of the earth. He had come to think she existed for their one night together in a magical dreamscape. A night that had changed his life and saved him from a lifetime filled with little more than bitter resentment and jealousy.

Linness had saved him.

He supposed he would always look for her in every woman he saw. Like now. And yet, no matter how beautiful or tempting, all other women paled when set alongside the memory of Linness. . . .

Paxton came off his horse, staring still. "What say you and Simon find some other spot to bathe in?"

With chuckles and well wishes, they turned their mounts around and disappeared through the trees. Paxton lifted the bridle over his prized stallion's head, letting the magnificent creature go to the water. After unbuckling his sheath and sword belt, dropping them to the ground, he began removing his heavy haubert. His back was to the water—his first mistake.

A barbarian! Perhaps an evil Saracen or wizard! Jean Luc's feet touched the silted bottom of the river as he rushed out of the water onto the river-bank, where he picked up his sword. With weapon raised, he turned to the knight. "Raise thy sword, barbarian, and stand to answer to mine!"

Paxton turned with a start, his keen gaze falling to a young lad, barely waist high, completely naked and obviously meaning to slay him. With a wooden sword, no less. The boy had light brown hair and large, dark blue eyes. A handsome lad and obviously a brave one.

Clair came quickly through the trees to rescue the boy, but she stopped, catching sight of the bright amusement sparkling in the man's dark eyes. He bent down to retrieve his sword and slide its long steel band from a jeweled sheath. Sunlight streamed through the trees overhead, glinting off the metal. The knight smiled, but the boy remained undaunted still, his hand clasped firmly on the wooden sword.

"Before we draw blood, young man, tell me what has grieved you. I have done you no harm that I know."

"You were staring at my mother."

"Your mother is a beautiful woman," he replied with barely suppressed laughter. "You must find many men who stare at her."

"Aye," he admitted, "but she is naked." He looked out over the water where his mother swam far away now, as she did every day. Turning back to the tall knight, he stated the fact as he knew it. "You cannot stare when she's naked."

Paxton threw his head back and laughed. "I see. Well, young lad, what be thy name?"

"I am Jean Luc."

Surprise fitted onto the handsome face. "Jean

Luc? Jean Luc, be you the young lord of Gaillard, Jean Luc de Chamberlain?"

"I am."

Hands on hips now, Paxton changed his expression in the instant. "My brother's boy! Jean Luc, I am your uncle, Paxton!"

"My uncle?" The boy's eyes widened at last to encompass the wonder of the famous knight's presence. And his famous uncle Paxton was a wonder John and his father always talked about. He had always thought of his uncle as a knight in a fairy tale, a man as noble and brave and real as Lancelot or Gawaine, King David or Apollo. "My father and John always speak of you! John says you are famous! He says you are the best knight in three lands! Be that true, milord?"

Paxton just stared, now seeing the family resemblance. He wondered if it bothered Morgan that Jean Luc looked far more like himself—with his light brown hair and large, dark blue eyes—than his father. "Well," he chuckled, lowering himself on a bent knee, "I have not fought every knight in three lands to know."

Though it felt that way at times. How he longed for peace, so bitterly fought for, so brutally won. Yet won it, they had, and Francis had rewarded him with a huge land grant in Alsace, a land he meant to make into the richest wine country in all of France. This would almost certainly be joined at some point with more land in the Duchy of Milan. That was if dreams came true.

"I am going to bathe and then dress to meet your father. Would you like to come with me?"

"Aye! I would indeed."

Paxton laughed at the boy's precociousness, but

the sound died the instant he caught sight of his nursemaid. The woman had both hands clasped over her mouth, looking at him with alarm and fear. He might have been holding the boy's head in his hands for all of it. "Are you quite well, madame?"

She nodded slowly.

"I'll take my nephew with me. We'll present ourselves shortly at Gaillard—" He stopped and snapped, "Confound it, woman, why do you stare like that?"

She slowly shook her head. She swallowed. "I . . . I just remembered something . . . I . . ."

"Yes?"

Struck mute, Clair shook her head helplessly.

Paxton didn't know whether to laugh or box the woman's ears. He did neither as Jean Luc quickly pulled his tunic over his head and pulled on his hose and boots. Gripping his sword, the boy followed Paxton as he retrieved his horse from the bank.

Paxton took one last look at the lady who was Morgan's wife. She swam against the current, which was swifter now, swollen with spring rains. Smooth, strong strokes gave her small progress. She looked beautiful; the scene was sensual. Morgan was a lucky man. He wondered what kind of husband Morgan was. "So the Lady is your mother?"

Jean Luc nodded.

Knowing boys well, Paxton asked, "Jean Luc, you look strong and able. Would you mind riding Tasmania, my horse? I am weary of the saddle."

Jean Luc could scarcely believe his luck. No one,

not even his father, had ever let him ride atop the warhorses. "You'll let me?"

"You would be doing me a favor, nephew," he said as he bent down to lift the boy and swing him up into the saddle.

Clair watched the two disappear through the woods. Her heart hammered unnaturally as she waited for a coherent thought to emerge in her mind. There was none, past *Lord, have mercy . . .*

Lord, have mercy . . .

For all these years Linness had convinced her, John, and Father Gayly—those who knew—that they would never get caught. She had always believed it. Even when John had inadvertently discovered the deception, he had chosen to remain silent about it. And simply because it was impossible to condemn someone you loved.

And everyone loved Linness.

First off, she had the sight. No doubt about it. Even she, an old, skeptical waiting woman, had come to believe in Linness's gift. True, Linness's clairvoyance was an indefinite talent—certainly, she had learned over the years, not a thing to be wagered upon—but it was nonetheless a miracle at times. Just the other day she had stopped everyone in the kitchen with the announcement, "Jean Luc just fell from a tree."

"Be he hurt?!" Vivian asked in alarm.

She had shaken her head. "Nay, a scraped knee and sore hands, 'tis all . . ." Sure enough, minutes later the boy came running in to proudly display these very wounds. And then Linness could always be counted on to tell when a storm was coming, predictions Morgan and John had learned to rely upon for the vineyards.

But even more than Linness's mysterious prescience, it was her aura of wisdom mixed with genuine kindness that worked magic. Somehow she could ease Morgan from his worst tempers, relieve John's biggest worries as he saw to the administration of Gaillard and the township, make Father Gayly's head spin with her extreme idealism, send children into fits of giggles. She lent her ear to the people's complaints, offered sound advice and was well known for her tireless effort to ease the burdens of the most needy.

And yet, despite these magnanimous gifts, Linness's hearty peasant stock shone through. Unlike any others in her lofty class, Linness had no pretensions or airs. Just the other day she was found sitting with a circle of women in a flower-filled meadow, making daisy chains with their girls, while they discussed the best means to remove stains from their linens. What other lady would condescend? So, while the people honored her for her saintly gifts, they also felt she was one of them and they loved her for it.

Over the years, the enormous fear of being caught had lessened day by day, year by year, until it had completely disappeared. She never thought about it anymore, not even when they wrote those letters to the baron and baroness de Beaumaris. Until now.

Until Lord General Paxton de Chamberlain returned.

Perhaps he wouldn't remember her. After all, he had been fighting a battle, his wits addled and dazed from all the killing. It had been only one night, hadn't it? Surely a man such as Lord Paxton had laid with dozens, perhaps hundreds, of women, and Linness had been so young, so terribly young. . . .

Still, it seemed to her, her lady would be hard to forget. . . .

Linness swam back to the shore, coming quickly out of the water. "I am numb with cold!" she said. "I should not have stayed in so long! I shan't be warm until supper. Where are my clothes?"

Clair came to Linness with a drying cloth and a gown. Her hands still trembled. She didn't know what to say, because if Lord Paxton remembered, nothing could save them.

She had to warn her! She had to . . .

Linness swung her long hair forward and dried the cold moisture from her skin, before wrapping the wet mass up and rubbing vigorously. She swung the warm robe around her shoulders and held it tightly, shivering. "I shall never be warm again," she repeated as she removed the towel and plopped down in the only spot of sun on the bank. Despite these complaints, she laughed with the exhilaration of her venture.

After donning her undergarments, she pulled her long, wet hair from beneath the folds of the beige day gown and felt Clair's hands lacing up the back of the dress as she dreamily stared off at the river she loved. Sounds of male laughter came from downstream. She wondered who else had plunged into its cold waters. . . .

Clair anxiously rubbed her chubby hands against her dress. How could she tell what she had just seen? Paxton Gaillard de Chamberlain, in the flesh, standing in the very spot where she now sat.

She would never believe it herself. Lord Morgan and John had unknowingly convinced Linness that

Paxton would never appear at Gaillard again. Ever. Each of Lord Paxton's letters brought an argument, one Lord Morgan always won. "I will not ask his forgiveness!" Morgan's voice would thunder. "Never!"

"But now you correspond with Paxton as if you never said those hateful words," John would say. "*Mon Dieu*, Morgan, you are taking his advice for the vineyards! I am old now; I cannot be working so hard. You will need Paxton's help when I die. Do it for me. I want to see him again before I die—"

"Ah, you old codger," Lord Morgan would dismiss him, "you are bound to outlive the both of us. . . ."

So Linness never thought she would see Paxton again. "I have Jean Luc and our one night to cherish my life long. 'Tis enough, Clair," she'd say. And while she knew Linness often dreamt of the man, it was for the best. No one could want the disaster it would bring if Linness was ever presented to Morgan's estranged brother.

A disaster that had just arrived.

Linness found her gold hair band and pushed it through her hair. "Where did Jean Luc run off to? His tree fort?"

Jean Luc and his friends practically lived in the forest; they knew it better than the game master. Her boy knew every tree that might be climbed, and which trees had lark nests, bluebirds, or squirrels; he knew every rabbit warren, where the hedgehogs hid for winter, the favorite grazing spots of the deer. The forest was his home, as it should be with a boy. . . .

Where? Mercy, where? She cast an anxious gaze

to the forest and back. "Mi . . . milady . . ."

The queer catch in Claire's voice alerted Linness. She turned around to stare at her. "Clair, what's amiss?"

"Milady, I have something to tell ye. Ye won't believe me, but—"

She stopped as hearty male laughter, horses' hooves, and heavy boots sounded through the forest behind them. Clair turned toward the sound. Linness rose to her feet, clutching the gold robe tight about her form.

Morgan appeared first, to make sure his wife was dressed. He had long ago issued a warning to all of Gaillard that if any man or boy was caught spying on the Lady Linness as she swam, he would be banished from his land and all his properties confiscated. The people of Gaillard took this warning seriously, and after four summers of daily swimming, no one had ever dared violate it.

He had been brought the word of Paxton's arrival just this last hour. He had rushed out to meet his brother. And here he was, little changed after six years, at least in the measure of appearance. He was, in fact, greatly transformed; they both were. For their animosity had disappeared over the years, a gradual progress that occurred, oddly enough, through parchment paper and pen, their secret exchange of letters. So that they were able to embrace with laughter and well wishes just as brothers should.

He was well pleased, more as his gaze came to Linness at the riverbank. She looked like a burst of spring warmth in the beige day dress. Long flowing sleeves covered her arms, and the modest bodice was made of a dark russet velvet. A pleated underskirt of the darker color showed through the outer skirts. A matching headband held the long hair back.

"Milady! I have a great surprise for you." He turned back to the forest and called, "Come and meet thy brother's wife."

Thy brother's wife. The words brought her a brief moment of bewilderment, until Paxton appeared alongside Morgan and Jean Luc. For one wild moment she thought she was dreaming, but no, he stood there. Paxton.

Six years had changed him. A wet lock of light brown hair fell over his forehead. He wore a dark chestnut doublet, informal garb, a wide brown belt and lighter suede breeches, and tall brown boots, but more than anything, he seemed harder, taller, more than she remembered. And she did remember. She knew every line of his face, every mark on his body, she knew the exact shade of those beautiful dark eyes. She knew because he appeared faithfully every night in her dreams. Paxton.

She didn't realize she had stopped breathing until she started again with a sharp gasp. Her hands went clammy. Her heart pounded as if she were running. She wondered wildly if she would faint.

Paxton's smile disappeared the incredulous moment he understood who it was that stood in front of him. His gaze rushed up and down the lovely figure in a desperate search for the crucial flaw that would announce it was not her. That standing before him was not his virgin witch-child. Thy brother's wife. Linness.

"Paxton." Morgan slapped his back. " 'Tis my great pleasure to introduce my wife, the Lady Belinda, though she goes by the simple name Linness." He then turned to Linness and said, "Milady, here is my long-lost famous brother, Lord General Paxton de Chamberlain."

A loud ringing sounded in Paxton's ears. He only heard Morgan pronounce her name, and until that moment he didn't believe it. Linness. His brother's wife.

She was as beautiful as he remembered. More so. The long, wet hair pulled straight back, held by a gold band that accented the lovely silver eyes, the depth of her shock giving way to pain even as he stared. The delicate Celtic features of her face had lost the sharpness of youth, softening with time and motherhood. Linness.

"Milord, I am honored," she said, and only because the silence had stretched too long. His next words could easily condemn her, separating her from Jean Luc and her life forever, and that fact pressed so heavily on her every nerve, it nearly dropped her to her knees in terror.

Staring still, much too long, Paxton approached her slowly, cautiously still, as if at any minute he would discover the mistake here.

Linness. Thy brother's wife.

His large, warm hand reached for and took her cold one. He brought it to his lips. She felt the press of her hand to his lips and she closed her eyes briefly, to savor the touch and stop from throwing herself into his arms. He bowed slightly with the word "Milady . . ."

Clair came to stand by Linness in a silent offering of support. The two women clasped hands tightly. Yet it was Jean Luc who saved her. Or so she thought at first. He rushed to his mother and threw his arms around her waist as he looked up at her, giddy with excitement. "Mother, Uncle Paxton let me ride his warhorse!"

She managed, "Did he?"

"Aye!" The boy laughed as he turned back to Paxton. "Did you not, Uncle? He said he will give me lessons, too, that I am strong enough now!"

Morgan laughed and began telling Jean Luc that his uncle was the greatest horseman in the world, that Paxton knew as much about horses as God himself, maybe more. War, horses, and grapes, he was saying, ridiculously listing Paxton's known accomplishments. Neither Paxton or Linness heard any of Morgan's high praise, which now sounded as if he never remembered the vicious fight or had uttered those fateful words. They stared still, lost in the clash of their warring emotions.

She knew the exact moment he understood everything. Paxton's dark eyes suddenly shifted to Jean Luc. They widened perceptibly before they shot back to her with the question. She panicked and, trying to hide it, her gaze lowered.

"Paxton," Morgan was asking, "is not my boy a hale and hearty son? Everything a man could want in a boy?" Jean Luc smiled up at his father's praise, and Morgan ruffled his curly hair with affection. "Why, the boy's as smart as you ever were!"

The dark eyes darkened more as he stared at her. "Is he now?"

"Aye, he can already read French and is starting Latin. He knows all his sums!" Morgan beamed, full to bursting with paternal pride. Linness had always been amazed and somewhat startled by how deeply Morgan loved Jean Luc. "Nor is there a boy in all of Gaillard that can shoot as straight as

Jean Luc. Where is your bow, Jean Luc? 'Tis a foot taller than himself and yet he has no trouble drawing it, do you now?" Jean Luc shook his head. "Ah, that's my boy. . . ."

Paxton's gaze shot to Morgan's laughing face. For one wild moment he thought this whole thing was his brother's idea of a sick jest, an unspeakably cruel ploy to enact the most punishing revenge.

Yet Morgan's expression was as innocent and ignorant as a pig led to slaughter.

The dark eyes came back to Linness.

"Jean Luc," Paxton said, forcing a smile. "How old are you? Seven? Eight?"

Jean Luc could hardly believe his uncle thought he was so old and he laughed, "I am but five."

"Five. I'll wager you'll be six soon?"

"This month," he announced, amazed by how well his uncle guessed things. "The fifteenth of May. My father says I shall get my first pony!"

Paxton's head raced with these numbers. He knew the exact day he had been banished from his home, one day after he had lain with his virgin witch. The boy had been born nine months to the day. To the day . . .

Paxton patted Jean Luc's lightly colored curls and said something encouraging before he returned his gaze to Linness. She understood his shock and disbelief, emotions that quickly gave way to fury. She clutched the skirts of her dress tightly.

"Ah, Paxton," Morgan was saying, ignorant of the turbulent current of emotion running between his brother and his wife, "nothing's been the same since you left. Certainly not the harvests! God's teeth, but I can never pick the right day—I'm always too late, despite paying the best astrologer in

France. Aye! And look, Paxton," he began, pointing out the brown spots in the fields across the river and continuing to lament the changes that had occurred since they had separated. . . .

Paxton didn't even pretend to listen. He couldn't.

That life was cruel, Paxton knew well. That life could turn into a previously unimaginable nightmare, individually shaped to bring a man's private demons dancing in the light of day, was what wise men had always believed was hell.

Linness was his brother's wife. Linness, the woman who haunted his dreams and who had changed his life. The only woman in the world whom he had ever wanted as a mate. Linness, his brother's wife.

"Come now, milady," Clair said, placing her arm protectively around Linness and drawing her away. "Ye are trembling with the cold. Ye need to draw close to the kitchen fire."

"Ah, your wet hair again," Morgan laughed affectionately and with husbandly solicitousness. "Paxton, let me take her back on this fine horse—"

"You cannot," Paxton said flatly. "The horse will accept no man's weight but mine."

Morgan's dark brow rose with wonder. "How the devil did you train him to do that?"

"A hard whip each time another weight was accepted."

"And how many times?"

His stare rested on Linness. "Until I owned the creature's loyalty."

Morgan petted the fine head. "Ah, but this is the finest horse my eyes have ever seen. You'll let him stud my mares, won't you, Paxton?"

"Indeed," Paxton replied.

Morgan admired Tasmania. He had always envied Paxton's ability with beasts. "My stallion has been worthless," he confessed. "We've not had a colt in years; no one knows why—even the seasoned mares cause no excitement." He looked back at Linness. "Well, Paxton, you take Linness back, then. I'll meet you in the hall. You must be starving. You can tell me your adventures as you eat. Wait till our uncle lays eyes upon you!" He laughed heartily at the thought. He had dispatched their uncle to the neighboring town of Clission, where many barons of Northern France had met in secret to unite against the church's new higher tithes. "He will be back tomorrow for the feast in your honor. Come, milady." Morgan reached for Linness's hand. "I'll lift you up."

Paxton turned to Linness expectantly.

"Nay." She shook her head, alarmed by this. "I should rather walk. A walk in the sun will warm me more than ten fires—"

"Huh!" Morgan said. " 'Tis bad enough, this insistence on plunging into these frigid waters, but I will not lose my son's mother to a chill."

She backed quickly away, retreating before Morgan could force her. "Please, I insist on walking. Clair." She motioned to the other woman to follow her. "A good day, milords."

The men watched as Clair hastily gathered their things and the two women started down the trail that followed the river back to the château. Linness heard Morgan say, "Ah, well," before he whispered conspiratorially, "Saintly, aye! But she is the most stubborn woman I have ever known." And he slapped Paxton's back affectionately.

Paxton stared at her retreating back as they followed behind. The faintest trace of her scent lingered in the air. Her long, wet hair swung like a pendulum; her dress brushed her legs. He noticed the imprint of her bare feet in the dirt.

Then he stared straight ahead, seeing none of the forest as the dark future wove itself tightly around him; each breath seemed to threaten to choke him until he drew her scent deeply into his lungs. His head swam with the faint trace of her sweet perfume that haunted his dreams.

He realized Morgan was talking, that he waited for his reply. "Paxton." Morgan stopped, an alarmed expression on his face. "You seem troubled. Is it—"

Paxton cut him off abruptly. "I am fatigued," he lied. "It has been a long journey after all." It was all he could do not to turn to Morgan and announce that the woman he called wife was the condemned witch he had rescued before laying her to the forest floor and owning her virginity, that the boy he loved as a son was the product of his joining—

He stopped all at once. He felt he was going mad, that this couldn't be happening. Morgan was assuring him he would have plenty of time to rest for tomorrow's feast before he stopped to capture his attention.

"What say you about my wife?"

"She is beautiful."

"Aye." He nodded. "As beautiful as my own saintly mother." When he realized to whom he was speaking, he added with a slap on the back, "As *our* mother."

The words drew Paxton back with incomprehension. He did not recall their mother as beautiful.

Quite the contrary, he remembered a large, ungainly woman of little humor and no warmth. A woman who wielded her shrewd and often cruel intelligence as a butcher uses a sharp knife to carve hides. He still felt the scars of dozens of pricks.

Linness evoked heat, lust, temptation—desires that were thousands of leagues from anything he associated with the word and meaning of *mother*. The only similarity between his mother and Linness rested in the frightening fact that, by sorcery or black magic, Morgan owned the affection of both of them. And while he had at last come to understand that not having ever known his mother's affections had made him stronger and, ultimately, wiser, it was not so with Linness.

He had only known her one night. One blessed night. Now Morgan's whole life was blessed with the joining of hers. He felt a near murderous rage at its injustice, an inequity that would weave unanswered desire into his every day....

His hand gripped his dagger to stop its tremble.

The following afternoon the trumpet sounded, waking Linness from the reverie of her prayers. She rose at once and stepped over to the alcove, peering out the opened window to the courtyard below. She watched as Morgan, Michaels, and old Father Gayly, her favorite, rushed to meet the coach being led by two fine mares.

The door opened, Michaels rushed to put the steps in place, and John Chamberlain emerged from the handsome coach. Morgan embraced his uncle, bursting with the news of Paxton's arrival as his arm swept up to the stairs. She did not have to see the stairs to know Paxton stood there, for she watched the look on John's face change as he beheld his long-lost nephew.

Paxton came down the stairs, the rich sound of his laughter filling the air as he embraced the old man until John stepped back to view the face that he loved. She could see his tears. As if sensing her eyes upon him, Paxton suddenly looked up to her window and she stepped quickly out of sight.

For several long seconds she leaned against the solid stone wall, her eyes closed, willing her heart to slow. One look from him had the awesome power to quicken the beat of her pulse and take the air in her lungs. How could she face him once, yet alone the year he meant to stay at Gaillard as his own château was being built and his vineyards planted in Alsace? *A year!* 'Twas not possible!

She had managed to escape seeing him all of yesterday and today. Tonight's feast had already been planned to celebrate John's birthday, and while there were a hundred things to attend to, she had pleaded a headache and withdraw to her private chambers. But tonight Morgan would certainly insist she at least appear at the feast in his uncle's honor.

"Mary, help me now. . . ."

Paxton finally entered his chambers in the afternoon to dress for the night's festivities. Yesterday when Michaels had showed him to the guest chambers in the solar, he had demanded his old room. "Milord, 'tis not possible," Michaels had said.

"Why not?"

" 'Tis Milady's private chamber now."

He had kept all emotion from his face. "Linness?"

"Aye, milord."

"She does not reside with Morgan in the large chamber?"

"Nay." He had shaken his head, coloring with embarrassment at the intimate subject. "Shortly after the marriage ceremony, she had her things brought to your old room."

He kept turning this fact over in his mind. What did it mean? Did it mean anything? Perhaps it only meant the sounds of Morgan's slumber disturbed her sleep. Or perhaps something more . . .

Thinking on it again, he stepped over to his window and peered out. The entire anatomy of the inner court spread before him. His gaze found the small chapel. Stained-glass windows had been put in since he left, and these appeared to tell the story of a woman. The Virgin Mary, no doubt. Little else had changed. He saw the enormous kitchen, smoke pouring from its two tall chimneys. Forming a semicircle against the outer wall were the stables, the cow braes and mews, the armory, the lofts and well, the smithy and kennels, and finally the knights' and servants' quarters.

An enclosed garden had been added just outside the wall. Climbing vines of roses, heliotrope, and ivy covered the walls in green. From his window he could also see a far corner of this flowering space. Beneath two leafy trees sat a stone bench and ivy-covered cistern. Water lilies and lilacs floated in the water where a half dozen birds flew up and around the stone fountain. 'Twas an enchanting place, and without a doubt, he knew it was a labor of her love. . . .

He looked away. Despite his family animosities, Gaillard had been a paradise for him as a boy. He knew every inch of the complicated labyrinth made of these stones; he knew everything, everywhere, all the smells, good climbs, soft lairs, secret hiding places, jumps, slides, and nooks. A hundred times, no less, he had climbed out his window and onto the narrow stone ledge that connected three of the four solar apartments.

So he knew how to reach her. The only question was when.

Morgan knocked softly but did not wait for a response before swinging the door to his wife's room open. With a gust of cool spring air, he stepped inside, only to find Linness kneeling in prayer at her small, candlelit altar to Mary.

She turned to see him. "Morgan . . ."

He came directly to the point. "Milady, the hall is full of our guests, and Clair tells me you do not intend to make an appearance tonight."

"Aye," she replied, turning back to the altar. "I believe she told you my reason."

"A head pain, she said."

His hand came over his beard; he looked for a moment frustrated, always burdened when a command failed to exercise his will. Which seemed to only happen with her, the strange and beautiful woman who was his wife. He had never once heard her complain of a physical ailment. Not once. So no doubt 'twas a bad head pain. On the other hand, she must make an appearance.

"And I am sorry to hear of it, milady," he said with genuine sympathy. "But can't you make a brief appearance at the table tonight?"

She paused, anxiously looking to the bright, warm light of the fire. She could not sit at the table with Paxton. Not yet. Probably not ever, but especially not before she somehow gained a measure of control, which seemed impossible. She kept praying he would announce an early departure to save them both. Until then, or until she found this miracle of control, she was not ready to face him. "Truly, I do not feel well, milord."

"Ah, but 'tis not often that a man sits with his brother after so long a separation. Confound it, milady," he said, "can you not feel poorly at the table as well as cloistered in this room? I do not ask you much, but—"

He stopped as she swung around to face him, unable to veil her feelings on this. "Nay," she replied with a hint of some long-suppressed anger in her voice. "You do not ask much of me, and yet, I have never once denied you anything."

The words were suffused with meaning. She had never denied him anything. While he might have claimed a part of her heart, if only from her deep appreciation for all he had given her and Jean Luc, he did not want it. He had never wanted it.

He preferred the low women of the township and the neighboring villages to his wife, which, admittedly, had always been a great relief to her after the mercifully few unpleasant experiences in their marriage bed. And if it were only that, she might find a measure of peace in their uncommon marriage. Nay, twas the shameful manner he conducted these liaisons that upset her. He always promised them riches and gifts which he never delivered, but far worse, he promised to care for the dependents got from these illicit matings as all decent men would. Yet this never happened; he would leave these women and children to the uncertain charity of the cruel world, sometimes in shocking poverty. There were three bastards so far. As soon as the woman quickened with child, he dismissed them from his attention as if they no longer existed. She herself had to see to their small needs in secret, usually through Clair.

Morgan had no inclination to ponder subtle allusions and hidden meanings; they were wasted on him. She always wondered if he was just dense or if he ignored it on purpose, and she suspected the latter. She was not surprised when her words produced no effect. He just stood there, heaving a sigh and rubbing his beard.

She returned to the point. "I only ask for this one night's respite for my suffering. I do not think it is too much."

"Oh, very well," he relented, vexed, always nettled by her quiet dignity. "But I order you to come down and bid everyone a fare night, 'tis all. Then you may take this respite. I'll send your woman up to help you dress."

She suffered a moment's shock, which he used to walk out of the room, shutting the door behind him.

He had never ordered her to do anything before.

She felt dizzy with apprehension. Nothing could happen in a crowded room, she told herself. Nothing. She would not even have to look in his eyes. That was, if she could resist the temptation. The temptation of beautiful dark blue eyes, soft and clear, as compelling as life's mystery, and just as deep. "Paxton, what have I done to us?"

Paxton watched with interest as Morgan reappeared in the crowded hall. The servants, with their long napkins draped over their shoulders, proudly bustled about, serving the high table the first course of steaming goose-neck soup in warm bowls, trenchers made of hollowed-out shells of bread, French pies, and bountiful plates of early spring fruit. Three English musicians serenaded the gathering from the gallery above, competing with the loud and raucous noise below. He watched Morgan quickly find Clair in the lower tables, and after passing instructions to her, Morgan returned to take his seat in the middle of the table on the dais.

Barely listening to his uncle, Paxton drained his goblet and held it up as a servant rushed to fill it. Morgan probably had to force Linness to appear. He did not wonder at her agony, for he felt the same. He half wished she had refused Morgan's command.

Morgan was distracted with Edward, the sewer, who managed the wine tasting. Too young to sit at the table, Jean Luc appeared in the upper galley with two other young boys, spying on the proceedings below. Paxton caught sight of him and smiled at the boy. He turned to his uncle and interrupted with a question. "What of Morgan's wife, the Lady Linness?"

John's gaze softened in the instant. "Ah, the Lady Linness. You have met her?"

"Briefly."

"She is as fine a lady as I have ever known, loved by all for her kindness and charity." Of course, he would not mention the secret he had discovered a short month after her marriage, having inadvertently overheard an arresting conversation between Linness and Clair. He didn't know why he had kept it to himself, all the while spending endless ·

hours dwelling on its ramifications, before at last he confronted her.

It was too late by then. He, like Morgan and indeed most all of Gaillard, had fallen under the spell of her wholly unique and wonderful charm, and to condemn her was impossible. It became unconscionable after Jean Luc was born and Morgan had a son. As the years went by, his gratitude for the wisdom of his silence grew, and it seemed to him it was all meant to be. . . .

With an edge of exasperation, Paxton said, "Everyone seems to think she is a saint."

"She is! Why, her charity is famous—"

"Her charity?"

"Aye," John answered, "she has given a tidy fortune to the Saint Leonard de Noblat hospital for the sick and infirm over the years, and she has bestowed rich dowries on the poorest girls. Now everyone turns to her with their sad stories." He sighed with a smile. "How Morgan complains about her generosity! But he is helpless to stop her."

"And why is that?"

"Paxton," he chuckled, "you will find it hard to believe, but Morgan is that rare creature—a husband who is mad in love with his wife. He grants her every wish. The lady can do no wrong. She has no faults. She is nothing but virtue and shining goodness."

"That is difficult to believe," Paxton said, draining his goblet again.

"The lady deserves his affection," Father Gayly added, overhearing the conversation as he broke bread and passed the basket on. "She has a depth of character quite uncommon among her sex."

"Father Gayly and the lady are quite close," John added.

Paxton looked over at the middle-aged priest. Short-cropped dark hair covered the sides of his balding head. He wore the beige vestments common to those orders that took a vow of poverty, but this virtue was contradicted by his enormous girth. He recalled John writing to describe the new priest of Gaillard; his uncle had said the man revealed his religiosity only upon the intimate probe of an agile mind, otherwise he was far more likely to be found playing cards or chess, or drinking with the guards, than lighting the candles at the altar or kneeling at vespers.

"You are surprised, I see," he said to Paxton. "Well, the dear lady's enormous faith counsels me through each of my dark periods of doubt, doubt which my enormous cynicism subjects me to. I had once been in audience with the pope and any number of cardinals; indeed I have spent my whole life among the faithful, and yet . . . I have met no one whose faith is as strong a light as the Lady Linness's."

Then John continued, "Whenever Linness is missing, we initiate a search in the forest, where we inevitably find Father Gayly and Lady Linness deep in communion, sometimes lost in their wonderings, oblivious to night falling, oblivious to everything but the weight of their conversation."

"Do you?" Paxton questioned mildly.

Father Gayly nodded, smiling, first with fondness and then with uncertainty. Lord Morgan's brother seemed irritated or angry at the mention of the lady's name. He noticed how tightly the man held his knife. Why? Everybody loved the Lady. . . .

"Paxton." John changed the subject. "Do tell us now—we have heard the story of the Florentine battle many times—"

"Aye." Morgan joined the conversation, adding eagerly, " 'Twas the bloodiest battle since Agincourt! Imagine my pride when we received word that you were one of the last two knights left, with still over twenty-five Florentines to fight. Put the tale in your own words and let us hear it, brother."

The men within hearing range agreed with this and a hush fell over the lower tables. The musicians drew softly on their bows and lute, but Morgan's raised hand made them stop completely.

"There is little to tell." Paxton shook his head, and like most men who fought at Florentine, he felt loath to tell of it. "You can believe I find no pleasure in recounting that gruesome day."

"Milord's reluctance is a shield for his modesty," Simon, his knight, said from a lower table. Paxton protested, but this was ignored as Simon launched into an exciting recounting of the last leg of the famous battle.

With mild surprise, Paxton saw that Morgan took enormous pride in his battle success, as if he were somehow responsible for it. The idea was both irritating and laughable, when it used to be that his smallest success usually sent Morgan into a rage of jealousy. Once his mother announced she had a craving for venison; it had been several months since the game master managed to produce any. In a desperate and futile attempt to please her, he had hunted through snow-covered forests for a week. He finally came across four deer and he felled the old buck.

He had left the prize only for an hour as he care-

fully set bags of grain out for the remaining creatures, a common practice to help the animals get
through the winter and multiply. When he went
back to retrieve his game, the buck was gone. Morgan and his page had followed him and carried off
his prize. With boyish indignation, he accused Morgan of stealing it and tried to explain to his mother
he had felled the creature for her, that Morgan had
stolen it. His mother never believed him, of
course. . . .

All of Morgan's jealousy, all the rivalry, was
gone now, taken away by time and circumstances,
perhaps Paxton's very absence in his life. Now
there seemed only a true brotherly affection left,
and this was forcing an adjustment in his perception of Morgan. Though many other things had not
changed.

No one had ever considered Morgan a particularly thoughtful man. Quite the contrary, Morgan
had always been bored with any subject he found
tedious, and these subjects were many, ranging
from astrology and theology to battle history. True,
Morgan had a commanding air about him, the kind
that arises from a lifetime of watching people jump
at every command, but now he realized there was
something different about his brother, as well.

Paxton watched his brother across the table,
abruptly realizing Morgan was a bit of the buffoon.
The thought startled him. After a lifetime spent
competing with Morgan, he saw at last that the
man had been undeserving of the attention.

Until now. Until he had married a woman
named Linness.

He still could not reason how it had happened.
The idea of a young maid somehow convincing the

world she was a noble Lady seemed impossible.

He intended to find out. . . .

The story of Paxton's heroism left everyone heavily laden with emotion as they broke into enthusiastic applause at the end of the telling. They turned their gazes to Paxton as if he would now make a speech. He did not. He was staring across the room. One by one, heads turned to behold the sight.

He had never seen Linness draped in finery, and while her beauty did not require any enhancement, the sight of her at this moment was startling. The blue velvet gown was edged with gold embroidery but otherwise remarkably simple. The low-cut bodice opened to a vee at the middle. A white silk chemise showed beneath, laced tightly over her bosom from her small waist, while its long, loose sleeves were gathered tightly at her wrists. Her hair, held back by a matching blue and gold band, had been plaited with gold ribbons into two loops on either side of her head.

He noticed the ring draped from her neck.

Linness forced herself to smile at the familiar faces turning to look at her, stopping to clasp hands as she made her way across the hall to the dais. The men rose as she assumed her seat at Morgan's side. Compliments flew about the table but finally settled as she inquired of John how his trip was, pretending normalcy, a pretense betrayed only as her gaze stopped at the man seated across from her.

She tried to listen to John's response, but this was not possible as she felt Paxton's eyes bore into her with undisguised intensity. She reached for Father Gayly's hand and clasped it firmly, feeling his affectionate squeeze.

She could always count on Father Gayly for security.

Linness pretended to listen to the lively conversation around her. Paxton related exclusive news of King Francis and the French court; his anecdotes amused everyone, Morgan most of all. Morgan interrupted to hint at the liaison they had heard about between Paxton and the duchess of Milan, which Paxton ignored as he neatly sliced an apple. She pretended to eat. She even managed an occasional response when it was required. Yet not a second passed when she was not fully aware of his gaze upon her. She was about to beg leave when suddenly she heard Paxton address her.

"Milady," he said while he raised a goblet. "That you are sitting across from me is still . . . How shall I say it? Such a great surprise. I find there are no words to express my emotion upon having caused the tragedy you endured when first arriving at Gaillard."

Silence came swiftly over the table. Startled eyes shot to Paxton before she cast an anxious look to Morgan, who pretended not to hear his brother's mention of the once volatile subject. Morgan appeared engrossed in carving a piece of the broiled venison.

"I was greatly relieved to hear you had emerged unscathed from your ordeal, and had arrived safely at Gaillard." Paxton boldly continued, "It seems nothing short of . . . a miracle."

He tempted the fates, too bold by half! She looked to John for help, but he, too, appeared deeply engrossed in his food.

Paxton paid no mind to the sudden tension at the table. "So, milady, I wonder how it is that everyone calls you Linness instead of Belinda."

She drew a deep, uneven breath and heard herself reply, her voice sounding far away. " 'Tis my pet name, is all."

"Is it?" he questioned as if this were highly improbable. "Odd too," he said evenly, "but if I recall correctly, you don't look exactly like the portrait Morgan was always displaying."

Father Gayly looked from one to the other, sensing something amiss. He thought he knew everything about Linness, and while he knew she had known love before the astonishing pretense that got her married to Lord Morgan, there was such a deep sadness around the subject, he had always assumed the man was dead. Could it be Lord Paxton?

He dismissed the frightening idea. That was not possible. There must be another explanation. "Ah well," he said, leaping to her rescue, "no painter could capture milady's beauty."

Morgan agreed with laughter, relieving the worst of the tension.

Then John added, "She had been ill at the time of the sitting, is that not true, milady?"

A servant set a bountiful plate of grape-stuffed boiled chicken on the table. Inexplicably Linness found herself staring at this. A chicken. Her vision turned white like a canvas for a second, no more, and then returned to normal.

She shook her head to rid herself of the strange effect. The light preceded or warned of her sight. What was it about a chicken?

"Milady, is that not true?" John inquired again.

Linness nodded as she found Paxton again, and watched with fascination and nervousness as he set ripe blueberries inside the curve of the apple slice before lifting the whole treat to his lips. He made the same again and, in acknowledgment to her interest, he set it on her plate.

Her silver eyes widened as she stared at the gift. He would make love to her at the table! She could take no more. She placed her hand on her forehead and started to make her excuses when he neatly interrupted again. "So have you come to love Gaillard?"

"Aye, milord," she answered honestly. "Very much."

Morgan reached over and squeezed her hand.

"And how do your parents fare in faraway Montegrel?"

She returned his stare, her eyes pleading. "Quite well, thank you."

"And does milady hear from them often?" Paxton continued.

Linness could not guess why he asked these less than innocent questions. As if he wanted her to reveal the whole of her long intrigue. Didn't he know or couldn't he guess that if Morgan ever discovered it, she would be made to pay with her life?

"I pen a letter faithfully on the last of each month, and my . . . mother does the same."

"You must miss them very much," he commented, sounding deceptively casual, so casual. "They have never been to Gaillard to see their grandchild, have they?"

"My father is unable to travel so far. He has the gout. Naturally, my mother is unwilling to leave his side."

"They are always sending Jean Luc fantastic gifts," Morgan added. "The boy will be richer than the both of us."

"A fine boy," Paxton said with feeling, and then forgoing any decency because he no longer felt any, he wondered out loud, "And why have you not had more children, madame?"

A tense silence greeted this remark. Linness colored sharply, her eyes lowered as she searched for a way to answer the question.

"Perhaps God will grant that happy wish in time," Father Gayly speculated, a sharpness to his voice. The intensity of emotion between the lady and Paxton was baffling. The man was behaving beastly to her! As if it were the lady's fault she did not give Morgan more children! He was not the only member of the household who understood the prick caused by the cruel remark.

Paxton was staring at Morgan.

" 'Tis her only defect," Morgan said, a strange gentleness to his tone. "But after giving me perfection in Jean Luc, I do not fault her any for it."

Paxton saw the subject had put a sudden tremble in her hands as she abruptly stood with a rash clutch at dignity. "Excuse me, milords," she managed tightly, "I find at last I must withdraw. A good night to you."

The men rose. With a lift of skirts, she exited quickly, quietly, feeling Paxton's gaze upon her until, at last, she disappeared out of the room. Clair, too, rose and left with her. They knew not to speak until safely behind closed doors. With dozens of servants and people under the same roof, they had learned the art of secrecy. They needed it now more than ever.

Chapter 5

The entire table appeared quite drunk when Paxton made his excuses, rose, and left the hall. Certain things never changed. One could always count on Morgan being drunk by the tenth bell and passed out by the eleventh.

He quietly made his way up the stairs to the solar apartments. Hearing the voices from within, he stopped outside Linness's door, which was barely open by a crack. Casting a quick look behind him, he leaned toward it.

"He asked about ye parents?"

Clair was undoing the back buttons on Linness's dress before helping her step out of the gown. She carefully folded it to fit back in the trunk as Linness removed the chemise, her strained voice rising with anguish. "Aye! As if he wanted to trap me in front of Morgan. He must know—surely he must understand!—'twould be my death sentence! 'Twas worse than anything I ever imagined!"

Clair produced a long gold robe. "What are we to do?"

"I do not know!" Linness buried her face in her hands. "I do not know. I am so scared. . . ."

Paxton moved away. She had reason to be scared.

He returned to his darkened room, lit only by a fire blazing in the large stone hearth. The servants were still down in the hall; many had retired. He poured a large glass of water as he waited.

Sometime later he heard Linness's door open and close shut. He opened his door to see her waiting woman exit down the stairs. At last, she would be alone.

He locked his door and moved to the window.

Linness was kneeling at her candlelit altar.

She never heard him enter through her open window. Wearing soft suede boots now, he made no sound as he crossed the space of the chamber and, leaning against the cold stone wall, he hid in the shadows. Minutes gathered and collected as he drank in the sight of her alone in her room.

Once upon a time this had been his chamber. She had changed little of it. Dark blue curtains, bearing the gold crest of Gaillard, draped the canopy bed. His childhood bedcover lay neatly folded at the end. Her trunks were different, but oddly, they occupied the same spots as his once did, one at the end of the bed, another along the far wall with cushions on top to serve as a bench. There was a long shelf with leather-bound and precious books, an elaborately hand-carved armoire, and a matching table.

A lace cloth covered the table. He could barely discern various metal tools, wood carving tools, and bits and pieces of material and cloth. A number of unlit candles sat on brass plates there as if she often worked at night. The room offered an alluring glimpse into the mysteries of this woman.

His gaze came to rest on the small altar opposite the hearth where she knelt. Candlelight lit her face, giving her an angelic appearance with her eyes closed and her hands clasped before her in supplication. Her hair had been unraveled and it was now gathered loosely in back with a ribbon. She looked more beautiful each time he saw her.

With a small, anguished sigh, she stood up shakily, and just as she was about to get in the bed, she heard the soft echo of her name. "Linness . . ."

She swung around as he stepped out of the shadows.

A scream rose in her throat, but before it could sound, his hand came over her mouth. Her frantic eyes searched his face, and when she saw it was he, she collapsed against him, her stomach somersaulting. He removed his hand slowly, distrustfully, watching to make sure she would hold her scream.

"Paxton!" Her frightened gaze swung around the room, as if half expecting to see someone spying on them. "How did you . . ." The words stopped as she realized he must have climbed along the ledge from his apartments. "If anyone finds you here—"

"I will die, I know. Because I am communing with my brother's wife, alone in her private chambers." His gaze filled with emotion as he stared down at her. "And yet holding this private audience with you is worth the risk, any risk." The back of his hand, callused knuckles, caressed the soft skin of her face. She closed her eyes and briefly leaned against that hand.

She lost herself to the joy of his touch. Paxton's hand on her skin was like a tonic; the potent pleasure of it spilled into her and nearly dropped her to her knees. If the moment could but stretch, it would be heaven. . . .

His hands came to her arms, circling the luxurious material of the robe, while her hands clasped his muscled forearms. An inexpressible sadness expanded within her, like frost on a windowpane, as she stared at the face she loved. "Paxton . . ."

"My God, Linness, I keep thinking I will wake from this nightmare."

"I can explain—"

"Explain?" he questioned, his fury rising like a waking monster, flooding into his whispered voice. "You say you can explain? Explain how you became my brother's wife? You, the woman who has haunted my every waking dream, a woman I have searched this godforsaken country for years to find. Years, Linness! My God, I had half my men looking for the poor and beautiful maid of Sauvage."

The idea of his devotion made her gasp painfully.

"And after all these fruitless searches, after losing hope twenty times and again, I return home to have my brother present you to me as his wife? You can explain this madness to me?"

"I was alone! I had not shoes on my feet or a decent cloth on my back. I had nothing, and when I woke you were gone. Gone as if you never were."

"I was coming back. This I told you as you lay in my arms!"

"I did not know! I never heard this!"

A mist appeared in her lovely eyes as she absorbed the tragedy of these words. If only she had waited. If only she had known he would come back. If only . . .

"Paxton, I did not know what to do—"

"So you married my brother. For the life of me, I cannot reason how a maid presented herself as a lady and married a man with half as many titles as the pope. How on God's earth did it happen?"

"The Holy Mother watches over my life and made it happen. I know 'tis a fantastic tale, but 'tis all the truth. I was going through the forest and I came upon the dead Lady Belinda and her knights. One knight was still alive and told me the purpose of the lady's travels. Because of my silvered speech and my fairness, he said I should present myself at Gaillard as the Lady Belinda, that no one had ever seen her before and that her parents would not ever come to Gaillard. He said I would be married and well cared for forever if the ploy worked. I thought I would die otherwise; I was already half-starved for want of food."

He searched her face, first trying to believe it and then trying to understand it. A woman alone and unprotected, with neither shoes nor cloak against the winter, half-starved already. Dear God, she hadn't known he would return to her. Still . . .

She stopped with a gasp of pain as his hands tightened more around her arms. "Did you know Morgan was my brother when you married him?"

Her face drained of color; he saw her fear. She tried to turn away, but he pulled her up sharply. "Answer me!"

"Yes," she cried. "Yes . . . but you had gone off to fight the Italian campaign. I did not know how to find you, and Morgan thought I was Lady Belinda. I would have been condemned again, executed, if I tried to run away. You were gone, Paxton. Gone . . ."

Only to return now.

He released her all at once, turning away in a desperate attempt to grasp this reality. He could not. A lifetime spent trying to understand this cruelest of fates would not be enough.

"Jean Luc?"

"Paxton . . ." She said his name in a plea.

He swung back around. His large hands fitted under her arms, as if he needed to hold her up now. "He's mine, is he not? Jean Luc is mine."

She had to be strong now. For Jean Luc. She stated the unalterable fact. "He is Morgan's by law."

Paxton's face blazed with sudden viciousness. "He is mine in *fact*!"

"It does not matter—"

"Say it, Linness. Jean Luc is mine!"

"Yes," she cried, and then in a whisper suffused with sadness, "Yes."

He just stared at her then, just stared, taking in the emotional pain in her eyes as she looked up at him; the flush spread across her cheeks, her whole manner, everything, pleading with him for understanding.

He suddenly realized that it was not his understanding she wanted but rather his acceptance. Acceptance that she was his brother's wife. Linness.

She held perfectly still as his eyes changed and his gaze fell to the gold chain around her neck. He lifted it and turned it in the firelight until he made out the small engraving of his initials. Morgan had never noticed this, it would seem.

He dropped the jeweled token and found her eyes. For a long moment he just stared down at her. She didn't know what he was thinking until she heard his words. "God forgive me, but I still want you."

She was not prepared for his kiss. Nothing on heaven or earth could have prepared her for this kiss. As his lips came over hers and her head fell back, white-hot lightning exploded through her as he took her mouth with unrestrained force. There was no end to it. Her desperation, their warring emotions, and all that fueled these vanished in the wild ravishment of this kiss.

In the space of it she died a thousand times.

Only to be reborn a thousand more.

A mindless desire surged through him, so swift, so strong, it obliterated the dark reality of the world beyond the touch of their lips. He slipped his hands inside the robe to draw the slim shape against him, needing to feel all of her and all at once . . . and still there was no end to this kiss until—

Reality stabbed a warning jolt through her and she tore her mouth from his. She backed up, nearly falling over in her desperation to escape this, him, and what that one kiss unleashed. "Oh no . . ." She shook her head, her mind and soul focused on Jean Luc and Morgan, and the disaster ignited by this kiss. "It is too late for us!"

In a fierce whisper he said, "Nay!"

She didn't hear. She spun around as the door opened and her heart leaped in terror. "Clair!"

Clair looked from Linness's face to the open window where a shadow disappeared. Though she never saw him, she knew. "Lord Paxton?"

"Aye!"

A gentle breeze blew through the opened window, swirling through the room and making the candles leap and flicker. Linness rushed to the open window and shut the panes, closing the latch to secure them before she collapsed like a paper doll to the floor.

"Merciful heavens!" Clair whispered. " 'Tis madness for him to come here. What did he want?"

"Everything," she cried. "He has my soul, but 'tis not enough. He wants everything Morgan has. . . ."

Paxton stood as still and unmoving as a lion on the ledge outside her window. The blackest night surrounded him; a rage filled him. Rage against his brother. Rage against the woman who had long-ago claimed his heart, then married his brother, stealing from him his only living son. Rage against this binding fate in the darkest hell . . .

That night Linness did not dream of Paxton.

That night she found herself walking in a darkened church. She was staring up at the marble statue of Mary. Mary's hands were clasped in prayer, and her marble eyes were not empty nor cold, nor made of stone. Her eyes were filled with sadness. Sadness for her . . .

Linness tried to see what caused Mary's grief. She knew it was somewhere in the church. Frantically she searched the pews. She suddenly noticed the chickens there. Chickens everywhere. Clucking and screeching, they leaped about her feet, pecking at her skirts. She covered her ears to escape the screeching, growing louder and louder as she climbed on a pew to escape their sharp pecks.

Suddenly Bonet, Gaillard's poultry cook, appeared with an ax. The tall man began hacking off chickens' heads. Blood spilled onto the pews. Father Gayly emerged from the darkness. He looked over the carnage, well pleased, rubbing his hands together in anticipation of a feast.

Something was terribly wrong. Terribly wrong. A sense of doom permeated the dreamscape. Linness looked to Mary for help. A tear fell from her marble eyes, sliding down the stone. She looked back to Bonet. She screamed as the familiar face turned into a long-ago demon from her past.

'Twas Bishop Peter Luce and he held a torch as he came toward her. He held the hand of another. The veiled woman in black. They were coming toward her. . . .

Linness woke with a start. She sat up dazedly and surveyed the empty room. Nothing and no one stirred. Her eyes came to a lump in her bed. Jean Luc.

He must have had a nightmare, too.

She gently drew back the covers to see his sleeping face and lovingly caressed his cheek. He did not stir.

She lay back against the pillows. The strange dream tried to warn her of something; 'twas the only thing she knew. Yet it had been years since she had thought of Bishop Luce, the man who had chased her from the comfort and security of the convent so long ago. Why would she suffer nightmares of him now? Now when the very beat of her heart had been altered by Paxton's arrival?

Jean Luc snuggled against the warmth of his mother's form. His blue eyes opened as he felt her arms come around him. They greeted each other with smiles. He laughed sheepishly and asked with innocent surprise, "How did I get here?"

"I would pose that question to you! I only just woke to find this lump in my bed. I almost screamed, I thought 'twas one of your father's hounds."

The idea made him laugh. They fell into a fit of laughter and tickles, and as their laughter quieted, and some boyhood dream stole his thoughts, she twirled an errant curl in her fingers. 'Twas almost blond, his hair. He looked so much like Paxton, it seemed a wonder no one guessed the secret of his paternity.

As she lay there, staring at Jean Luc and loving him so much, the blessing of that one night washed over her with force. How much love had come from the ecstasy in Paxton's arms!

"Mother . . ." he beckoned uncertainly, "will I leave Gaillard on my seventh birthday? In one year?"

The question gave her pause. Jean Luc had never spoken of it to her before, though Morgan and John often spoke of it—the passage to squire that young boys had to take. Jean Luc knew how much the subject grieved her; she wondered if he had ever overheard one of her arguments with Morgan about it. 'Twas the only thing Morgan said he would refuse her.

She would have to give him up in a year. When he turned the tender age of seven, he would be taken from the comfort and security of their home to go to another where he would be taught by another man. No matter that the child was usually placed with a relative, this time-honored custom of the nobility struck her peasant soul with fear. It seemed a hateful and stupid practice of no good purpose, devastating to both mother and child.

"Mother," he began, carefully watching her expression. "I heard my uncle tell my father he would be honored to take me as squire." He did not want to say the rest, that the idea of living in his uncle's household excited him. He would ride his uncle's warhorses all day. "Father says I must go, that it will make me strong and . . . well, if I must go, I do not think I would mind so much if I went with my uncle."

She lovingly touched her lips to his forehead, closing her eyes to savor the tenderness filling her heart. The idea had never occurred to her before— that Jean Luc might go with Paxton. Of course, it was meant to be; Mary had arranged the whole thing. He needed Paxton. Paxton would love and cherish him as no one else could. Yet it still did not mitigate the pain of giving her son up for all the years of his growing.

Mary, why could I not have had a girl?

For Jean Luc had always been her comfort and solace for losing Paxton. A comfort she needed now more than ever. She could not bear the thought of losing them both, of not having either.

She remembered the flame of Paxton's kiss last night.

Jean Luc did not see the tears appear in his mother's beautiful eyes. "Mother, shall we watch the sunset tonight?"

'Twas their habit to watch the sunset together from the battlements. No matter what they were doing in the day, if it was at all possible, they met in the same spot on the battlements and watched the sunset together. It was their quiet time for sharing thoughts and adventures and stories; a daily ritual that was more sacred to her than vespers.

"Aye." She smiled.

He spotted Maid Belle, his mother's favorite cat,

sitting in the window of the alcove. The morning sunlight streamed across her shiny black coat. Jean Luc leaped out of bed and, knowing not to frighten the skittish creature, he slowly approached the spot. The cat did not seem to mind. He gently reached to pet her and, after a few strokes, he felt over her midsection. "Mother, I can feel her tiny kittens inside. You were right!" With hardly a pause of wonder, he looked down to the courtyard. "There's my uncle and father! They're going to the stables!"

The boy bolted out the door.

There was nothing she could do but pretend it was a normal day, and pray her emotions would not betray her every time she beheld him. She rose to go about dressing. She was just lifting her hair as Clair stepped into the room, her hands behind her back.

She saw the distressed look on Linness's face and said, "All ye troubles came out in ye dreams, am I right?"

"Aye." She nodded, turning to her friend with brows crossed in perplexity. "Strange dreams. I felt as if Mary was trying to warn me of something."

"Ye cannot wonder what?!"

"Nay, 'twas about Father Gayly and . . . chickens."

"Chickens? Ah," Clair dismissed this, "the stuff of madness and nonsense. Look what just arrived," she said, holding out the sealed envelope.

"Another letter? So soon?"

This did not bode well.

After all these years and the continuous exchange of letters, and Clair's amusing anecdotes of the Lord and Lady de Beaumaris, Linness felt she knew them. A deep affection had sprung in her heart; she understood her vision of Belinda. At the time, she had imagined the vision's reference was to Mary, but no, 'twas to the Lady de Beaumaris. One of her deepest regrets was that she would never meet this great lady.

She quickly tore the letter open and, recognizing the familiar script, she read the contents.

My dearest daughter Belinda,

I dispense with all formality as the news my letter bears is urgent. I deeply regret to inform you that your father's illness has taken a turn for the worst. His hours left are numbered. As I wrote last time, we have solicited the help of Vienna's finest surgeon, Monsieur Niccolo Spinelli, but to no avail. Neither the leeches, the bloodletting, nor the many vile potions poured down his throat has alleviated his pain. God is calling to him, and I anxiously await the trauma of his departure.

He begged me to convey his growing affection and love for you, a love that, as you know, has blossomed like a summer rose since you left us. It is so strange, he thinks, that this should be so. Like a seed carried far away from home and dropped on fertile foreign soil, you have grown from a selfish, complaining girl into a woman of virtue, generosity, and piety. How marriage and childbirth have rewarded you! How God has blessed us!

So now, in your father's last hours, his only regret is that he never had the opportunity to view his grandson, Jean Luc, or to embrace the shining creature his daughter has become. I fear that by the time you read this, he shall have left us and this

*world for another, as he seems only to be waiting
for our seal to be on this letter.
    With all my heartfelt affection —*

Linness passed the letter to Clair. Clair read it
once, then twice again. "So," she said slowly. "The
old jackdaw is leaving us. . . ."

By now Linness had grown accustomed to Clair's
blunt and unsentimental view of the world. "Shining creature, generous, virtuous . . . Oh, Clair, how
the sweetened prose doth stick in my throat! Sometimes I feel so . . . so deceitful."

"Little wonder. The stunt ye pulled was the
grandest deceit my ears ever heard."

"And you were the next most elemental player
in this grand deceit. Do you not feel bad about it,
as well?"

A comical expression crossed Clair's face; she appeared aghast at the idea. "Why should I? 'Twas,
after all, me who gave them the daughter they deserved, instead of the death they didn't. I made 'em
as happy as pigs in a cabbage field. They truly love
you! And now he's going to die thinking of his own
flesh as good and angelic and . . . what was it?"

"Pious," Linness supplied.

"Aye. Why, I even gave 'em a grandson!"

There was a truth to it. Linness spent a good deal
of time wondering which truth was greater: the
shared love between Lord and Lady de Beaumaris
and herself, or the deceit on which it was built. She
prayed it was the first.

"You're impossible," Linness decided. "Well,
come. Help me write a letter back."

From the start they had devised a system for
writing to Lady Belinda's parents. Lady Belinda

could not write; apparently this had been just one of her numerous faults. She had trouble reading, as well; letters appeared as indecipherable blurs to her eyes. The convent she had spent several years in had given up trying to teach her shortly before the sisters had sent her back home, "because," Clair had explained, "the lady's less than shining personage disrupted the peace and sanctity of the convent just as she did in her good parents' home. . . ." So Linness simply wrote the letters herself, while the baron and baroness naturally assumed the words were penned by a scribe, and instead of signing them, she drew a big heart, which Lady Belinda's dear mother said had brought tears to her eyes when she first saw it.

Sometime later another letter to Lady Beaumaris was sealed. . . .

With her hair still wet from a swim, Linness, shivering, lifted the pitcher of goat's milk and poured it into the wooden bowl, intending to bring it up to her apartments for her cats. She drew close to the great wide oven where venison hung on a spit. The kitchen boy, Oscar, turned the spit, while Edwin, his brother, stood washing the ladles and brushes for the basting. Unlike older kitchens, the château's kitchen had two more baking ovens, and Linness savored the delicious scent of Vivian's fresh bread that sweetened the air.

She caught sight of Michaels trying to sneak away with a hot piece of bread. This was her cue to start the game. Normally she would point out his shenanigans to Vivian, who would scold him, often threatening him with the ever-present spatula or spoon, and as the elderly cook was so engaged, she would slip the loot of food into her apron pockets and later meet Michaels outside to share in the bounty over laughter.

Not so today. Today she was distracted. . . .

So Vivian caught Michaels at once, moving her great girth in front of the hot baked bread protectively. She pointed not a spatula, but the long-handled rake that was normally used to clean the ovens. "No dirty hands on me bread till I set it on the table!"

Michaels waited for Linness to save him. Instead he heard her curiously subdued voice request, "Vivian, I need some scraps of meat for my cats—"

"Do ye now? Those cats will be the end of meat on Gaillard's tables, they will," the woman complained even as she began heaping a wooden plate with scraps. "Over a half dozen living up there now, and with Maid Belle's lot coming soon, ye will be needin' a wheelbarrow to bring up these precious scraps. . . ."

Despite her complaints, the elder woman had a soft spot for the creatures. Linness had won her affection the day she refused to move a mother cat and its kittens from the comfort of the linen closet. They had been allies ever since, an allegiance that grew stronger with the friendship between Jean Luc and Vivian's grandson, Pierre.

Michaels winked at Linness conspiratorially before he reached over to the tray and quickly stuffed his pockets with hot bread. Linness was looking past him. Vivian held out the plate of scraps, but she, too, stopped as she saw the change in Linness's gaze as Bonet stepped inside the kitchen, warmly greeting everyone.

He held three plucked chicken carcasses in his

hands, preparing to wash them in the big basin before he hung them on a spit over the lesser oven. Linness stiffened visibly as the strange and awful dream came back to her. The crowded room went suddenly white.

She opened her eyes to see the familiar faces staring at her. Michaels's hands had caught her up when he saw her stumble. "Milady, did you faint?"

"Nay." She shook her head slowly, staring still at the chicken carcasses in Bonet's hands.

The concerned gazes of everyone were upon her. "Milady, are you well?"

"Aye . . . I am fine. I—" A chill raced up her spine. She turned to see Michaels's kind face. "Michaels, would you come with me? There is something I must see."

"Of course, milady. Where to?"

"The chicken coop."

The chicken coop sat alongside the dovecote, and the mews. She hated the mews, where the hooded merlins and one prized falcon lived in large wired cages. She loathed the caging of the winged creatures. It seemed the cruelest fate for flying birds who were meant to make their home in the blue sky, to know freedom as no man ever could, to live out their lives in foul-smelling, dark cages. She sometimes had dreams wherein she slipped inside the mews, opened the cages, and watched joyously as the creatures took flight into the night heavens.

The chicken coop was another story. Michaels and she had to bend to enter the smaller space. The afternoon sun lit the space from a window above. A hen led a half dozen chicks across the straw-covered floor, pecking obsessively for specks of leftover grain. Hens sat cooing contentedly on nests while the ducks and geese generally preferred the yards outside. A basket of freshly hatched eggshells lay discarded at her feet. Four roosters preened about, occasionally flying up to the nests. Unlike the hens, the roosters were assured a long life. The Gaillard children had given them names.

Michaels stood, hands on hips, surveying the place. "What is it milady wanted to see?"

A reasonable question, but she had no answer. Her sight did not always, or even often, come through dreams, but she recognized it those few times it occurred. Mary was trying to warn her about a chicken. Something about a chicken. "I do not know really. I had a bad dream about these creatures."

"About chickens?"

"I am trying to make sense of it, too," she replied. "I thought if I came here and looked at them—" She sighed and shrugged. "Ah well. Perhaps it was no more than the nonsense made of any dream." She shook her head and smiled at her apparent madness. "Somehow I felt 'twas trying to warn me of something—"

They turned at the sound of the trumpet outside. They stepped back into the brighter light of the courtyard space. At first they didn't see anything, then the sound of flying hooves was followed by Paxton and Jean Luc riding Tasmania at full speed toward them.

Linness was about to scream, but stopped herself. Like all mothers of boys, she had considerable practice at catching her screams, so as not to burden his irrepressible courage and boyhood fun with her own fear for his safety. She exercised this prodigious fear cautiously, like a precious medicine, using it only when absolutely necessary. Not now.

Jean Luc was safe with Paxton.

Paxton drew back on the reins. The horse lifted into the air, then crashed back to the ground. Her son's wild peals of laughter joined with Paxton's. She stood very still, watching, as he lowered the boy to the ground and swung off himself.

Jean Luc's face flushed with excitement as his uncle embraced him. Paxton's laughter stopped as his eyes came to hers. Morgan and the rest of their party rushed in on horses behind them. Paxton stood up slowly.

She wore a work dress of green and gold stripes and a white apron prettily embroidered with green flowers. 'Twas cloth a peasant might wear, but he understood it hardly mattered what she wore; tattered rags or a colored silk, the effect was the same. The wet hair told him of what he had just missed. His gaze fixed on her breasts, where his ring hung, and he remembered their fullness against his chest long ago, the lush temptation of her nudity against his hot skin. . . .

He suddenly cursed this uncharacteristic boyish agitation; it was irritating, to say the least. He pointed her out to Jean Luc.

"Mother." Jean Luc ran to her. "Mother, did you see me? My uncle let me ride his horse again! We went so fast! The wind blurred my eyes and I thought we were flying. My uncle says he will help me train my pony, that he will get me a saddle finer than any in all of Gaillard! Mother, are you listening?"

Michaels looked curiously from Linness to Paxton and back again. Their gazes had locked across the distance; she seemed unable to look away. She finally looked down at her son with a start as riders crowded into the courtyard. "What? Oh, aye, I saw you. It gave me such a start!"

Paxton removed his gloves as he stepped toward them. Then she knew how much trouble she was in, for his nearness caused her blood to rush from her head, giving her a brief wash of dizziness, which she quickly recovered from. Only to find a slight shake in her knees.

Oh, Paxton, Oh Lord . . .

"So," Paxton began in a pretense of indifference. "Are you anxiously awaiting your husband's return, milady?"

The words were like a slap to the face.

Paxton, do not do this to me . . .

She wanted to say it out loud, not realizing the pain on her face said exactly that. The truth was, she never anxiously awaited her husband. Ever.

Jean Luc was talking to her, and she realized he, too, had asked her a question. Without having a clue as to what plot or scheme she agreed to, she replied, "Aye, go on now."

The boy ran off to the stables.

Paxton's attention shifted to Michaels as he struck a conversation with him on the subject of horses. She realized she could leave, that she should leave but somehow her mind had focused on his hands; his large, beautiful hands holding the suede gloves at his waist. Without warning, she was remembering the unholy pleasure of his touch. . . .

They were forbidden thoughts.

Her cheeks flamed with color and she forced these thoughts from her mind. Morgan and the others approached, greetings were exchanged, and then the whole group turned toward the stables. She watched their retreating backs. Paxton had not wanted an answer to the question. He only meant to torment and punish her because she had slept with his brother. If he only knew . . .

A chicken wandered at her feet.

She thought of Father Gayly. . . .

Linness sat at her small table working on Jean Luc's knights. Over the years she had found a strange comfort in carving wood, chipping at it bit by bit to make something useful or pretty or amusing. At first she had carved only tools: brushes, combs, the handles for hammers. Then a bow, a doll for Tera, a cottager's little girl, a pretty frame for an embroidered prayer. Talent had aided her growing skill. This year she felt capable enough to make Jean Luc a set of toy knights for the gift giving on his birthday.

The room had darkened and four candles lit the table where she finished one of the pieces. She had already made one good knight and one bad, a princess and a magician. She wanted the magician to be good, for the fun her boy would have finishing off the bad knight. Yet somehow the form emerging in the carved wood kept having an ominous shape. This was her third attempt.

She refused to join the household for supper in the hall. She claimed fatigue and told Clair to tell Morgan she was asleep, that if he pressed, to say she had a fever. She needed to find the necessary armor in which to breathe in the same room as Paxton. So far she did not have this strength.

She felt like the sleeping princess in the child's

tale. She felt as if she had been in a deep slumber all these long years of his absence, her slumber interrupted only by her dreams of him. Then he had returned and had touched his lips to hers, awakening her to a new world where miraculously he lived and breathed alongside her, a world of bright colors and acute sensations, a world where each moment belonged to him. Only him.

Paxton . . .

She found herself examining each breath and gesture and stolen glance, evaluating it for hidden meanings and subtle allusions, as if she and Paxton lived in a secret world known only to each other. The secret world of forbidden desire . . .

She had to find strength to overcome it. Perhaps over time the effect he had on her would wear away; she prayed fervently for this to happen. She suspected it would not.

The noise from the hall drifted up.

A chill raced around the room like a menacing spirit. The fire did not chase it away. She found herself staring at the face emerging on the carved figure of the magician in her hand. Abruptly it took shape in her mind. 'Twas somehow familiar to her. Who did it remind her of?

With a start she saw it resembled Bishop Peter Luce.

The wooden figure fell with a clamor to the table. She rose in horror and backed away. How strange! Why was he haunting her now? After all these years?

She closed her eyes and remembered all the fury seething inside the man, Peter Luce. His anger was a thing so painful, he had buried it deep inside where it had grown; monstrously, it had grown.

Now as a man, this monster had to be fed the pain of others. She had sensed all this at a tender age long ago. She had known he was a man to be feared.

She would never see him again. He might even be dead now. Praise God that it be so and forgive me the sin. . . .

She impulsively picked up the doll, rose and rushed to the fireplace. The figure was tossed into the flames. Fire lapped around its hateful form before the fire went suddenly white. And on the white canvas before her she saw Father Gayly choking.

Her silver eyes opened in fear. She remembered Bonet carrying the chickens. The chickens were for supper. Father Gayly would be eating them.

She ran out of the room. Sheer panic gave her speed as she flew down the stairs and through the corridor to the hall. But it was too late. She heard the sickening crash of a bench toppling, the men and women rising, a rush of cries.

"He's choking! He's choking!"

Linness burst upon this scene. Everyone had gasped in horror as Father Gayly stood, his hands on his neck, his face reddening. "Save him!" she cried. "For the love of Mary, save him!"

As everyone else stared helplessly, Paxton rushed into action. He leaped over the table and behind the man. He slapped his back, once, then again. Nothing happened and not knowing what else to do, Paxton grabbed hold of his head, tilted it back, and reached his hand inside his throat. He pulled the fatal chicken bone out and tossed it to the floor. Too late. Father Gayly was unable to catch his breath, and as a blinding pain seemed to explode inside him, he clutched his chest and sunk into Paxton's strong arms.

Paxton laid him gently to the floor.

"Nay." Linness fell on top of him. "Nay! Don't leave me! Please to Mary, don't let him leave me...."

She set her head against his huge chest and willed herself quiet, listening for the beat of his heart. For too long a time no sound came to her ears; his body was as still and quiet as a winter night. And warm, so warm still...

A strange rhythm came to her ears. For one merciful moment she thought it was life returning to his body. Only to abruptly realize it was the sound of her own soft sobs.

She remembered little after that. Someone finally came with a blanket to cover his body. Someone else was whispering a prayer for the dear man they all had grown to love. Hands came to her shoulders to pull her away. The hands shook ever so slightly as their warmth penetrated her grief. She saw they were Paxton's.

Morgan leaned over and took hold of her arms, leading her away. He was saying something; she couldn't hear. Her grief echoed in a roar in her ears, wave after wave cresting through her. She couldn't stand, unable to perform the simplest function. Morgan caught her up in his arms. Clair was there suddenly, taking her hand as they entered her solar. Morgan laid her on the soft cushion of her mattress. She was hardly aware of his awkward sympathy expressed in a jumble of platitudes. "He was a fine man and a goodly priest, the best I have ever known.... He will be sorely missed...." and so on. Or even Clair's that came afterward.

Finally the door shut and she was alone.

She lay perfectly still on the bed in the darkened room, and at first her tormented thoughts centered on her guilt. If only she had realized sooner what the dream had meant. If only she had the sight two minutes sooner, she would have been able to save her friend. If only she had gone down to supper, she might have put the pieces together in time to have saved him. . . .

Then reality began settling over these thoughts.

Father Gayly was gone. No more long afternoon walks. No more celebration of their faith. No more laughter. No more deep and shared understandings of the divine.

Their afternoon walks had started when she was large with Jean Luc, and had continued to his last days. They were marked in her mind by the stages of her son's growth. First she had carried him on these walks strapped in a large scarf tied at her shoulders, close to her heart. Then in a saddlebag on her back. When he became too heavy for her to manage, Father Gayly carried him. Then Jean Luc would walk part of the way. By the time Jean Luc was three he walked the entire distance at their side, though at the end of these long sojourns, Father Gayly always made him forget his tired legs or his hungry stomach by telling Bible stories, or the tales of the Round Table, which he especially loved.

Father Gayly's keen intelligence probed and pricked at her understanding of her faith. Like a sculptor, his questions shaped her comprehension until it came to gild her life, the celebration of the force of love on earth. She in turn renewed his faith, so sorely tried by the folly and stupidity of his fellow man and the cynicism his intelligence bred. They had both needed each other, finding solace, comfort, and camaraderie.

I shall miss you, my friend . . .

Grief descended, sad and deep and quiet, over her heart. Grief made of longing. Longing for a last word, an embrace, a good-bye. A last touch . . .

She felt suddenly chilled. So cold. She tried to burrow farther down into the covers. Shivers raced up and down her spine. She dreamt of snow.

The window was latched shut. She tried to struggle up from the shallow depth of her sleep. To no avail. As if her soul demanded the brief respite from grief, it refused to let consciousness intrude on her sleep. A chilly draft raced into the chambers from the cold night, and she turned toward the pillow, trying to find a measure of warmth.

A man stood over the bed watching her as she slept. Her robe had parted and he stared down at her naked figure. As fear seized her, a soft cry escaped her. She tried to cover herself, but the more she tossed, the more tangled the bedclothes became. She struggled to open her eyes to see him, but they refused her will and she was falling, falling into blackness.

He had to see that she was all right.

Even asleep, her grief showed on her face. He stared at the long hair spread across the pillows, the slim lines of her neck, the lush offering of her round full breasts, and he gripped the dagger in his hand tighter as his body flushed with a heat that was almost painful. His gaze roamed over the flat stomach and dramatic curve of her hips, the lush tuft of hair between her thighs, and her long legs. Where the blazes was Morgan? On this night when she surely needed the comfort of an embrace more than any other, he found her alone in her bed. Again. Why?

He had to know why. If he had found Linness surrounded in marital bliss, he might find the strength to leave her be. But this puzzle teased him unmercifully. Twice today it sent him flying to his feet, pacing the floor like a caged creature, mad with his longing. And this morning, when he had woken from a lustful dream of this slim form pressed against his heat, he had rushed out Gaillard's gates and into the frigid cold waters of the river. It did not bode well; here he courted a disaster far more deadly than any battle.

Drawing on his great will, he drew the covers over her form and turned away. He imagined he was strong enough to resist the need to come again. But this thought brought no comfort as he disappeared into the night. . . .

"Where are you going?"

Linness turned with a start. She looked up the stairs of the castle keep to see Paxton and Morgan and a number of men, merchants from Gaillard, filing out of the entrance hall. They had just finished the afternoon meal, after spending the morning in the vineyards. Everyone talked of Paxton and his new methods of vineyard production, a fertilizing method he had discovered in Italy. There was still time to implement it this year, and Morgan was already convinced these new methods would save the harvest. The predictions of a rich harvest put him in a fine mood, punctuated by loud laughter, back slapping, and a childlike giddiness.

The men came down the stairs. Linness stopped, searching faces for a clue as to why the question was asked. Paxton's question made her feel as if something was amiss. "I am going for a walk."

Paxton's gaze narrowed. He looked incredulous. "Not alone."

"Aye. Alone."

The loose trailing burgundy skirt swirled about her feet. The long hair was covered with a thin, almost sheer, maroon cloth. A thin braided band of the dark burgundy color sat like a crown over that. She held a basket on her arm. She was about to turn and walk away when she was addressed again.

"You will not walk about unescorted."

She turned back around. "I am perfectly safe."

"That she is, Paxton," Morgan said as he tested a new sword his armorer just produced, slashing it about in the air. "I would kill the man who dared."

"Aye," Paxton replied. "And the killing would be after the fact. I will escort you, milady." Without taking his gaze off her, he added, "With your permission, Morgan."

"Suit yourself," Morgan laughed. "As I recall, you always do." Just like that he forgot them, turning to his armorer with his compliments.

Emotions trembled through her as Paxton came to her side. She thought of saying she changed her mind about the walk, but stopped herself. She lived in terror of giving herself away. An action, glance, or word could reveal the intensity of her feelings for Paxton, and she saw at once that to refuse might draw unwanted attention.

Yet to be alone with Paxton was to step into a forbidden world. A world where desire was an unmerciful tease. Even now as they walked out the gates and onto the road, she was focused on the tall man at her side. She was aware of him and everything about him: the darker color of his brows, the tiny creases at the corner of his eyes, the errant lick of a chestnut-colored curl on his forehead. And she noted his fine clothes too. He wore a black woolen houppelande with leather padded breastplates, perfectly fitted across the wide breadth of his shoulders and belted at his waist with metal-studded leather. Instead of the fashionable hose, he wore cotton breeches for riding and black boots that reached all the way to his knees.

She was acutely aware of where his gaze rested. His ring burned against her skin, and she reached a hand across her bosom and toyed mindlessly with it. He stopped suddenly and she turned to stare up at him. "You are afraid of me."

The gray eyes—made grayer by the cloudy sky—stole swift glances around as if someone might be watching. "You cannot wonder why!"

"Nay, there is no mystery in your fear. Yet you know I would not hurt you?"

"I never thought that. Not in the way that you mean. To be alone, though—"

"God's curse, girl, I will be at Gaillard for nearly a year, and every time I draw near you, you grow mute and breathless and more frightened than a deer caught in the aim of a crossbow." Anger suffused his tone; his stare was level, direct. "You must overcome your aversion to me or our secrets will be betrayed."

She did not trust herself to give voice to her thoughts. She turned away to prevent their sounding—there were too many people about and too many gazes upon them. 'Twas not possible to maintain a friendly air of indifference. 'Twas madness to even try. Best to stay separated as much as possible.

They were passing through the township now. People stopped their chores and called out to her, and she replied in kind, mostly about the clouds and the promise of rain and the prediction she would soon be wet.

"The townspeople appear to love you."

The comment brought a smile tugging at the corner of her mouth, despite everything. He saw that it pleased her much. Yet this disappeared as she caught sight of the woman watching from an upstairs window above a common tavern.

Paxton looked up to see a young, beautiful woman boldly staring at them. Long golden braids fell over a silk undergarment that was all she wore. Her hands lay proudly across her swollen belly as if she were flaunting her fertility to Linness. The cloth she wore was practically transparent.

"Who is she?" Paxton asked.

"Her name is Amber."

"Amber?" Paxton questioned, and then laughed. "That was Amber? Why, I remember the girl as a little street urchin, the baker's daughter, am I right? She was always trailing behind the boys, chasing after them in play."

Linness said nothing, but he watched the color leave her face. He could not explain how, but he knew the woman solicited a barrage of emotion from Linness.

"Linness, what is she to you?"

"She is nothing to me."

He gently took her arm, drawing up her attention. "You are lying. Why, I wonder?" He studied her face; understanding filled him, startling him. He could see into her mind as if her thoughts were an emotion that passed between them. " 'Tis your sight, am I right?"

She looked away, unnerved by his hand upon her. The slight touch caused a tremble of awakening. The need to touch him was like a thirst borne of standing beneath a hot summer sun. Every night she woke from erotic dreams drawn from their one night of ecstasy six years ago. Dreams wherein her heart pounded and her blood rushed hot and she imagined she felt the imprint of his lips upon her . . .

Forbidden dreams . . .

"What is it your sight tells you?"

"That she is a danger to me."

The idea of anyone harming her was of extreme interest to Paxton. "How is that?"

"I do not know how."

She was aware of his scrutiny as they walked along. "Who is her husband?"

"She is unmarried."

"Then who is the father of her bastard?"

The question made her nervous; too nervous. Hastily she said, " 'Tis not my place nor is it in my nature to pass along common gossip."

He sensed something of import here, but he did not know what. He wanted her at ease. Desperately he wanted her to find ease with him.

"Your sight. Everyone talks of it. Morgan said at first he thought it was little more than fancy, but now he says he has learned to believe you."

She smiled. "Father Gayly always said Morgan mixes truths and falsehoods into an absurdly amusing reality."

"Aye," he said, laughter lighting his eyes. "Despite all the evidence to the contrary, even the explorer Columbus's famous journeys, the man still believes the earth is a flat rock, and that the sun circles around and around the earth, that it is populated in parts by horned, dark-skinned pygmies, and that Eden actually exists in the Far East surrounded by a great wall of fire."

She shook her head at Morgan's obstinately closed mind. "Father Gayly used to argue with him until he was breathless and blue in the face. He finally decided Morgan's mind was as unreachable"—she laughed—"as a cloistered virgin locked by the chastity belt."

Their laughter quieted before he stopped again. and, in a whisper that conveyed the wealth of his sympathy, he said, "The sadness is in your eyes still. You loved him very much."

"Aye," she said, and as they walked he prodded her to tell him about this man she had come to love. In a voice heavily laden with grief, she told him about the sharpness of his intellect, the complexities of his mind, and the thing that drew them together more than anything, the ambiguities of his faith. "Our friendship was a blessing in my life. I will always miss him."

"Did he ever suspect what had happened to you?"

A sad smile changed her face as she remembered his incredulousness and laughter when she told her fantastic tale. "Aye, he had always, or almost always, been in my confidence." In a whisper she added, "John, too, you know."

"John knows?"

"Not about you, but all the rest. He discovered

the secret by accident. He overheard Clair and me talking once, but up until about two years ago, he had never revealed to me that he knew."

He was contemplating this when, to his surprise, they left the main road for a worn path through the vineyards. The path took them into the forest. She realized the mistake as soon as they entered the darkness brought by the entwined branches of the trees overhead. She stopped and turned to face him as if he, too, understood they were truly alone with no eyes upon them and no ears listening. She saw at once he did.

He stared down at her, his eyes soft and dark and so beautiful. A hand reached to caress her hot cheek. She closed her eyes and said his name in a whisper of yearning, confusion, and fear.

"The night he died I came into your room. I had to see that you were all right." Her silver eyes reflected the sympathy in his. "I wanted to comfort you desperately. Yet as I stood over your bed, I knew I could not touch you and leave again. . . ."

Fear won out. 'Twas madness to speak freely, even if they were alone. Shaking her head in negation, she hurried forward along the path, terrified of what might be said now. The path wound through the forest, coming out on her private spot at the river's edge. It was completely isolated. A small bank surrounded by trees, set before the roar of the river.

She leaned against a trunk and closed her eyes, willing her heart to a slower pace. She heard him approach her. For several long moments he was silent as he stared.

He understood her anxiety all too well. His gaze traveled over her closed eyes, the high, flushed cheeks, the wine-dark lips slightly parted. Her bosom, tightly bound, pushed up the creamy softness of her breasts where his ring always sat. A maddening tease; his fingers ached to free this treasure, to take her in his arms and bury his hot flesh in the sweet mercy of hers. . . .

"When I was a boy we used to play a game called 'truth.' A simple game where one person asks four questions of the other. And the only rule is that truth must suffuse every spoken word of the answer." His hand reached for the band on her head and he withdrew the sheer cloth to see her long hair wrapped around either side of her head in loose braids. "Will you play with me, Linness?"

Her silver eyes pleaded with him, but it was too late. It had always been too late. He asked the first question. "Why do you deny Morgan your bed?"

She hesitated, coloring sharply, and to his shock, he saw the question shamed her.

She dropped her gaze to the large booted feet beneath her, pausing with uncertainty. Morgan did not view her as a man views his wife. Despite Morgan's possessiveness, he thought of her only as his son's mother, though this was a lofty elevation indeed. He treated her with the utmost deference and respect always. Over the years, this, taken with her sight, had a queer effect on the way other people thought of her: untouchable, saintlike, a Madonna.

Morgan never bothered to hide his numerous liaisons and affairs; he gave no consideration to her feelings or shame, no consideration to decency. This made them the favorite subject of everyone's gossip as the sheer number of his liaisons boggled the mind almost as much as the unchivalrous manner with which he conducted these affairs. He could have any woman he wanted and yet he always seemed to pick those whose morals had sunk so low, they lay with any man who showed the slightest interest, then he discarded them and his children as easily as if they were worn hose.

She shook her head, first slowly, then more certainly. "Truth. There could be no more dangerous game between us. We cannot afford truth; 'tis a luxury fate has kept from us. Paxton," she pleaded, "truth will hurt us."

"Us," he questioned softly, a bitter edge to his voice, "or me?"

"How can you even ask that? 'Twould hurt us both, me, I think, even more than you. If you don't believe me, then I will prove it. I will answer your questions."

Their gazes locked. "Why do you deny Morgan your bed?"

With no hesitation she stated the fact. "I do not deny him my bed."

Paxton could not hide his shock. He was stunned into silence and felt as if he had just been sliced with a hot blade.

She had warned him.

"Does he ever insist on his marital rights?"

"Paxton, you are tormenting me—"

"Answer me. . . ."

"Nay," she whispered. "Not since the beginning. 'Twas but two weeks, less, before I had the morning sickness. Never afterwards."

"Do not tease me, Linness," he said as he seized her arms, pulling her up. "I could not bear it now."

" 'Tis true," she cried. "You wanted the truth and I said it."

The memory of those few awful times emerged

in her mind. Lying with Morgan had been nothing like lying with Paxton. Morgan's bed had been like stepping into a whirlwind made of wet lips and hot breath, grunts, and harsh hands. Her only mercy had been his quickness with the couplings. He never used a toothcomb, and his breath was most foul, and while that might seem a slight fault indeed, 'twas so bad, she had stuffed tiny drops of bees wax up her nostrils and piled the bed with sachets of fresh scents in order to endure the ordeal.

As soon as he knew she was with child, he had stopped bedding her. Then, once, two years after Jean Luc was born, she had tried to share Morgan's bed again. She closed her eyes as she remembered his groping hands and lips, his mounting desperation and frenzy, the embarrassing unwillingness of his flesh. With as much tenderness as she could muster, she had tried to help, but it was no use. Nothing worked. His last words were, "Like the Madonna herself, you are. I will not subject you to this indecency again, milady. . . ."

As Linness finished her story, Paxton slowly released her, the stinging words giving way to a far greater relief. He felt a sudden profound surge of joy, as if a burden he had been weighed down with had suddenly lifted from his shoulders.

Yet he didn't understand. Why didn't Morgan want her?

Paxton's gaze found her in the instant. She was not just beautiful but more desirable than the next thousand women, and she was Morgan's wife. His wife. Morgan had always had a lusty appetite, hardly discriminating between women at all. He used to tease Morgan that he'd bed the four-legged creatures if he didn't have so many two-legged ones from which to choose.

Suddenly he understood. "Amber . . ."

In a pained whisper she told him, "She is one of his women. 'Tis Morgan's child she carries. She flaunts her belly. She tells everyone how pleased Morgan is with her and the child she carries, that though it is a bastard, Morgan will spoil him and his mother with riches. She tells everyone how sad it is that I am barren and can bear him no more children, that it is the very reason he came to her. Morgan tells all his women these things, and then as soon as they get with child, he abandons them. . . ."

"His dependents? He leaves them nothing?"

She shook her head. Truth, he wanted the truth, and she would give it. "You don't know what it has been like all these years without you. With only the memory of our one night to feed the longing in my soul. The terrible longing. I could not have lived if it were not for Jean Luc. Paxton, after you were gone, Jean Luc was all I had of you. As he grew and thrived and I realized he would be taken from me soon to be squire to some distant lord, I began to dream of another child. I prayed every night to Mary to give me another child, a girl this time. I . . . I tried to approach him and—"

"Nay, Linness." His voice was firm, threatening, as he took her by the arms again, silencing her with a gentle finger. "Nay. Please to God, do not put visions in my head of you trying to coax my brother to your bed. Not after I have just learned the nightmare I have lived with since I first heard him introduce you as his wife has just been miraculously lifted."

He studied her lovely face and saw, unbelievably, that she was still tormented. "Dear God, I cannot believe it. You think Morgan's rejection is, rather than the bizarre expression of my brother's perversity, somehow your fault; a failing of some kind. That you have a figure not luring enough, or a face not pleasing enough." The silver eyes shot to his face as he chuckled bitterly. "Aye, Linness. For there is no other man I know who, if married to you, would trade the treasure of his marital bed for another. The idea is laughable, and yet, yet it pricks at me like a jagged piece of ice and makes me ask my next question. Do you love him?"

The question surprised her more than any other. "Never."

"Never?"

"My heart was stolen before I met him; you know this."

Fat drops of rain began to fall around them and yet neither moved, neither dared to breathe, as she stared up at him, and he, down at her. "Say it, Linness. Let me hear you say the words."

"I love you." And then in a whispered rush of utter agony, "I have loved you always. I will love you always. My curse is a lifetime made of longing and unanswered desire—"

"Nay," he said, "not as I draw breath!"

He lowered his mouth to hers as his arms circled her small waist and drew her tight against his body. Not a gentle kiss. Beneath the falling rain the wild ravishment of his kiss made her pounding heart explode in one fiery burst that sent her swooning and helpless in his arms.

Her surrender allowed him deeper access in the succulent recesses of her mouth. He answered her yearning and, fanned by its flames, he pressed her slender hips against the very heat of his passion.

Fire curled in her belly, and yet with it came the image of death. Their desire was death; its unleashing, the slow march to the executioner's scaffold. She tore her mouth from his and slipped from his arms. "Nay, Paxton! We are held hostage by our fate!"

Rain fell unnoticed all around them. Passion shined in his eyes as he stared at the girl who just stepped out of his grasp. "Your fate changed the moment you spoke those words to me. I will have you, Linness. In secret or no, I will have you. . . ."

"Nay." She shook her head, desperate to make him understand. " 'Tis madness to court our love! 'Twill bring our deaths!"

Paxton was a seasoned warrior, a man who had faced death too many times to still fear its threat. "Death," he scoffed huskily. "I have lived through years of facing death every day, many times a day; it no longer has the power to move me. Every moment I still breathe is extra and to be celebrated now, today," he said with feeling. "So that denying my desire becomes the monster I cannot, will not, fight—"

She backed away as if he might advance. "Nay. I'll fight! I will! I must—"

He reached her in two steps, his arms wrapping around hers as she stared up into his fierce eyes. "Fight me?" The whispered question hinted at his amusement as he leaned over, his lips brushing against her forehead. "You don't have armor enough to fight me." His lips lowered to the nape of her neck where her pulse beat wildly. He heard her sweet gasp. "I shall prove it to you, love—"

"Paxton..."

Terrified, she tried to shake him off. Images of Morgan's rage swam dizzily through her mind. Surrender meant death, and while that dark threat might no longer move him, she felt its full power. Perhaps they could escape the threat the first time or even the second, but 'twas a path that would eventually lead her soul to hell. For, even if Morgan spared her own life, it would only be to punish her more by allowing her to live in a world where Paxton did not.

As she backed away, she vowed with a fierce conviction, "I must fight you ... I must—to save us!" She stepped back, stumbled, and turned to flee down the river path.

He watched her disappear before lifting his face to the darkened skies. He let her run. For now. Until she understood they had no more choice of path than the moon chose to circle the earth or the earth circle the sun. Until she knew every merciful step of the journey would be worth the price they paid in hell ...

This was a battle he looked forward to. ...

Chapter 6

A cool spring wind swept into the solar apartment through unseen cracks and ill-fitted
doorways, interrupting the cloak of quiet with a
soft whistle, while Linness waited impatiently for
Clair to leave and shut the door. Then she broke
the seal and unfolded the letter. She heard his voice
in her mind as she read the bold script:

> *By day we are theater actors, but beneath this shal-
> low exterior, I am made of longing. Longing for
> what can never be, longing for a violent transport
> into the glimpses of what life should have been. I
> see the same longing in thy eyes. Answer thy long-
> ing, my love. Tell me denial has become as awesome
> as death; desire has become thy life, dictating the
> beat and pulse of your heart. . . .*
>
> *Tell me, Linness. . . .*

She read the note again and then twice more.
Glimpses of what life should have been . . .
She saw him every day now, many times a day.
Each and every afternoon Paxton escorted her and
Jean Luc on sojourns to the river, and these were
the glimpses of what life should have been.

161

Glimpses of the family they might have been. Longing and desire were stirred by nothing more than the music of his laughter, his storytelling and wit, the intimate probe of his questions. Witnessing his natural ease and love for Jean Luc plunged her into a depth of feeling she had never known before. It was impossible now to separate the force of physical desire from the emotional, and she did not try. Every time he stepped within the circle of her vision, she felt as if she were floating, buoyed by the indescribable sensations his nearness brought her: a pounding heart, racing pulse, a fluttery feeling in her abdomen, so that her breath caught each time, her thoughts fled, her whole body felt like sparks of fire. . . .

Glimpses of what should have been . . .

She constantly sought him in secret, too; she could not help it. She would listen for his door opening or the sound of his boots crossing over stones. At the table his laughter would reach across the distance separating them to rush over her in a warm caress. She would watch from her window above the courtyard as Paxton parried and fought his men, his half-naked body glistening with sweat and strength. Or under the pretext of some domestic chore, she would spy through the stable doors as he returned from the fields and managed the horses, spellbound, his every movement and gesture a source of endless fascination.

She crushed the note in her hand. Each beat of her heart echoed in her ears, shattering the silence, each labored breath seemed to demand conscious will, and she felt fear. Enormous fear. Nightmarish scenarios of witnessing Paxton's death played through her mind. She saw Morgan's rage, his pain, his revenge; Morgan's knights rushing at Paxton to execute his death. And 'twould be her death too; Paxton was her heart and, therefore, her life. Her very life.

She began pacing the floor. Did he not understand where their forbidden love would end? That to have her once was the first step on the journey to hell? To have him once was to want him always; one night of love would lead to another and another, desire and love growing each and every time until—

They were caught. Until Paxton died.

These thoughts wove a dark and menacing cloud about her. Could she fight him? Could she resist the temptation of his solitary presence in this room?

She closed her eyes and imagined the scene that would transpire. She imagined all the tension exploding at the feel of his lips upon hers. A kiss of salvation and damnation both. She imagined falling against the pillows and his hard, warm flesh coming over her body. She imagined being bathed in fire and washed in chills. . . .

'Twas the path that led to death. The darkness of a world where he no longer breathed. And she felt herself sinking into this dark night, falling in the fires of certain hell. . . .

'Twas so unfair, so terribly cruel.

Yet the maddening tease of Paxton's presence in her life drew her closer and closer to the flame he offered. It frightened her, more as it seemed his every look and movement promised what was to come.

Until the dark hours of night, like now, as she

lay tormented and waiting for him, and as the hours stretched and gathered into the night; her thirst for his salvation mounting and growing with each breath. She thought she was going mad; sometimes knew she was going mad.

Then, like a capricious wind, the madness became fear. She felt the steely talons sinking into her. Warning her. Darkness waited just behind the salvation he offered.

Paxton, leave me before it is too late. . . .

She had to stop thinking about him; she had to!

She looked to her table where her wood carvings waited. She rose at once and headed out the door. . . .

Paxton lay in his bed. 'Twas the hour of enchantment, the bewitching hour. A half dozen candles and two lanterns illuminated the precious manuscript spread before him. Soft footsteps sounded, footsteps that belonged to a woman of grace and elegance. Linness's footsteps.

Where would she be going at this hour?

He rose quietly and made his way out the door. Torchlight lit the stairway and he caught a brief glance of her dark gray skirts swirling behind her as she walked down, lantern in hand. He followed quietly. The whole château was still and quiet with sleep. He had realized she had irregular sleeping habits, especially since his private war with her had begun. He might awaken to hear her pacing hours after midnight, then discover her awake at dawn. She might retire with the sunlight or sleep past the tenth bell. She was restless with unease.

None more than I, my love . . .

He followed her through the hall and into the kitchen. She stopped suddenly, stiffening with fear before turning to look behind her. Paxton ducked into the shadows as she held her lantern up high to cast its illumination.

With more caution, Linness continued to the cellar storeroom. Tomorrow was Jean Luc's birthday. She needed a cup of oil to put the finishing shine on the statuettes.

She needed to get her mind off *him*.

She descended the small, wide stone stairway to the bottom. She held up the lantern, flooding the shelves of foodstuffs with light, all of it attesting to the wealth of Gaillard: sacks of oatmeal, barley, and flour, dried ham, smoked beef, expensive imported salmon, venison, cod, two barrels filled with green and tart spring apples, onions, a butter churn half-full, pickled herring in small tubs, hemp maize, bags of duck, geese, and hen feathers, drying herbs, tubs of almonds. Two shelves were lined with all of Vivian's cooking spices: mustard, salt, pepper, ginger, cinnamon, nutmeg, mace, cloves, and many others. Far up on the uppermost shelf, among various odds and ends, sat the scented oil.

She breathed deeply of the pungent mix of scents as she set the lantern on the shelf to reach up for the oil jar. A slight sound made her spin round. She gasped as a mouse scurried across the floor, disappearing into the pile of sheep fleeces in the corner. Washed in a wave of strange relief, she turned back to the shelves.

Hiding in the shadows, Paxton could only wonder at the unending lure of her beauty. Two pearl-handled combs held the long hair back; it fell in rivers of curls down her back, its rich color contrasting dramatically with the dark gray of her skirts. Her face was pale and circles underlined her eyes, yet this did nothing to offset her beauty. The dark gray gown laced tightly in front over a white cotton chemise, its long, loose sleeves gathered at her small wrists.

He soundlessly stepped forward until he stood directly behind her. He let his lips lightly graze the nape of her neck where he drew deeply of the perfume of her skin. He felt her spine tremble; the jar dropped with a soft clamor to the rush-covered stone floor and she spun around with a gasp. "Paxton!"

"Linness . . ."

He stood so close, so terribly, terribly close. Her eyes searched the handsome features of his face. A day's growth of beard gave him a threatening look. He wore only light cotton breeches and a beige tunic, belted at his waist, and soft suede boots. Her senses filled with a masculine scent of leather mixed with the musky scent of his soap.

Her heartbeat galloped in sudden fear. "You followed me. . . ."

"Aye. I followed you."

"To see where I was going?"

"Nay." He smiled as he watched her try to recover from her scare. "In hopes of finding you alone somewhere. I want to assess how you fare in this battle of . . . wills between us. I wanted to know if you read my letters or burned them without opening them. . . ."

Her arms came over her bosom, a gesture of

prayer or perhaps to shield herself from the effect of his dark gaze. "Your letters . . . You want only to torment me more."

"Are you tormented, love?"

His voice was a whisper-soft lure. The answer was aye, though she would not arm him more by telling him this. For two weeks she had lain in bed every night, terrified he would come to her. Like tonight. Two weeks of madness, of being tormented by forbidden fantasy that left her panting, trying to catch her breath, to slow the race of her heart, to ease the fiery ache that spread and grew in her loins. And with little success, she fell into an uneasy sleep each night, only to find herself suffering worse with erotic dreams that woke her even more unfulfilled . . .

Yet she was just as tormented by the waiting darkness.

"Let us see how tormented you are, love. A test . . ." He lowered his lips, lightly touching the curve of her neck, barely touching. She felt a heated chill on that spot. "Lower your arms, love. . . ."

Her breathing quickened. Her heart pounded. By cursed magic the command stole her will; she slowly lowered her arms.

She stood perfectly still, the heat of his gaze penetrating her gown. Anticipation was keen, heightening with each breath. She trembled with it. As if she had lived her life for the moment his hands touched her.

Callused fingers grazed her shoulders, teasing, testing. The warmth of her skin saturated his senses. His hand lingered just above her breast. He felt each sharp intake of her breath, the wild race of her heart. His fingers toyed menacingly with the laces of her dress. He watched the tightening tips of her breasts beneath the cloth.

"Shall I loosen your laces?"

The question was asked as he lowered her head and gently bit the sensitive lobe of her ear. A hot shiver rushed through her.

"Say aye . . ."

Another test. Her hesitation filled, not with indecision, but with a titillating expectation that was indeed torment.

"Aye," she whispered heatedly.

Deft fingers slowly untied the thin strings. His large hands rested lightly across her bosom as they worked, their heat a sweet balm on her taut nerves. She came undone with the laces. He pulled away the cloth, revealing the thin, transparent undergown.

He kissed her ear, her closed lids, then brushed his lips across hers, idly kneading her lower lip until she gasped. "Paxton . . ."

"Shall I touch you, Linness?"

"Aye . . ."

His hands slid beneath the cloth, parting it from the treasure beneath, and smoothed the rounded lift of her breasts. She drew a sharp breath. The pleasure was acute. Fiery shivers spiraled between her legs as his thumbs slowly circled the tightened peaks. She threw her head back against the wooden beams, arching into the heat of his palms. "Paxton." She murmured his name as if in prayer as her hands reached up to span his shoulders, searching for support.

He rewarded her response with deepening strokes as he whispered against her mouth. "Linness . . . how many times have I imagined feeling the weight of your breasts in my hand, hearing your cries, seeing your eyes shine with passion." He kissed her lips. "And, Linness, how privation doth sweeten the pleasure. . . ."

"Paxton." She said his name again as a demand for his lips. She did not have to ask twice. His mouth came over hers as her arms circled his neck. The brush of their bodies, the strokes of his hands, brought another rush between her thighs as she succumbed to the pounding sweetness of this kiss.

"Linness." He uttered her name as his lips traveled to the arch of her throat, making her gasp. His loins were hard and swollen, he was losing his mind. He knew only one thing. "Linness, I want all of you . . . I want . . ."

The words were left unsaid as his lips found her breasts. His lips moved back and forth over a nipple. The world started spinning and she closed her eyes, a helpless whimper escaping her lips as his tongue swept around and around the tightening bud. Her nerves went wild. "Paxton, Paxton, not here, not here . . ."

It was all she could manage.

He tried to slow the race of his pulse just long enough to get her behind closed doors. He swept her into his arms and carried her swiftly up the stairs into the kitchen. The world still spun, her blood ran hot. She tried to right her gown as he carried her through the outer hall and then he suddenly stopped.

Morgan stumbled into the hall.

She felt Paxton's muscles stiffen. Her gaze shot

up and her face lost all color. Morgan's precarious balance was evidence that he was quite drunk, and for one brief moment it seemed he wouldn't notice them. He often consumed prodigious amounts of spirits, though he rarely suffered from any malaise the next day—and he often toppled over at the table in drunken sleep, waking in the middle of the night to stumble back to bed. Like now.

Yet he stopped and spent a long moment trying to focus on their unlikely shapes. A look of confusion crossed his reddened face. "Milady, what has happened?"

No words issued from her throat.

"A mouse," Paxton said suddenly. "I was in the kitchen, fixing a late night meal, when it happened. She spotted a mouse in the kitchen and fainted."

With trembling hand she clutched tightly at her gown, while she reached over with her other hand and pulled out a comb, sending the long hair tumbling over her chest.

Morgan's mind turned in lethargic circles, but he abruptly caught the words. "A mouse!" He threw his head back, laughing with masculine amusement. "She has always been frightened of the little beasties." He shook his head and the movement made him sway. Righting himself, he added, " 'Tis why she has such a fondness for cats. God's teeth, but every time I open a cupboard, I see another mother cat and kittens. Here, let me carry milady...."

He made a movement towards Paxton. Paxton stepped quickly back. "You appear unsteady on your feet, brother. Best I carry the lady," he said as he stepped past Morgan and started up the stairs.

"Oh, aye, 'tis a woozy state I'm in," he said, slapping Paxton's back and laughing at his inebriated state as he followed behind his brother. Morgan's chamber sat to the right of Linness's, and he found his door first. "A good night to ye all!"

He disappeared through the door. The door shut. Paxton cursed softly, viciously, beneath his breath as Linness buried her face against the soft material of his tunic, the long string of cursing ending with "The drunken fool of an ox!"

Morgan apparently harbored no suspicions. It seemed as if his brother considered him above seducing his wife—

Nay, Paxton realized, suddenly staring down at Linness.

It had little to do with him. It had everything to do with Linness, the way he saw her as a saint, rather than a flesh-and-blood woman. Infidelity was quite beyond her; an impossible idea like purple horses or sweet lemons. And that was Morgan's shining mistake.

He carried Linness swiftly to her room, shutting the door behind them. As soon as he set her to her feet, she collapsed into a trembling heap on the floor, her gray skirts a pretty circle around her. "Linness," he whispered as he reached down to lift her back up. "Linness . . ."

There was no passion in her eyes now, only a dread where moments before fire uncurled.

"Mary sent him. 'Twas a warning. . . ."

"Mary?" he questioned, then realized she meant the blessed Mary. He was familiar with her mystical thinking; in fact, it often amused him, though until now, he had not known how far it went. Incredulously he asked, "Think you Mary sends Morgan about on tasks in the dark middle of the night?"

A hand covered her mouth, a measure of the emotions coursing through her. "I know Mary sent him," she whispered. "To warn us."

To say he was in no mind to discuss the philosophical or religious ideology underlying her ridiculous beliefs was an understatement. He had no thoughts above the hot blood still coursing through him; he was full to bursting with wanting her. The sound of her name alone could produce a hardening of his loins; holding and touching her had enlarged that effect dramatically. He only wanted to pull her back to his arms and taste the flesh beneath her mouth, feel her desire licking through him until he was driven mad.

He wanted the salvation only she could give him, and he reached to draw her back into his arms.

"Nay, I can't, I can't. 'Twill destroy us! Please, Paxton, leave me! I beg you, I beg you. . . ."

With a tender hand he brushed against her face in sympathy. At first she didn't understand the look in his eyes, but then she saw it was pity. "You are so frightened, love. Aye," he whispered, "I will leave you. For now. But there will be a time when I can't leave you. There will be a time when you won't want me to leave you. . . ."

She closed her eyes to absorb this message. His hand came under her chin. Exerting an exquisite pressure, he tilted her face up as he lowered his mouth to hers. The kiss breathed a tremulous spark of warm life back into her cold and trembling form and brought the knowledge, far more certain than any other, that his words of prophecy would come true.

"If I could let you go, I would. . . ."

Then he was gone.

That night the strange, magical dream visited her again. Of the lady dressed in black. The room surrounding her was as gloomy as her gown, her dark hair was lifted over her head. A black veil, transparent and mysterious, covered her face like the time before. Linness struggled to see her eyes, compelled, without knowing why.

Time seemed to stop as she felt the lady's stare. Slowly small hands reached up to lift the veil. To answer her wish. Finally Linness stared at the flawless olive complexion, the mild dark eyes. She was young and beautiful and tragic somehow. Kindness shined from the dark eyes, or perhaps sympathy for her rival.

And they were rivals, Linness knew this. A raging jealousy was sweeping through her. She did not know why. She felt as if the woman was everything she ever wanted to be, all that she had ever desired, and this made no sense! She did not even know who she was!

Who are you? Who are you?

Dreams have no words and the lady had no answer. . . .

She struggled to wake. The dream receded, just as it had every night; it was banished into the furthest reaches of memory.

Linness woke to the gray light of dawn. The woman had vanished. Only a lingering sense of foreboding surrounded the quiet of dawn. She searched her room and thought of Paxton, of longing and desire mixed fatefully with the threatening darkness of the future. . . .

*   *   *

Peace was the sound of rain falling and children playing by the fireside. Linness sat by the open window in the small alcove of her room, staring out at the rain. She could see the terraced garden on the far side of the courtyard wall, a small stone path that wound its way through bursting beds of violets, heliotrope, and poppy. Her herb garden was hidden behind this. The vineyards, too, needed their enormous thirst quenched, and as much as she did not care to be confined indoors, she, like all the people of Gaillard, welcomed the spring storm. She felt a tug on the yarn that she idly wound around her hands and she looked down to smile at her Maid Belle.

She thought again of Paxton and felt the longing in her heart. In absence, he seemed to grow larger in her heart. *Is this what you warned me of?* She carefully avoided contact as much as possible, as even the briefest encounter had disastrous effects. And the nights were the worst: Sleep found her in dreams spun with erotic yearnings. . . .

Her hand reached to the windowpane, as if to touch his face, and his words echoed in her mind. *How privation doth sweeten the pleasure.* . . . Aye and aye again. He would be here for a year. One year of agony. If she only could survive this year . . .

She forced her thoughts away from Paxton and tried to concentrate on the happy sounds Jean Luc and Pierre were making as they played with wooden knights by the fireside. The boys' voices were lively and animated as they took on the parts of the small cast of characters on a quest to slay the evil magician and free the princess.

She looked down into the courtyard and the smile left her face. A horse and rider were splashing through the mud toward the steps of the entrance hall, the wet horse wearing the livery colors of the Vatican.

The rider would be bearing news of Father Gayly's replacement, and also bishop of Gaillard. Neither Father Gayly nor any of Gaillard's three other priests had been considered for bishop. Men had to travel through the endless political morass of the Vatican to reach that lofty place. The church had reviewed the position upon Father Gayly's death, and had weighed into the equation Gaillard's growth and burgeoning trade of the township. Already there were seven guilds, and each guild's membership grew all the time.

The church decided Gaillard now offered a large enough diocese to support a bishop, rather than just its three simple priests. This new bishop would have four fathers and one scribe under him. Upon learning of this, Morgan was thrilled, until Paxton pointed out how much it would cost him. Poor Morgan had been in a foul mood for days.

Wanting to hear the names of the priests who would be arriving at Gaillard, she rose to meet the messenger. She flew down the stairs, stopping at the bottom just as Michaels showed the messenger inside. He removed his wet cloak to reveal the black and red vestments of the Jesuits, the Vatican's famous soldier priests.

The priest looked up and stopped, just to stare at the beautiful lady. In a burst of color against the gray and wet day, she appeared in a dark burgundy-colored gown. It was trimmed in rich ermine along the bodice and had long satin sleeves that gathered in three places along her arms. A gold chatelaine wrapped three times about her small waist. A matching circlet held back her long hair. Yet 'twas her eyes that captured his, large, gray eyes that revealed the shadow of a secret anxiety or pain.

Michaels introduced her as the Lady de Chamberlain. "Milady," the priest said smiling as he took her pale hand and kissed it lightly. He introduced himself as Father Thomas.

Sometimes when she first met a person, her sight washed a wave of emotion over her, an emotion that was attached to the person like a physical feature. This man sent her a wave of blackness, not his, she sensed, but someone close to him. It passed so quickly, she hardly had time to register it before it was gone.

"You bring news of Gaillard's new bishop, Father Thomas?"

"Indeed. I have ridden from the holy see of Cardinal Duprat in faraway Notre Dame."

The most powerful cardinal in France, this man was arguably as powerful as the king, harnessing the power of the church in France. Duprat, a pragmatist and pluralist, was far more a political creature than a religious one. It was rumored he kept more mistresses than even the king . . .

The priest's smile revealed stained teeth and a missing front one. A scar crossed his cheek in a streak. Yet his voice sounded soft and his eyes were fine and dark. He reached into a velvet-lined pocket in his cloak and withdrew a sealed envelope.

"And who shall we be welcoming at Gaillard?"

He smiled at the lady's eagerness. "Should I not present the news to your husband as well, milady?"

"Oh, of course. Michaels?"

"In the hall, milady."

She led the man through the corridor to the hall. Fires blazed in the hearths and the room bustled with activity. Servants rushed about, pouring ale and setting down fruit and cheese trays that signaled the end of the midday feast. Paxton sat at a table with his two architects, who had arrived from Alsace just yesterday to review certain features of Gaillard's château that Paxton wanted incorporated in his new home. Morgan and John were listening to a group of master craftsmen from Lyons, who were trying to explain why the wine prices were falling there.

She moved quickly to the head of the table, "Milord." She beckoned with a slight curtsy. Morgan looked up. The wine master stopped midsentence. Silence descended as people looked from the lady to the messenger waiting behind her.

Paxton's gaze found her and his breath caught. She looked more beautiful than a summer dawn at sea. And yet she was changed. Over the last few weeks he had used every ounce of will to resist coming to her. He had wanted to teach her the cost of denial, a cost that escalated and grew until it finally crested with the understanding that they had no choice.

And seeing the pale pallor to her skin, and the dark circles under her eyes, all accenting her struggle, he knew his wait was over. He would end it tonight.

With difficulty he forced his gaze from her.

"Father Thomas is here to announce the appointment of the new bishop to Gaillard."

"Ah," Morgan said, rising to display his fine *chamarre*, a formal loose gown made of a rich brown material, heavily decorated with gold braids and buttons. Linness stepped back as the introductions were made all round before Father Thomas presented the envelope. Morgan ripped it open and read the formal announcement. The names meant nothing to him. Yet his brows crossed as he read the expensive requirements this bishop demanded for his arrival. With a reddened face he immediately passed the letter to Paxton, and Morgan's furious brown eyes found the priest in demand for an explanation.

Linness looked from one to the other in confusion.

"I see you are displeased, milord," observed Father Thomas, as he tilted his head slightly and, with hands behind his back, stood tall, his gaze narrowing. The bishop had told him to expect this reaction, that it was all too common in these pending days before the Armageddon. . . .

"This is preposterous!" Paxton stated the fact bluntly as he quickly handed the letter to John, watching his uncle read it quickly and his face change with shock. "My brother can ill afford new plows this year, let alone afford the fortune necessary to build this monument to some bishop's grandiose ambition!"

"What is it?" Linness asked.

Morgan did not look at her as he answered, "The church wants me to build this fine bishop not just a church but a monastery as well! For thirty monks, no less. And he wants a huge land grant to go with this monastery. 'Twould cost me my next ten years to pay for such a scheme—"

Father Thomas suggested, "One lifetime for eternity seems a fair price."

A delicate brow lifted as Linness asked, "And since when did God anoint the good bishop with the power to bargain for men's souls?"

Paxton and John were not the only men who admired the comment. Morgan often thought Linness's high-mindedness and religious beliefs—while often different from the strict teachings of the church—made twice as much sense. He nodded with an appreciative grunt.

Father Thomas's gaze darkened with anger at the woman's foolish comment. "And would you dare advise me on religious doctrine, milady?"

"Nay," she said in a pretense of innocent shock, "I would never do that, Father. I was just surprised to hear that the clergy had the authority to guarantee eternity in return for service to the church. Because, you see, I had always been taught that only God has that glory."

Averting his mirthful gaze, John reached down to stroke one of the hound dogs. The lady's wit was sharp, her charm alarming and yet wholly irresistible. How many times had he wished for the nerve to say such to the greed of the holy church?

The priest bristled with anger and decided to ignore the impertinent lady and the steward. Addressing the lords Paxton and Morgan, he asked, "What price a man's salvation? Gaillard is growing. Already the township is a community of nine hundred, and by God's grace that number will triple in five years." With sudden passion he said, "The people need the spiritual center of God's church as much as they need bread and water."

Paxton dryly replied, "Only the well-fed man would think so."

" 'Tis a moot point in any case," Morgan added. "The Gaillard vineyards have not been producing half as good as in days past—all the world knows this. Thanks to my brother, we are starting crop rotation and this year we will be fertilizing the soil better—"

"All at great expense," John pointed out.

"Aye," Morgan agreed. "You go back and tell your bishop that Gaillard has a good enough church, that we will all rejoice that I can afford to feed and house him and his legion of fellow brethren, but that is all. I do not have a fortune with which to execute his grandiose plans."

Father Thomas's mouth pressed in a fine line as he looked to Paxton. "Surely there is some wealth in Gaillard. . . ."

Paxton laughed, unnerving the man more. "The holy plot thickens, I see. This bishop imagines I will pay for all these new buildings. I suppose you shall offer me eternity as well?"

With an amused chuckle, Simon added, "The gates of heaven doth open, but only for a price. . . ."

"Aye," Paxton said, smiling at Linness. "But then I believe the lady already pointed out the fallacy of the statement."

Father Thomas's eyes blazed, his face reddened with humiliation. The bishop would be furious, and this fury would spill over into his growing certainty that this was a sign of impending Armageddon. He believed the faithful were fewer, their numbers diminishing daily, that new blasphemous ideas kept creeping into the holy doctrine; holy men and laymen everywhere were questioning the strict teachings of the church, and with arresting ideas. Despite his enormous faith, Father Thomas found himself struggling in secret with many of these new ideas. . . .

He searched for the scathing answer his superior would deliver to these good people, but for several tense moments no reply came to mind. Of course, no one, not even the pope, could guarantee eternity, but that did not mean service to the church was not measured.

"Do you dare mock the grace of godly fear?"

"Nay," Paxton said as he shook his head slightly, leaning over his strong arms on the table. "Yet neither do I quake with a peasant's ignorance and foolish superstition. But I tell you this: Look not to me nor my brother for monies to finance the bishop's hopes. If it is to be done at all, I suggest the church reach into their own vast and boundless pockets. And that, my good man, is final."

Linness watched as the man paused, then nodded curtly. She sensed his own struggle, but there was a darkness surrounding him, pulling him into . . . pulling him into a crisis of faith, into despair. . . .

"Bishop Peter Luce will not be pleased, but I shall put the matter into his infinitely more capable hands."

The sound of that name shot through Linness, like a hard blow to her chest. Her face went pale, her hands numb. Bishop Peter Luce. Bishop Peter Luce.

Dear God, she could not have heard right!

"Show the good father to Father Gayly's old room behind the chapel," Morgan was telling Michaels, wanting to get rid of the unpleasant man. "If there are any of that dear man's things left there, have them bundled up and . . ." He paused to look at Linness. "And bring them to my wife to dispense to the poor or keep as heartsakes." Morgan's brow creased with confusion. "Milady, you look so pale a sudden. What's wrong? If it's Father Gayly's things—"

Paxton had come round to her side.

She had turned to Father Thomas and, staring hard, asked, "What name did you say?"

"Why, the noble Bishop Peter Luce. Do you know him, milady?"

'Twas what Mary had been trying to warn her of in the dream of Father Gayly's death! 'Twas the reason she kept carving his face in the wood! He was coming here, to Gaillard, to damn her! "Nay," she managed a whisper, "I have only heard of him."

Father Thomas nodded and turned to follow Michaels. Michaels, who cared for his lady, stood looking at her with concern a moment longer before escorting the man out. Linness waited until he was gone.

"Milady, what is wrong?" Morgan asked.

"Please, I . . . I need a private audience."

That was all she had to say. Morgan signaled the people, all but the family, to leave. Everyone but Paxton and John filed out of the room, and then she dropped to her knees before Morgan.

For no reason he knew, John turned from the lady to Paxton. He suffered a confused moment's shock as he recognized the harsh emotions on Paxton's face, saw Paxton's fists curled into tight balls at his sides. He looked back to Linness, kneeling before Morgan. Understanding dawned as he realized with a sharp intake of breath that Paxton was in love with his brother's wife.

"Milord," she begged, ignorant of everything but the threat of Peter Luce coming to Gaillard, to her home. "If you care at all for me, you will not let this Bishop Peter Luce come here!"

"What's this?" Morgan looked down with confusion. "Do you know this man?"

"I . . . I have heard of him. In the convent. He is hateful, well known for cruel and harsh judgments. He will never make the people of Gaillard happy or content with his relentless preaching of evil and its damnation and never telling of heaven or salvation. You know his mold of man—filled with fury and anger. Oh, please, Morgan, do not let him come here!"

"Milady, I cannot stop him from coming here. The cardinal himself has already made the selection, it says right there." He glanced at the thin sheet of parchment as if it were stone. "Oh," he said, waving his hand dismissively, "you know how it goes in the church corridors—the cardinal no doubt owes this man a favor, or perhaps this Bishop Luce has paid handsomely for our small, rich tithe . . . well . . ." He sighed, amending this with another scowl. "What they think is a rich tithe anyway. They will see soon enough that Gaillard is like all other places in the world these days—"

"Please, milord, please. I cannot live in a household with this man. Nor do I want him or his priests tutoring Jean Luc; they would poison his young mind with hate and fear. I know this man's reputation. I know he would choke the happiness from me!"

"I believe I could help," Paxton began calmly, expertly managing to keep his desperation at bay. "I am good friends with Lorenzo Lotto, duke of Nantes, high steward to King Francis, to say nothing of my standing with Francis himself. And old Duprat, the rascal. Perhaps I exercise some influence there, as well. I would certainly be willing to try. For the lady and Jean Luc."

Morgan's smile widened. "Could you, brother? Think you that Lotto would intervene for Gaillard?"

"Aye," Paxton replied smoothly. "He would for me. I believe he owes me a few favors."

Gratitude shone in her eyes as she turned to Paxton. "Please, whatever it takes," she whispered, a hidden message passed to Paxton in her words. "I must stop him from coming here. . . ."

Morgan stared down at her with worried affection. While he had little hope of understanding the turns of her mind, especially the depth of her faith and religiosity, he had no doubt her happiness could be stolen by someone cruel. "Aye, you must, Paxton. Whatever you can do. For, you see, my wife has never asked me for anything. I believe we can all agree that she, of all women we know, deserves her happiness."

"Thank you," she said to both men.

The rain fell unceasingly through the afternoon. Jean Luc and Pierre made a fort in the stable's loft and were determined to eat supper there as well. "Only after vespers," she had agreed, hiding her anxieties, always managing to hide them from her boy. "And no matter what," she added in a strict voice, "no mirth! Absolutely no laughing!"

The command immediately rewarded her with the sight of two young boys trying desperately to suppress a giggle of mirth, their small chests puffing with the effort. Their quick and certain failure threw them into stitches of laughter. Vivian had agreed, as well, and set about making them some special treats.

After asking the two night guards to keep their eyes on the children, Linness finally returned to her room. Though it was not dark yet, the fires had been lit, casting the room in a dim golden light. Clair was not to be found. Clair often enjoyed supper in the knights' barracks, playing cards and dice as well as any man, and due to her lively spirits and keen wit, she was ever popular among the men. Tonight Linness was glad to be alone.

She desperately needed the peace she found through prayer.

Linness moved to the hearth and withdrew a kindling stick from the box. She set it to flames and, cupping the flickering light, she hurriedly brought it to her candles at Mary's altar. She lowered the flames to one wick, then another and another. She saw him when she lifted her eyes.

She stood frozen for a long moment, staring at his candlelit features, trying to assess his intentions. The blackened pools of his eyes reflected the small flame. "Paxton . . ."

He leaned toward her and blew out the kindling stick just before it would burn her fingers. Scented smoke rose between them. He gently slipped his long, warm fingers over hers and removed the scorched stick and tossed it into the fire. Staring down at the flames, he asked in a whisper, "Tell me what you really know of this bishop."

She forced her gaze from his to collect her thoughts. Of course he would have known there was more to her fear than she claimed. She could keep nothing from him.

"When I was but ten and one, he arrived at my convent to examine me. I told you of the old abbess and how she loved me, and I, her, how she was a mother to me. When she died the new abbess arrived from faraway Florence. I think she hated me upon sight; her animosity growing as she perceived the other sisters' affection and growing more as she heard more and more about my . . . sight.

" 'Twas Peter Luce whom she called to the abbey to examine me. He was already well known for routing out the devil's infiltration into the holy church, a task he committed himself to with the unreserved enthusiasm and determination of a zealot."

She paused before adding in a subdued whisper, "I overheard the sisters' worry. The numbers stuck in my mind all these years. He was known to have executed eighty-eight members of the clergy; his reputation reached all the way to the German states."

Paxton swore softly, viciously.

"When I first saw him," she continued distantly as she remembered, "he was so tall and handsome, magnificent and noble in his fine crimson robes. I remember thinking that he would do me no harm, that he could do me no harm, despite the sisters' worries. He was too fine. . . ."

Linness stood by her bed, her hand idly smoothing over the crevices of the carvings on the post. "I remember kneeling before him and that he held out his jeweled fingers to kiss. I was filled with a young girl's excitement upon meeting a powerful and handsome man. I never had a father, you know. I suppose I was thinking to charm him and win his affection as I had with the good sisters and the dear old abbess. . . ."

In a changed voice she finished, "I kissed his hand. He withdrew it, as if I had scorched him. Harshly, so harshly, he demanded an explanation of how I made his crucifix tremble. I was so frightened by this. The sisters hurried to withdraw me from his presence. He arranged a formal ecclesiastic investigation. With many tears the sisters helped me escape, and that night I stepped out alone into the world. . . ."

Paxton saw this was a dangerous situation. He had only one question by the end of this sad story. "Would he recognize you, Linness?"

"I don't know!" A distressed hand went to her forehead. "I keep thinking aye, he would know me immediately and remember me at once, but then rationally, I realize I was only one of hundreds of people he tried to condemn. I was only eleven too. He is large in my mind, but surely I would only be a fleeting encounter in his." She understood the huge mistake at once. "If only I had kept Belinda's name instead of using my own . . ."

She wondered wildly if she could change it back to Belinda now. She needed to change her name in the terrible event that Paxton's letter was unable to prevent Bishop Peter Luce from coming here. Clair would go along with it and so would many others. Most everyone called her by title in any case. Oh, if she could just keep Bishop Luce from hearing the uncommon name of Linness, she might be able to save herself!

"Paxton, I am so scared," she confessed. "The whole of this past month I have been having nightmares of him. I was carving Jean Luc's wooden statues and as I was making the magician, his face kept taking on a sinister air. I started anew time and again and still his face would look sinister. I couldn't think who he reminded me of. But the night Father Gayly died, I suddenly saw whose face I was carving over and over. 'Twas him; 'twas Bishop Luce. I threw the statue in the fire and as I watched it burn, I saw Father Gayly's death." In a frightened whisper, she added, "If he comes here, 'twill be my death too!"

"Never," Paxton swore passionately as he came to her and took her in his arms. Fire pulsed where he touched her; she closed her eyes a moment to savor it. "I would never let his hands touch you, let alone hurt you. I daresay neither would Morgan. Love, love, all of Gaillard would rise to protect you!"

"But if the church—"

"Hush," he said, quieting her fears. "If the worst happened, I would—"

What would he do? Slay the next fifty men until weakened and spent?

He stared at the hopeful look in her eyes as she waited to hear of his miracle. "I would snatch you up and carry you away to . . . to Switzerland—"

The silver eyes widened upon hearing this fancy. "Switzerland?"

Switzerland. The land of snow-covered mountains, emerald green forests, and crystal blue lakes. Switzerland, where good and simple folks lived between blue skies and the rich earth, where no punitive monarch could reach them and even the church was more or less the simple communal worship of peasants. She had always loved stories of faraway Switzerland.

"Aye," he said, smiling down at her, trying to keep his gaze from lingering at the place where the softest ermine brushed against her bosom. "And I would build you a house high in the mountains, overlooking a beautiful green valley and a deep lake, another mountain beyond. You would think it was heaven and I would pinch you each day to keep your feet on earth."

The pretty picture melted her fear suddenly and made her smile. "And how would we live in this pretty house overlooking the green valley and the blue lake?"

Her smile went through him in a rush of feeling, "Well, I . . . I would plant a field—"

The happy sound of her laughter interrupted him. "You? The great and famous Lord Paxton de Chamberlain, living a common peasant?" She laughed more as she said, "I can just imagine you cursing our poor old plow horse, the relentless weeds and foul weather. 'Twould be me who pinched you each day to get you to put on your boots and out the door into the bitter wind!"

The idea, like a distant dream, was too sweet to say good-bye to. He added, "I would come back to our small home tired and hungry and in a mood as foul as this bitter cold. Ah, but then I would see my beautiful wife and my mood would melt like the spring snows. I would know happiness."

"I would not be beautiful then. I would be as ragged as any tired and overburdened peasant's wife."

"Aye," he said with a teasing lilt to his voice,

"your dress would be patched and tattered, your hands would be raw from scrubbing and cooking all day, and you would be plump and cross from all my children tugging at your skirts." His voice softened as he stared into her eyes, sparkling with merriment at this fanciful idea. "And yet my love would paint you more beautiful than any other. . . ."

Her laughter quieted, her emotions rose in secret greeting with his as they felt the irresistible lure of the romantic dream of a common and simple life filled with daily toils, the happy sound of children, and all of it blessed by their love. That hundreds of peasants dreamed of their life did not occur to them. For their dream signified the escape to a magical time and place where they would be free. Free to rejoice in the blessing of their love.

Just as quickly the hopelessness of ever finding this magical place washed over them, and with this came desperation. The intensity of this emotion was fully expressed as his lips lowered to hers and he kissed her as if it were the last time he ever would.

With her eyes closed, she was breathing hard and fast when he finally broke this kiss. "Linness," he said in a ragged whisper, "I cannot wait any longer. Just following your sweet scent down the staircase, or the light trace of your skirt against my thigh, or your sleeve on my arm, seizes my senses and washes me in a hot chill—"

"Paxton," she whispered, feeling his moist lips on her forehead.

"You fill my every dream. The mere issue of your name makes my blood run hot. Linness." He cupped her face, tilting her for his kiss. "I want you. With each breath I take. Tonight, Linness. To-night . . ."

He kissed her, gently, tenderly, a kiss that beck-oned with a promise. Neither one heard the booted footsteps coming up the stairs nor even the first knock at the door.

The knocking came louder. "Milady, your lord begs entrance!"

Paxton broke the kiss with a start.

A small gasp escaped Linness; her next breath washed her in a wave of panic. She pointed to the bathing screen, a movable wooden panel to protect her modesty if dressing with company in the room, and Paxton swiftly stole behind it. She tried to still the wild race of her heart before she called out, "Come in."

The door opened and Morgan, Michaels, and the priest, Father Thomas, stepped inside the soft light of her chambers. "Ah, milady," Morgan said, not noticing her pale face nor the hot fear in her eyes. "I came to tell you it has been arranged. I have my brother's letters, signed and sealed and I will be sending these off as soon as the weather allows. Father Thomas here has agreed to carry them," he told her, not seeing the obvious problem with such an arrangement. He hesitated. "But the good Father does not believe Paxton or even Lotto has a chance of altering Bishop Luce's appointment. He claims the pope himself asked for it, that Francis would be helpless to change it. And Father Thomas here wanted to be presented to you again, to discuss this dilemma."

Michaels saw at once something was terribly wrong and he looked about the room in search of the source. He saw nothing. Just as he was to leave he spotted booted feet under the small opening at the bottom of the screen. His eyes flew to Linness in shock and, grasping the reason for her fear, he quickly stepped in front of the screen before anyone else noticed the same thing.

Then he realized whose boots they must be.

Linness was so consumed with the terror that Morgan would discover Paxton's presence that she could hardly follow what he was telling her. Yet his words slowly penetrated her stricken thoughts and she shook her head, a look of disbelief and horror revealed in her eyes. She shot her gaze to Father Thomas to measure his reaction. He stared stonily at her predicament.

She looked back at Morgan. The fool! Had Morgan told this Father Thomas everything? So that now Bishop Luce would be warned of her desperate disapproval, and dear Lord, he would be suspicious from the start. She could scarcely believe Morgan was that foolish. But then Morgan's mind was a mercilessly blunt instrument, sometimes as incapable as a child of the smallest intrigue or secret.

She turned back to Father Thomas, who now stood over her small altar to Mary, examining it. At the top of the table were expensive scented candles, a crucifix, her rosary, and a small white marble statuette of Mary that she treasured. It had once been the abbess's.

"So, milady, your husband tells me how much you dislike the bishop."

Still trying to recover from the fear of discovery, she managed to shake her head. "He is mistaken. I have never had the fortune of meeting Bishop Luce."

Father Thomas looked up from the candlelit altar. "Yet you have asked your brother-in-law and your husband to intercede; to stop Bishop Luce from assuming the vicarage of Gaillard."

Trapped. She had to say something. "I have heard he is a harsh man—"

"You have heard wrong," he interrupted. "The bishop is a just man."

"Oh?" she questioned, clasping hands together to stop their tremble. "Then it is not true that many people have been executed and, still worse, excommunicated, at his will?"

Excommunication was the harshest of punishments for the faithful. Death was nothing when laid alongside the awesome power of separating a soul from God for all eternity. While she harbored considerable doubt as to whether this possibility was real or not, for the devout it was far more terrible than the most slow and painful death by torture.

"Only those deserving of the punishment," he replied. "Only those whose sinful lives refused the holy word."

"I have heard differently," she said uncertainly. "The people of Gaillard are simple and decent and good; I would not want them to be the recipients of the bishop's . . . notions of justice. I would rather see the Gaillard vicarage go to a man who will show them the more holy grace of God's forgiveness and love. . . ."

"Aye, aye, aye," Morgan said, impatient with any conversation of things he could not get his hands around, especially abstract religious ideas. "Do not fret, milady. Paxton and I are still determined to try to get a new bishop for Gaillard. And the letters will be sent as soon as the weather clears, though Paxton may be unable to stop the arrival of this bishop. But after discussing this personage with Father Thomas, I believe he is not as harsh a man as you are imagining. I only tell you this so you will not be so concerned if the letter does indeed fail to merit a reconsideration."

Her silver eyes shimmered with anger. How she wanted to hate Morgan for this betrayal! And she would, too, if only she could attach malice to it. She couldn't, though; 'twas not Morgan's fault he could not see the disaster of this situation.

"I see you worship the Madonna," Father Thomas commented, after another glance at the table. A great debate raged in the church even now over the peasants who worshiped Mary, and neglected God. Many priests had begun seeing the reverence of Mary over Christ and the Holy Father as a sacrilege. Most priests, he knew, felt this unholy path must be discouraged. Bishop Luce himself felt it must be suppressed. . . .

He himself had always been struck with adoration and admiration and, aye, love for the Virgin, though he certainly never expressed this to the bishop. . . .

When the lady offered nothing in response, he added, "I have also heard it said that you tell people you are blessed with the sight. . . ."

"Huh!" Morgan said with a gust of enthusiasm, stopping as he turned toward the door. This he knew about. "My good wife always knows of things to come." Noticing the priest's skeptical expression, he added with a pointing finger, "When she first came to Gaillard I dismissed it all as feminine nonsense. No more," he laughed. "I have lived too long with her to harbor any doubts. Why, just the other day Paxton and I had decided to put off the new fertilization until next week. She said no, that a great storm was approaching—you see, the benefit to the grape greatly increases with rain. Even though the sky was blue and the day fair, I knew to trust this." He laughed with a glance at the window where the steady patter of rain continued unabated. "And so it came to pass!"

"Indeed," Father Thomas said, with a hint of amazement. "And to whom do you attribute these miraculous visions?"

"To no one," she said quickly, moving towards the door to hasten their departure. "It grows late. If you will excuse me so I might wash for supper."

"But of course, milady," Father Thomas said, and with a last glance about the room, he turned toward the door.

Morgan followed, his thoughts slightly disturbed by his wife's distress. He was not a man who was bothered much by a woman's capricious moods, things that fluctuated more frequently than wine prices, and he quickly dismissed her anxiety. No doubt the priest was harmless enough and her fears exaggerated. In any case, eventually his beautiful wife was bound to win the man over as she won every man over. He often thought she could cast some sort of magic or spell over men; his men were all so eager to sing her praises or win her favor. . . .

When Michaels at last joined the other men at the door, Father Thomas turned back to bid her good eventide and stopped. He, too, spotted the boots beneath the screen.

His eyes blazed with sudden understanding.

It explained everything. . . .

"You shouldn't fear Bishop Luce, milady, but

rather God Himself. After all, Bishop Luce is only exercising His will—"

She shut the door on his face, and leaning against it, her legs gave way and she collapsed to the floor in a trembling heap of maroon velvet. 'Twas bad and getting worse. She felt the talons sinking into her flesh again and darkness swirl around her.

Tonight . . .

She looked to the screen that hid Paxton. Only to see he was gone. She looked to the open window; a gust of wind blew rain through its opened shutters. He was gone and yet it was too late. . . .

Tonight . . .

She waited half the night, feeling, knowing, he would come. Yet, like so many nights before, he did not. Minutes gathered into an hour and then another and another. She paced, she sat, she paced some more. She stared at the darkened window, watching as the raindrops streamed down its panes. Every small and large sound made her jump.

The last thing she remembered was the sound of his name issuing from her lips, over and over, like a spell by which she called to him.

She fell into a deep, dream-filled sleep, a place where wishes come true. Lightning cracked against the night sky. The boom of thunder awakened her with a start. She looked dazedly around the night-shrouded room.

He stood over her bed, his face hidden in a mysterious play of darkness and shadows. She could not see his face. The rush of her breath came out in a scream, but his hand came over her mouth hard, aborting the sound. Terrified eyes searched for his face but she saw only shadows. The hand forced her head back against the soft cushion of pillows.

Her thick robe parted as she fell back and he beheld the naked beauty beneath him.

She heard the sharp intake of breath and her heart leaped. No words were spoken. The intensity of emotion sparked the air between them, forbade words, leaving them voiceless, just as storms forbid any glimpse of the sun until the earth has been washed, the river swollen and full, the soil quenched.

He held her hands on either side of her head and still said not a word as he came partially over her. The touch of their flesh was like fire.

A warm hand came over her side, sliding all the way down past her hip and back again, his touch summoning the long-denied need, then celebrating it before his hands came intimately over her buttocks. He fitted her tight against his hot staff and closed his eyes as he burned.

The slow thud of her heart echoed in her loins. She moaned as his hand slipped over the mound of her breast. Over and over. Her nerves went wild. She arched seductively against him and said his name in a plea.

His lips met hers. The pounding eroticism of the kiss sent warm licks of fire through her abdomen, opening the wellspring of her desire. She felt hot and shaky. His lips left her mouth to gently tease the arched line of her throat, moving lower and lower to her breasts.

The teasing of his tongue and mouth on her breasts drew fire to the surface. Her blood drained, drawn to the hot core of her pulsating center as his mouth moved lower still, gently kissing, tasting, circling the sensitive point on her flat stomach, his tongue as hot as the flesh that opened and welcomed him.

A swirl of purple exploded in her mind. She was vaguely aware as he lifted back up. Lightning cracked in the sky, illuminating their moistened bodies as he thrust himself deep inside. She was thrown off a cliff, spreading wings and catching a blast of wind. Colors and colors, a swirl of hot breath in hair, open mouths and arched backs, an ageless cry as the hot core of her sun burst deep inside, its light receding into darkness . . .

Chapter 7

~~~♾️~~~

"**B**ruises," Bishop Luce said to the abbot of Fontevrault. The room was dark, lit only by brass candles and a small fire in the hearth. The voices of a hundred priests raised in chorus echoed through the stone walls of the great monastery at Fontevrault. The distant harmony of the chorus irritated Bishop Peter Luce as he sat stiffly in the ornate hand-carved chair behind a polished desk.

Since arriving yesterday at Fontevrault on his way to his new diocese in Gaillard, he had discovered the acting administrators here selected members of their order with hardly a thought to anything but the sweetness of each man's voice, ignoring the weightier matters of the arduous devotion to the higher call. One priest he interviewed had gone from a bakery to the vows to Fontevrault with hardly a step inside a church.

"I beg your pardon? Bruises?" the tall, robust, elderly man questioned with confusion.

"Bruises on the kneecap. It is the most telling sign of religious devotion. The mark brought by the hours of supplication and devotion to prayer, you see. And there are no bruises here in Fontevrault."

The abbot saw he was serious. He wondered

wildly if the bishop had checked his priests' knees for this mark of devotion. "Well, no. At Fontevrault we celebrate His Holiness with our raised voices and hearts; our supplication and devotion come with a glorious harmony of prayerful music, not as arduous on the knees perhaps but every bit as . . . as meaningful."

Bishop Luce did not agree. "You take great pride in your chorus, do you not?" He stood up with hands clasped behind his back, pretending to study the pictures hanging on the wall. "Your chorus has been presented to the king himself, I've heard."

"We have in fact." He smiled, unaware of the trap here. "Twice now. The king is quite a music afficionado. I am very proud—"

"Indeed." Bishop Luce turned to him suddenly. "You suffer from this pride. I fear your chorus has become an exercise of vanity, the way you glory in all these raised voices. And"—his mouth tightened as his eyes reflected the firelight, and he spoke slowly to emphasize each word—"as you know, every vanity is an affront to God Almighty as it is the adversary's tool. It must be purged before Satan devours you with it."

"Purged? But—"

"I recommend a year of silence, fasting, and ardent prayer to rectify this—"

"A year?! 'Twould be my death—"

"It would save your meager soul and grant you the necessary humility your position demands. I shall recommend this to Cardinal Origo in Avignon—"

A knock at the door interrupted them. "That is all for now."

The horrified abbot was too shocked to realize

Bishop Luce had just dismissed him, until he abruptly stood and withdrew. Through the opened door came Bishop Luce's young servant, who announced, "Father Thomas, milord. He has just arrived from Gaillard."

"Show him in."

Father Thomas stepped into the faint light of the room and rushed to kneel before his superior and kiss his ring. All other formalities were discarded; the urgency on Father Thomas's face expressed the importance of his information. He first withdrew Lord Chamberlain's letter to Francis, another to his steward, Lorenzo Lotto, duke of Nantes, and finally a letter addressed to Duprat himself. One by one Bishop Luce ripped these open and read them before he dropped each one into the flames, watching the smoke rise and curl.

Father Thomas tried not to mind this obvious trespass—the reading and destroying of a lord's private correspondence. He tried to tell himself it was all for the greater good of the faithful, that it was necessary. Just as he knew he had to relate the specifics about the unusual Lady Chamberlain.

The light danced in his dark eyes as Bishop Luce listened to the vile details of the lady's life, and when this tale was finished, he at last understood. "At least now I know why God called to me to Gaillard."

Sunlight streamed through the canopy of green overhead and the air felt warm and balmy in the late afternoon as Jean Luc walked alongside Paxton; both were returning on the river trail after a day of hunting. Two hound dogs raced ahead of them, still excited by the catch of two pheasants.

They had not found the treacherous Diablo dragon, as Jean Luc was hoping, though for many miles they had followed a fox trail until they lost it, only to pick up a deer track nearby and lose that, as well, when they discovered a hawk's nest. Finally they spotted the two pheasants. His uncle shot one with a bow and arrow and then helped him shoot the other. He was still excited by his first catch; he could hardly wait to tell his mother and father. And Bonet favored pheasants above all other foul, and Pierre would be green with envy.

"So," Paxton asked as they walked along, "I heard Morgan speaking to you about sleeping in your mother's bed all the time."

"Aye." Jean Luc smiled sheepishly as if he had been caught in mischief. "My father said 'twould not do at my age to always be found in my mother's bed. He said I could lose my strength."

"Did that upset you, son?"

"Nay. I don't mind not sleeping with my mother. I love her so, but . . . but . . ." He stopped, not knowing if he should say or not that it was his mother's idea he sleep in her bed. "She wanted me to sleep with her."

Paxton knew this, of course. Since their night of splendor, Linness had Jean Luc sleep in her bed, desperate to keep him out of it. The ploy had worked. He might be angry if he didn't so completely understand her desperation.

For their love sprang not from Eden but rather a wilderness beyond. And this magical sphere was both savage and violent, a place where their souls joined, soared, flew, discovering the place where the sun was born. . . .

He wanted to travel there again.

Like all worthy hungers, Jean Luc carried his bow loosely in his arm with his fingers curled around an arrow fitted tightly in the bow strings, ready to shoot at any moment. "I shall tell my mother I cannot sleep with her every night. She will be sad, but 'tis for the best."

"Aye," Paxton said, a smile tugging at the corners of his mouth. " 'Tis for the best."

Jean Luc's thoughts turned to the day's excitement, reliving the moments over and over. This day had been more fun than any other day he remembered. "The only thing better than bagging a pheasant," Jean Luc said, racing to keep up with his uncle's long strides as they came out of the forest and headed toward the thoroughfare leading to the town, "would be a deer or a poacher—"

"A poacher?" Paxton stopped to look down at his son. With hands on hips, he asked, "And what would we do if we caught a poacher?"

Jean Luc knew this answer. "We would hang him!"

"Would we now?" Gentleness suffused Paxton's tone as he knelt down to the boy's level. "Yet what if the winter was hard on this man and he had hungry children to feed? Perhaps this man was only trying to feed his hungry family. Jean Luc, what if these children will all starve if we kill their father?"

The idea shocked Jean Luc; he searched Paxton's face. "That would be a sorry thing," he said, greatly subdued by the idea. "Still he must hang if he is a poacher!"

"Must he? Think, Jean Luc. Which is more important to a man: feeding his children or obeying a law that will make them starve?"

His quick mind turned this over. "Well, my

mother told me a man's first duty is to his wife and children; am I right?"

"Aye, 'tis true. So wouldn't it be a kinder thing to help this man?" He stood, and they resumed walking. The town was just ahead and he called the dogs back to his side so as not to let them get into any mischief. "Should we not let some land to this man and give him a plow, perhaps extending some foodstuffs to his family until the sweat of his labor could come to fruition?"

"That would be kind, and," he realized, "I think God, too, would be pleased."

Paxton smiled at his boy.

"But then, Uncle, why did my father say that poaching was a grievous offense and he would hang any poacher?"

"Well, Jean Luc . . ." Paxton paused, unwilling to say his brother was the type of man who probably never once considered the question from the poacher's perspective. "Times have changed, and Morgan, like many other barons, needs to change with them. You see, not long ago, during the time of the plagues, the great war with the English kings, and the schism in the church, chaos and upheaval reined in France. There were never enough foodstuffs for everyone. Sadly, many people starved; many of them children. During this time of desperation, most lords felt death was a fair punishment against poaching as they needed the animals of their forests as much as anyone. Things are different now. 'Tis a better time for France—"

Paxton stopped suddenly as they went through the château gates. A coach and a number of horses were in the courtyard, all of these displaying the livery colors of the Vatican. It could only be the new bishop, and yet 'twas too soon for Francis or Lotto to have overridden the man's appointment, too soon for a new replacement to have arrived. He cursed softly. He called back to Jean Luc as he raced to the castle steps, "Jean Luc, bring those birds to Bonet, then go wash up."

"Aye, Uncle!" The boy broke into a run, anxious to show off his pheasant.

Paxton ran up the steps and through the great wooden doors. He moved quickly down the corridor and burst into the hall, stopping in the archway when he beheld the crimson vestments surrounded by a number of priests. His brother had not yet returned from his trip to nearby Cahors, where he went in an effort to recruit a dozen more cottars. John stood talking with the bishop. Father Thomas was in attendance. One look at the concern on John's face said it was indeed the Bishop Peter Luce, and John was not enjoying his introduction to his Excellency.

Paxton stepped forward. The men stopped talking and turned to him while his uncle greeted him. "Ah, Paxton. Bishop Peter Luce has arrived . . . unexpectedly early." And formally turning to the bishop, he began, "May I introduce my nephew Paxton de Chamberlain, lord of Bordeaux at Alsace, lord general of the king's guard—"

The tall man waved his hand to stop the long litany of Paxton's titles. "Worldly titles are of no interest to me." He held out his hand to receive Paxton's courtesy and bow of supplication.

Paxton ignored this formality as his sharp eyes focused hard on the man. The man looked nothing like he'd expected, and because of this, he realized he had been imagining a small and miserable looking creature. The bishop was rather tall, long-limbed, thin, and many would say handsome with his neat, uniform features and unlined face. Unlined save for deep crevices at the edge of his eyes and mouth. Gray edged his thick blond hair, adding to the distinguished air about him. Yet his eyes were a light amber, the color of gold, and every bit as cold as the metal. Oddly, he held a long, carved wooden staff covered with tiny demonlike heads to ward off the devil.

Paxton disliked the man instantly.

John was introducing the other priests as the two men continued to stare at each other. Paxton abruptly noticed Father Thomas again and demanded, "You were carrying letters for me, I believe?"

"I passed it on to a Frederick Coursan, a messenger at the Anjou court, who assured me of their swift deliverance."

The name meant nothing to Paxton. "Did he now? And you," he addressed Bishop Luce. "I imagine you have been informed of the whole of their contents."

Everyone listening drew back with shock. Everyone except for John, who knew his nephew well enough to have anticipated just such a scene. Paxton's strength of character was mercilessly blunt; he never showed the slightest willingness to involve himself in any treachery or intrigue. Nor did he fear any reprisal, of any kind.

The bishop assessed these things at once. Only the most well-protected or conceited man would dare the outrageous suggestion that he had opened a private letter addressed to another. He suspected Lord Paxton de Chamberlain of both. "I am not in the habit of reviewing the contents of personal letters. I know not what you speak of."

"No, of course not," Paxton said, noticeably without feeling, for he had no doubt the bishop had in fact read the whole of each letter. "I sent a letter to Cardinal Duprat, to the king, as well as to Lorenzo Lotto, the duke of Nantes and steward to Francis, requesting their effort in replacing you with another."

The bishop appeared unperturbed; only an inquiring brow rose over his staunch gaze, though, God knows, the blunt attack said much. Cardinal Duprat was a pluralist, damned because of it, and it stood to reason an adversary would draw his name. Nor did the duke of Nantes present a threat to his purpose. "Ah." He finally nodded, as he smiled condescendingly, implying that this was quite ordinary and rather expected. "And now I suppose you shall enlighten me as to your motives for such rash impudence."

"There was nothing rash or impudent in my judgment," Paxton corrected as he stepped closer, hands on hips, an arrogance in his stance. "The matter is simple. Having had your reputation brought to my attention—"

"And who did this?" Bishop Luce interrupted.

"Why do you ask?" Paxton shot back just as quick. "Is your reputation a secret thing, guarded from scrutiny and public discourse?"

The bishop's hand tightened on his staff. "My reputation stands as testament to God, no other, Milord Chamberlain." His gaze narrowed just slightly. "I fail to understand why I am being persecuted in this rude and, some might say, outrageous manner. So do tell, what have you to gain from my dismissal from Gaillard, or what do you imagine you lose by my presence?"

Paxton eyed the man as if judging his strength and finding it wanting. "My objections are many and owe themselves to philosophical arguments as well as family allegiances. You are well known for your defense of papal rights and law, and the belief that it should supersede the rights and laws and inheritances of my king. I have read your arguments against the writings of Aristotle, and on the 'divine scourge,' the absurd idea that the plague was God's judgment unleashed on the unfaithful. I can say, without hesitation, that I object to every word you have penned. I object most of all to the strictness and rigidity with which you implement church law and practice." He did not smile as he concluded, "In truth, there is little I know that you have said or done that I do not object to. So you will not be surprised when I pen yet another letter requesting Duprat and Lotto intervene to have your superiors withdraw you from Gaillard."

A brow lifted; he was impressed. "I appreciate your honesty—"

"Do you? I am surprised. Most men like you are offended by my inability to hide my displeasure."

He went too far; even John saw that.

For a long moment Bishop Luce just stared at Paxton, appalled by his brazen antagonism, his enormous pride, the doomed sentence this placed upon his soul. The man needed a dose of humility, and he intended to see that he get this.

Paxton started to withdraw.

"Your antagonism is noted, milord." The bishop's voice made him turn around and face him again. "And in time I hope to ease this unwarranted antipathy towards me. For I assure you, I harbor none towards you."

Paxton greeted this pretense of benevolence with unmasked skepticism, a hint of amusement glimmering in his fine eyes.

"However, I feel I must warn you, your letters will result in nothing."

Paxton remained unconvinced. "An interesting test of power," he replied. "We shall see."

"*You* shall see. The king himself would not be willing to extend the necessary energies to have me removed."

The statement brought anger to Paxton's tone as he demanded, "Did or did not Francis's concordat with the papacy grant him full authority over church appointments?"

The bishop chuckled. The man was naive. "Indeed, but as you should know, there are . . . strings attached. The concessions our holy pope would demand for the favor would be too high, their cost prohibitive. The king may indeed grace you with his favor, but as I am sure you are aware, there are limits to every courtly liaison. Even the relationship of king and a favorite general."

Paxton's expression—narrowed gaze, tilted chin—neatly conveyed his ire but concealed his confusion. My God, was this a bluff? Or did the man's connections reach all the way to the pope?

He looked at John, who shook his head with the same question.

Bishop Luce pressed his advantage. "But then it occurs to me this entire tedious conversation is naught but wasted air as you are not the master of Gaillard, are you?" He did not wait for an acknowledgment of the fact and instead pronounced it as sentence. "No, you are not. And with your brother's son, and God's grace of health upon the boy, you never will be. So, while you might covet your brother's inheritance, and"—he paused before adding in an impassioned whisper—"any number of your brother's possessions, you cannot have them. Ever."

Paxton eyes widened as he demanded, "What the devil does that mean?"

"The devil indeed." Bishop Luce's voice rose with sudden viciousness. "I merely point out that, for all your pretensions, you are left with little more than the enormity of your . . . unanswered desire, a state of being described in hell, sometimes even as hell. And while I pity you this unholy state, it occurs to me your colossal and shallow pride is as vacuous and meaningless as rainfall over the sea."

Violence trembled through Paxton. Until that moment he hadn't grasped the nature of this man's game. He threatened not just him, but Linness. Those words made it perfectly clear that somehow the man knew about his love for his brother's wife. He would not wonder how until later.

For now he had to make his stance perfectly clear to this evil man before him. "I warn you now. Tread carefully into the examination of my motives and purpose, still more carefully into the state of my soul. For you might discover any number of things I would be willing to protect with my life." The dark eyes blazed with emotion. "I hope that is clear." And with that, he withdrew.

Quickly Paxton headed down the corridor and up the stairs. No one stood in sight. He stopped in front of Linness's door and quietly, so quietly, he pressed down the latch. With a quick glance down the staircase, he stepped inside.

Afternoon sunlight came in through the window and washed over the alcove Linness sat in. With startled eyes she looked up from her wood carving to see Paxton leaning against the door, staring back at her. The tool dropped to her lap and she rose anxiously.

His brow lifted as he watched her pale hands clutch at her beige skirts. The dress was plain and old-fashioned, forming a curve at the bodice, where the white lace of her chemise showed. The benign colors accented the red ribbon woven into her dark hair, the pale gray of her eyes, and the redness of her lips.

He slowly approached her and she closed her eyes, the memory of their night together swimming dizzily through her mind. The yearning grew, a yearning to be held against his strength and beneath his weight, embracing the passion and splendor of his consuming love. They were doomed, she knew. The branding he left upon her soul shined in her eyes for all to see. For Bishop Luce to see. 'Twould be too late.

She said, "Bishop Luce has arrived."

"I just left his company."

Anxiety made her large eyes even larger. "And?"

"He claims the familiarity and protection of the only man who could save his position."

She cried, "Who is this?"

"Leo the tenth."

She stepped back in shock. "The pope . . . dear Lord." An anxious hand went to her forehead. " 'Tis said the pope has enough power now to reinstate Satan with God. Is it hopeless?"

"I do not know. I rather doubt my letters were delivered."

"How?!"

"Father Thomas has guilt writ over his face, and the bishop smacks of self-righteous pomp and knowledge—I sensed it at once. I will write a stronger letter today, and send Simon himself to deliver it personally. We can still hope. In the meantime . . ."

"Aye? In the meantime?"

She was desperate, he knew. "You must maintain an air of indifference to him. When Morgan presents you, act with gracious fortitude and this quiet dignity that is one of your finest graces. Linness," he whispered urgently, "you must learn to hide your fear."

Her eyes lowered as she considered the wisdom of his words. He was right—she must hide her fear, and she could, she felt certain, if only he didn't remember her. "But what if he realizes who I am?"

"Pretend ignorance. He cannot prove it. And if he does recall who you are, by the time he gets proof, if he can get proof, then either he will be removed from Gaillard or . . ."

She turned back to face him. "Or?"

His gaze filled with fierce conviction, but he did not want to frighten her further. "We do not have to consider the alternative now. Linness," he whispered, as he stepped to her. She started to back away, to shake her head, but the compelling light in his eyes caught hers and she was mesmerized, held still and unmoving beneath the warm intensity of his stare.

She heard the swift, steady beat of his heart, felt his lips brush across her forehead as he drank the scent of her perfumed skin and small breaths. She could not resist. With a wounded cry, she reached her arms around his neck as she lifted on her tiptoes, while his arms crossed over her back to hold her securely against his frame. She clung tightly, as the security of his arms suddenly seemed the only refuge in a world gone dark. She lifted her head back to meet his eyes. "Linness." A shiver ran through her as he brushed his lips across her mouth. "Let me taste your sweetness before our time is stolen. . . ."

His lips touched hers and he called up all the gentleness he owned, but dear Lord, she tasted like succulent fruit, sweeter than life itself. Gentleness vanished, replaced by a surge of fierce hunger. He tilted her back even farther and widened his lips like a man dying of thirst. Her fingers dug into the padded leather shoulders of his tunic as her lips clung to him in need.

When he broke the kiss, he uttered the single promise for salvation. "Tonight, Linness . . ."

Her eyes pleaded with him helplessly, to deny their need, but it was too late. It had always been too late. He turned from her and stepped to the door. He opened it a crack and listened before disappearing.

Linness leaned against the cold stone wall and closed her eyes as the future wove its bleak darkness through her consciousness. Violence threatened; she could feel its waiting threat.

It would come tonight. . . .

She squeezed her eyes shut and held her head, desperate to see the cause and reason for this violence. Her vision went white. The image emerged bright and clear.

She whispered his name in a start of fear, "Morgan . . ."

Morgan was to escort Linness down into the hall to be introduced to Bishop Luce.

Clair had used every trick she knew to transform Linness's appearance. When one met Linness, one noticed her hair. The streams of dark hair fell in tight ringlets past her waist, so curly that its own heaviness failed to pull it straight, and it was beautiful. Everyone loved her hair. So Clair made it disappear. She pulled it into a tight crown atop her head. A red velvet square-cut cloth, trimmed in gold braids, covered the whole. The effect was severe and changed the delicate lines of her face, sharpening her features. Then she applied rouge to her cheeks and lips, coal ash to her lashes.

She wore her finest gown of a red brocade and black Venetian velvet. The brocaded material covered half the bodice and the opposite half of the long, flowing skirt, while black velvet covered the rest. The sleeves had a long black ribbon that dropped to the floor.

Linness wished she could measure the effect, but she did not have a looking glass. Not only were looking glasses very expensive, but the abbess always called them the devil's tool to celebrate vanity, and though she knew this was extreme, she still maintained a superstitious aversion to them. "Do I look much changed?"

"Aye," Clair said. "As much as it's possible. Though if Gaillard is to be his diocese, he is bound to see you as you really are someday. We can't go through *this* every day."

"I know. 'Tis just that the first impression is the most important, I think."

Clair clicked her tongue. "Well, what if he does remember you? How could he explain the transformation from a simple girl to the Lady Belinda de Chamberlain? 'Twould be impossible; I daresay he would dismiss it as coincidence."

She closed her eyes. "I pray this is so. . . ."

Morgan opened the door. Linness turned and stood up. "Well." He rubbed his hands together as he stepped in the room. "Are we ready—" He stopped midsentence, staring with great shock. She wore face color. She looked so changed! "What is this?" he demanded

Linness felt inexplicably embarrassed. "I just thought I . . . well . . ." she looked helplessly to Clair.

"A little change." Clair forced a smile.

"Why?" he asked with innocent shock.

"To look pretty."

"Pretty?" He drew a deep breath, and licked his lips uncertainly. Without his realizing it, the face paint reminded him of his trouble with Amber and he scowled suddenly. The foolish woman wouldn't leave him be! He had paid handsomely for her bed, but somehow she thought he was still lusting over her like a sick hound with the scent of a seasoned bitch. Just today, Giraud, the town butcher, secretly confided the woman was telling the townspeople that he would name her bastard after John.

It enraged him every time he thought about it.

Linness swallowed nervously, repelled by the way he stared at her. Yet just as quickly his gaze narrowed, and he shook his head. "I do not like it. You are as beautiful as an angel. I do not want you to"—he motioned with his finger—"do that. Remove it. I will wait outside."

The door shut.

Confused, Linness sat down heavily on the seat. A shiver raced down her spine and she stared distantly into space as Clair wrung a facecloth in the dressing water. "Clair," she whispered mysteriously, "I just know something terrible will happen tonight."

This statement gave Clair pause. She knew not to doubt Linness's premonitions, but on the other hand, that pompous old bishop had given the girl a goodly case of the jitters. She was probably just anxious.

"Ah, ye are just scared of that old goat. Come, let's wipe the paint from ye face and pray this Bishop Luce doesn't have a mind or a memory for women. Half the priests do not—everyone knows a whole lot of 'em be mollycoddled pansies, if ye know what I mean."

"Mollycoddled pansies? I'm quite sure I don't," Linness said as she wiped the moist cloth over her face.

"Queer as a purple lime," Clair explained.

Clair's lewd comments worked like magic. A wicked smile tugged at the corners of Linness's mouth and she released her fears in a sigh. "Thank goodness no one else hears your black tongue, for otherwise 'twould not be me who need fear the flames. . . ." Once done, she genuflected for luck as she rose and gathered her skirts. Clair opened the door and Linness met Morgan in the hall. He smiled as his gaze came to her rosy face, scrubbed vigorously and looking squeaky clean. "Ah, that's more like my wife. Shall we?'' he said, and he offered his arm.

You must learn to hide your fear . . .

Paxton's words echoed in her mind and she tilted her head up and smiled brightly, creating an air of regal grace as she and Morgan descended the ancient stairs, passed through the corridor and into the great hall.

The fires blazed, warming the room. Festive torches lit the space. The freshest linen decorated the tables. Vivian had constructed artful centerpieces made of fruit and flowers, which Linness had helped her with earlier. The best pewter dishes and goblets sat neatly atop the table along with bowls of fruit and cheese and the special basins and cloths for the feast washing.

The most prominent citizens of Gaillard, dressed in their finest clothes, stood along the lower tables. Knights and priests sat at another table, the priests on one side, the knights on the other. From the corner of her gaze she noticed Simon was not there.

Paxton noticed the change at once as Morgan escorted Linness to the main table on the dais, stopping every few steps as Linness greeted friends and clasped hands with others. She was playing the part of the beautiful and well-loved lady of the manor, and playing this well. Relief washed over him in force; laughter edged his grin.

He looked to Bishop Luce, startled when he saw the man watching him watch Linness. Paxton's brow rose inquiringly. Bishop Luce turned back to Linness as John, acting as steward, introduced her. And as he always did in formal situations, especially with members of the church, he repeated her

Christian name. "May I present the Lady Belinda de Beaumaris Chamberlain.

"And, milady, may I present Bishop Peter Luce."

Linness gathered her pretty skirts in hand and gracefully swooped into a curtsy. He held out his hand for her supplication. Trying not to remember the last time this happened, Linness lightly touched her lips to the ring of Christ.

"How do you do?" she asked softly as she dared a look into his eyes. A tingling alarm shot up her spine. He stared at her with unmasked confusion.

The bishop was stunned by how familiar she looked. Where had he seen her before? He could not but stare at her. And something told him to beware of the pull this woman had on men.

The bishop continued to eye her even as John called the names of the rest of the members of the bishop's party. Her curtsies solicited bows from each of the priests. The party gathered in their assigned seats and took their places. The butlers, in charge of drinks, rushed to fill glasses, and still she felt the unnerving scrutiny of the bishop across the way.

"Milady," he finally said. "I am baffled. I have the queerest sense of having met you before. You seem . . . somehow familiar. . . ."

She suffered an anxious moment's pause, but this disappeared as she took a deep breath, which she released in a smile. "Do you?" she asked in a perfect pitch of politeness. "Perhaps you know my parents? The baron and baroness de Beaumaris of Montegrel? Have you journeyed there before?"

"I have not," he replied. "Have you traveled elsewhere?"

"My wife's travels have been limited," Morgan

answered for her. "She is content to stay close to home and hearth."

"Content?" She tossed a light and teasing gaze to Morgan. "Oh no, my husband, I am in bliss to stay at our home."

Morgan's pleasure at this answer showed in a smile and an affectionate squeeze of her hand.

Paxton realized, too late, the price of this intrigue; he stared stonily at Morgan before forcing his gaze away.

The servants carefully began serving the two distinct meals. Bishop Luce and his brothers maintained the restricted diet demanded by the rule of Saint Benedict. This forbade the meat of quadrupeds. Shortly after his arrival, the bishop had appeared in the kitchen to discuss the requirements he demanded for meal preparation, of which, to Vivian and Bonet's dismay, there had been many. Vivian made the mistake of mentioning that Father Gayly had never even mentioned this obscure rule. Bishop Luce seized this chance to express his opinion—expressed it as a fact—that this laxity on Father Gayly's part was what brought down the divine retribution that killed him.

Vivian was still upset about it. . . .

Paxton was reminded of the man's ridiculous zealotry as the special plates of Lenten stew and sundry fish were set before the priests. "So, Bishop Luce," he inquired, "I suppose the German monk, Luther, and his attack on the church's practice of issuing indulgences is well known. I have not heard the church's formal defense of the practice. Do you know it?"

The bishop's brow lifted, Linness forgotten as he replied, "Since when does the holy Roman church need to answer to a German monk of no distinction or repute?"

"Since his words captured the passion and inflamed the ideas of the faithful," replied Paxton.

From across the way, a guard called for Michaels, who rushed around the table and through the doors.

Linness knew at once what Paxton referred to; they all did. Priests accepted money for passing out "indulgences," an absolution for a sin not yet committed. For instance, a man who desired to have an affair with a woman who was not his wife could buy an absolution from a priest and then commit adultery with a clean conscience, supposedly guaranteed God's forgiveness—on the off chance he died while committing the sin. Father Gayly had refused to issue these licenses for sins, though most other priests' pockets were full to bursting from the collection of coins for indulgences; thus all manner of sins—adultery, thefts, deceits—were being wiped away for a pretty price.

"My dear man, are you now questioning church law? Do I really have to explain its holy purpose? Indulgences are absolutely necessary to lift people from purgatory; all the world knows this; certainly the faithful know it." His tone managed to imply that Paxton was not likely among this group. "If a person dies without benefit of absolution, he is condemned to purgatory. Indulgences have saved countless souls from that unpleasant state. Their purpose is holy and noble."

"Really," Paxton responded. "And I thought their purpose had to do with the pope's effort to rebuild Saint Peter's."

Morgan and a number of the other men laughed

openly at this frank assessment, while Linness hid her smile in a hasty gulp of water. Even Bishop Luce smiled and yet he asked, "You would not question the church's right to spend these coins for the glory of God?"

Another priest rushed to point out the profound effect of the church's greatest architecture on the masses. Chartres and Notre Dame, these glorious buildings, dropped common folks to their knees in awe and supplication, no easy feat to do to sinners. But as fine dishes were being set before them, few listened to the man's rather undistinguished and long-winded speech.

Michaels rushed back into the hall and straight for Morgan. He came directly behind him and whispered into his ear, "Milord, a . . . a woman is outside the doors, insisting on speaking to you now."

Michaels did not attach a name to this person; he didn't have to. Linness demurely wiped her mouth, pretending not to have overheard any of this. Yet, to her horror, the whispered words received Bishop Luce's full attention—causing all the priests to fall silent and observe what had caught their superior's attention.

Linness looked anxiously to Paxton.

Paxton rushed to fill this silence and save his brother this embarrassment. "Yet how do you reply to the German monk—"

Too late. Morgan's face had reddened, more as he slammed his fist to the table and shouted to Michaels, "Curse her. Send her away! How dare she interrupt me in my hall. How dare you bring her claim—"

Michaels, obviously frightened by this, hastened

to lean over and explain, "She says she shall kill herself if—"

"Begone before I do it for her!"

Michaels drew back, stunned. Humiliated and upset, he rushed away.

Color came to Linness's face. She was not embarrassed for herself, but rather for Amber's pathetic attempts to engage Morgan's paternal interest in her child. Clair had gleaned from the local gossip that Amber had given birth last night. But Amber should not be out so soon, even though the birth had apparently been an easy one for her. She had not yet gone through the ceremony of ritual cleansing after childbirth, which would cause even more gossip.

Adultery was still a sin against the sacrament of marriage, and while this was hard to forgive in the best of circumstances, many of the townspeople might turn a cheek to Morgan's infidelities, if he conducted his affairs honorably. He did not. He flaunted these liaisons as if he were an unmarried merry prankster, deceiving the women and, unforgivably, abandoning his bastards. The other day one of his children was seen in the rain and mud without shoes, barefoot like a beggar. This was too much, and when this news reached her ears, Linness, that very day, sent the woman a bag of coins, foodstuffs, shoes for the child, and some warm woolen scarves and hats for the winter.

Of course, Amber was aware of Morgan's past abuses of peasant women. Somehow, Morgan always convinced these women that each was special, that he would love her all his days. Yet, even in her distress over Morgan's abandonment, Amber should have stayed in bed. If she knew Morgan at all, she would have realized that, as with so many men, one did not press forward when they turned the other way.

Angry, Morgan drained his goblet and held it out for more. Everyone knew to leave him alone until this storm passed. Paxton asked his question again and saved him from any of the bishop's inquiries. The bishop decided to ignore the obviously upsetting subject, whatever it was, and he replied to Paxton. Within minutes a furious debate raged at their table. The food was practically forgotten as Bishop Luce's unrelenting fundamentalism met Paxton's rational and logical challenge, which he cloaked in a considerable wit.

Linness remained silent, tearing off small bits of bread. Despite the animosity between the two men, or perhaps because of it, they seemed to relish the heated exchange. She might have enjoyed the exchange as well if she were not sensitive to Morgan's still-seething fury.

Which gradually diminished as the minutes passed.

She lifted a succulent slice of apple and a piece of cheese to her mouth but felt a sudden and sharp jolt seize her body. She gasped in a small, startled cry. Instantly all gazes came upon her and she saw Paxton rise in alarm. Her hands went numb, the food dropped to the table. A noisy scuffle sounded outside the door. The musicians stopped, turning to see what it was about.

A harrowing scream sounded from the corridor, echoing through the hall. Michaels shouted a warning. The hall went silent as everyone turned to see the commotion.

Amber made a mad dash through the doors.

She burst upon the hall and stopped, breathing heavily, her terrified eyes flying about the grandeur before her, unable to suppress her awe. The woman held a bundle in her arms, and with dread, Linness knew it was her newborn child. A tingling of fear shot along her spine again. She felt rather than saw Mary's worried presence, hovering over the child. Her alarm increased.

Michaels and Clifford rushed in behind Amber, and when their hands came to her person, she cried, twisting from them as she sought and finally saw Morgan at the head of the main table. She rushed to him.

Morgan rose as well, but it was too late to stop the woman. She fell on the steps leading up to the dais, her plain green skirts fanned out behind her. "Milord! Milord!" she shrieked in a maddened voice. The crowd murmured its shock and outrage, but quieted when she spoke again. "Ye would not come to see ye babe. So I brought him to ye."

Through clenched teeth, Morgan spoke, his voice like a low growl of a bear. "You stupid simple whore—how dare you!"

For a moment she looked as if his reaction surprised her. "Ye are ashamed of me! Of ye own Amber!" She cast a glance to the people behind her. A trembling hand went to her flaxen hair, smoothing it as if it were her disheveled hair that brought Morgan shame. "All ye mighty and pretty lords and ladies here. Ye think I am not good enough, do ye?" She looked back at Morgan with fury. "I was good enough to warm ye bed and ease the ache in ye loins! I was good enough to bear the product of ye seed!" She rushed on, "And here he be, milord. Ye must see him, ye must—" Trembling hands removed the cloth from the child and she held him up as an offering. All those who could see drew back in horror.

The baby was hideously deformed.

The tiny head was swollen, his eyes white slits that could see nothing of the world. There was a mangled stub of flesh where an arm should be. It was a miracle that he still breathed.

Morgan's lip curled in revulsion; he stared in shock.

Linness was seeing beyond. Mary's light was bathing the child, and her own wealth of sympathy and compassion washed over her, so powerful, it nearly dropped her to her knees.

"For the love of Mary . . ." Linness pleaded.

Save the child, Mary cried to her, the words echoing so loudly in her mind, she thought everyone heard them. . . .

The bishop saw the stamp of Satan and felt the righteous indignation. The child had been condemned by the Almighty God. For the sins of his parents.

Amber's eyes narrowed. "Ye looked so surprised, milord. Surely ye knew what curse ye hateful wife would put upon our babe!" The mad eyes suddenly turned to Linness and with viciousness she cried, "Ye and all ye witchery! Ye did this! 'Tis ye own evil mark upon my poor doomed babe! To feed ye never-ending jealousies. Ye poisoned our love and turned him away from me. Ye made sure he wouldn't come back to me! Ye did . . . this!"

A collective gasp sounded.

Linness's vision went white, then red with blood.

Paxton shouted to Michaels and Clifford, "Get the woman out of here now!"

The command suddenly snapped Michaels out of his daze and he stepped forward. She swung around to him, a knife manifesting in her hand, which she had retrieved from the folds of her skirts. A number of women screamed. "Don't touch me or I'll kill it!"

"Amber, I beg you," Linness cried. "I beg you don't do that. For love of Mary! For mercy's sake—"

The words enraged Amber; she swung toward Linness. "Ye! Ye did this to me!" Tears fell down her face; she was gasping each breath. "Ye stole his love, with all ye fine ways and pretty clothes and silvered tongue." Her eyes turned vicious. "With all ye witchery," she cried, "and then did this to my babe. . . ."

Amber's startled gaze turned to the child, as if seeing him for the first time. The child lay unnaturally silent before her. Her eyes blazed in bewilderment, fury—a fathomless pit called madness.

Linness knew what was to come next. "No, no," Linness cried, moving towards her. "Someone stop her!"

Michaels ran toward them, and Paxton leaped over the table, but too late.

Amber stared into the baby's face, and blinded by tears, she raised the knife and thrust it down with all her strength. And then blood, blood covered Amber's face and her hands and spurted over her dress as she lifted the dead child and crushed it against her heart, her anguished cry echoing loud and long through the hall. . . .

Chapter 8

Paxton found her at last. He stopped short, breathing hard and fast, staring at her. Waiting for him, she lay in a meadow bursting with a profusion of bluebells. Laughter, made of anticipation, joy, and love, sang in the stilled morning air. Sunlight fell upon her naked beauty, bathing her white skin. One arm was raised over her head, shielding her eyes. Careful to keep his weight from her, he came over her and stopped her laughter with a kiss.

Dear Lord, he wanted her, more as he found her hot skin, slick with desire. "Dear Lord, Linness . . ." He would die—

"Aye," she said with strange urgency, her eyes feverish with worry and fear. "Aye, you will die. You will die and I with you. . . ."

He bolted up in bed and stared at the still dark room. The gray light of dawn filtered through the silence. He fell against the bed and sighed, sighed because it would be some time before his body made the necessary distinction between a dream and reality.

I want you, Linness, with each breath I take, I want you. . . .

227

It had been two weeks since that night of blood and murder, and Linness had retreated, receiving no one, not even Jean Luc. He did not trespass upon this solitude. He understood, better than any other, the depth of Linness's devotion and reverence for life and all that was holy; he would not intrude upon her period of healing prayer and silence.

Meanwhile, Morgan walked around like a belly-up dog, sheepishly stealing glances into faces as if to assess their condemnation. Everyone pretended not to notice this; everyone happily pretended nothing had happened that night. Except, of course, Bishop Luce, who had demanded an outrageous price to have the madwoman, Amber, cloistered in a nunnery where the nuns might care for the deranged creature. Morgan made the payment without hesitation. Paxton had viewed this change in Morgan with contempt and occasionally pity, until recently.

The other day as they were returning to the château from the fields, they came across a well-made cart heading into Gaillard. It was Alberti and his sons, moneylenders who were setting up shop in Gaillard. The man was very pleased to meet Lord Morgan Chamberlain, but his young sister more so. The eighteen-year-old woman, Arianne, flirted and pranced, tugged on her dress to present an offer Morgan somehow would not refuse. The girl's morals were brazenly displayed in her manner. . . .

Somehow nothing excited Morgan more. That was all it took. Morgan's mood rebounded as he arranged a private tryst. The situation with Amber had taught him nothing.

Not that he wanted Morgan to learn anything.

He didn't. For the last thing he wanted his brother to discover was the treasure he had in his wife, and even less, the virtues of marital fidelity.

The heat in his loins seemed to increase with deprivation; he had reached his limit. He bounded out of bed and moved to a table where he splashed chilled water from a bowl over his face and chest before pulling on breeches and a tunic. He grabbed a dagger and slipped out his window.

'Twas still dark....

He reached her window and found it open. Thinking she still slept, that he might wake her, he slipped inside quietly. He stood up in the alcove and stared.

She was kneeling at the candlelit altar. Her gold robe was spread in a neat half circle around her. With eyes closed, her face looked pale and angelic, otherworldly somehow. The long hair was gathered tightly in the back of her head, accenting the delicate lines of her face. She was changed, he saw, and it scared him, this transformation. As if she were slipping away from the world where mortals lived. As if she had slipped away from him . . .

He stepped forward. Not wanting to startle her, he kept his voice whisper-soft, "Linness . . ."

She opened her eyes. "Paxton." She said his name in an echo of longing. In the still gray light of dawn, he appeared as a shadow brushed with faint color. His beautiful eyes appeared like shining pools of black. She now knew the blue color of his eyes shone only in the bright light of the sun. 'Twas her sad fate to rarely see him beneath the bright and sharp colors of day. Forbidden lovers faced a lifetime of whispers, stolen glances, and longing, the terrible longing that had awoken her as she slept and brought her to the altar in a desperate attempt to find peace.

" 'Tis been too long," he whispered. "Tell me, Linness. Tell me what has happened to you."

Her heart surged forward, and her senses flooded with the play of light and shadow on his face and the faint trace of his masculine scent of musky oil and hard-worked leather. Her arms ached to reach around his neck and bring his strength against her skin, his lips on her mouth, the caress of his hands. . . .

Forbidden desire. Did it grow because it was forbidden? She had asked herself that question a thousand times, and always the answer was the same. Nay. It grew as the physical manifestation of love, not an easy or gentle love but a dark and passionate disease that would steal the life from them. . . .

She had to end it now. Once and for all in this lifetime she had to stop it, to turn back the tides sweeping them away, back. She prayed she had the strength to do so. For him, for Paxton.

He took her hands and she stood up, tilting her head to meet his concerned eyes. " 'Tis easing, the ache in my soul. Mary's love is easing it bit by bit." She turned her head away as she struggled to find words to explain all she had passed through.

"At first I felt ripped apart. That night, Mary was there, in the hall, calling to me to save the child. I tried . . . I—" She shook her head. "I felt I had failed her. . . . For many days my thoughts ran as mad as that poor woman's. Morgan's pathetic looks, like a misbehaving child, begging me for forgiveness, and the hateful bishop probing and pricking at everyone in his senseless search for a truth that shall always elude him. Anger and bitterness tore at me until I suddenly understood its source. 'Twas my own guilt for having failed Mary that was ripping me apart."

With feeling he swore, "You could not have saved that child!"

"I know that now. For as I prayed I felt it. Mary's sorrow, Paxton." Her voice was changing in wonder at her mystical sight. "It is an awesome thing that dropped me to my knees and washed over me in wave after wave. Mary's sorrow is as boundless and deep as the ocean waters. It is not for mortal contemplation and I could not have borne it if it did not carry with it the revelation of her love. And in this blessing of her love is forgiveness."

He stared into her eyes a long moment. "Linness, love, what do you need forgiveness for?"

"How can you ask me thus? I came to Gaillard and married Morgan in deception. I bore you a son and gave him to Morgan in deception. And now, now I deceive him more every day that I live. Paxton," she cried, "I am in love with you, his brother!"

The words did not stun him, but her anguish did, and before he knew how to answer that, his gaze came to rest on her neck. There was no necklace. He reached for the place where his ring had sat over her heart. Fingertips brushed the cool skin. She drew back. His gaze blazed intensely and he swallowed his fear as, at last, he understood what she was telling him. Good-bye.

Something dark and dangerous came into his eyes. "Linness—"

She shook her head. "Please, Paxton, please. Let me go. . . . Just let me go before 'tis too late."

Tension and anger seized him, like a great lion

before a fatal strike. She felt it threatening her with its quiet restraint and unholy control. In a soft vow of feeling he answered, "Never."

All she knew was that she had to make him go. She had to convince him the path they walked on led to hell, a vicious hell where death would be no mercy, but the start of the torment. Mary was warning her; it was all she knew.

"You must, you must. It is like being forced to march to an execution; I cannot bear it. The lost child was the first wave of a dark future spreading across our sky, like an ink blotch over parchment. . . . It will destroy us—"

"Enough," he said sharply as a hand came to her mouth and another to her thin arm, drawing her close. "Enough." The black pools of his eyes stared down at her. "I can feel your fear, Linness. Again. I can taste it, and a bitter taste it is. Again. Have you learned nothing?"

"Paxton, please, 'tis not death I fear, but life; living in a world where you do not!"

"This fear will increase until you understand the true meaning of this death that so terrifies you. Beginning now, I vow not to come to you again."

Surprise changed her eyes as she frantically searched his face.

"*You* will come to me. Aye, love," he whispered. "You will come to me when you are weak from the relentless pounding of your heart, the breathlessness no air can ease, when your body is soaked in nothing but longing and the sweetened scent of your desire." Softly he told her, "I will wait until you realize that this same desire is coursing through my veins even now. . . ."

He released her as he stepped back and turned

to disappear through the window. She stared after him before she sank slowly to the floor. A cool morning breeze blew in through the window. The struggle to generate the unnatural strength to resist the pounding sweetness of forbidden love had just begun. . . .

A battle she was doomed to lose . . .

Tom Boswell found much to admire as he walked through the streets of Gaillard. No pillories, for instance. He thought he might stay here, at least for a spell, if only he could remain honest for a change. Or if he could just be dishonest on a more modest scale. The trouble, of course, was that God created more fools than the lice that plagued them.

The sun was bright and shadows were sharp. Signs of industry abounded everywhere; the streets were full of people bustling about their chores. Tom smiled widely, tipped his head to all, even a group of unkempt cottars heading toward the fields. He drew deeply of the scents wafting from the bakery, before stopping to read the banner proclaiming an upcoming fair, one that promised fortune readings from the lady of Gaillard. The tailor glanced up as he passed and smiled. A most friendly town, Tom saw as he passed the smithy, where a man was shoeing a new coach. A group of men bent over cobblestones being laid into the street. There seemed as many people milling about the goldsmith shop as the butcher's. Coins were passing from hand to hand everywhere he looked. Vineyards stretched as far as he could see. And he had a taste for what vineyards produced. No beggars here either, another good sign. 'Twas perfect.

Gaillard had more industry than any English

town he knew, and he knew many of them. He had been chased out of every English village east of London, until at last a sheriff put him on a boat crossing the channel. "So ye can try ye hand at emptying the pockets of the frog-faced French . . ."

Tom still chuckled every time he thought of it. " 'Tis a fine thing by me," he had shouted back. "No doubt the French have as many fools as merry ole England!"

Besides, he knew the language well enough.

So here he was, a man without a country, looking for a few rich pockets and already holding the introduction to one in his sack. He shielded his eyes with his hand as he looked down the thoroughfare to the gates at the Château Gaillard. Perhaps he would soon be wrapped in the comforts of this wealthy provincial court.

He stepped into the shady dark comfort of a tavern. A woman was sweeping the rushes thrown over the floor. "How do ye do, sir?" she asked pleasantly.

"As fine as Adam afore the fall. How about a mug of some nice cool ale."

She cried with surprise, "Oh, ye be an Englishman!"

"By no fault of me own," he said. " 'Twas my mother's doing. God rest her soul. . . ."

The woman laughed as she set down the broom and stepped behind the counter. She grabbed a mug, opened the barrel and tumbled cool ale into a cup. This was set before the man as she looked him over. "Ye be wearing a monk's cloth?"

"That I am, good woman, that I am. I've come with a sorrowful news for Lord Chamberlain."

"Oh?" she inquired. "Which one would that be?"

"Be there two Lord Chamberlains now?"

"Ye must have just arrived if ye have to ask. There are indeed two. Brothers. Twins at birth."

"Ye don't say? Well, I'm seeking a Lord Paxton Chamberlain, who until recently had in service a knight named Simon."

She drew back. "Did some mishap befall the goodly man Simon?"

She held her breath, bracing herself for bad news. She had liked Simon. Everyone did. He had shown them how to better roof their tavern, spending a whole two days here to do it. He had learned carpentry from his father, a high-minded architect with connections to the crown. He said he had always meant to follow in his father's footsteps, but somehow, after he was knighted and with the king's wars and all, he never had the chance. Still, he couldn't keep his hands from any building going on and he had been anxious to quit Gaillard for Alsace with Lord Chamberlain. . . .

"Aye." The monk shook his head sadly.

The woman waited for more to be said, but the monk remained silent. She supposed she'd learn about it soon enough. Nothing but bad news and evil deeds seemed to be coming to the Chamberlains these days. Two weeks since the mad girl murdered Lord Morgan's doomed bastard, and people still talked of nothing else. . . .

Poor Lord Paxton. Never had it easy despite his riches and title. Always in the shadow of his brother. Now more than ever, she suspected, the way Lord Paxton and the Lady Linness were always seen together, the love between so tangible. Some said they saw its sparks flying from the château's windows at night.

"God save us," she whispered, and she told the man how to press a request for an audience with the lord general, murmuring again, "God save 'em all. . . ."

With a sweep of skirts, Linness stepped into the hall. It was so very quiet. Soft summer sunlight filtered through the stained-glass windows and the enormous skylight overhead. The air was cool. Four priests sat at the table on the dais with two open Bibles. Papers, the bishop's seal, ink wells, and feathered quills crowded the tabletop.

The bishop stood, his hands clasped behind his back, staring up at the stained-glass depiction of Mary and Child, a gift Linness had ordered for Morgan at Christmas gift-giving time. God appeared as a golden light above her. It was an unorthodox vision the Lady Chamberlain herself had ordered the artisan to make.

Linness knelt before the priests in supplication. "You called to speak with me, Bishop Luce?"

He turned from the stained-glass window to see the lady kneeling there. She was beautiful, but then, so was Satan. So was Satan. Women were the source of original sin and weak vessels particularly liable to vice. This lady more so; unholy demons had seized her soul; he knew this now. She tempted more than one man to vice.

As for her unusual beauty, it was a ruse, a clever trap for the obtuse man. Like Lord Paxton. And this one wielded her beauty with particular skill. He had noted this from the start. She never let her vanity reveal itself in the normal pretensions of her sex; no coy sighs and batted lashes, indecent bodices, provocative hair arrangements, or fashionable shoes. The theatrical air of melancholy about her was most irritating, and deceptive. Half the people of Gaillard, including her own husband, saw it as a signature of the depth of her feeling for the sordid scene played out here that night.

The town's gossip had led him to a series of startling conclusions. What the simple folks didn't know was that, no doubt, the lady had caused her husband's impotence through witchcraft, which explained Lord Morgan's infidelities. Now she was free to copulate with his brother, entangling that man in her godless ambitions. He had guessed it all. This, in turn, brought about the sordid triangles of adultery and fornication, which ended in the devil's own horrific spectacle played for the entire court of Gaillard. He had never witnessed anything quite so diabolical.

He meant to uncover her deceit and bring her to her knees before God's judgment. He meant to see the fear of the everlasting fires of damnation consume her whole. Beginning now. "So," he began. "You have emerged from your meditations today."

"Aye," she said quietly.

"The day that marks the pagan solstice."

She looked confused for a moment. "Is it now?"

"Would you pretend not to be aware of the date or its unholy significance?"

"I would not pretend," she replied, speaking in a cool, detached voice.

It infuriated him, her calm.

For a moment he said nothing. He turned back to the stained-glass depiction of Mary and Christ. "You had these made, I am told."

"Aye. For my husband. It was a gift."

"This obsession you have with the holy Mother. From whence does it spring?"

That was an easy answer to give. "From the everlasting bounty of my love."

"So you say, so you say. The reverence for Mary is specious at best, false and illicit at worst. It steals your prayers and soul from God—"

"Mary brings me closer to God!"

His eyes blazed with sudden wrath, though his voice remained calm as he replied, "The worship of Mary over Christ and God is an evil ideation that directly contradicts the teaching of the holy church!"

Father Aslam stood and read three Scriptures from the Bible, including the first commandment and ending with a more ominous one. She hardly listened. The Scriptures, she knew, were a mirror held against the soul; what one found there revealed the nature and inclinations of one's heart. Father Gayly used to say it best; there were as many ways of reading the Bible as the sun had of shining, and that as man thinkest in his heart, he finds in the Scripture.

"Yet you know this, do you not?"

"I have heard those passages many times."

The bishop added, "You have thus been warned, milady. I shall not suffer the impertinence of your false ideation again. You shall remove all false images of Mary and replace them with the cross. You shall begin directing your prayers to Christ and God. You shall delete any reference to Mary from your mind. Is that understood?"

She made no reply, save for her eyes. How dare he? He wouldn't know God if He knocked him down with a lightning bolt! This was too maddening. . . .

"Now I shall direct my questions to another matter. Did you know the serving woman, Amber?"

"Aye."

"How did you know her?"

"Just from passing."

"Is that all?"

"Aye."

"Did you know she was your husband's mistress?"

Linness paused and in a whisper she said, "Aye."

"So you knew her a bit more than just in passing?"

"The common gossip had been brought to me."

"Who brought you this news?"

"I heard it from a number of different people."

"Name them."

"I will not. They are of no consequence to your questioning."

The bishop slammed his fist on the bench. "I will determine what is and is not of consequence here. In the name of God, state the names of the people who told you this."

Bright rebellion flashed in her eyes. She would not involve any other in the man's malice. No matter what. "Then, I do not remember who. . . ."

His gaze bored into her. "You would lie to protect these people. Another abomination before God. Very well. Did you or did you not consider your husband's mistress a rival for his affection?"

"I did not," she replied.

"Yet you knew he was conducting an affair. How do you reconcile this disparity?"

"I do not see it as a disparity. I have always had my husband's regard and affection. What he did or did not do with another woman concerned me not. I have no moral authority over my husband."

"Perhaps you have another reason for ignoring your husband's affairs."

She made no reply to that.

"You have no answer, milady?" he pressed.

"I did not hear a question."

"Do you have another reason for ignoring your husband's affairs?"

"Nay," she lied for the first time. She had to. To save Jean Luc. To save Paxton. To save Morgan. Firmly, she said again, "I do not."

"And would you swear to this on the Bible before God Almighty?"

There came the briefest hesitation. "Aye . . ."

"So now how do you answer the woman's charge?"

"What charge is that?"

"The charge of witchery!"

"I say not guilty to that mad accusation."

"Do you? And if you were guilty, would you not also deny it?"

A trick, she knew, of course. "Aye."

"So do you admit you are lying to save yourself?"

"Nay!"

"But you at least admit that we cannot trust the veracity of your word?"

"Nay!"

He paused a moment, having proved her denial meant nothing. "And what of your well-known reputation as a seer of men's fortunes?"

Linness frantically searched the stone and marble

squares around her, then lifted her gaze. The brightness of the afternoon filled the hall with little lights and quivers, dancing across the walls and floors and lighting the bishop's thin face with frightening planes and shadows. Perhaps she was only imagining this, for the question truly scared her. How to answer it? To deny it was impossible. It was indeed common knowledge, but then to admit to the gift before a man such as Bishop Luce was to set fire to the kindling sticks beneath her fate. He would declare her guilty of witchery no matter what.

"Do you or do you not see into the future?"

"Aye, occasionally."

"And to whom do you attribute this 'miracle of sight'—as you have been known to call it?"

"To no one."

"No one?"

"No one."

"Are human beings capable of orchestrating miracles?" When she made no reply, he demanded, "Are they?"

"Nay," she confessed.

"Then I ask you again. To whom do you attribute these miracles—"

Mary, save me now. . . .

The answer was Mary, the long-ago bump on her head, a child's flight to heaven. He had already equated Mary with Satan, and her love for Mary would be seen as love for the Great Deceiver; her sight would be declared of a darkling, sinister nature.

"I am waiting!"

Mary, save me now . . .

* * *

The three riders, Paxton, Morgan and Jean Luc, rode through the township as workers dispersed to their various homes through Gaillard. Paxton drew his horse to a stop, turning to watch Jean Luc expertly do the same. The boy was a quick learner, and even better, his mother's reverence for life had embedded in the boy a great love of the creatures. He was congratulating Jean Luc on his new skill when Michaels's voice beckoned his attention.

Paxton turned to see an odd-looking monk standing behind Michaels. Beige robes hung on his corpulent frame, a thin rope gathered at his waist, accenting his girth. He carried a sack tied to a pole on his back. Neatly cropped dark hair covered the sides of his balding head. The man was tall, almost as tall as himself, and his eyes were as blue and mild as the afternoon sky.

Jean Luc chased after the grooms and disappeared in the stables. Michaels cast a nod in the man's direction. "Boswell, milord. From England. He's been traveling about France and, well . . ." His gaze brushed the ground as he withheld the tragic news. "He needs to speak with you."

Morgan came up to Paxton's side.

The two men were an imposing sight, but Tom Boswell was not easily, if ever, intimidated. He bowed and, in a loud and booming voice, introduced himself.

A tremor of alarm passed through Paxton. "Aye, what news have you?"

"Sad, methinks, milord. Very sad." He looked away, mentally deliberating on how best to begin the story. "It concerns a knight by the name Simon. I witnessed his death at the violent hands of a band of lecherous thieves."

Paxton's eyes blazed with emotion. Morgan put his hand on his brother's shoulder as if to steady him.

"Simon, dear God, not Simon . . ."

"I am sorry to bear the news. I was walking along the road to Amboise. I stopped by a stream to cool my feet, and while I was sitting on the bank, I heard shouts and the clang of steel in the distance. I hurried to the spot to see what it was about." Actually he had imagined it a common jousting between men and he had hoped to amass some coin in wagering on the outcome; he was famous for his ability to pick winners in battles and fights.

Only he saw it wasn't a joust at all.

"Well, the man, Simon, was outnumbered by these robbers. Three men attacked him. I hid in fear . . . you understand, having sworn holy oath to God never to raise sword or arms against another man in honor of Christ. And . . . when 'twas done, he lay in a pool of blood."

Paxton couldn't speak. Not now. Simon was a dear friend, his favorite, a man he dearly loved.

"You say they were thieves?!" Morgan demanded.

"Well, there's an odd bit. The evildoers searched through his saddlebag and over his person. They seemed to be looking for something. I do not know what. They left all this." He brought out a bag and untied the ends, spreading it open. "They did empty his money bag but left his jewels."

Simon's purse contained two of his rings, a velvet doublet, and an envelope with a broken seal; that was all. Paxton knelt down to pick up one of the rings. 'Twas a platinum band with a large oval in the center. The Lady Joan of Orleans, lady in waiting to the duchess, had given it to him as a betrothal promise, the year before she had died. Simon had worn it always in her memory.

"Did you see what they did take?"

Paxton asked the question in a controlled whisper.

"The money, 'tis all, and oh, the man's sword. I was . . . hiding, you see, and there was a good distance between me and the robbers."

"This"—Paxton picked up the letter—"was Simon's letter to his father—"

"Aye." The monk nodded. " 'Twas how I knew to come here."

"He carried two other letters," Paxton said.

"I did not see any, milord. I searched the body. I gathered his things up before I buried him."

"They took my letters," Paxton said.

Morgan wanted to know, "What would robbers have to do with a worthless piece of parchment?"

Paxton gave no clue of his thoughts. He struggled to believe the bishop's treachery went deep enough to kill an innocent knight carrying a letter. Was he that devious, that determined to thwart Paxton's attempt to get him removed from Gaillard? What twisted mind would allow him to kill for it?

Perhaps he was wrong, though. Perhaps the bishop had nothing to do with it.

Not that he would take the chance; he couldn't.

To Morgan he said, "It could be treachery—"

Paxton abruptly caught sight of Clair racing down the steps of the keep to where they gathered. Morgan turned, too.

"Milords, please come!" Clair screamed. 'Tis the bishop. Linness went out today for the first time since . . . since the incident with that madwoman, and the bishop caught her on her way back and demanded an audience. At first she refused, but he insisted. She's in the hall now, and she has been with him for some time—"

Morgan searched Clair's face before he drew a deep breath. For a long moment he stared at her, trying to understand what her words meant. His gaze lowered uncertainly then, and she realized he felt guilt and shame. It was just as Linness said; he skulked about with the pathetic look of a naughty child, all but begging for her forgiveness. Clair wondered if Linness hated him for it.

But Paxton would not endure his brother's cowardice now; he couldn't. Linness needed him, needed both of them, in a show against the bishop. He needed Morgan to appear with him in the hall, to demonstrate they were united in protecting Linness from the bishop's threat. In a voice that was sharp and clear and commanding, he said, "Morgan, you must be strong. You must protect Linness now!"

Morgan's dark eyes lowered to the ground with hesitation. It wasn't that he was afraid of the bishop; he wasn't, and God knows, he did want to protect his wife. But would no one ever let him forget that wretched night? He just wanted to forget it happened, the whole sordid incident with that stupid mad wench. The outrage of her appearance in his hall with that hideously deformed child—

He muttered to himself, "God's teeth, but I do loathe the day I parted those thighs!"

"Morgan . . ." Paxton said his name in a warning.

"Oh, aye, I will appear with you for her. But you

do the talking. I have no facility with words as you do."

Paxton patted his shoulder before telling the monk to wait for him in the guards' quarters, to not speak a word to anyone. He turned and raced inside, followed by his brother.

They stopped in the arched entrance to the hall and stared. He saw only her back. The long hair fell in a dark cascade over a pale blue gown, held back by a darker blue band. The gown made a pretty circle of color.

"Answer the question!"

"That's enough," Paxton interrupted as they stepped inside the hall.

A hot wave of relief washed over her as she turned to see Paxton step inside the hall. There was no mistaking the natural authority of a man who commanded whole armies of men. He wore it in his stride, his raised voice, the depth of his stare, as he looked over each priest in turn, as if dismissing them. His hand held a jeweled dagger as though he might use it; Linness had long ago noticed that he always had a weapon in hand or within reach, a remnant of too many wars fought in one life.

"Milords." The bishop's brow rose questioningly. "I am conducting an investigation of the tragic affair the lady played a part in, and I would ask you both to leave—"

"You may ask till doomsday and our feet would remain planted." Speaking for both of them, Paxton said, "We demand an explanation for this investigation. Now."

The bishop stared stonily for a moment, then at Morgan, who stood behind his brother, an air of uncertainty about him. He had to concede. For now. "As you see fit. This is a preliminary investigation only. I have not yet called for a formal ecclesiastic court to hear this case—"

Paxton stepped alongside Linness. "What case would that be?"

"The case to consider and assign guilt for the unspeakably hideous crime of murder."

"And, I believe," Paxton responded, "we all witnessed the hand that committed the tragic deed."

"Did we?" the bishop asked rhetorically. "And I am quite sure there was a diabolical force employed behind the hand that murdered."

Paxton's eyes blazed with emotion. "She was mad. It was a horrid misfortune for sure, but no more."

"I am not convinced. I am interested in the diabolical motives behind the wretched act—"

"That is enough!" Paxton said with the strict authority used to direct and dispatch a dozen bloodthirsty warriors. "Quite enough." He stepped over to Bishop Luce, and met the man's brass stare. "You forget whom you are addressing. This lady is no cottar's brat or lowly servant. She has the full protection of her husband's title, her parents before him, and the lawful protection of the king of France!"

"Aye," Morgan verified with a nod of his head.

"By Jesu!" Paxton's voice thundered, "I have already warned you. You will not accuse the lady or subject her to this imbecilic form of harassment again!"

Anger bristled through the bishop. Lord Paxton would openly threaten him and, therefore, the authority and strictures of the holy church, of God

Himself. He had sunk so low! All for a woman. She had pulled him down into the deep and filthy cesspool of her own lusts and sins, and he was blinded by his wicked appetite. Blinded. So help him God, he would get around this man. This woman would be made to fear the indictment of the holy Church.

Especially for practicing witchery!

He saw immediately he would have to address the issue in his report to the Vatican. The details of the lady's idolatry and witchery grew; he would collect them all until even the pope would want the matter resolved by ecclesiastic trial. He would get the authority, so help him God. . . .

Morgan reached a hand to Linness. He felt her tremble as she rose. "Milady." Then with apology and affection, "Linness," he said to her, his voice lowering to a whisper. "Withdraw. You need not answer any more of his questions. Ever."

A shock went through the bishop.

Linness, he had called her Linness.

Linness. He knew that name. The distant memory burst upon him, riveting his attention to the woman as she rose to leave.

In one graceful movement, Linness curtsied ever so slightly before she rushed from the room. Paxton stepped alongside the table, moving slowly across the row of silent priests, his gaze condemning. These men, arms of the bishop, had not been picked randomly. Each man met his stare with icy condemnation. He let his hand rest on the hilt of his jeweled dagger, the threat so explicit, it might have been voiced.

He stopped, realizing what he should do. He would ask the monk for his silence and then pretend he had not heard of Simon's tragic fate. He would send yet another letter, but this time in secret. And this letter would reach its destination.

The bishop was so lost in his startling train of thoughts, he failed to notice Paxton until he heard his low and threatening voice. "I will not warn you again that there are things and people both my brother and I would protect with our lives, that foremost among them is the lady. . . ."

As Paxton withdrew, the name continued to echo eerily through the bishop's mind. He waved away the priests who rushed to his side. He needed to understand. He needed to understand how an orphaned and penniless convent girl, a girl who did not even have a surname, a girl accused long ago of witchery and evil ideations and who had slipped from the church into the darkness of night, how this girl could reemerge many years later as the Lady Chamberlain of Gaillard.

Long ago he remembered being brought to the room where the girl slept. He had stepped out to the window from which she had escaped into the night. He remembered thinking it was God's judgment, that no child would survive long in that night.

How terribly wrong he had been.

She was a great pretender indeed. . . .

Only one explanation came to his mind. She, either alone or with the aid of treacherous beings, must have killed the real Lady Beaumaris. It must be so! Yet would not someone have discovered this secret? How could she possibly maintain all the pretenses?

His thoughts spun over this awesome dilemma. Satan's dark powers must be growing! 'Twas so awesome! So incredible and unbelievable. It occurred to him no one would likely believe him. No one but his own priests . . .

Perhaps he was mistaken; there might be another explanation—

He immediately squashed these doubts, the devil's tools. She was the same girl! Somehow she had managed the impossible, murdering the true lady and taking her place.

How was he to expose her?

He stared unseeing at the stained glass depiction of Mary with Child. Was not the dowager Lady Beaumaris still living? Aye, he had heard her name mentioned. Did she not correspond with her daughter at least? What did she make of the pretender in place of her daughter? How could she not know?

If the letters were penned by a scribe. Perhaps that serving woman! The lady would never guess . . .

Well, he would send for her at once!

The bishop felt his heart pound with the revelation of how he would make everyone see the true nature of this pretender, and reveal the murder of the real Lady Beaumaris, God rest her soul. He would insist the dowager Lady Beaumaris come for a visit, not giving an explanation other than that the journey should commence at once.

'Twould mean the death sentence of this Linness, one richly deserved; she would burn in the everlasting fires of hell. Morgan would be free. The boy Jean Luc would be known as the bastard he was. And Lord Paxton, too, would at last be free of her evil bewitchment. . . .

Feverish eyes, filled with the weight of his understanding, encountered Morgan's hulking form,

apparently still waiting for him. He was surprised
Lord Morgan had the necessary spine to confront
him alone after all that had happened. For the man
was a world apart from his arrogant, prideful
brother.

Or so he thought.

He questioned, "Milord?"

Morgan struggled for a long moment, feeling
wretched and embarrassed. He had to make the
man comprehend, though; no matter what, Linness
was innocent. The thought gave him courage. "I
want you to accept fully that my brother and I are
of a like mind. You are not to attack my wife in
this matter. I will not abide it. Please to God, she
alone is undeserving of the horrendous and horrific
things you seem to be accusing her of."

The bishop did not smile. The poor cuckolded
fool. Pathetic, he was. "Indeed?"

"She is innocent and as pure as an angel. She is
even touched, methinks, by God Himself. Her
sight, it is only good—"

"Milord, you are greatly deceived," he replied in
a low and threatening voice. "God alone ordains
and divines the future; He grants the gift of prophecy only to the saints and apostles. No other. Certainly not a"—his hand waved in scornful
dismissal—"a woman! Which leaves us with the
diabolical forces of deception to account for her so-
called *gifts*. I mean to root these evils out. To save
her soul or damn her forever. For the good of all
the faithful at Gaillard."

Until that moment Morgan had never grasped
the deep and inexplicable hatred the man harbored
for Linness, and it came as a shock now. He had
neither the patience nor the inclination to evaluate

supernatural claims—they made his head spin like a child's top—but that this man was threatening his wife was not to be tolerated. Ever. "I grant that I do not know about these things," he confessed, and yet his gaze narrowed with his own threat, "but hear me, Bishop. My wife is not to be subjected to accusations of witchery and whatnot. I will not abide it!"

Morgan started to turn away. The bishop stopped him. "Your brother has said he will protect the lady with his life. Why is that, do you think?"

Morgan turned around, his face darkening with emotion. "Because Fate has made him my brother! We are joined by blood, and by God, he would not be my brother if he did not swear to protect what is mine!"

"You are a fool, milord. It is because he is in love with your wife!"

The bishop fully expected the man to become enraged by this enlightenment, but this did not happen. He knew the extent of the lady's power of bewitchment when Morgan replied, "As is all of Gaillard! 'Tis as simple to comprehend as the changing seasons; to know the lady is to love her. All the world loves her." With a furious warning glance, he added "And my brother is not the only man who would die protecting the lady. Tread carefully into her life."

The bishop fully intended to. He would start by obtaining proof of the colossal scale of her deception—proof that the dowager Lady Beaumaris would provide—and this would open Lord Morgan's sadly deceived eyes. And that proof would be the condemning evidence.

* * *

The women's fury fueled their pace as Linness and Clair swept through the Gaillard gates and into the courtyard. Chickens *bawk*ed and scattered, and Michaels, from high up atop the battlements, saw trouble fast approaching. "Milady," he called down. "Is something amiss?"

"It is indeed. I need to speak to my husband. Where is he?"

Morgan's head suddenly appeared alongside Michaels.

"I'll be right up," Linness called, and the two men watched her violet skirts and Clair's beige ones billow behind them as they rushed up the stairs.

She emerged on top and stopped. For her gaze came to Paxton. He looked so darkly handsome in black: a black doublet, leggings, and boots, a thick silver belt. His hand rested on the hilt of his sword. He was turned sideways, telling the Gaillard merchants gathered around him that he had put four more men on night watch to catch the thieves who were robbing everyone. The thieves brought by the flood of people into the town for the Gaillard fair.

Her heart felt as if it suddenly stood still, as though it were a queer mechanism that stopped and started by the measure of his proximity. She understood now how it was impossible to stop loving him and nearly impossible in the dark dead of the night to stop herself from going to him. *When you are weak from the relentless pounding of your heart, the breathlessness no air can ease, when your body is soaked in nothing but longing and the sweetened scent of your desire . . .*

Aye, Paxton, every night . . .

Morgan came to her side, asking what trouble

she found, but she hardly heard him as Paxton had turned to look at her and she knew she must be going mad! For she could only be imagining that strange and compelling light in his eyes that said he was fully aware of her predicament.

She turned her confused gaze out over the battlements and drew in the breathtaking vista. Rooftops stretched in the distance, the vineyards and forest beyond, the sun slanting in a gold arch over the whole. The river carved through the forest-covered hills. People had come from miles and miles away, flooding into Gaillard for the festivities of the fair tomorrow. The streets were packed. Colorful tents, with bright banners, stretched for miles along the river. There would also be wild bear wrestling, merchants selling wares of all kinds, jugglers, acrobats, a singing choir, all manner of entertainments and amusements.

A larger, dark red tent had been erected on the outskirts of town. The traveling theater troupe was erecting a private box for the lord and his family. They had invited her up to examine the enclosed seats, lifted above the rest, and the uninhibited view of the stage this seclusion offered.

That was, if she could help the troupe.

When her silence stretched too long, Clair nudged her. She turned to Morgan, remembering the fury that brought her to him, and she demanded, "You must do something."

"About what?"

She brushed an errant curl from her face, pausing as Paxton dismissed the merchants and approached the place where she stood. "The traveling theater group. For tomorrow's performance. They accosted me as I was returning, some of them crying but most of them just plain angry." Her silver eyes narrowed. "They have just endured a visit from Bishop Luce, who has informed them that they cannot perform their play because he has not had the opportunity to review the material, and since it is not a Bible story, he is certain it will be scatological." With exasperation she said, "You must tell Bishop Luce he cannot dictate what play will be performed; they have rehearsed for weeks. Besides, they assure me there is nothing in the play offensive to the church or indeed any Christian mind."

Morgan rubbed his beard and cursed, "Blast the man. Hands into everything. This fair has been more trouble than it's worth. . . ." He looked to Paxton for help.

Paxton suggested, "Get the bishop the copy of the play. He can read it tonight if he's so concerned about protecting the good people from any scatological material—"

"That's just it," Linness said, "the actors produced it for him, but he told them he has neither the time nor the interest in reading it; he said they had to either produce a biblical story or keep their doors closed."

Paxton actually smiled at this. "Then we shall give him another chance." He turned to Michaels and ordered, "Michaels, get your hands on the copy of this play and present it to the bishop. Tell him that Morgan has decided if he doesn't have a meritorious and intelligent objection to truly offensive content after he reads it tonight, the play shall go on."

Morgan nodded in agreement, and Michaels raced off on his quest. Linness and Clair squeezed hands. They had looked forward to a modern play.

The Three Wise Men or Noah's Arc became old after one saw it the twelfth time.

No one at first noticed Jean Luc waiting patiently for his parents' attention. Enormous fear filled his chest and threatened tears. But he would not cry, no matter what.

His father said only cowards cry. He was not a coward.

He braced against the pain. The more he braced, the more he felt its sting. But he would not cry for it.

When Linness started to leave she noticed her son and stopped as she saw something was wrong. A bright, hot wave of pain washed over her mind, leaving a sick dread in its wake. She stepped quickly before him and knelt down. "What's wrong? Did your schooling not go well today?"

Seeing his mother's love and concern made the threatening tears come forward. He tried to stop them, but 'twas too hard. He wanted to fall in her arms. He struggled not to, and in the end he had to look away.

The two men and Clair came up behind them. Linness knew something was terribly wrong. She reached her hand around his arms. With his own concern, Morgan reached a hand to his shoulder.

Jean Luc winced, shrinking away.

Alarmed, Linness stepped behind him. His neck was red, and she knew, somehow she knew. She ripped off his belt and lifted his tunic.

Angry red scratches covered his back.

She drew in a shocked breath. "Mercy—"

They beat him! Those wretched monsters beat him!

And Jean Luc was in her arms. His small frame

leaned against her warmth. Her arms held him, carefully, without touching the angry red marks. He buried his face against her, feeling ashamed and not knowing why. He heard a vicious curse before his uncle demanded, "Who the devil did that to you?"

He heard his father say, "I'll kill him. I swear, I'll kill the bastard—"

The anger frightened him more; he clutched at his mother. "No, no, Jean Luc, not you. Not you, my love." She shot a warning look at Paxton and Morgan. "Who did this to you?"

"Father Aslam. He did not want to, but Bishop Luce said he must."

"Why did he do it, Jean Luc? Were you behaving badly?"

"I was," he said with his startling honesty. "I could not help it. I tried, but—"

"What did you do?"

"I made mistakes. I was thinking of the fair. Pierre ran off to see the bears." Tears filled his eyes as he said the worst part. "Father Aslam said I cannot go. That bad boys cannot go. I must stay and copy the lesson, over and over on my slate, until the fair has gone. . . ."

Linness looked up at Paxton and Morgan, both furious as Jean Luc gave in to his tears at last. "Jean Luc, darling," she said softly, "this was a terrible mistake. Father Aslam was very wrong to have beaten you."

A choked whisper asked, "He was?"

"Aye, your father and your uncle will straighten him out. They will explain that we do not beat our animals in that manner; that we most certainly will not ever abide the beating of you, who is most precious. Do you understand? He was wrong; he is to be brought up for it."

Clair guessed the real fear pumping in the young boy's heart. "Poor Father Aslam's all mixed up!" the older woman declared, hands on hips. "What can he be thinking saying ye are not going to the fair on the morrow, that you have to do lessons instead? Why, he must be daft!"

Jean Luc turned hopeful eyes up to his father. His father smiled and nodded. His mother hugged him again. He looked at her smile as she wiped his eyes. He drew a deep breath.

"Come," his mother said, "let us go to the kitchen and try to steal some of Vivian's honey cakes. . . ."

She cast a meaningful look at the men, both of whom nodded back. Morgan slapped Paxton's back and said, "Shall we toss for who gets the bones of this Father Aslam . . ."

"And his superior rat, Bishop Luce," Paxton added.

Torture often led to death, and fear of death often produced a heart seizure. Bishop Luce remained unconvinced of this common wisdom. As far as he was concerned, God ended the man's miserable life once he finished serving His purpose.

Tom Boswell's crimes were many and grievous; he was the devil's puppet, culminating in the impersonation of a priest, which, after suicide, was the gravest of all sins. He spent his life cheating people through the devil's games: The man had denied this to the end, but he knew. He knew it all, including that Tom Boswell had pledged an oath to Lord Paxton, who richly rewarded the reprobate for it. For he had found enough gold coins in Tom Boswell's pockets to last his lifetime.

Bishop Luce toyed with these coins in his vestment pockets as he stared down at the miserable leech, now covered hideously in blood. Apparently Boswell had brought Lord Paxton the news of Simon's death at the hands of robbers. This had apparently greatly alarmed Lord Paxton, filling his mind with suspicions and intrigues. He knew Lord Paxton had secretly sent yet another knight to deliver his letters to Cardinal Duprat and Francis. It was all part of *her* diabolical plot, he knew. Unfortunately Boswell had died before he could name the new messenger or the route he would take.

He stared down at the body with disgust. The night fell fast around them. His new liaison sent by the Vatican, Father Andrew, now spoke the burial rites over the dead man. He watched the new priest offer up the familiar Latin in a slow and halting voice.

The rush of the river drowned out his words.

Father Andrew had been raised to the church in one of the more severely ascetic monasteries in northern Germany. He spoke little. A feverish intensity surrounded him, that of a zealot awakening to his call, and thus he sensed the man would be a great ally in the upcoming battle for the very souls of the people of Gaillard. Tomorrow he would send him to spy on the woman who had wickedly stolen the title of Lady Chamberlain.

The letter urging Lady Beaumaris to Gaillard had been sent. She would not be able to refuse. The bishop expected her to arrive within the month. The pretender of Lady Belinda would be revealed at last; her demonic presence would be punished by death.

Father Andrew concluded the rites and genuflected, as did the other four priests. The body was turned in to the shallow grave. The last prayer was said with a toss of dirt and then the priests began covering the hole.

Father Thomas felt a tremor of shame and anger. This was not right. No matter that the wretch surely deserved his death; or that the death was not Bishop Luce's intent. No matter. Death, he knew, should not be delivered by the holy church. . . .

There was nothing he could do about it, though. . . .

They silently turned and followed Bishop Luce into the darkness. Father Andrew, like his silent brothers, hid his long, thin, trembling hands in the folds of his robe. The whole tragic scene of the poor ignorant man's death reminded him of another. . . .

The single row of darkly robed priests reached the road to Gaillard, less than a mile away from the township. Moonlight and shadows played across the road. The bright orange glow of campfires and torches rose in the distance. Hundreds of people camped along the river and road, waiting for the morrow's fair.

The bishop stopped, staring off at the swelling numbers of country fools, their tents and tired pack animals. In a low, impassioned voice, he whispered to his fellows, "How corrupt and odious be the common man's love of shallow entertainments! Look how they gather! Hundreds of them!" He shook his head, his narrowed eyes filled with pity. "They are so stupid, worshiping the frivolous and meaningless bursts of false thrills: a wrestling bear or a poorly writ play, even a fire-eating fool!"

Father Aslam nodded in agreement, staring off at the distant lights blinking gayly in the night. "Few churches ever see the same numbers as a town fair; the faithful are few...."

"Aye, but so, too, will the fires of everlasting hell swell with their numbers, damning them all for eternity," Bishop Luce continued. "That foolish Lord Morgan refused to honor my directives and stop the play; indeed he refused to stop any of the necromancy attractions. He especially refused to stop his wife from sinking to the damning pit of practicing her witchery in public—"

The sound of a rider coming at a fast clip from behind made the bishop swing around in the opposite direction to look. He and his priests watched the fast-approaching horse and rider. As the man came closer, the bishop made out the bright livery colors of the crown. He held up a hand.

The rider slowed and finally stopped before them, drawing up his horse. He examined the bishop's crimson vestments. "Milord?"

"Evening tides. You have ridden from...?"

"Paris. With orders from the king!"

"And who would the royal command be for?"

The horse shifted nervously. "Lord Paxton de Chamberlain, milord."

"Ah, I am seeing him now. I will take it to him directly."

The man hesitated but briefly. He had orders to drop it in Lord Paxton's hands, but then he knew the content of the letter and he supposed all the world would soon know its secrets. Besides, he hardly had the rank or right to refuse a bishop's favor. "Very well, milord."

He withdrew the sealed envelope from his saddlebag and handed it down.

"Very good," the bishop said. "Follow the road straight to the château. A groom will see to your horse and accommodations. May God be with you."

The rider bowed and kicked spurs to mount. Dust rose in his wake. The bishop slipped the envelope into the folds of his robe. He needed light. . . .

Chapter 9

"I see questions of health are worrying you."
Widow Moulin drew back in surprise.
The lady had uncanny insight, surely divine! " 'Tis
the source of all my woes!"

Linness nodded as she let her gaze go blank, pretending to be lost in a deep mediation on Widow
Moulin's problems. Her dark hair had been pulled
tightly back into a single braid, woven with a gold
ribbon that matched the Turkish costume she wore.

Linness, and four of her waiting women, had
worked for a month to make the costume, drawing
upon illustrations from a precious illuminated
manuscript of Turkish treasures. This had been
shown to her by a traveling merchant, and with
delight, she had bought the book for a fair price.
Manuscripts were becoming more and more common now. She had finally convinced Morgan to
start a collection for Gaillard.

Clair and she had studied the drawing endlessly.
Many of the townspeople asked to see the book as
well, and today it seemed just as many people came
to see the Turkish costume as to have their fortunes
told.

All earnings were to be given to the leper hospital in nearby Saint Bertrand de Comminges, though this was not generally known. Common folks did not like their monies going to lepers, who, most people felt, deserved their wretched fate. Having heard she worshiped the Virgin Mother, three sisters from that hospital had traveled all the way to Gaillard, seeking her patronage. After a brief audience, their sad stories of suffering had captured Linness's sympathy.

Sunlight filtered through the gold tent, casting the Turkish fortune-teller in that illuminating light. Inside, the sounds of the Gaillard fair seemed subdued. Like a trick of magic, the noise of the crowds, the music of the wandering band of minstrels, the wild applause rising from the bear-wrestling ring, the constant hawking of vendors, the slow pick of steady pack animals weaving through the crowds, were muted.

Linness spread her jeweled fingers over the silver cloth that covered the low table where they knelt. The woman's worries were for naught, and in fact, she was blessed with rare good health, but she knew better than to tell her so. Widow Moulin was one of the wealthiest women in town. Her family, free people for as long as anyone could remember, had built and run the two mills in Gaillard for over a hundred years. She had only one son, Peter, whose late wife had remained sadly barren. Peter ran the mill now. Widow Moulin lived in a handsome house alongside the busy place. She had two servants to do her work. She had little with which to fill the many empty hours of her day but all these imaginary worries. The town gossips claimed she had called her overworked son to her deathbed so many times, he had begun sleeping on a cot along-side her to save himself the trip.

Linness whispered, "The spirits are speaking to me."

Widow Moulin looked about as if to see these disembodied beings before she nervously adjusted her elaborate maroon gown. "By the saints, spirits?"

"Aye." Linness appeared confused. "The spirits are telling me your health, especially your . . . your . . ."

"Arthritis?"

"Aye." She nodded. "Your arthritis and your . . . your . . ."

"Digestive problems?"

"Aye. Your arthritis and digestive problems . . ."

Widow Moulin could hardly believe the lady knew her exact problems. She was a marvel! "Oh," she cried, rushing to explain, "they are so bad some days that—"

Linness held up her hand to cut her off, as if hearing other voices. "The spirits are saying these problems will be much improved if . . . if . . ."

Widow Moulin leaned forward, listened intently. "Aye, aye?"

"If you cease eating heart-beating creatures."

A skeptical look fell over the older woman's face. Heart-beating creatures? That would never do. She liked her meat as well as any, perhaps better than most.

"They are urging you to eat more bread, cheeses, and fruits. They suggest a glass of wine with your supper, too."

"Oh, I never indulge in spirits," the widow divulged. " 'Tis so costly, you see! Two ducats a barrel some days."

"The wine shall be less expensive than the meat, and besides," Linness added, "the benefits shall outweigh the costs." She closed her eyes again. "Why, I also hear them mentioning in particular the fruit of one tree that grows near your house—"

The woman gasped, "That would be an apple tree!"

"Aye." Linness nodded vaguely. "You are to fast for a day and night. On the dawn of morning where a waxing moon hangs in the sky, they say you should break the fast with two of these apples. This will cure your fatigue, and replenish your energies."

Opening her eyes now, Linness presented the older woman with a charmed smile.

Widow Moulin sat absorbing this amazing information. She could fast. After all, she fasted during the high holy days of Lent, did she not? 'Twould be grand if it replenished her energies and cured her fatigue too.

"Does the good widow wish that I look into her future?"

An expression of fear drew the plump woman up again. She shuddered slightly. Only a deathbed could be in her future, she knew. Yet her son would no doubt be glad to have the exact date. Then he could make arrangements to have extra workers at the mill, slowed as he'd be by the weight of his grief.

She nodded, bracing to hear the worst.

Linness appeared to go into another trance. She

swayed and rocked. A low humming sound came from her.

Clair bit her lip. She shifted restlessly as she watched.

"Why, I see a remarkable event happening to you."

"Ye do? My deathbed!?"

"Nay, not that—"

"*Mon Dieu*, a long illness!?"

"Nay," Linness shook her head. "There is . . . Mercy! I see the blessing of love coming to you in your sunset years."

Nothing could have shocked the woman more. "What? Love?" She laughed nervously, "At my age?!"

"This love is . . . how strange, 'tis already in your life, but you do not perceive it. You walk blindly past this good man almost every day, never realizing the design God has placed before you. Do you know who this could be?"

Widow Moulin sat on the edge of her seat, a look of intense concentration on her face as her thoughts raced over the familiar faces she saw each day. The idea struck her like a lightning bolt from the sky. "Why . . ." She drew back, quite shocked. "Not the . . . why, ye couldn't mean Hansberg, my son's old mill worker!"

"Is he kindhearted?"

"That he is! He always has a kind word for me in passing and he's good with the creatures, but he's just a poor man—"

Linness said only, "He thinks of you often."

Clair could hardly believe it when the old bat blushed like a maid in her first bloom. After the first few customers to come to the tent, Linness had confessed with vexation, "My sight has fled today. I shall have to draw upon intuition and common tricks."

These common tricks were a kind of magic themselves. Almost every person left the tent thrilled with her miraculous powers of prophecy. Many based decisions, which changed their lives, on the things Linness predicted. Like old Widow Moulin.

For Clair, 'twas more fun witnessing firsthand the foolish gullibility of her fellow citizens than the last ten fairs she had been to. She peeped outside. 'Twas almost over. Only one man left in line outside her tent. Everyone was preparing for the play.

Widow Moulin fluttered with excitement. "Does he really care for me?"

"Aye. I believe he would welcome an invitation to sit at your table. And I see there is someone else, too. A child is calling to you. How strange!" She closed her eyes and appeared deep in thought. "The spirits are telling me this child needs you."

"Needs . . . me?" She asked, amazed.

"Aye, you were picked for this child. To help on her long road through life. In return this child will be a comfort to you in your old age. 'Tis a little girl, I see. She has no mother. Who could that be?"

"Hansberg's granddaughter! Why, she has no mother, and I am always thinking the child needs someone to dress her proper and find shoes against the winter cold. They are so poor, you see, and I know the old man tries, but he is rarely picked for work anymore. He has back trouble." Widow Moulin never really gave much thought to the little girl always peeping from behind Hansberg's legs, her curls ruffled and in need of a comb. She might be a little angel if someone only dressed her up proper.

She had always wanted a little girl. . . .

The young, tall man outside the tent watched the old woman emerge with a huge smile and a glossy, bewitched look on her face. The old woman paused to tighten her loosened purse strings before drawing a deep breath and tilting her head to the late afternoon sunshine. She hurried into the thinning crowds of people.

Clair pulled aside the flaps of the tent and motioned for the man to step inside. His shrewd dark eyes searched the queer surroundings. Gold and silver and white, everything gleamed like a treasure. A dark velvet cloth covered the low table Gaillard's lady sat behind as she told the fortune seekers the secrets of their lives.

A heathen celebration, absolutely godless . . .

Not absolutely, he saw. A small gold crucifix hung on her neck, over the modest gold bodice of her remarkable costume. Gold, flared pantaloons, gold slippers, and a white and gold bodice—all of it indecent. It was against church law for a woman to wear pantaloons, even at a fair.

Just as he was studying her, Linness was studying him. Middle-aged. Long, dark hair. Shrewd brown eyes. An unlined face marked by a childhood bout with the pox. She sensed the intensity of his thoughts; he was not here for a frivolous amusement, but perhaps in search of an answer to a specific question. He wore plain clothes, neither rich nor poor: a beige tunic and hose, no jewels or weapons, and brown boots. He was not from Gaillard. His appearance gave no clue to the secrets of his life.

She cast a meaningful look to Clair as her hand touched her forehead in a signal that she would fail with him, unless she managed to get him to speak. "Please have a seat, Monsieur . . . ?"

The man lowered his tall frame with surprising grace and offered nothing more than his name. "Garret." Not his real name either, she sensed. He stared back at her, and in his eyes she saw condemnation.

Her silver eyes narrowed suddenly as she felt a bright wave of hostility. "You do not want to be here," she first said. A tingling alarm shot up her spine, and she paused and looked away. The world went white before her eyes and then burst with images drawn from this man's life. "Garret is not your real name. Your real name begins with a C. Charles. No, 'tis been changed and now begins with a . . . I cannot see this as the change does not fit you."

She paused as more images piled into her mind. "I see the world you grew up in," she said slowly in a voice much changed, weighted with a sadness that was rapidly overwhelming her. " 'Tis a monastery far north of here. Snow fell endlessly, aye, 'twas a world of snow and darkness and many, many miles removed from a township. The warmth of the sun rarely shone there. Your nature was gregarious and loving as a boy. You were your mother's favorite child. I see how she fought your father over your placement at this monastery, but your father ripped you from her arms. Mother in heaven, how she missed you."

These words mixed movingly with her startling compassion, especially on a subject that was so close to her heart. This produced a curious effect on the man. He sat with his back ramrod-straight with absolutely no emotion showing on his face. Save for his eyes. There was a flash, a confused wave, a stir of something buried deep in his heart.

She continued after a moment. "There was little happiness in this place. You were so young." As young as Jean Luc, she saw. "The monks were usually in silence. This was very hard for you. You wanted to speak so badly, to ask a hundred questions, to discover the answers to them. I see . . . mercy, I see the beatings that took place here. They beat the joy out of you; frightened and scared and, dear Lord, ever so alone, you withdrew into yourself."

Clair realized Linness's vision was real. She stiffened and shot her gaze to the man when Linness paused. Anger and confusion shimmered in the man's startled gaze. Whatever reason brought him to this tent, he had not been expecting these revelations.

"A secret love touched you in this cold world once when you were ten and four . . . or five—I cannot tell for sure. For the first time in ever so long, you were touched and loved by an, an—" Her silver eyes opened to look at him, but she did not voice his secret out loud. She didn't have to. He knew what she saw, for he had lived it.

Linness closed her eyes again. "Aye, you were happy for the first time since leaving your home. You knew joy with this person. And yet something happened, something . . ." She gasped with the next hideous image that came to her mind. "Heavens, you were punished for this by watching this person you loved—" Her lovely eyes filled with unspeakable anguish as she held her head to stop the echo of a long-ago scream.

Alarm shimmered in her eyes as she understood the full magnitude of what had happened to him. "They were wrong!" she told him. "They were wrong to do that! Can you not see thus? How cruel they were; the worst part of their cruelty was in making you feel as if his death was your fault! Your fault for finding a measure of human warmth and love—"

"Enough! Enough!" He stood up abruptly, his gazed filled with agony. "I will not hear any more—"

It was too late. Understanding dawned . "You have been sent by another. Mercy, 'tis Bishop Luce who sent you to spy on me! You are a priest. Yet you are filled with doubt. The German monk has thrown your faith into confusion. Like many others. I see you sharing these doubts with Father Thomas in secret. This monk has given a voice to your doubts about the church. You are still torn. You were sent to Bishop Luce to temper this struggle with your vows—"

The man refused to hear any more. Unwanted emotions trembled through him and he turned his back, rushing from the tent as if it were on fire.

Linness fell against the pillows as Clair whistled. "Well, now we are in trouble."

"Aye." She nodded. "That we are. He will not go back now, and Bishop Luce will blame me for his disappearance."

Hands on hips, Clair announced, "As if that weren't bad enough, the treacherous sod did not even pay ye fee."

Jean Luc stepped inside the tent, glancing back as the flap closed. "Mother, you made that man angry! He knocked a juggler out of the way, the man lost three balls and fell—" He noticed his mother's costume and then Clair's and he forgot the angry man in the next instance. "Mother! You look so beautiful!"

And laughing, the boy fell into her arms.

The magical story mesmerized Linness. 'Twas the story of a great nobleman who had three daughters. When he became aged and infirm, he thought to divide his wealth into three parts, one for each of his beloved daughters. Yet the youngest and most beautiful daughter's profession of love was not as honeyed as her sisters, though it sounded much truer. The old nobleman loved his youngest daughter the most, and so her words cut deep. In a rage he disinherited her, leaving none of his wealth to her when he died.

Now, as the first act concluded, the two remaining sisters turned on the younger one after their father's death and treated her cruelly.

She sat on the edge of her high seat. The stage was lit, though the curtain had fallen over the first act. The theater was dark. Hundreds of people paid the billet price and sat on the neat rows of benches below; it was so crowded. A wooden balcony had been erected for the Lords and Lady Chamberlain, high above the rest of the crowd. John sat beside her, only mildly interested in this story. Jean Luc sat on Clair's lap in a soft cushioned chair. The soothing darkness and the day's unceasing activity had sent them both into a soft slumber. Morgan was nowhere to be found.

Paxton stepped quietly up the stairs and pulled back the flap to step onto the balcony. His gaze spotted Jean Luc sound asleep on Clair's lap and he smiled. A smile that changed as he saw Linness beside his uncle.

In the semidarkness he leisurely examined her strange costume. Like a harem girl, she was. His gaze traveled up from the gold slippers with the tips curving ridiculously upward, to the billowing gold pantaloons which fit tightly over her backside. He released his breath in a silent growl. A white chemise appeared beneath a gold bodice, the skein of long hair dropped over the back.

He had to see the front.

He had to see all of her. After reading King Francis's order, he had to see her. He had a need to lay eyes upon her. To find solace in her proximity. And to force himself to face the full awful reality crashing all around them.

How paltry were the rich clothes of wealth, fame, and success! How pale even the greater bounty of health, wits, and strength! Pale when laid alongside the treasure seated before him. Linness.

He had long ago discarded the idea that his love was inflamed by the unalterable fact that she was his brother's wife. The burning had been there always. He wanted her now as then, with each breath he took, and for the long rest of his life, he would want her.

King, country, and family be damned, he would claim her again. And again until through death they would part. She fought against the same tide sweeping over their life, and those times he viewed her struggle from afar, he might confess it even amused him. She could not resist their passion, he knew, and only because he had fought the same battle, fought it armed with superior will, and still he lost to the mystical pull between them.

He would show her again tonight.

John turned to see him in the darkness, and though not a word was said, an understanding passed between them. John returned his attention to the actors as Paxton stepped behind the place where Linness sat. She turned with a start. "Paxton!"

She pretended mild surprise, no more, and this was an effort. He looked so tall and darkly handsome in his fine gray velvet doublet, black belt, and riding pants. His riding cape was draped over one arm; she wondered where he had been all day. She struggled to see his eyes in the darkness but couldn't.

"Milady." He bowed slightly, his expression wholly unreadable. "Uncle." He nodded.

Was there a coldness to his tone? Or was she imagining it? And yet her intuition produced the idea he was amused by her. Amused? By her struggle?

Aye, she realized with a shiver of sudden nervousness.

John moved to the next chair, so Paxton could sit between them. "An old story," he said casually as Paxton assumed the seat. "A much-abused maid. Two cruel sisters. No doubt a familiar ending of mistaken identity, a prince, and, of course, the marriage ceremony . . ."

Linness took this in with surprise. She had not been anticipating this ending, but in the next instant she forgot the play entirely. Her senses heightened as Paxton lowered his impressive height into the chair alongside her. She felt a subtle shift in her fear. The effect was powerful. A familiar excitement uncurled in her stomach.

She closed her eyes for just a moment, her senses flooding with anticipation. In an attempt to maintain an air of indifference, she drew in a deep, uneven breath, which brought her the familiar masculine scent of him, soothing and stirring like a tonic. She felt his penetrating warmth, the brush of his arm against her.

She could not be near him. . . .

"Are you enjoying the play, milady?"

She turned to him with confusion, her eyes questioning. What emotion sat behind his mild tone? "Aye. I never guessed this ending John predicts. . . ."

"Ah, the prowess of our local fortune-teller has at last begun to fade," Paxton said.

His tone was light and teasing, and instead of being a comfort to her, it threw her into confusion.

"Really?" John questioned in a surprised whisper, his amusement plain. "I thought all ladies were raised with this tired old tale. Did your mother never sing it to you?"

"I don't remember such a story."

"Lucky for you, milady," he said, bemused by his boredom and her innocent interest. He knew it was time to leave. For Paxton. For Linness. Their days were numbered, their time together but an hourglass turned upside down. The sadness of it weighed heavily on his mind. True love was as rare and precious as a just and good king, and he had lived long enough to know the treasure of what Paxton and Linness shared. He would not let his presense steal a moment from their mercilessly short time together.

He stood up. "I was afraid I'd have to endure this story yet again. I find that, like Madame Clair and Jean Luc, I am fatigued. I will carry Jean Luc to his bed, if you do not mind, milady?"

She paused for a second, only to realize there was no way to keep John here. The idea of being alone with Paxton terrified her. She looked to the sleeping Clair. Almost alone. "Aye, if he's not too heavy."

John stepped to her sleeping boy and, leaning over, he lifted him to his arms. The movement awoke Clair, who, after a sleepy assessment of her situation, and either ignoring or not seeing Linness's sly shakes of head, decided to take leave as well.

Linness was alone with Paxton.

The curtain was drawn up again.

Linness turned back to the play and pretended to watch.

Paxton watched her for a moment before his gaze dropped to the front of her bodice. Modest. A row of neat gold buttons between the tempting swell of her breasts. It reminded him of her gray dress and their encounter in the cellar storeroom.

She could feel his gaze upon her. Color slowly suffused her cheeks and she shifted in sudden discomfort. A tingling sensation shot up her spine and she lowered her eyes with a small audible sigh.

"One should learn to control one's breathing, milady."

She turned to the intensity of his gaze. "How do I do that, Paxton?"

Her beguiling honesty surprised him and he gave her a pitying smile. "Think of the play set before you."

She looked to the stage, seemingly so far away suddenly. She tried to concentrate on the heroine's speech, but this was impossible. Her nerves were

drawn as taut as a harp's strings and she closed her
eyes again, remembering his mouth on her breasts,
the gentle draw and play, the shimmering pleasure.

"You should not have come here."

"Indeed," he whispered as he leaned slightly toward her, his mouth dangerously close to her ear.
She could feel the teasing warmth of his breath.
"Are your sentiments for me so painful as to render
my presence unbearable?"

Silver eyes, dark in the light, turned to him.
"Aye."

To her surprise, he only chuckled. "And just
what is it about me that you struggle to endure,
milady?"

He would tease her now. She stood in sudden
agitation and took one step toward the ledge. "I
just cannot be near you."

She stared off at the stage, unable to hear a word
with her heart hammering so. He stood up as well
and came directly behind her. She closed her eyes.
If she but leaned back an inch, she'd be against him.
He was tormenting her, and yet . . .

Her back aligned with his front. The tiny space
between them was charged and heated, like the air
before a storm. He peered at her over her shoulder.
She felt his gaze, like a lover's caress, resting on the
swell of her breasts. She opened her eyes, still pretending to watch the theatrical proceedings below,
but all she could think was how close he was, the
quiet lift and fall of each breath he drew into his
lungs, the warmth emanating from his hard frame.

"Love," he whispered as his finger toyed at the
nape of her neck, light as a feather. "I vowed to
wait until you came to me. I intend to keep it, but

you are a fool if you think I will make it easy for you."

The threat was explicit. "Paxton, you would torment me. . . ."

He did not deny it. A shiver raced along her spine in a warning or anticipation, or both. They might be alone on a star-filled night for all she knew now. She tried to resist, but—

The prince stepped onstage and the audience applauded with anticipation.

Paxton, too, took an imperceptible step forward. With her next breath her backside pushed against his frame. The hard outline of his chest and hips and thighs brushed against her. She suddenly gripped the banister as his heat washed over her in a sensation of tingling pleasure.

"Surrender, love . . ."

The whispered words brought her firmly against his magnetic warmth. She felt his desire. A rush of fire shot through her, and she gasped his name. "Paxton . . ." His warm lips skimmed her neck, his strong hands crossed over her front to enfold her against him. Her hands came over his forearms to keep him there or push him away, she didn't know. "Paxton . . ."

She went still as his lips gently teased between neck and shoulders. Shivers rushed from that spot down to her breasts, where a hot congestion grew, an ache only he could assuage. His hands came to span her ribs just below the soft swells. She drew a sharp breath that shifted the warmth into his palms.

"Again," he said.

He rewarded her by cupping the soft flesh in his hands, sculpting the form until he felt her pulse race. "Do you feel that, Linness?" he whispered against her ear, his mouth as warm as the flesh he caressed. "The heat in my loins?"

She did and it was madness. She shifted slightly, nestling her buttocks against this heat. She heard his sharp groan. His warmth disappeared for the briefest moment and then suddenly his riding cloak surrounded both of them.

One hand held her seductively against his heat, while the other deftly unbuttoned her bodice. The cloth parted. His hands slid over her breast, massaging it until she was a mass of trembling pleasure. Warm serums were heating her blood.

His hands came behind her and there came a few anxious minutes of separation before he brought her back against him. The hard swell and heat of his naked sex pressed against a sliver of opening found in her unlaced pantaloons. She nearly swooned. He pressed her hips tight against him. A hot lick of fire shot between her thighs. She drew a sharp breath, shifting to ease the tension, only to hear his response, and feel another hot lick. She was suddenly gasping.

She felt suddenly hot and weak. "Paxton . . ."

"Lean over, love. . . ."

She complied in slow motion. As if in a dream. His strong arm lifted her slightly at the waist. His leg nudged hers shamelessly apart. She closed her eyes as she felt his sex sliding against her, his huge body tense with pleasure. Each breath shot fire from the spot. His seeking heat crested at her moist opening, stroking her. A bright wave of ecstasy grew, straining for the blossoming each smooth movement promised. His hand slipped between her thighs. Deft strokes, heated pants, until—

The audience burst into thunderous applause.

She opened her eyes, startled, and abruptly straightened; his warmth vanished, replaced by shivers. The curtain dropped. His cloak came over her shoulders as her trembling hands hurriedly began buttoning the bodice of her costume.

"An arresting performance," she heard him say. Then he added in a whisper full of meaning, "The ending felt abrupt, though. Would you not agree, milady?"

She nodded. Abrupt. Too soon, precious seconds too soon. Yet a lifetime would not be long enough. And they did not even have a single night to call their own.

Tension still enslaved her breathing and claimed her deepest part, which throbbed in gentle insistence for more. She could only wonder how she would possibly manage the short trip back to the château. For she stumbled with her first step. . . .

"Paxton." She said his name in a plea as he helped her to her feet. His gaze was black and shining with unleashed passion.

"Tonight, love. Surrender tonight."

She knew then she could not deny him. Resisting him was like fighting against a strong and powerful current sweeping over her life and promising only to carry her to bliss. To heaven on earth. Resisting him became a hell, the death he warned her it was, a constant struggle wherein she lost ground inch by slow inch, and yet fought on and on until she could not remember against what she was fighting.

"Aye," she said, seeing the darkness swirl all around her as she reached this decision. "Tonight . . ."

"And when you come you will wear only the

gold necklace with my ring beneath your robe. . . ."

She paused as she absorbed this and then she assented with a quick nod . . .

She fingered the ring about her neck as she waited in her well-lit chambers until at last she heard Morgan stagger into the entrance hall below. His voice, raised in a drunken song, stumbled through the absurd lyrics. She heard him climb each step, a tumble and a clang of spurs, a shuffle. He righted himself and continued on his way up.

She made no sound as she went to the door, pausing there to listen. She closed her eyes, her senses flooded with heady anticipation. *Paxton*; his name echoed in her mind.

Morgan's boots paused outside her door.

She stiffened in sudden fear. What was he doing outside her door? Mercy, was he checking on her? Did he know? Did someone tell him? Yet who would dare?

The lightest of knocks sounded as if to check if she was sleeping. She stepped back in panic. Should she pretend to be asleep?

Nay, 'twould not do.

In a breathless rush she said, "Come in."

Morgan stepped into his wife's room.

With one hand fixed on the ring, she stood there staring at him. She tried to look calm, but her face was drained and her eyes were wide with trepidation. Her other hand clasped the robe tight about her neck.

Paxton heard Morgan enter her room from behind the stone wall separating them. Within the next minute he was pressed against the ledge; seized by his rage, he gripped his sword tightly,

his mind filled with thoughts of blood and violence . . .

Yet he waited outside her window, listening. . . .

Linness saw immediately that Morgan was quite
intoxicated. Once upon a time he could drink the
night long and remain seemingly unaffected. No
more. It seemed he became drunker on ever smaller
amounts. Clair said this was the progression of
many drunkards; she swore she had seen it happen
thus a dozen times. . . .

Presently Morgan's eyes were red and his skin
blotched. Blood vessels appeared prominently on
his nose. It was a struggle for him to focus. With
an unsteady hand, he wiped his mouth. He seemed
quite unsure of himself. Nothing could have frightened her more.

Why had he come? Tonight? He rarely entered
her chambers alone. He appeared only with Michaels or when Clair was with her.

Surely he did not come for . . .

Dear Lord, please not for that . . .

"I saw the light through the door," he explained
obliquely as he rocked back on his heels, then
righted himself. "You are well?"

She nodded. "Yes. And you?"

"Aye." He smiled with a pleasant memory of the
night. A smile that vanished as he focused again
on Linness. "I did not see you all day at the fair,"
he said, his words slurred. "Paxton and I were . . .
Never mind that. I understand Jean Luc had a good
time with my uncle?"

"Aye, the two of them had a fine time."

He nodded and seemed to drift off. He rocked
back again, teetering, and his hand went to the wall

to steady himself. "I, ah, want you to know something. . . ."

She saw suddenly he was afraid. "Aye?"

"This . . . bishop. You were so wary of his coming, and I see why now. He is . . . like a darkening storm cloud. . . ." Deep crevices furrowed his brow, disappearing as he said, "Aye, but Paxton will save us. . . . Milady, I, I know I am not the best husband, but I want you to know . . . I will never let him hurt you."

Emotion sprang to her eyes and shimmered there as this sentiment touched her. No matter what, he cared deeply for her; in his own sad and distorted way, he did care for her.

She nodded, her eyes filled with sympathy. "Thank you for that. It means much to me. . . ."

He smiled gently at her words and then hesitated for a moment. With an unsteady hand he reached into the folds of his cape, struggling to find something in his pockets. "Here, I bought this for you."

He presented to her an object wrapped in a frosty pink velvet and tied with a white ribbon. Linness reached for it. She untied the ribbon and pulled the velvet cloth from the object.

It was a small hand-carved wooden statuette. Of Mary. She studied the fine, smooth lines, like nothing she had ever seen before. She gently traced the graceful folds of Mary's cloak, the delicate and beautiful lines of her face. Somehow, the artisan had captured the love Mary offered the world.

She studied the small wooden reminder of Mary's love and she held perfectly still as her thoughts raced. Was she wrong to love Paxton and not her husband?

Yet how could she not love Paxton? 'Twas not

possible! Like altering the course of the planets around the sun, she did not have that awesome power. Each breath in her body declared this love. . . .

Her gaze lifted to Morgan, then dropped back to the statuette, to her fingers still sliding over its smooth lines. Mary's love stared back. Mary would not ask the impossible of her humblest servant.

And Mary's light would protect her from the darkness Bishop Luce was surely bringing into her world. . . .

Her hands trembled slightly; she clasped the statuette against her heart as she lifted confused eyes to Morgan. He smiled tenderly at her. "I thought maybe I should get you a new dress or ribbons, but when I saw it at a little stand on the edge of the fair, I thought this might please you more—"

"Aye," she said in a heated whisper, and she reached up and gently kissed his cheek. "Aye— thank you. 'Tis so beautiful. More treasured by my heart than a thousand dresses."

The answer pleased Morgan. He nodded as he turned and left the room. The door shut.

Outside on the ledge Paxton's hand relaxed at last from the hilt of his steel. He drew a deep breath and confronted his madness. He would have killed Morgan. Killed his flesh-and-blood brother for touching his own wife . . .

He looked up at the star-filled night but saw no beauty in the distant pinpoints of light against the black velvet. A warm breeze whispered in his ear. No solace in the future. For he knew the tables were reversed, or would be soon.

Forgive me, Linness. . . .

He swore softly, viciously. He could not save her;

he had always been too late to save her. He had no choice. Even if he did not have to save Linness from the bishop's vengeful malice, and get him gone from Gaillard, he could not save Linness from his king's edict . . .

In truth he wouldn't save her, even if he could.

The idea that he would soon be losing Linness filled him with urgency. He wanted her to damn his brother's bumbling gestures and come to him tonight. He wanted her to answer his urgency with her own.

They had so little time left. . . .

He slipped back inside his chambers. A fire had been lit in the hearth, despite the mild night air. He set down his sword, unclasped his belt, and pulled off his tunic. He sat on the bed to remove his boots, and when he had taken both off, he caught the faint sweet scent of perfume: lilacs and oils.

His dark blue eyes searched the shadows of the room.

She stood across from him, leaning against the wall.

'Twas a dream spun in a waking state, she looked so beautiful. She wore only the long gold robe. The thick braid of her hair fell over one shoulder. The delicate Celtic features were marked by a lingering flush of anticipation.

In a husky whisper he said, "Drop the robe."

The robe slid off her bare shoulders to fall in a neat circle of cloth over her bare feet. She drew a deep, unsteady breath and closed her eyes beneath the intensity of his gaze.

"Come here."

Tension increased with each step she took slowly toward him. She stopped just in front of him.

"Dressed in firelight, you are my desire in flesh," he whispered as his gaze moved over the thrilling beauty of her nudity. His warm palms reached behind her thighs and slowly traveled up, pleased with the shiver this caused. His firm lips caressed her flat stomach and she held her breath, her hands braced on the wide span of his shoulders, his flesh warm and vibrant beneath her fingertips.

Hot shivers raced and echoed in a rush of heat between her legs. "Paxton . . ." His hands slid over her sculpted back, sliding forward over her bare breasts to cup their softness. She rewarded him with small heated pants. His hands, behind her now, slipped over the dramatic curves of her slender figure, caressing the rise of her buttocks, massaging, kneading her flesh until her legs went weak and her weight needed the support of his shoulders.

His mouth found the hard tip of a breast.

"Paxton, Paxton." She said his name in a plea.

His hand threaded between her legs, testing the richness of her moistened sheath. Her breath came in small gasps and she flushed with a wave of hot suspense. A husky growl sounded briefly before he gathered her to him and turned, lowering her backside to the bed. A shudder of heat passed through him at the feel of her slim, naked body beneath.

"I want to hear your love cries," he whispered as his mouth lightly brushed her lips. "I want to feel your lips beneath mine, the swell of my sex in yours. Linness, I want you. . . ."

And he kissed her. The kiss was a prelude, the beginning, an opening to the heaven that followed. The heaven was like nothing she ever imagined, for it was her surrender. . . .

* * *

Clair peered over Linness's shoulder to see the statuette of the Virgin Mary while Linness hurriedly dressed for the feast that marked the last night of the fair. "Tsk, tsk." Clair shook her head. "Isn't that just like the man? Saved himself a pretty coin buying ye that, no doubt. Pretending ye'd like it better than a new dress! Like we'd be fooled by that bit of theatrics!" She laughed at the thought. "Either the old bones are gettin' addled or the man's more of a miser than I guessed."

Linness frowned angrily at her. "Clair, sometimes you're really quite wicked."

"You mean honest."

"No, you're wrong. This means more to me than a thousand dresses. Truly."

Linness shook her head as she pulled the violet and rose brocaded gown over her head. Clair began buttoning up the back. A rose-colored chemise appeared around the edges of the darker violet bodice. Billowing sleeves gathered at her wrists. Her long hair was decorated with violet ribbons and piled into a soft crown atop her head. The color was not a good one on her; she looked best in darker colors and she was just about to ask Clair for an opinion when she noticed her stare. Her hand went nervously to the gold necklace that draped over her throat.

She met Clair's stare and saw the compassion and worry in her eyes. Clair looked away and went to the trunk to fetch the matching caul. "Nay," Linness said softly, "the ribbons are enough."

"As ye wish."

Much meaning clung to those simple words. She knew Clair was afraid for her, and yet there was nothing she could do. There had never been anything she could do.

She closed her eyes as images drawn from the previous night's passion danced dizzily in her mind: swirls of exploding colors of ecstasy. She drew a sharp breath. Her vision went suddenly white and against the white background she saw *her*. The lady in black.

Clair looked in bafflement at Linness. "Milady?!"

"Who are you?" Linness asked in a heated whisper.

There was no answer. Just a haunting doom emanating from the sad creature, and then she was gone.

She was stepping into her life now.

Nay, Linness realized, she had already arrived.

"What is wrong?"

The vision was gone. Linness looked up at her friend and, with a hand to her forehead, said, "I keep seeing this strange woman. . . ."

Clair swallowed nervously as she looked around the chamber, quiet, perfectly normal, not a thing out of place. "Where do you see this . . horror?"

"Just in my dreams. Sometimes I think I see her every night in my dreams. A vision of a lady dressed in black. Somehow I know she is to be a part of my life, that she is sad for me." She shook her head. "But I do not know what it means."

"It means ye are not gettin' enough sleep, is what it means. Are ye quite well?"

"Aye. I am fine. Do not worry so." Dismissing the strange dream as she did every morning she woke remembering it, she headed for the door. "It will all work out in the end," she said. Yet her voice echoed with uncertainty as she whispered, "Somehow . . ."

Clair nodded skeptically, watching as Linness went through the doors in a swirl of violet and rose. If only it could work out, but it couldn't, she knew. If the bishop's malice weren't enough to threaten the lady, someday, somewhere, the lovers would be caught and made to pay the price for their love. Only Morgan's death could save them, and for all of Morgan's drunkenness, the man was as hale and hearty as many a man half his age. Besides, even she could see that Morgan did not deserve an early death.

Try as she did, her imagination failed to generate a happy ending to this love story. There was something else as well. She used to see Linness as a charmed and enchanting heroine of a fantastic tale. No more . . .

The older woman's mind traveled over the dozen courtly tales of romance she had heard over the years. Lady Beaumaris had been particularly sentimental, and she had paid many minstrels to sing these romances at Montegrel. Now she realized how few of these love stories had happy endings. For fate never rewarded so rare a passion as that between Lord Paxton and Linness. Quite the contrary, like an overlooked law of nature, the magnitude of love between Paxton and Linness was like a too bright fire, burning hot and bright only to be quelled, extinguished, gone, leaving only ashes. And the memory of its once bright and shining light for the minstrels to sing to sentimental old women . . .

No matter how Clair looked at the future, it ended in darkness and tragedy. She felt a chilly draft sweeping in through the opened shutters and she shivered. In the middle of a warm summer night, she shivered for the want of a happy ending.

Everyone stood as the bishop said grace.

Linness hardly heard a word. She stood between Morgan and John and across from Paxton. His unwavering gaze rested on her, while she kept stealing glances at him. He was so bold now! He might have echoed the words of last night, "Again, Linness, I will have you again." They sang so loud in the heat of his stare. Her color rose. . . .

Then suddenly she felt something ominous between them. She struggled to make sense of the emotion emanating from Paxton. What was it?

It came to her in a confused rush. Pity. He felt sorry for her. She closed her eyes in a desperate attempt to shut out the world, long enough to understand this.

The image of the lady in black came to her mind. . . .

Morgan shifted his feet uncomfortably as the bishop went on and on in an annoying exercise in verbosity. This prayer not only taxed his thirst and his hunger, both ferocious, but it began to tax his temper. Father Gayly always said a simple prayer at mealtime; that was enough—not this monotonous spew of Latin no one even knew anymore.

John hid a yawn in the sleeve of his green doublet.

Morgan's heated glance demanded he finish. The bishop paid him absolutely no mind, the Latin song rising, lowering, continuing; it might be a whole high mass. The man continued it just to irritate him, he was sure. Just as he had insisted on retaining

Father Aslam after he had beat his son . . .

Morgan cast an angry look at the very priest standing at the lesser table below and he gritted his teeth against the incessant, grating noise spewing from the bishop. He thought again of the previous day's findings.

The man was insufferable! He and his less than merry band of priests had all but taken over his hall. John and Paxton said 'twas to convince him to spend the monies for their own residence, but curse it all, he did not have any monies for new buildings.

The bishop and his legion of priests, numbering ten now, gathered in the hall every hour of every day not used in church or prayers, and like a black blight, their robed presence stole all humor and merriment, and dropped a somber, dour mood over the whole. He had not enjoyed a feast since the man arrived. He could not play a game of chess with his son, let alone meet with the town's burgeoning guilds and merchants or his own vassals, without hearing the man's scathing and dire warnings of fire and everlasting hell or whatnot, or a directive about this or that. His endless directives. Monday it was on the indecent dress of the women of Gaillard. The man objected to the curved tips of their shoes, of all things. Claimed it was a display of vanity.

And there it was, the frightening contradiction. He could think of a woman's shoes as sinful, when he raised his hand to stop the beat of another's heart and think it as just. The man's malice was cloaked in his empty ideology.

He was a danger to his wife. . . .

Linness had been so right! She had known he

would ruin everything. He remembered her saying he would steal her happiness. Happiness was not all the man tried to steal. He was trying to steal her very life.

"I know you are scared, Morgan," Paxton had said yesterday when they had discovered Boswell's body. "I am as well. But we cannot just kill him. If something were to happen to you or me, if an ecclesiastic trial found us guilty of murdering a bishop, Gaillard would go to the church until Jean Luc comes of age. By then our boy's precious life would not be worth a brass ducat. We must find another way...."

The bishop ended at last. A disgruntled Morgan sat across from the man at the head of the high table. He hardly noticed the special dishes the servants set to the feast: the goose soup, delicately stuffed eggs, roasted beef, pheasant and venison, the plate of ripe summer fruit ingeniously made to look like the biblical arc, the delicious scent of warm trencher bread. He poured another goblet of wine and drank it whole.

"So, Lord Paxton," the bishop began in a mild tone, "I understand you recently received a letter from our good king."

Linness tensed slightly as she felt Paxton's sudden consternation and watched his dark gaze turn to the bishop.

"Aye," Paxton said suspiciously. "I received a letter just yesterday."

"And pray tell," the bishop continued, "what news comes from the royal court?"

Paxton's suspicion was now a certainty. The man had read his missive. He had not carefully inspected the seal. Michaels had brought the letter, informing him the messenger had been paid. He had not inquired further, assuming Morgan had done so.

He cast a glance to his brother, who shrugged, conveying he knew nothing about it. John looked just as bewildered. He looked back at the bishop. "I must rid myself of the apparently archaic understanding that a man's letters are private."

"I'm sure I don't know what you are referring to," the bishop said innocently. "But tell us, was it a private directive, then? Perhaps an order regarding your future? Now, what could that be?" He wondered out loud, "One of Francis's favorite lords, his most successful general. Is it a new campaign perhaps? Will you be leaving Gaillard soon?"

Linness watched with heightened interest as Paxton picked up the carving knife and, though the task belonged to the servants, he began slicing the venison. John and Morgan exchanged apprehensive glances. By this point everyone sat poised, listening and waiting to learn what order had arrived from the king.

Paxton's glare did not stop the audacious man. Nor did his intentionally deft strokes of the knife on the meat. There was no stopping him now.

He had always been too late. The thought allowed him to rein in his temper. He finished the carving, lifted two slices onto his plate, and sat back in his chair, appearing indifferent, almost bored now. Save for his eyes. Eyes that focused now on Linness.

The bishop thought to nudge Lord Paxton from this rare inarticulate stupor. "The Italian campaign is over with. France, the greatest Christian country on earth, is at peace. Surely all Francis wants now, like every king who ever lived to end a war, is to join the two countries: the Kingdom of Naples and the Duchy of Milan with the greater kingdom of France. The marriages will be starting soon, no doubt—" He stopped in a pretense of sudden realization. "Why, of course! You are land-rich and conveniently unmarried. No heirs hath been issued by your loins, none that you have claimed in any case, and you would no doubt be one of his first candidates, am I right? Did he present you with a marriage contract?"

John felt the shock pass through Linness; he reached under the table and took her hand. She clasped it firmly, as she felt the blood drain from her body.

"My God, brother, is that true?" Morgan asked, with a burst of sudden laughter. "Has a marriage been arranged?"

With lowered eyes, Linness stared at the artful presentation of sliced pears, apples, and berries that Vivian had prepared for her. Her vision blurred and the woman in black appeared, like a mirage over the plate of fruit.

She was Paxton's future wife, his betrothed, by orders of the king. No one could refuse an order from the king. Not even Paxton. He would be married. . . .

The lady in black would be his wife . . .

She had had the vision since the very first night she gave herself to Paxton. Because the lady in black was to have everything she ever wanted in life, the only thing she had ever wanted in life. The lady in black would be his wife. . . .

"You have indeed guessed," Paxton said, his voice amazingly calm. "My king has arranged a marriage to the Lady Beatrice Lucia Calabria, duchess of Nuovo in Naples."

"Ah," the bishop said, watching Linness, "an arranged marriage. The best kind, decreed by God himself, rather than the trite sentiments brought by lustful emotions. May God bless your marriage."

Morgan was thrilled. "My God! And what do you know of her?"

There was a brief hesitation. For he knew everything and nothing about the lady. She had lived her life cloistered in a nunnery; she was said to be extremely pious and devout. She had chosen to remain in the nunnery until he decided to send for her. Francis had regretted he could not send a portrait, but no one had ever seen the lady.

"The lady is orphaned," Paxton replied in a dispassionate tone. "And she has only an aging steward, her late father's brother, to oversee her properties. The man is said to be on his deathbed. There are many problems with her estates. Landrich, aye, but it has not been productive for nearly half a century due to the unending wars between the church, the Kingdom of Naples, the Duchy of Milan, and, of course, France. The people are suffering, a hairsbreadth from starvation. Francis imagines I will remedy the half century of neglect inside of a year and soon be replenishing not just the peasants' stomachs but his own treasury with its wealth."

Morgan laughed at this. "And he is probably right! And what of the good lady herself? Be she young or old?"

"Young. She is but nine and ten."

"Not in her first blush, then," Morgan commented. "But young enough to get you sons."

No one but John heard Linness's stifled gasp, as a napkin covered her mouth. He asked the only question that mattered. "Has the church committed the lady to the marriage?"

"Aye," Paxton said at last. This, of course, meant that once he put his signature to paper, they were legally married. "Francis has demanded my signature on the marriage contracts. I am to send them within the week."

"And when does he want you to leave?" John asked.

A pause. Then he announced, "Immediately."

"Immediately?" Morgan questioned, alarmed. Paxton could not leave immediately. He could not leave until they got rid of the bishop.

"I was considering sending Rialto," Paxton said, referring to his steward at Beaumont in Alsace. "Despite how much I need him to oversee the building at Beaumont."

John understood this at once, and in the next moment a perfect solution presented itself to him. "Paxton," he began, "let me go. I could leave at once. I would be there within two fortnights. I could assess the damage and problems and begin the construction, if it needs such, while arranging for the purchases of plows, chattel, and seeds. And I would be more than happy to present myself to the lady as your representative."

Paxton met his uncle's anxious gaze. He had not dared to hope for his uncle's generosity; it was the perfect solution. It would be a hardship to send Rialto when there was still so much work at Beaumont, and he could not leave Linness as long as the bishop's malice still threatened her. Still, "Uncle, you are not as young as you once were——"

"Nor am I too old for the task. Paxton, I would welcome a journey abroad. God knows I have been too long in one place. I need both hands to count the number of friends I might see on my way, which I would welcome. I have been across the Italian borders only once—some of my fondest memories are of the numerous pleasures found in that country. And more than anything, we are so close in mind; you know me as the one man you could trust with the awesome responsibility of this important task. Let me go, Paxton."

The bishop watched his hope crumbling about him. "And why is it you cannot leave Gaillard now, milord?"

"Ah, well," Paxton said, leveling a heated gaze in his direction. "You see, I will sign this marriage contract, and so Francis will naturally feel more inclined to answer my most recent request with his favor. I would like to stay at Gaillard to see the result."

The bishop stared stonily at the lord. He had not anticipated this turn of events. He should have known, for Satan does not rest.

"So it is settled," John said with a note of triumph on his face. "I shall begin preparations to depart immediately."

Morgan was well pleased and held his goblet out for more wine.

Linness could not absorb the shock of losing him, let alone bear the idea he could sit so calmly discussing the details of her execution. Color had drained from her face; her eyes were filled with emotion. "Congratulations, milord," she managed somehow. Her skills at falsehoods and pretensions were so terribly acute now, she could say those words as she felt the very life flowing from her limbs. "I fear I must withdraw suddenly—"

The bishop stood in a pretense of concern. "Milady, you look so sickly suddenly."

She ignored the glee in his tone. Her hand went to her forehead as if bracing herself against an aching pain and she said, "My head has suddenly started pounding. . . . If you will excuse me . . ."

"By all means, milady," Morgan said in confusion and worry as all the men stood for her withdrawal. The men watched her rush from the room in a swirl of violet and rose silk, her perfume lingering in the air.

Paxton drew the faint scent deeply into his lungs, as if to hold the small part of her close for a precious second more. She would be pulled from his grasp. Soon. He always knew it would happen; he just had not known when. Now that the time approached, he felt a numbing sense of doom. Some called it fate.

The fate of star-crossed lovers.

Forgive me, Linness. . . .

To the great relief of all others remaining, the bishop and his priests left the table soon afterward. Paxton waited until Morgan's eyes were red and his speech slurred, staying to discuss the details with his uncle for his departure. Finally he managed to exit. He saw Michaels in the stairway. The young man's face searched his questioningly, stricken by the news.

Paxton grabbed his forearm and squeezed, his request understood. Michaels nodded and moved to the bottom of the stairs as Paxton went up and opened the door to Linness's room.

She was leaning against the wall, waiting for

him, her eyes closed. Pain and anguish marked her face and echoed in a whisper. "Tell me it is not so! Tell me you will not do this to me!"

He stepped toward her. Silent.

She opened her eyes; with desperation she said, "You could refuse!"

"Not if I ever expect Francis or Duprat to rid Gaillard of Bishop Luce."

"I do not care about him! He is nothing when laid alongside that woman—"

He snatched her hand, drawing her up as if needing more of her attention. "You are a fool, my love, if you do think that man is nothing. Remember the monk who brought me the news of Simon's death?"

She nodded.

"He disappeared shortly afterwards. Morgan and I were suspicious. Yesterday we sent the hounds out after his scent. And we found him, love, buried in a shallow grave by the river."

Silver eyes searched his face with confusion. "What?"

"Aye. The man was murdered. No doubt the bishop wished to discover what he had told me and who I sent in Simon's place. Linness," he said with feeling, "the bishop had him murdered."

The shock of this registered on her lovely features, changing her expression to one of confusion. Murder and the bishop, she did not care. She could hardly think long enough to care. . . .

"There is no limit to the man's malice," he continued. "And this malice is directed at you. I will not leave you until he is gone. And I need all of my king's favor to make this happen. Accept it, Linness—"

"Nay! I cannot, I will not. There must be another way—"

He pulled her up again, his face cruel with its insistence. "But there isn't."

A hot fury uncoiled and trembled through her as she abruptly realized the only thing worse. "You want to marry her!"

Paxton could not deny it.

For a long moment she stood frozen in a panic, waiting for the denial. When he did no such thing, the humiliation of it and fury demanded a vent. Hot, tremulous, vengeful, she raised her hand to strike his face.

He caught her hand, and then the other, pulling her hard against his frame. With a pained cry, she gasped for breath, struggled but briefly before she went still and lifted her pain-filled eyes to his face. Only to see his own struggle there: his own anger and pain and sympathy.

"Listen to me, Linness," he said, demanding she listen to the unalterable facts of his life. "Listen. Even if I went back to that first night and found you had waited for me, even if you had never married my brother, I could not have offered you the sacrament of marriage. You would have always been my mistress. No one with my landed rank is free to choose a wife. You know thus!"

She stared up at him as she tried desperately to deny this. "That's not true! If you renounced—"

The look in his eyes stopped her short.

"Aye," he said, "if I renounced. Renounced my land, my king, my country. Renounced my life. Forced you to renounce our son, his inheritance, my brother, the church. Nay," he said with feeling, "nay, not even for you, my love. Not even for you.

All that would be left of me would be a worthless skin of a man, empty and hollow inside, a man who had nothing left to give you."

The impassioned words melted her fury, replacing it with raw and tragic sadness. They had nothing but their love; they never had anything but their love. . . .

Tears filled her silver eyes and his tone softened with his sympathy as he finished his say. "Linness, I have spent the whole of my life either preparing for war or waging it. I am so weary of it. I long to ease my hand from the sword, to sleep through a night without waking at every creak and slight sound; I want to walk through the rest of my days and never see bloodshed again." He gently kissed her forehead, closing his eyes to drink in the sweet scent of her. "I want to join that lady's land with Beaumont, Linness. I want to spend my life raising the people from poverty. I want to see their fortunes rise with mine and my king's. Linness," he said, "I want this peace so badly. . . ."

He had freed her hands and she reached up on tiptoes to bring her arms around his neck, clinging to him tightly, passionately. She struggled desperately to accept this, the fact that they would never have anything more than forbidden love: a love made of stolen kisses and whispered words, of denied longing and desire, a love that never shone beneath the bright light of the sun, but she couldn't, she couldn't . . .

As he held her closely against his strength, she saw *her*. The lady in black. She understood her pity at last. For that lady had everything Linness had ever wanted, the only thing she ever wanted. To be Paxton's wife . . .

"Kiss me, Paxton." She whispered the forbidden words. "Kiss me as if it's the last time you ever shall. . . ."

Chapter 10

❦❦❧

"And why should I?" Cardinal Duprat asked from the sidelines as Francis and Lord d'Etampes parried back and forth across the lawns of the rose garden. The clang of metal sang in the stilled afternoon air. Normally the entire court gathered to watch a display of their king's famous swordsmanship, but after last night's gala, those few lords and ladies of the court who were awake by noon chose to remain indoors with shades drawn against the bright sun and cool, damp cloths pressed to their foreheads.

Francis advanced, swung, and struck, but Lord d'Etampes parried neatly and countered. Francis knew this game with Duprat, his voracious, infuriating, yet absolutely irreplaceable cardinal. Nay, not a cardinal, not really. Rather, Duprat was a shrewd, brilliant administrator dressed in a cardinal's vestments; his faith in the holy doctrine was as honest and convenient as a condemned man's. No matter. He knew exactly what Duprat wanted, what he was willing to give him, and how to play the game out in hopes of winning from Duprat the minor but costly concessions.

Yet today he did not have the energy for this. So

he said as he parried, "Because I am your king!"

Duprat, an enormous man both in height and weight, only laughed with a shake of his graying hair. "Indeed, Your Majesty." With a hint of amusement, "So is this a command?"

Lord d'Etampes was gaining the upper hand.

Francis stopped suddenly and turned to Duprat, lowering his sword to inquire, "And what if it was?"

"Ah well! As your humblest servant, I would comply, of course. That is, after warning you about the consequences, the potentially dire consequences. The bishop has earned the high favor of a certain fanatical segment of the Vatican, which is, not coincidentally, the same faction that brings me, and therefore you, constant trouble. I suspect it would be more than a thorn in their side. I would remind Your Majesty—"

"Aye, aye, that precious papal concordat." 'Twere treacherous waters, these, Francis knew. The pope, Leo the Tenth, had granted him the right to control church appointments, a precious agreement that came at the conclusion of the most harrowing and fierce battle of the king's young life. He knew now that he'd rather raise his sword against a hundred warring Goliaths than to meet a single Vatican lawyer in debate.

"And besides," Duprat continued, pressing his king's uncertainty, "why would you want to rob the court of the high amusement brought by those priceless letters our faithful servant keeps sending?"

Duprat referred to the letters from the zealous Bishop Luce. Letters that seemed to imply all of Christendom was threatened by a single obscure lady no one had ever met or heard of before. Lord General Paxton Chamberlain's sister-in-law of all creatures. The poor lady was a Jezebel, deceitful, scheming, and perhaps, the last letter suggested, evil incarnate. She was a practitioner of witchcraft and a killer of babies, able to bewitch men with nary more than a glance or a look. The madman even went so far as to claim the lady was a pretender to her modest title, that he would be providing proof of this soon. As if the great towering ranks of French nobility would be set to trembling by a pretender to the Lord General Paxton Chamberlain's brother's wife . . .

There was apparently some truth to the assertion of the powers of bewitchment, as Lord General Paxton's letter had followed, signed by his lesser-known brother and his good uncle. It seemed clear that the lady had won what all the other ladies of court had found unobtainable: the prize of Lord Paxton's affection.

He grinned every time he thought about it. A love-struck Paxton—how he would love to see that! How he would love to meet this lady.

The bishop's letters had become high entertainment. The whole ridiculous affair might be dismissed with the court's laughter, after he had pressed Lord Morgan to present his beautiful wife at court so they all might meet the infamous lady, if only the bishop had not also sent these letters off to the Vatican. Those hallowed halls took an entirely somber view of such absurd accusations.

Still breathing heavily, and tired of this dance, Francis got to the point. "Confound it, Duprat. Paxton signed the marriage contract. We owe him. We both owe him the favor."

Laughter erupted from a group of ladies nearby, and Francis looked over at the gathering and spotted his mistress, the beautiful duchess d'Etampes. She was showing off his latest present, a tiny six-pound dog shrouded in long white hair. The miniature dog had been brought from faraway Malta, and it had cost a good deal more than his weight in gold. Today the duchess wore a pale orange silk that matched perfectly the tiny creature's ribbons, but more alarming—at least to his treasurer—the duchess had told him she was having her jeweler create a gold and diamond necklace to match the little dog's new collar. . . .

He turned back to Duprat and with a capricious change of thought added, "Besides, Paxton claims the bishop's treachery was responsible for Simon's death!" He pointed to the hilt of his sword. "And you know what that means!"

Indeed, Duprat knew exactly what that meant. Simon's father was the head architect of the magnificent château at Chambord, Francis's latest architectural project. The architect had to stop work for his grief.

Duprat sighed, thinking on this. The huge estate was just one of many projects Francis had started to execute. Apparently his king wanted to be remembered as the greatest patron of the arts; he had begun discussing plans for a new *collège de France*, a place that would attract scholars—"real scholars," Francis had said, "not those despotic fanatics of church doctrine!"

He had already begun attracting the continent's greatest artists, including the old eccentric and revered Leonardo da Vinci. For Francis wanted to be remembered as the king who saved the world from the Dark Ages and brought the sun upon the age of learning and glory for France. . . .

Duprat drew in a deep breath; he understood his king's tone. Francis always rallied to calls for justice; the man was filled with romantic, archaic notions of chivalry.

"The Dark Ages are over," Francis declared again. "If Paxton wants to get rid of the fatuous zealot, then get you rid of the bastard!"

Duprat contemplated this, weighing it against the costs. Vatican relations were strained, and since the concordat with the Vatican at Bologna, they were more strained than ever. He even imagined it was possible that the bishop's dismissal could rally the extremist wing of the Vatican to press for reneging the concordat. " 'Tis not so simply solved, Your Majesty—"

Too late . . . Francis had already made his decision. "It is if I say it is." And that was that. Or so Francis always thought. He turned back to his mistress's husband and his friend, d'Etampes, and raised his sword again.

"Very well, Your Majesty." Duprat sighed, and clasping his hands behind his back, pretended acquiescence as the furious battle of swords resumed. Afterall, he had not reached his lofty position without learning how to manage things. Things like his king. He knew well how to mediate between conflicting issues and desires, his king's direct command and the starker reality in the messy political chambers of the Vatican.

Like all bureaucrats, he would simply stall. . . .

Bernard looked up at the setting sun, then at the lady riding in front of him. She wore a pleasing

blue riding habit with slit sleeves that revealed a
lace underdress of snow white silk. Tiny drops of
mud spotted the expensive cloth. Her dark and
graying hair was lifted into an attractive crown
atop her head. She sat straight and majestically on
her prized mare.

She was a wonder, the Lady Eleanor Marie Beaumaris.

Every bone in his body ached from their long
days of traveling, from his skull down to his ankles
bumping against the horse's side. He was convinced he would never walk straight again. His
face was burned and his hands were raw from han-
dling the leather reins. He never did like horses.
He liked riding them even less. He could sleep ten
days and still be tired.

Yet there sat Lady Beaumaris bouncing sprightly
in her saddle, hardly a hair out of place. She was
almost forty, and she was burdened by the weight
of her great worries. All the bishop's letter had said
was that God had called her to Gaillard, that it
would be the most important journey of her life
and she was to leave at once. The bishop had not
said her daughter was dying, but they all knew otherwise. What else could such a letter mean?

Though, oddly, no one else had written. Not her
son-in-law, nor Belinda's good servant, Clair. They
could only deduce the situation was so dire, so
tragic, these loved ones were too distressed to pen
a letter, leaving the chore to the church servant.

So, after spending half the night in prayer, quite
certain she would arrive at Gaillard to learn her
daughter had died before she had the chance to see
her again, the indomitable Lady Beaumaris had left
the next day. She took no coach nor pack animal,

nothing to slow them down—her trunks would arrive later. The lady was escorted by only two young men from the ranks of Montegrel's fourteen knights, Gregorio and Paul. Bernard was serving in the capacity of steward since the death of his distant cousin, Lord Beaumaris, and she had asked for his companionship on this journey.

Lady Eleanor Beaumaris allowed no sign of her inner turmoil to show as she pressed her mount tirelessly forward. Sweat glistened on the creature; the horse was tired, but she could not rest until she reached Gaillard. There was a bitter irony in the situation, she knew, for once upon a time she would not have grieved very much to discover her daughter had died. In fact, as incomprehensible as it would seem to most mothers, she might have felt a twinge of relief that her daughter had at last found peace in death. For she had none in life.

This was not so now. Now she was losing something very precious to her soul, and she felt the full weight of a mother's grief threatening her. The miracle of Belinda's transformation still seemed so strange and novel to her. Belinda no longer suffered from "black spells," had no more violent fits and tantrums, or periods of a despondency that used to leave her bedridden for months. No more blind and cruel disregard of others. She had been cured. . . .

For the birth of Jean Luc had brought Belinda an inspiring devotion to Mary and the church, which had saved her. Belinda wrote over and over how very sorry she was for all the trouble she had caused her loving parents. Now she found happiness through love, and she was often overwhelmed by feelings of gratitude to God for the blessings in her life. Just before her father's death, she had written, "Gratitude, I have come to recognize, is one of the most undervalued emotions. Knowing gratitude is finding a heavenly joy...." Her intelligent letters were full of love and goodwill now; it was as if they were written by a different person.

Tears appeared in Eleanor's eyes as she thought of these things and confronted the idea that it might be too late to see her daughter again. She was fond of saying she had not fallen in love with her daughter until after she had lost her. Her husband's death had washed her in grief and she had just begun toying with the idea of journeying to Gaillard to see her precious daughter....

Now it would be too late....

From the corner of his vision, Bernard caught sight of the tears in his lady's eyes. He pulled his horse from a muddy puddle brought by recent rains just as bells rang from the distance ahead. He sat suddenly straight in the saddle. "Do you think a church is up ahead, milady?"

"Let us see!"

She set her boots into her mount's sides and spurred the creature forward. They rounded a bend and she stopped the horse and stared.

A breathtaking view spread before them. The sun set behind a low mountain range. A river carved through a deep and green valley. Vast, tree-lined meadows were washed emerald green by a summer rain. There were no buildings nor signs of civilization, except for the white stucco walls of a small monastery.

"We can stop there, milady, and water the horses," Bernard suggested, trying to keep the pleading from his voice. The two knights who accompanied them waited expectantly as well.

She was not looking at the three men staring at her, or even the distant monastery. She was staring off at the river.

"Gregorio? That river?"

"Aye, milady." Gregorio grinned. " 'Tis running to Gaillard. 'Tis but a day's ride from here. We should spend the night and ride through on the morrow. We should reach the place sometime in the afternoon."

Jean Luc and Pierre crouched behind a gangling vine heavy with fruit, peeping up to view the lecherous black knight and his two men riding alongside. He carefully kept his fingers wrapped around the arrow strung to his bow. "Be you ready, red knight?"

"Aye," Pierre replied. He was the red knight, Jean Luc was the blue. Irrepressible excitement filled the two boys as the black knight approached ever closer. The black knight would be shot straight to hell with one arrow. "Look! A lady's with them! Kidnapped, I bet!"

"Aye. " Jean Luc nodded. "Ransomed, too, I wager. We'll—"

"Rescue her," Pierre cut in, looking to Jean Luc for his approval.

Jean Luc nodded. His blue eyes narrowed. "Here they are! Aim true! Aim true! Ready! Fire!"

Lady Beaumaris's gaze fixed intently on the township just ahead when two wooden arrows flew past her head, dropping to the ground on the other side of the road. Gregorio and Paul drew up their horses; Bernard and the lady reined their mounts just behind. "What the devil—?"

Two small heads appeared in the grapevines. The boys could not believe the riders had actually stopped. Even the old tinker had not bothered—he had only shaken his fist at them.

"We are doomed," Pierre whispered, amazed and scared now. His gaze shot to Jean Luc, he wanted to run but did not want to be a coward.

Jean Luc leaped to his feet and demanded, "Halt in the name of law!"

Lady Beaumaris sat regally on the saddle as her mount danced a bit. "Well, now that you have us, what shall you do?"

He looked back at Pierre, who crouched even lower, terrified. "You must say your names and state why you have come," he said boldly. "We are stopping all knights of the Black Prince. We shall rescue all ladies in need."

"We are not that," the lady said with a smile. "We have come from Montegrel to see my daughter, the Lady Chamberlain. So, if it is quite all right with you, good knights, we shall continue on." And she kicked her mount's sides. Her knights chuckled as they moved forward.

His *grand-mère*! The one who sent him all those presents, most recently the saddle, one better than his father's and almost as fine as his uncle's.

He leaped forward, racing alongside the horse, excitement on his young face as he shouted up, "Milady! Milady! I am Jean Luc! You are my *grand-mère*!"

"What?" Lady Beaumaris pulled tight on the reins, stopping her horse. She stared down at the boy, who smiled up at her. In the next instant she had dismounted and was now kneeling in front of him, her gloved hands on his arms.

Tears shone in her eyes, her smile shone with love. "Jean Luc, you are Jean Luc?" The boy nodded. "You are just as she said, tall and healthy and so beautiful!"

His blue eyes widened upon hearing this. "Beautiful? *Grand-mère*, I am not that! I am a boy!"

She laughed at this, hardly able to believe this was her grandson. "Handsome, then. Oh, Jean Luc, I have longed to see you ever so long!" She hugged him tightly and for a long moment she just held the precious boy against her heart. Jean Luc pretended he did not mind. She drew back and asked softly, "Your mother, how is she?"

"Hale, *Grand-mère*, hale." He was happy to tell her this.

She was confused; her dark eyes searched his face. "She is fine?"

"Aye! My father says she is too hale, that she never catches my head colds. My father always catches them."

A sweet wave of heady relief washed over her as more tears filled her eyes. Belinda was fine; thank God for that. Surely Jean Luc would know if she was ill or injured? No one could keep that from a child.

He told her, "No one told me you were coming to see me!"

"No one?" The boy shook his head. She began to sense a mystery here. Why had Bishop Luce called her here if Belinda was fine? Why was it a secret? Perhaps Jean Luc was too young to know what was wrong. "Perhaps your mother wanted to surprise you?"

"She would have told me. She tells me everything about you. She reads me every letter you send." Quite suddenly his eyes turned sad, like a capricious whisper of wind. "*Grand-mère*, I am so sorry about my *grand-père*. I never got to see him. It made my mother sad, you know. . . ."

The boy was so sweet! She nodded with a smile, her heart so full of love. " 'Twas a sad thing. Even though he never got to see you, he loved you very much."

Jean Luc declared, "And I loved him, too! We had a special mass sung for him," he added, thinking this would please her as it had pleased his mother.

"Well, come," she said, standing up and taking his hand in hers, hardly able to take her eyes off him. "You can escort me to the château, can you not?" The three men dismounted and Paul rushed to take the lady's mare. Hand in hand with her grandson, a smiling Lady Beaumaris asked, "Will your mother be there?"

He shrugged. "I do not know. She swims in the afternoon, when the sun is high, you know—"

Lady Beaumaris stopped, shocked. This was, perhaps, the most jolting of all the strange things that had happened to her daughter since arriving at Gaillard. For Belinda had been deathly afraid of water. She bathed infrequently and only upon the most outrageous threats imaginable. Then she only let the great wooden tub be filled two inches, no more. She would measure it with her hair comb. "My daughter swims?"

"I do, too! I love to swim in the river. My mother says I am as good a swimmer as she is! And she swims better than my father. But not as good as my uncle. He has rescued her more than once. I think she was teasing him, just pretending, because she never needed to be rescued in the river until he came, you know. No one is to know they swim together every day," he whispered confidentially. " 'Tis our secret, so do not tell anyone. Look, *Grandmère*, there's the château gate. Can you see it?"

Bishop Luce waited from atop the battlements, watching for the Lady Pretender's return. The sun set behind the township and the mountains beyond. The breeze held a whisper of fall. Soon it would be harvesttime; the end of one cycle and the beginning of a new one. The end of the devil's reign and the beginning of God's.

She was late today; she usually returned earlier. Just after or just before Lord Paxton. She always had either her serving woman, her son, or Michaels with her. To avoid suspicion. The serving woman and Michaels would always part on the river trail, leaving her alone for her illicit tryst with Lord Paxton, before rejoining her on the way back. The nights were easier managed. Lord Paxton simply slipped into her room, somehow always leaving just before dawn. Lately they were so consumed with their wicked lust, perhaps because Lord Paxton would have to leave after the harvest, that they no longer waited for Lord Morgan to retire anymore.

Father Thomas waited at the gates in the event she was with the serving woman, to stall her. Nothing and no one would spoil this. For Lady Beaumaris had arrived. Morgan and the lady and her knights were gathered in the hall, waiting for Linness's return.

Ah, 'twas the serving woman, he saw.

Father Thomas stepped out to meet her. He would tell her Jeanroy, an acquaintance, had asked to see her immediately upon her return, that it was important. Clair would not find this person, however. He had been sent to town on an errand.

He watched as the serving woman absorbed this message, and hurriedly rushed off to the guards' quarters. The lady stood still and unmoving, staring back at Father Thomas. She turned to stare at the château, then back at Father Thomas. He could not hear what she was asking him, but that she was suspicious, he had no doubt.

Her diabolical intuition again.

He was lying, Linness knew. She could always tell when falsehoods were uttered. Why would he lie about Jeanroy wanting to see Clair? Obviously to separate Clair from her, but why?

She looked back at the château. A chill raced up her spine, and not from the lingering aftermath of Paxton's love play. Something was wrong . . .

Father Thomas stared at her, hatred in his eyes. 'Twas not the priest's hatred she felt. He was anxious, as if he were secretly worried for her. Lately she had begun to sense a change in Father Thomas. His friend's departure had awakened his sensitivities and doubt, and this uncertainty was directed at his superior. She longed to speak with him about it, but she didn't dare, afraid it might make him rally back to Bishop Luce.

Yet she felt hatred shooting at her, like invisible hot stones slung from above, and she looked up to where Bishop Luce stood, watching her from the battlements high above. Another shiver passed through her. The bishop turned away, disappearing. She looked back at Father Thomas, but he, too, had left.

Something was wrong.

A vague image of four riders sprang into her mind. A woman in a blue riding habit. Anxiousness. Worry. Who were they?

She didn't know. The feeling of foreboding remained, and with a shake of her wet hair, she headed for the stairway, a basket of bluebells in her arm.

'Twas cool and dark inside. The fires had not been lit. Voices came from the hall, Jean Luc's and Morgan's among them. Michaels was waiting for her and she smiled, brushing lingering bits of brush from her plain green dress. "I know that look," Linness teased. "That is the look you get when Vivian has made something sweet and special."

Michaels laughed and shook his head. "Something much better than a treat, milady. There is a big surprise waiting for you in the hall!"

She froze; another warning chill shot up her spine. "What is it?"

"Do not look so scared." He grinned, excited. " 'Tis a wonderful surprise!" He took her arm as they turned down the corridor, leading to the hall. "You will be thrilled, I promise!"

Michaels led her into the hall. She stopped in the doorway, taking in the gathering of people: Morgan, Jean Luc, a lady, a number of men she did not recognize. Bishop Luce stood there, too, along with a number of his priests. Everyone stopped and turned to look at her. Smiling, Michaels grabbed her hand and pulled her forward.

With a look of bewildered amusement, Linness approached the crowd. Jean Luc held the lady's hand and she was smiling at her, unaware. Completely unaware. Michaels stopped in front of this woman. Silence. Everyone stood staring, waiting for an exclamation.

The two women stared at each other, confused.

Jean Luc laughed and said, "*Grand-mère* has come!"

Morgan laughed and announced happily, "Milady, 'tis your dear mother. Your mother has come to Gaillard at last!"

"Mother . . ."

The word was uttered in a whisper. A whisper like a horrified gasp. Linness stopped on the word "mother," the idea that this at last was the Lady Beaumaris, that she would now be sentenced and condemned, that nothing but heaven could save her now. Nothing—

The basket of flowers slipped from her numb fingers and onto the floor, bluebells spilling over the marble and wood squares. Linness followed in a faint.

It was a beautiful faint, dramatic and absolutely convincing, a slow sinking to the floor, like collapsing into the protective folds of her green dress, a trail of long, wet hair falling to her side. Anger and incredulousness blazed in the bishop's gaze as he watched the amazing theatrics. He had been expecting hysterics, a scream, a cry for mercy, anything but this. His gaze shot to Lady Beaumaris, who appeared confused and shocked, hands over her heart, staring as Jean Luc fell on top of his mother with alarm. "Mercy! Mother!"

Then the bishop realized the faint was so convincing only because it was real. She had fainted!

Morgan was lifting her up with a whispered, "*Mon Dieu . . .*"

Bishop Luce's gaze shot back to the Lady Beaumaris. She continued to stare with bewildered confusion. A hand went to her mouth. She was trembling.

He would not let this opportunity pass. Faint or not, unconscious or not, he would hear the lady declare the creature an impostor. He stepped forward. "Milady." He stamped his long staff. "Now you have seen why I sent for you!"

Morgan was carrying Linness from the hall and crying out, "Milady just never thought she'd see her mother again. She was so glad. Someone find Clair." Servants were rushing away to fetch water, some pepper, and Clair.

Michaels rushed after his lord with concern and worry. "*Mon Dieu*, we should have prepared her! She is so delicate!"

Lady Beaumaris turned to the bishop. She looked at him hard, her eyes searching, questioning. No words came from her mouth. She didn't know what to say; what she could possibly say! There had to be an explanation for this, there had to be. Someone would explain how this had happened, or at least what had happened.

The bishop's gaze turned fierce, and he demanded, "Say it! Say it out loud for all to hear in the name of God Almighty! You know why I sent for you!"

She drew back as if slapped. She felt his hatred washing over her, an unrelenting force, like the sting of scalding water. She suddenly understood what he wanted of her. The woman's condemnation.

In the next moment she grasped that her daughter was dead and this woman had, dear Lord, all these years, pretended to be Belinda. She knew in that instant that she was the authoress of each letter that had filled her heart with joy and given her love again. More than that, given her late husband love and joy, the idea that they had a grandson . . .

She cast her gaze to where Morgan had disappeared with the lady through the entrance to the hall. With a lift of her skirts, she rushed after them. The woman might indeed deserve her condemnation, but it would not be given until after she was made to understand how this had happened, exactly what had happened. . . .

"I will not let her get away with this, so help me God—"

The bishop's threat echoed eerily after her. She wondered if God Himself had given her a choice: the bishop and his condemnation, or the woman and her son. She did not have to think long on that one. . . .

After a baffling and fruitless search for Jeanroy, Clair stepped into the entrance hall as Morgan raced up the stairs with Linness in his arms. Servants crowded the stairway. "Oh, Lord! What has happened—?"

She stopped as Lady Eleanor Marie Beaumaris appeared in the corridor. The reality drained the blood from her limbs. The tremble started in the pit of her stomach and spread out. She started to back away, shaking her head.

"You! Clair!" Eleanor understood Clair's shock quite well now as she continued up the stairs. "Attend me at once in the lady's chambers. . . ."

For the first time in five years, Clair genuflected. For help. She had never believed in the direct intervention of God, but then, 'twas the only thing that could save her now. . . .

*   *   *

Nothing was said while Morgan and a number of other servants were in the room. Linness lay in a stupor, protected by those around her. Clair sat on the side of the bed, her mind racing over the questions that would be asked and the answers she would attempt to provide. Only the truth would do, but the truth seemed pitifully inadequate to the task. The good woman would not believe it; no one could believe this fantastic story who hadn't, like herself, actually witnessed it from the beginning.

Finally Morgan and the other servants left to wait downstairs. "I hope she wakes in time for supper." He shook his head with a chuckle. "She was just so surprised. Next time, milady," he said to Lady Eleanor, "you will have to prepare us in advance for such a happy occasion."

Eleanor managed a nod. The door shut. She turned her gaze to Clair, who stood up, her bright blue eyes hot with worry and trepidation. "My daughter, my real daughter, Belinda?"

Clair's gaze lowered.

"How, Clair? How in heaven's name did this happen?"

Clair fell onto the trunk at the foot of the bed. She drew a deep breath as she tried to find the place to start.

She began the story with Belinda's death. Clair spared no detail of the gruesome attack. As Eleanor listened to the incredible series of events, she stared at the unconscious creature lying in bed. She could not stop staring. As the story of Linness of Sauvage unfolded, Clair reached the part wherein she, too, faced the choice between condemning Linness or linking her fate to the pretense.

" 'Twas her eyes," Clair said. "Her beautiful silver eyes. There was such kindness there and hope of youth. She was so young, barely ten and five. Milady, you cannot blame her, for she had nothing before this, past her flawless tongue; not shoes against the winter nor her next piece of bread. And Lord Morgan would surely have condemned her, too, if I said she was a pretender. I felt in that moment that I might as easily put the knife in her heart with my own hands ... and I couldn't do it...."

Eleanor absorbed this, indeed she even understood this except for the single most damning fault. "*Mon Dieu*, Clair! To keep me from knowing Belinda's death!"

" 'Twas wrong, milady." Clair shook her head. " 'Twas the thing that always grieves Linness the most. We have no excuse; I have no excuse."

Subdued, Clair went on to describe their life at Gaillard. A good life. Linness brought happiness to everyone who knew her, save for certain unnamed members of the clergy. Eleanor knew this much was true, for her own life and that of her late husband had been so touched by this unusual woman.

Yet her mind kept returning to Belinda. Her daughter was dead, and yet when she greeted this idea, she felt ... nothing. Shock certainly explained some of the absence of a mother's natural sentiments when confronting the death of an only child, but not all of it. No, not all of it.

For some small part of her had known, had always known. The cruel and unpleasant child she had raised had disappeared long ago, died long ago, alive no more. And though she had viewed this as a miraculous transformation, rather than death, the two seemed somehow interchangeable, a jumble in her mind. . . .

Memories of Belinda played through Lady Beau-maris's mind as Clair went on describing Linness and their life. She told of her sight, her devoutness, her recent trouble with the new bishop. Eleanor re-membered vividly Belinda's more famous tan-trums, all rising from the expectation, the demand, that all the world turn on her whims, of which there were many. She had been only ten when she took a knife to a child's doll, chopping it to pieces, just to spite the poor servant because the little girl had loved that doll and had refused to give it to Belinda. Another time Belinda had ripped ribbons from a servant's head, taking a clump of hair in her fit, claiming the servant had stolen the ribbons from her box—this after the distraught servant produced the vendor who had sold the ribbon to her just the day before. So many ugly incidents. Perhaps the worst aspect of Belinda was her own unhappiness. Her despondency went deep. She went through periods when she could hardly lift herself from the bed, succumbing to tears, endless tears, and for no reason she knew.

With a small shudder, she remembered her hus-band's words, uttered in a half-sleeping state, ut-tered in the darkness of night. She had just returned to bed after spending half the night trying to com-fort her girl, worried, at a loss as to what to do. The last in a long series of expensive surgeons had just left the day before, and he left them with the sug-gestion of an exorcism. Demonic possession, he had concluded. Her husband had gathered her into his arms. "She would be better off dead, she suffers so. . . ."

Her own thoughts had joined him secretly, wick-edly. Aye, Belinda would be better off dead. There was no rest for them until the day Belinda had departed from them, and even then they had been so afraid, certain really, the marriage would soon be annulled and Belinda returned to Montegrel. . . .

Linness woke with a small start.

She sat up slowly, bringing the covers with her. Lady Beaumaris sat on the bed. She looked about the room. At Clair. The lady. No one else was with them. She looked back at the lady.

In a rush of movement, she came out of the bed and dropped to her knees before her. "Milady, milady," she begged, tears springing from her gray eyes, "I am so sorry you had to find out this way about your daughter's death. No words can ever excuse what I have done to you. Ever. There is no excuse for denying you the knowledge of her death!"

The lady made no response at first to these anxious words. Then she nodded. "I do not know how you managed a . . . a deception of this . . . this consequence," she said, still confused by all of it. "All these years, all those letters, those beautiful letters. I should have known they could not have been penned by Belinda. . . . Somehow I feel as if I did know, but they were such a sweet comfort and joy to us. . . ."

Mother and child. Mother and child. Linness's face drained of blood as these words echoed in her mind. She reached for the lady's hands, imploring, "*Mon Dieu*, did Morgan renounce Jean Luc?!"

Lady Beaumaris looked confused for a moment before she understood. If she spoke, Morgan would have to renounce Jean Luc. That charming boy would not inherit. He would be a bastard. The boy, the beautiful boy.

How could she do that?

"Did he?"

"Nay, no one knows. Save for Clair, of course. She told me everything: Belinda's death, how you appeared at Gaillard, everything—"

"My son, madame. I do not deserve your forgiveness and I would not ask, except for my innocent son—"

The door opened with a violent thrust. Linness and Eleanor rose with a start. The bishop and four priests appeared. Morgan and Paxton followed. The room shrank with their masculine presence.

Tension filled the room as the bishop absorbed the scene in a glance. He drew a deep breath, preparing to condemn Linness, but he stopped, seeing Eleanor's face change with a smile.

"My daughter has recovered from her shock." The words sounded as she offered Linness the loving embrace of a mother. Linness accepted, and from it, she knew gratitude.

The bishop watched this tender scene with disbelief, his incredulousness boiling over to fury. A red-hot fury that knew no limits, it trembled through him. With his mouth pressed in a hard line, his long staff punched the stone floor and he spun on his heels, turning away. His startled priests followed, more than one questioning their superior. . . .

"By Jesu!" Morgan watched this in confusion. "He insisted on meeting with you, milady. He said you had a far bigger revelation for me than your mother's surprise visit." He shook his head. "A passel full of trouble, he is. . . . Now, what could he mean by it?"

"I believe I will be staying here through the harvest," Eleanor said. "Or do you think he could have guessed the present I brought?"

Paxton drew his first easy breath and eased his grip on his sword. Since learning of the lady's arrival and taking in the bishop and his priest circling Linness like vultures, he had faced the certainty of upcoming battle. The question was Morgan; whose side would he join? The side to save Linness or the side to condemn her? He suspected the former, except that he had no doubt the bishop would have related tales of infidelity as well. Then he couldn't guess what Morgan would do. Nor the Gaillard guards. Many of them would no doubt go with Morgan, but there were more than a few who would go with him, if not out of loyalty to himself, then out of devotion to Linness.

He would have had to send her far away, to some place where the church could not find her. Somewhere in Scotland or the northern states of the Holy Roman Empire. She would lose not only himself and Jean Luc but her whole life, all that she knew and all the people she loved.

The dark scenario melted away. His intense relief made him want to drop to his knees and kiss the lady's shoes.

Morgan dismissed the bishop and turned to introduce Paxton to Lady Beaumaris. She knew at once who else among these new faces had joined the conspiracy. For the light of gratitude in Paxton's fine dark eyes said so much. . . .

"You see, milord, the positions of Mercury and the sun are coming into alignment. Within one week, Mars, too, will join the perimeters of the orbit, which means—"

"Enough," Paxton said, interrupting this long-winded speech made of nonsense. "Enough. We have heard this all before. You may leave the hall to wait for your lordship's decision outside."

Pol Saint Jude looked angrily back at Paxton, but he nodded and gathered up his precious charts and maps before he and his three young assistants left the hall. The famous astrologer arrived every year in August to offer Morgan the best date for harvesting the vineyard's grapes. Every year these predictions had been a disaster.

Selecting the harvest date was like walking a tightrope over a deep and treacherous valley. The longer one waited, the sweeter and more potent the wine, but one day too many and whole fields could be lost. If an unexpected storm arrived, the whole harvest could be wiped out.

Morgan always waited too long. Last year he had waited until almost half the yield had gone to rot. The year before he had waited for a late harvest, and though Linness herself had warned him of the approaching summer storm, he had delayed the date again and lost almost three quarters of the yield. So it went. Every year Morgan picked wrong.

"Do not listen to that old fool," Paxton said. "Now is the time. Tomorrow . . ."

Still Morgan hesitated. Paxton thought the grapes were ready. Just today they had found one field with four rotten bunches, another with five. This was the first sign they must act quickly before it was too late.

Yet Morgan so loved a sweet, potent wine. The sweeter and more potent, the better—and the higher price the barrels fetched. The astrologers guaranteed a week of good weather and a bountiful harvest on the date. "Three more days," Morgan said, but in a voice weighted with uncertainty.

"Nay, brother." Paxton shook his head. "I am warning you—the rot has started; we can wait no more. One more day and we could lose twenty percent of the yield. Besides, the cottars are waiting, and the wine press is ready."

Morgan appeared to consider all this. "Aye, but the astrologer—"

"That man has been wrong five years now," Paxton pointed out. "I have no more faith in astrology than I do in chance, less even when considering that man's record. Morgan," he tried to reason with his brother, "if he has not been right so far, why would you listen to him now?"

Morgan nodded slowly. His brother's words rang true, and they lay against Pol Saint Jude's excuses for why he had been wrong. Of which there were many. The man had promised that this year was different. This year he guaranteed his prediction, and had offered half his fee back if he was wrong.

Paxton placed his hand on his forehead and looked away. 'Twas his life's thorn, always having to defer to Morgan's decision when he knew better. The dark shadow in his life.

The light in his eyes changed as he found Linness. She clutched the folds of his favorite dress, watching Morgan with the same anxiousness as all the other people gathered in the hall. The skirts were made of a pale violet cotton, the tight bodice made of a purple velvet, trimmed in gold. Short, puffy sleeves left her thin arms bare. Aye, the dress was his favorite because it was the easiest to remove.

He remembered the musical echo of her laughter when he had told her this. The memory of what had followed played in his mind. He drew a deep breath as heat rushed to his loins at the thought.

He had spent the last three days separated from her as he had left to secure enough laborers for the harvest, a thing John and the wine steward normally managed. It had been a week since Lady Eleanor had arrived and took up residence in Linness's apartment. Despite numerous attempts, they had not been able to find a moment alone. Over a week had passed since he last felt her sweet, pliant lips beneath his, the incredible softness of her breasts in his palm, watched her eyes shine with passion or heard her love cries, over a week since he parted her thighs and slipped in the damp mercy of her sheath. He was losing his mind with desire. . . .

'Twas an echo of their dark future, of what life would be without her. An emptiness filled only with longing. And while he tried to fill the emptiness with the wealth in his life, enough wealth for dozens of men, the responsibilities and labor put into his land and estates and the hundreds of dependent people it could neither touch the emptiness nor alter the longing.

He sometimes imagined what life would be like with Linness at his side. He imagined being free to love her: the joy of waking up in the morning with her breath against his skin, her warm softness pressed against his, free to talk and laugh and tease all the time, to share all the small and large joys and triumphs, disappointments and frustrations. . . .

The future that should have been . . .

Paxton forced his thoughts back to the task at hand. Morgan appeared deep in thought; he was indecisive still. "Morgan," he continued, "this year's wine already promises to be the sweetest and most potent Gaillard has ever produced. It could be the best wine Gaillard has ever produced!" He patted his brother's back and said meaningfully, "You will be rich. . . ."

"Oh, do say aye, Morgan!" Linness said, as she stepped over and squeezed his hand affectionately. " 'Twill take four days to harvest the fields, and on the last day of the feast, there will be a harvest moon for the celebration! The harvest feast will be on the night of a harvest moon. Surely that is a fortuitous sign, more potent than anything the astrologers can find?"

Morgan absorbed the anxious hope appearing in his wife's gray eyes. A full moon, aye, 'twas a good sign. And wasn't she always right about things? "You think we should harvest now, too?"

"Aye," she said, "I do."

He smiled at her. "Ah, well," he agreed at last, "if you really think one more day might cost us some yield, then let us harvest the crop. The grapes are sweet enough already, are they not?"

Applause broke out. Everyone breathed a sigh of relief. Linness laughed gaily and squeezed Clair's hand. 'Twould be a grand year for their wine. Morgan would be rich. She laughed, "The king himself will be ordering barrels of our wine!"

Morgan started naming prizes to the pickers: The man who filled the most barrels would get two young plow horses; the woman, a bolt of velvet cloth; the child, a chess game or a pick from one of his hound's litters, and so on.

Linness did not hear. For she met Paxton's gaze. All she saw was his desire, the heat of it reaching across the space separating them to quicken her pulse. She understood his want because it was hers as well. Erotic dreams filled her head every night, so she woke three or four times with her heart pounding and a breathlessness no air could ease. She drew a sharp breath, and thought she would slip out tonight, somehow. . . .

Too late. Now that Morgan had made the decision, he swung into action, shouting out orders to everyone, including now his brother. "Paxton, will you oversee the harvesting of the northwest fields?"

These were a half day's ride away. He would have to leave with the workers today. He would not return until the harvesting was done.

"There's no one else I trust," Morgan added.

A strange light shone in his brother's eyes; he looked fierce, unreadable.

"Will you?"

"Aye." Paxton nodded. "I'll leave at once."

Linness's disappointment felt sharp.

The harvest day moon . . .

The grapes had been picked. The sweet, succulent fruit sat in huge vats outside the wine press, alongside the river near the château's gates. Tomorrow the grapes would be conveyed to the wine press, which would crush the succulent fruit into juice for the fermenting into wine. It would take weeks for the barrels to be filled and years for the finest of red burgundy to age. The first thousand empty barrels had been brought up from the storehouses.

The ancient tradition of the wine artisanal was called "forcing the cap," but it was more popularly referred to as the "wine dance." The custom dated back a hundred or more years to the days before the wine press. Dozens of giant wooden vats were positioned in the courtyard where the feast was held. Yves, the wine steward, had spent weeks selecting the best grapes for the Gaillard special reserve.

A hundred invited townsfolk gathered for the harvest feast and music. Dozens of women, young, strong, and healthy, had been selected weeks ago as well. They sat off to the side of the vats for the foot scrubbing. Their hair was lifted, sometimes netted, and they wore light and loose dresses, not their best dresses but their oldest and most worn, for they would be turned to rags after this night.

Excitement hung in the air. Ceremonial torches lit the courtyard, flickering wildly in the light breeze. Banners emblazoned with the colors of Gaillard flew overhead.

Morgan finally stood up; his raised hand held last year's best bottle of reserve. Linness, seated alongside Morgan and Eleanor at the high table, had never seen him so happy. The harvest had indeed been the best in nearly six years.

In a loud, booming voice, he began the prayer of thanks for the bountiful harvest. It used to be a mock salute to Bacchus, the ancient god of wine, until the church put a stop to that. He tilted dangerously back, and forgot the next words before he burst into hearty laughter with the rest of the crowd.

"Methinks your husband has enjoyed his bounty a bit too much," Eleanor observed.

Linness nodded as she whispered discreetly, "Bacchus doth drown more men than Neptune—I fear it is just so with Morgan. . . ." Everyone knew Morgan was becoming a drunkard. No one knew what to do about it, though. There was no cure for the age-old malady, the unfortunate weakness of kings and peasants alike.

Exasperated, Morgan gave up trying to remember those elusive words. "Well, well, God makes only the water, but we made the wine!" The crowd cheered with wild applause and laughter.

Eleanor's brow lifted; a smile followed. "Thank goodness the bishop is not in attendance or Milord would be called up for the remark."

"Aye," Linness agreed.

The applause changed to a rhythmic clapping, faster and faster, urging Morgan to break the bottle open and start the festivities. The bottle was smashed over the wine barrel, signaling the dozens of musicians to start playing. The dancing followed.

The moon shone bright on the laughing faces of the wine makers and dancers. No soft lutes or harps here, nothing but the swift draw of violins and faster drums. The people danced around the vats as the women, with skirts hiked over bare legs, danced in them. Faster and faster until they felt his heart pounding with the beat.

With laughter sparkling in her eyes, Linness watched these women, her foot tapping away beneath the table. Morgan never let her dance to the madness, swirls, gyrations, the abandoned rhythm of the harvest moon. Eleanor clapped happily to the beat, more than a bit tipsy herself.

A pretty woman suddenly appeared behind Morgan. Linness took in her silk brocaded gown—

much too fine for the rigors of a harvest feast—and the loose arrangement of her hair. She had never seen her before and she knew at once she must be Morgan's new mistress. The woman laughed seductively as she coaxed Morgan up from the table to join the dancing.

Linness pretended not to notice as Morgan, drunk, stumbling, and laughing, was led through the gates and out to the barren, moonlit fields where many couples ended the night. Clair herself had long since disappeared with Galazz, a man at least ten years younger than herself.

She turned back to the feast.

Michaels's gaze fell to Linness's foot, tapping away to the music. He smiled as he tossed the remains of a goblet and pointed Linness out to Clifford. Both men laughed as they headed toward her. Linness laughed as Clifford bent down and, ignoring her protest, removed her slippers. She screamed as they lifted her and carried her off to the vat. The two men set her down in the enormous wooden tub of grapes just as a tired maid climbed out. Linness hiked up the skirts of an old cotton dress as grapes oozed between her toes and up her bare legs. The music sounded loud, the beat fast, and she laughed with abandon as it suddenly carried her crazily into motion. . . .

After the three-hour ride to get back, Paxton finally led his horse through the gates. The courtyard was full, the music loud. His gaze searched through the throngs of dancing people, stopping on the high table. Lady Beaumaris, Michaels, two of Gaillard's guild leaders and their wives, and all of them laughing and clapping. No Morgan. No Linness.

He looked to the wine vat.

Desire exploded through him, riveting him to the spot.

Moonlight bathed her dancing form. She tossed her head back and forth with the rhythmic stomp of her long white legs, her dark skirt hiked to her thighs. The long hair fell in chaotic array all around her form, her slim, seductive form spinning round and round with alluring velocity.

Gone was the demure and beautiful lady of his brother's court. In her place was the bewitching wood creature made of earth, wind, and fire. Here was Linness dancing with joy and abandon as he first saw her over six long years ago.

He stepped closer. . . .

The pounding of the music reached through him, fast and hard, as he stared up at the wild creature. His gaze locked suddenly to hers. She stopped with a small shock. The blatant desire on Paxton's face knocked the air from her lungs. A tingling awareness shot down her spine. He looked discreetly at the stables, that was all.

Then he was gone.

Breathing hard and fast, she managed to climb out of the vat. For a long moment she feared she had imagined him, that he appeared from her desperation and longing to see him.

The music roared in her ears as she looked confusedly about the darkened surroundings: the flickering torch line, the wild dancers everywhere, the few remaining seated. She spotted Lady Beaumaris dancing with Michaels and the others. No one else seemed to have noticed his presence.

She slipped into the huge vat of water to rinse the sweet and sticky juice from her legs before she ran to the stables in a rush, the music becoming fainter with each step. No one was here. She looked to both sides, pushed open the huge wooden door and stepped inside.

'Twas quiet, so quiet. The pungent scent of freshly mowed hay filled her senses. Frantically she searched the darkness, her heart pounding. A bat flew with a sudden screech, drawing her gaze up to the hayloft where the disturbed night creature circled out the roof window. Moonlight poured inside. A shadow fell over the ladder leading up. She moved to it and climbed up to the top.

She looked about the darkened space, seeing nothing and no one. She stepped to the darkest corner.

Nothing. No one.

Breathing hard and fast, trying desperately to slow the wild race of her heart, she leaned against the wall and closed her eyes. She had been imagining him! Like every night since Eleanor had come and inadvertently separated him from her. Like last night. She had dreamt of waking to his kiss, to the warm, firm lips claiming hers as his huge, warm body came over her, his forearms gently pinning her arms over her head as she felt the sweep of his tongue in her mouth. She couldn't move, she didn't want to move, as he parted her robe and she felt his lips on her neck and ear, sliding to her breasts. . . .

She woke to find it was only a dream. . . .

Suddenly she felt the whisper of his warm breath against her ear. She nearly collapsed with joy. A hot shiver raced from the spot. Her senses flooded with the sweet taste of him, the clean masculine scent of hard-worked leather and just him.

"Linness . . ."

The easy way his long arms braced against the wall landed her on the very real shores of her dream. She felt the leap of her pulse and his name came in a husky cry. "Paxton . . ."

Shadowed and lit by the light of the harvest moon, his face was intent, a look that somehow registered in the lower part of her body. His eyes appeared as black pools in the night. Desire mixed feverishly with joy, relief, and a twinge of fear, for the agony of their brief separation spoke of the dark future. "Merciful heavens." She felt strangely like crying as she threw her arms up and around his neck. "I thought I was dreaming. I thought I was imagining you! How I've missed you—"

"No more than I, you. No more, Linness." He lowered her to her feet, savoring the sight of her lovely upturned face, the feel of her slender form in his arms. "*Mon Dieu*, you are a fever consuming me," he said as he brushed his lips against hers, then gently kissed her mouth. "I am past care, mad with wanting you . . . Linness." He said her name as his lips sought her flushed cheek, his fingers sifting through her hair. "Linness, my sweet witch . . ."

The kiss expressed more, so much more.

He held the sides of her head as he studied her upturned face, the blush staining her cheeks, the satin arch of her brows and closed eyes, the fine small nose and the slightly parted lips, the quick rise and fall of her bosom. Hunger for her ran like brandy through his veins, strong and potent. Like the first time, he was afraid he could not manage the gentleness she needed.

Yet this concern disappeared as she said, "Kiss me, Paxton. Kiss me, again. . . ."

His mouth lowered to hers in the instant.

His lips molded against hers, his tongue slipped into the moist recess. Dear Lord, she tasted of sweet ripened grapes. He needed more. He brought her head back, drinking until his senses flooded with the sweetness of her.

He gently pulled her against him. Her breasts were a soft weight against his chest as he broke the kiss and let her draw in air. He gently kissed the corner of her lips where yearning made them tremble, and then he closed his eyes, trying to temper the race of his pulse.

She was shaking. She reached up and took his hand, first stroking it tenderly with her lips before placing it over her breast where her heart beat wildly with heady anticipation, the lingering abandon of the dance.

She reached for his large brass belt, fumbled for a minute before pulling it off and dropping it at their feet. He helped her pull his tunic over his head. She watched avidly as the fine fabric exposed the tightly corded muscles of his stomach and then the rise of his chest. Her fingers ached to feel his sun-washed skin, her toes curling into the hay as if to steady herself. She helped him out of the rest of his clothes, her impatient fingers trembling as she did so. Once done, her gaze went hot with the masculinity before her. He caught her hand and lightly tasted her fingers, soothing them and stirring the sensitive tips. "I want you so badly, I'm afraid . . . Linness help me, help me be gentle with you."

She shook her head, for she felt the same desperation and urgency, and she was certain she could not endure a gentle hand. Her throat felt thick and hot, too hot for words. Agonized by her own mounting arousal, she took his hand and returned it to her aching flesh, gasping as he cupped her breasts. Through the thin cloth his thumbs sought her nipples, prodding the peaks to tighter points.

Her breath sharpened as his hand slipped around her ribs to the buttons down the back. The warm night air brushed her skin as he pulled the fabric apart. She held perfectly still as his hands came to her shoulders, caressing the sharp curves there as he slipped the dress from them.

His eyes widened in response to the beauty unveiled and bathed in moonbeams. He cupped the softness and took her mouth, kissing her until her knees went weak and they were sinking to the hay-covered floor. His arm reached behind her to cushion her fall as he laid her to the soft ground.

In minutes he had slid her gown off altogether. She felt his hand curling gently around her thin ankle, his lips lightly bathing her skin there. He discovered the remnants of the harvesting on her legs. "My God, you are shrouded in sweetness, Linness." He tasted more and more and more, and chuckled because the last thing he needed with her was a rousing taste on her skin. "Everywhere ... sweet and luscious ..." Skilled fingers began to massage her calf, while the other hand stroked higher.

A shuddering gasp escaped her as his palms and fingers spanned the back of her thighs. His fingers grazed the swell of her buttock while his mouth danced over her skin, drinking in her fragrance, the taste of grapes blended with the dew of her awakening.

In desperation she pulled him back over her. The

joy of having all his flesh against hers swept through her, and with trembling emotion, she sought his lips. All restraint vanished with the kiss as he pulled her lithe form against his hard warmth. Like an avalanche, it was, the swift rush of lust. "Easy, love, easy," he said more to himself than to her. "You are not ready yet. Linness, Linness, here, let me show you. . . ."

She felt his hand sweep away her hair from her neck, before brushing the highest spot on her spine with his open mouth. Stinging pricks of pleasure raced to the base of her spine. A small cry escaped her. She felt his breath halt and come more quickly on her skin.

"Aye, love, aye . . ." he whispered as a sweep of movement brought his hand down her spine, soothing the shivers there to come just below her breasts. He cupped their swelling weight, his thumb teasing the nipples.

"How many times I imagined making love to you," he said huskily. He massaged her taut flesh to pliancy before slipping lower to feel the dew-rush of wetness. His lips found her neck, drawing sparks of fire to the surface. "And how my imagination pales to this reality. . . . Linness, I love you. . . ."

His mouth captured her nipple, massaging it with a tongue as hot as the flesh it was licking. She was softly crying, falling over the cliff again as his sensitive fingers coaxed her to a fever, his palm lightly cupping the silky curls, molding her to a fiery ecstasy that made her cry out sharply. And still moist kisses covered her breasts before finding her swollen lips, taking them hungrily.

Small moans issued from her throat. With heart-wrenching slowness, he filled her with his erotic heat. Under the shower of a harvest moon, they moved with the ancient wisdom of their bodies, joining their souls in a triumphant rapture, and like a giant star exploding, the ecstasy blinded them to the dark future fast closing around them. . . .

Chapter 11

"She's not feeling well," Clair whispered, with a cautious glance down the stairs.

"Oh?" Paxton inquired, alarmed. "What's wrong?"

Clair looked away. It was impossible to meet his intense gaze: it probed into her very thoughts. He looked ruggedly handsome in his riding clothes: a forest green doublet and black riding pants, tall black boots and spurs. She rested her eyes on the fine gold spurs as she replied, "A touch of the flu, is all. A slight fever, and weariness, you know."

With alarm he started towards Linness's door.

"Nay." Clair reached an arm out to stop him. "She begs you to give her a day or two alone. She's not feeling well and she looks a sight really. . . ."

Paxton's sensitivities were acute, and as he stared at Clair, he realized she was lying. He had only just returned from a week's absence, having overseen the grapes being pressed into wine in the northern section of the vineyards. He would have to leave Gaillard in two weeks' time. The parting weighed heavily on his heart and mind. He did not want to waste a minute of their time together.

Meantime, tensions within Gaillard escalated. An

armed guard of forty men from the Vatican was said to be less than a day's ride away; they would reach the gates by tomorrow. The bishop was collecting stories from peasants and townsfolk of Linness's "sight."

Paxton had received a letter from Duprat promising to expeditiously see the bishop reassigned. Expeditiously meant two or three months, if ever, and he cursed Duprat for stalling.

"She'll be on the mend tomorrow, no doubt," Clair added.

"Very well," he said smoothly. "If you will assure me that there is no reason for alarm?"

Clair's head bobbed up and down with feigned assent. "Oh, aye. She'll be up and about in no time."

"I eagerly await that good news," he said formally with a slight nod of his head.

With a faltering smile, Clair turned her back, slipping inside Linness's room when she heard Lord Paxton's door shut.

Paxton stepped to his window, where the last light of the sun slanted across the panes and fell in a gold stream to the stone floor. The shutters opened to the courtyard below. Agilely he climbed out onto the ledge, his back pressed against the warm stones, and made his way to her window.

Everyone was still in the fields for the harvesting of the wheat, barley, and corn, which had begun last week. From the battlements he could see the barley fields, sharply divided by the river; the workers appeared as distant specks against the ripe gold plains. He saw none of it, though, not really. He was focused instead on the question of why Linness would lie to him.

To protect him from something, he knew, but what?

He reached her window. Latched. She had latched it to keep him out. Peering inside, he saw that Linness stood with her back to the window, talking to Clair. He removed his dagger and slipped it between the shutters, underneath the latch, until it lifted. The shutter opened a few inches; their voices drifted through.

Linness's hands held Clair's arms. "He believed you, then?"

Clair nodded.

"I just need time," Linness said, a hand weaving distressfully through her hair. "I need to think." She wore the long gold robe; her unbound hair cascaded around her shoulders and back. "If only he would leave now. I cannot believe I am saying it, after spending every hour of every day terrified of the time when he would actually go—"

"Ye should tell him," Clair said decidedly, in her way of reducing every complex feeling to its bare point. "He deserves to know."

She shook her head. This was out of the question. "Not now, Clair."

After a disapproving shake of her head, Clair slipped out the door. Linness clasped her hands over her mouth and turned. She stopped with a gasp.

Paxton stood in the alcove, his towering frame outlined in the setting sun. He stepped to her, quietly, so quietly. She was shaking her head as her hands clasped the folds of her robe tight at her neck. She backed up, unaware that she did so until she felt the stone wall on her back.

He had heard. He would have to be told something. . . .

With frantic silver eyes she searched his face as her thoughts clamored to produce a believable explanation.

"Tell me, Linness."

His voice was a gentle whisper, filled with confusion, curiosity, and a hint of pain. His nearness, like a great enveloping warmth, threatened her resolve. He abruptly understood. "*Mon Dieu*, you are afraid of me. Why, Linness?"

"Paxton, please, I, I just need time, I—"

"What aren't you telling me?"

"I'm not feeling well, truly—" Her hand went to her mouth, as if she herself were unable to bear the falsity on her lips.

His gaze turned fierce as he warned, "Do not lie to me, Linness. By the heavens, anything but that."

His gaze swept over her; an intimate caress. She looked pale and, aye, terribly frightened. The gold chain and the precious ring hung just above the thick cloth of the robe, which she clasped ever so tightly. As if shielding herself. Shielding herself from him.

Understanding penetrated his senses. His hand came over her cold one. He gently brought it away, parted the robe to reveal the startling naked beauty beneath. The fullness was a subtle change, but he knew every ounce of her slim figure and he perceived it immediately.

He remembered vividly the slim shape of the woman-child he had first known: her bewitching eyes and sweet taste, the sharp lines and the feminine softness of her first blush, tempting beyond reason and yet not as beautiful as the woman he found six years later. And when he made love to Linness now, he savored every tiny mark and diminutive imperfection of her form that made her the flesh-and-blood woman he would die loving.

And how motherhood had rewarded her beauty!

A tremble came to her hands, tears hung in her eyes like a morning mist over the river. She felt the wealth of his love cascading over her, and indeed, never had he loved her more. Their emotions surged together and she reached her arms around his neck, and he held her tightly against his strength.

She knew the child was a girl. The girl she would never have to give up. Mary sent her this blessing, to ease the ache in her soul when the time came for Paxton and Jean Luc to leave. And she had never wanted anything more in her life.

She closed her eyes as she felt his lips upon her forehead. "I am so scared, Paxton. . . ."

"Linness, Linness, it will be all right," he said. "What can he do now? He is not the first man who faced this situation and he won't be the last. Life will go on. He has no choice but to accept it." He thought of Morgan's pigheadedness, his unwillingness to dwell long on troubling situations. Aye, Morgan would come to accept it. "I dare say he won't even think long on it. I'll return when your time has come, to be here. Linness, I love you, I love you. . . ."

The shocking words drew her back slightly. She searched his face, scarcely able to believe this, the masculine simplicity of his reasoning. He imagined Morgan would just accept it.

He would not. Never. At the very least it would bring him the unendurable pain and grief of betrayal, and strike away the harmony in their lives. And then, if he did not renounce her and the child, he would almost certainly turn his animosity against the innocent babe.

At the worst, it may compel him to act with violence.

For a brief moment she was dumbfounded, alarmed, confused, but enlightenment dawned quickly. Paxton could not bear the reality of what she would have to do; it did not even enter his mind. All this time she imagined he would want her to rid her womb of his seed—there were potions for this—and she had been trying to guess how to explain that she could not, could never do that, but no. That had not occurred to him at all.

Paxton's ignorance was a blessing, she saw at once. There was only one way to make Morgan think it was his child, and the only thing harder than that was the idea of the unbearable pain her actions would cause Paxton if he were to ever find out. . . .

He was smiling at her as he lowered his head to kiss her. So tenderly did he kiss her at first, she felt a bewildered kind of agony. She would have to carry out her plans soon. Tonight. Paxton would never know. He would never have to know what she did. No one would have to know. . . .

She felt a sudden surge of gladness and relief, expressed in the pliant melding of her mouth beneath his. Paxton saw it as her passion meeting his and he was suddenly kissing her as if it were the last time he ever would. . . .

Logistics. She figured she would not actually have to lie with Morgan, thank the heavens. She would wait until late at night, until he was inebriated. He would pass out on his bed. She would sneak into his chambers, disrobe, and climb into his bed. He'd wake to find her. She would kiss him tenderly on the forehead, make an inane reference to something that had happened. He would have to assume he had made love to her.

Then she'd slip back to her chambers when no one was looking. 'Twould be done and over. And when the child was born, Morgan would think that she, too, was his.

Paxton would soon have Jean Luc at Beaumont. Morgan would allow her to visit a month each year, perhaps longer. Paxton assumed he could spend two to three months of the year at Gaillard. She tried to tell herself that this was enough, that it had to be enough, and when she thought of having a daughter, sometimes she actually believed it.

The room was dark. She pretended sleep as she waited for Eleanor to doze.

The soft sound of the good woman's slumber soon filled the chambers. Another hour passed and there was still no sign of Morgan going to bed. He sometimes passed out at the table. After yet another hour, she imagined that was what had happened. It could be a long wait.

She heard Paxton's footsteps. She tensed instinctively as she heard his door open and close, his every movement unusually graceful and quiet for a man of his stature.

Paxton, forgive me, forgive me. . . .

How he had loved her this afternoon! As if he had needed to engulf every part of her body with his soul, undressing her in the still-lingering light of the sun, whispering his love as he flushed her body with warmth, carrying her to the sky-bound heights until, losing control, his adoring hands caressed the tremors of her surrender. . . .

I love you, I love you. . . .

He had been playing chess after dinner, she knew. She had told him she would sleep through the night, that she was so tired. She had promised to meet him at their special place by the river tomorrow afternoon.

A curious numbness crept into her limbs, part fear, part apprehension, as she thought of Paxton, sleeping so close. A numbness that intensifed as she waited . . .

The sound of Morgan's heavy footsteps sounded on the stairs at last. There was a scrape and a clang; she abruptly guessed one of his spurs must have come loose. He sang a ribald song in a wine-sodden whisper. The song stopped. The door opened and then shut.

The beat of her heart roared loudly in her ears— the only sensation she felt through the numbness that was claiming her.

Perhaps she should wait another hour or so. Perhaps she should wait until dawn. Morgan never rose before dawn and usually not until the tenth bell. Why spend any more time in his chambers than necessary?

If she fell asleep, though . . .

Stalling, she was stalling.

Mary, help me, for this is so difficult.

She finally sat up, swung her legs over the cot, and rose, silently making her way to the door. She stopped, glancing down at the lovely gold and white robe that just this afternoon Paxton had parted. She bent over and rubbed her hands over her hair to mess it up. She hesitated still.

She was so scared!

She had to do it, she had to. 'Twould be over and done by morning. 'Twas but one night of sleeping in his bed. One night for her child's life and well-being!

Morgan would never touch her . . . he never touched her . . .

Soundlessly she stepped out into the darkened hall and to Morgan's door. Just as quietly she opened it and slipped into his room.

Morgan's snores were loud. Frantically her gaze searched the darkness of a room she almost never entered. Brightly colored banners hung on the walls and canopied the large bed. Morgan lay there with his legs together and his arms stretched out, like a man on the cross. His large bare feet pointed up at the end of the bed, and it surprised her that he managed to get his boots off. His tunic, too, had been discarded, tossed carelessly to the floor. He wore only hose.

A hand went to her heart as if to slow the hard and irregular pounding. She drew a deep breath and marched to the bed slowly, like a condemned prisoner, and sat on the very edge.

The smell was strange and unpleasant, the rot of too much drinking, and the pungent odor of the faint sheen of masculine perspiration. A wave of nausea swept over her; by force of will she pushed it back. Without making a sound, she laid her head down next to Morgan's arm and curled into a protective ball on the very edge of the bed.

The canopy overhead flapped lightly in the slight breeze blowing through the open shutters. Two flies buzzed round and round. She found herself staring through the dim light at the chessboard that sat on the trunk: the white queen and her knight lay flat on the wooden checks; the black king and bishop stood ominously over them.

It was only then that she realized the salty taste in her mouth was brought by the silent fall of tears. She closed her eyes and tried to dream of Paxton. She tried to imagine Paxton looking at an emerald green valley surrounding a deep blue lake, the place she always sought when she was troubled. A place where she imagined the joy and freedom of loving him.

No pictures formed in her mind, as if the dream had already faded beneath the cruel and harsh light of reality. . . .

The days were still warm, but the nights grew steadily cooler. The breeze blowing through the opened shutters carried a hint of fall chill. It stirred the banners draping the canopy of Morgan's large bed.

Morgan stirred beneath the sunlight filtering into his chambers. Yawning, raising his arm to block the light, he touched something.

Alerted, he opened his eyes.

He sat up in alarm, his heart leaping with sudden upsetting energy.

Linness! Linness was asleep in his bed.

He stared at the tousled mass of dark hair, the pale beautiful sleeping face, the slight parting of her robe as she slept. He saw at once she had nothing on underneath. His mind turned slowly over how it was possible, how she had come to his bed.

She must have come while he was sleeping. But why?

The idea that she sought his bed produced a curious tingling throughout his body. Not Linness, his beautiful and saintly wife, the one everyone loved. She would not have such inclinations. Surely!

Yet there she lay, sound asleep. . . .

He found himself staring at the soft swell of her breast beneath the robe. His heart began to pound hard. He felt a sudden rush of heat through his veins, a familiar tightening of loins.

He remembered the first time he had lain with her. Before Jean Luc. She had not been so saintly then. Quite the opposite. Then she was a woman a man wanted only to sink his flesh into.

The memory pumped his blood harder and faster through his veins.

He pulled his hose off his legs.

He lay back down beside her. She stirred in her sleep. He reached his hand under the robe and over the tempting swell, encompassing her breast in his large hand, slightly flexing his fingers into her soft flesh. And again. He grew hotter.

Her gray eyes flew open with a startled gasp. A hard hand gripped her shoulder, turning her. The night came back in a rush of memory. Her eyes went wild with fear as his huge weight came over her with a husky grunt. She was shaking her head, a loud, frantic denial in her throat. The negative declaration changed to a scream, but it never sounded, for his mouth was over hers and she felt the wrenching pain of his body's first thrust. . . .

Clair knocked softly on the door and opened it. Lady Beaumaris stood by the alcove, already dressed and brushing out the length of her hair.

Black hair streaked with silver, beautiful hair, startling when it was let down.

"A good morning to ye," Clair said after she ascertained that Linness was not there.

"Good morning, Clair," she said brightly. "Linness must have already risen and left. Where did she go off to so early?"

"I do not know," Clair said, wondering herself. Lord Paxton was in the hall, and she had assumed Linness had shared her happiness with him at last and would have been with him; they never lost a chance to be together these days. After a quick inspection, she had seen that only Michaels was with him, and a few servants milling about. She had rushed upstairs to tell Linness where Lord Paxton was, only to find Linness not here either. She hoped she wasn't asleep in his room still; that could be a disaster. "I just woke myself," she continued. "Mayhap she's helping Vivian in the kitchen or is off to her garden. She wanted to finish picking the cloves before the first chill."

Lady Beaumaris nodded, though she knew it was a lie. Linness had no doubt slipped into Lord Paxton's room and had fallen asleep there. The love between Paxton and Linness seemed such a huge and grand thing, so perfectly obvious to everyone. As long as she lived, she would not understand how it was kept a secret at all. She suspected most of the household knew anyway; the only exception seemed to be Morgan. She kept trying to hint to Linness that she need not keep it a secret from her, that she had lived too long to pass judgment on a matter of heart, especially one so obviously consuming and sweeping. But somehow these words were never said. Somehow it was easier to pretend she didn't know. . . .

"Can I dress ye hair, milady?" Clair asked. Eleanor assented and, once it was done, the two women made their way downstairs to the hall.

Eleanor hid her surprise at finding Paxton there, apparently just finishing his meal. After passing morning pleasantries, Paxton inquired, "And I suppose Lady Linness is still sleeping?"

Eleanor and Clair exchanged confused glances. Clair said, "Actually she must have left bright and early this morning. She was gone when we woke. Methinks she's tending her garden." Booted footsteps sounded and she looked past Lord Paxton to the entranceway. "Oh no, here comes the devil. . . ."

Paxton swung around as the bishop appeared in a bright burst of crimson. He approached the table with several priests following behind. The tension had become so acute in the last weeks, Morgan had finally banished the man from the hall—by threat of guards. The bishop had bought an old grain storage house in town and turned part of it into living quarters for his entourage. Mercifully, they had seen much less of him lately.

"I see Lord Morgan has not risen," the bishop said as he faced Paxton across the table. "I find I must speak to him. Would you rouse him?"

Paxton folded long arms easily across his chest. "I'm afraid he had a long night. I am loath to disturb his slumber."

"The matter can only be resolved by your brother, I fear. It concerns the Jesuit knights who have arrived. I was told last night your brother refused them lodging here at the château—"

"You were told wrong," Paxton neatly interrupted. " 'Twas I who refused the courtesy to extend shelter, not my brother. Though, of course, he naturally agreed to the measure."

The bishop's eyes blazed, before narrowing menacingly. "I thought as much. I demand to see Lord Morgan. If you will not wake him, I will—"

In one fluid movement, Paxton leaped across the table, his dagger manifesting from thin air to touch the startled bishop's throat. The room drew a collective gasp. Wide and now frightened eyes met darkly cold ones as Paxton said, "Do not threaten me again, because, I swear I would just as soon cut your throat."

The dagger did not waver. Paxton understood his reaction; it had been building for days. Life was going dark, and quickly. Not just the idea that the bishop's warriors now outnumbered Gaillard's meager force and the danger of that—'twas impossible to know what side the people would come in on if it ever went to battle—but he now understood Francis and Duprat were not going to help him.

Beaumont was finished. The harvest here was over. It was time for him to leave. Yet he could not leave Linness with this malicious man's threat against her.

"Now I will indeed rouse my brother," he told the terrified man. "But only so he can tell you we will not house any guard that comes to Gaillard with the intention of raising swords against my brother or his own. Only so he can tell you that we will not stand by for an ecclesiastic trial, indeed any trial or further torment to his wife. Only so he can tell you it's over . . ."

Paxton slowly lowered the knife.

The bishop stumbled back, gasping, his mind turning over the words, the shocking words. The lords of Gaillard would spill the blood of the church to protect that witch! *Mon Dieu!* The Vatican would not stand for it. Not with the evidence he would soon be sending them. This man would live to regret his unholy liaison with that woman!

Paxton ignored the scathing condemnation on the bishop's face and he withdrew. He rushed through the corridor and to the stairs, pushing back the violence trembling through him. He was stopped by an odd retching sound he heard coming from Morgan's room. A tingling bolt of energy rushed down his spine.

Linness was bent over the water basin for nearly a half hour now, unable to stop the violent retching of a mercifully empty stomach. Morgan had passed out again.

Only one thought sustained her: retreat from this room.

Finally she stood up, drawing gasping breaths as she wiped her mouth. She took two unsteady steps toward the door before her knees collapsed beneath her weight and she fell with a stifled cry. She stood up again and stumbled to the door. A violently trembling hand touched the latch, and she stumbled out.

She made her mind go blank to protect herself from the horror of what had just happened. She had no awareness of seeing anything until two tall black boots suddenly appeared before her. She looked up to see Paxton staring down at her. A look of startled confusion changed his features. For a long moment she just stared up at him, a cold chill sweeping over her. The world went gray; she realized she was sinking. His arms caught her up. He jerked her head back; the wild mass of hair dropped back with the movement, but all she could perceive was the violence in his dark eyes.

Paxton just stared down at her, not understanding at first, and simply because he didn't believe the obvious. Her eyes were shining gray pools of a fear edged with hysteria. She was gulping for breath. Her robe parted slightly. Red marks appeared on her skin.

He caught her up in one arm, and with a twist, he pulled the robe from her trembling form. Her bare breasts showed brutal marks of another man's hands. She was speaking. "Paxton . . . no, I can explain, I . . ." He never heard.

A blinding murderous rage filled him. He only knew he would kill him; once and for all, he would kill his brother.

His hands left her and Linness fell to a heap on the floor. She stumbled up and rushed after him, crying. She gripped his arm and he pushed her away. She fell again. He pulled his dagger out, and seeing this, she started screaming.

Morgan woke to Linness's screams and Paxton's vicious howl as he flew on top of him, the dagger raised and descending, mobilizing him in a rush. He twisted beneath Paxton's straddling weight, altering the weapon's entrance into his flesh. The dagger went through his arm, tearing off a piece of flesh with the movement. Morgan's howl of hot stinging pain was hardly heard against Paxton's rage as he pulled the bloody dagger from the bed and thrust it into Morgan's shoulder.

In desperation to stop him, Linness leaped onto the bed. Paxton's arm shot back with fatal force,

hitting her in the abdomen and chest. She never felt
the pain. Blackness exploded in her head as she fell
off the bed. Paxton paused, startled, and that saved
Morgan's life. Morgan sucked in a breath as he
jerked from underneath his brother and came to his
feet. He stood for the briefest moment before he fell
in a pool of blood.

Michaels and Clifford burst into the room and
stopped. The bishop, Father Thomas, Eleanor, and
Clair crowded in the doorway behind them. Startled gasps and screams sounded; more people
rushed into the room. Yet no one could move as
they stared at the shocking sight.

Morgan lay unconscious in a pool of blood on
one side. Linness lay unconscious on the other.
Blood rushed between her bare thighs. Paxton knelt
over her, pulling the gold robe over her naked
body, gathering her precious form in his arms and
burying his face against her warm flesh. . . .

Mary's light shone before God's benevolence, a
beckoning, enveloping light of love. Linness felt it
washing over her as she knelt, crying before Mary,
who held the child in her arms.

Linness reached out to touch the child. To hold
her just once. The baby girl with dark hair and blue
eyes. The child she would not have now but whom
she would always love . . .

For she was with Mary now. Mary's light fell in
a cascade of sadness and love over her as she cried.
She could not let her go, this girl she loved, and
she reached out again to take the child back to her
arms. Yet the light behind Mary intensified and
seemed to absorb her and the child.

The light was too bright to look at steadily as it

reached to her as well, beckoning, touching the middle finger of her right hand. Time and self disappeared in the light, and it was merciful beyond words. For in the space of the light she felt all things in the universe at the same time: It was like perceiving every grain of sand on every planet and knowing why each grain was in its place. And she was with Mary and her child. . . .

She could step into the light forever. . . .

She looked back across the distance, far, far away, like looking through a kaleidoscope to another time and place. She saw Paxton crying over her lifeless form. Paxton. Desire to touch him again pulled her away from the light. . . .

And then the light was gone.

Morgan lay in his huge bed. Bandages wrapped tightly around his arm and shoulder, blood still trickled out every time he moved. Still he would mend, the surgeons said. He would probably not lose much use of his arm either. The dagger had mercifully missed bone and tore only muscle, which heals, they said. Eventually.

Linness had saved him. The fact weighed heavily in his mind. . . .

He stared up at the ceiling, counting the rows of timber that held it up, waiting for sleep to claim him. A soft knock sounded on the door. He did not move. Somehow the hesitant sound of the knock told him it was Paxton. He had been expecting him. Yet now that his brother had come, he felt an anxious moment of fear.

For some part of him knew. Some part of him had always known, but the very idea had been too painful to bring into the light of scrutiny. So he had ignored it.

"Come in . . ."

Paxton approached his brother lying in the bed, naked, wrapped in bandages, covered in a bright blanket. His dark blue eyes filled with emotion as he stared at what he had done. He turned suddenly away, moving to the window.

He had prepared a short speech—words without meaning. No apology. For though he regretted the violence deeply, he could not apologize. To apologize was to regret loving her, Linness, his brother's wife.

He could not do that.

Once Linness had told him that her sight brought her a montage of many different aspects of his life: the endless training as a boy, his love of the creatures and the horses. She saw him in the midst of battle, and yet she also glimpsed him laughing with children and mourning the death of his first wife. She saw everything, she said, including the dark shadow over his life.

His brother. From the day he was born, Morgan's presence shadowed his life. In a powerful way Morgan was the reason behind everything he did and had become; Morgan was the reason for the self beneath his skin. He would never have become the man he was if not for having to reach beyond his brother. And it was Linness who pointed out this curious paradox of living in his brother's shadow; this had been the driving force in his life, and it had been very good.

The understanding was a humbling one.

There was only one thing in the whole of his life he could honestly claim had nothing to do with his brother, and that was his love for Linness. The force of his love had been there that first day he had rescued her from death, and it had grown even in the long years separating him from the shining memory of that one time together, increasing every blessed day he had known her. The cruel fate that she was Morgan's wife did not alter, change, or touch the deepest sense of his love for her. . . .

Except that it had come at last to separate them . . .

"Morgan, I—" Paxton stopped and said in a soft admission of frustration, "In truth I do not know what to say."

Morgan lay perfectly still. A burning began in his ears from all the words that would never be said, that could never be said. Emotions gathered in his chest, and it was strange and certainly unexpected that he should understand how much he loved his brother at this moment. As if the final violence between them had washed away all lingering traces of the hatred that always hid their brotherly love.

The one thing he could not blame Paxton for was falling in love with Linness. Michaels, Peters, John, Father Gayly, it sometimes seemed as if everyone fell in love with Linness. While his mind was not one to contemplate or understand people's motives, he had lain here in bed thinking on this, on how he could not blame any man, not even his brother, for falling in love with Linness. Then he had thought of the bishop.

It had struck him that perhaps the very same force of emotion was behind the man's hatred of Linness. Perhaps he, too, had found something in Linness that was better, softer, more beautiful and good, than anything in his own heart. Linness was a reality that shook everything he believed in, threatening the very foundation of his beliefs. So he had to destroy her.

So no, he did not blame his brother for falling in love with her. "But she is my wife." He finished the thought out loud; without really meaning to, he stated the unalterable fact.

The words were not without impact. Paxton straightened suddenly and nodded. "Aye," he agreed in a voice of inexpressible sadness, "she is your wife."

It seemed suddenly the summary, the whole, the reason of their life, was all a mistake. Morgan suffered a moment's confusion as he wondered at the sense of shame and guilt filling him. As if a great rock were being lowered to his chest. He shifted with discomfort.

"I am leaving," Paxton said.

And Morgan, of course, knew this.

Paxton scoffed suddenly, "Much to my surprise, the bishop was not unaffected. He has agreed to see his knights returned and gone from Gaillard if I leave. Morgan, I just need you to promise—"

"I will," Morgan said firmly. "I will never let him hurt her. Never," he swore.

Paxton nodded. "If ever he even comes close—"

"I will send for you at once."

"And do so in secret. The man has a habit of killing off messengers."

"Aye." Morgan nodded.

Paxton fell silent with the last request. The most important one. He did not know how much Morgan knew now; the question mattered little, he supposed, except as it affected him and Jean Luc.

He turned back and approached the bed. In a

whisper that conveyed his fear, he began, "Morgan, about Jean Luc . . ."

Paxton's fear filled his pause; Morgan desperately wanted to remove this fear. "Paxton, despite all that has happened, I do not know anyone else who I would trust to see Jean Luc to manhood. I have already told him he will be leaving with you."

Paxton shut his eyes as gratitude washed over him in force. "Thank you, brother."

Morgan reached his good arm across his chest, and in a startled moment, Paxton saw his own hand reaching out to meet his brother's. Long-dormant emotions rushed to the surface as they clasped each other firmly, a moment stretched in meaning; brothers by fate, and now, at last, brothers in heart.

With unsuppressed feeling, Paxton said the last. "Keep Linness safe, Morgan."

"Aye," he said.

Paxton nodded and turned. The door shut.

Linness had been prepared.

Lady Beaumaris retreated to the alcove, where she sat on the cushioned seat. Voices came from the hall outside the door: Jean Luc's high, youthful voice filled with excitement and questions, Paxton's deep voice answering each one in a pretense of the same excitement. If she closed her eyes and listened very carefully, she could perceive the veiled hint of Paxton's fear. The emotion hung over the room, the air grew heavy with it, and each breath seemed to demand conscious effort. . . .

Shaking her head sadly, she picked up her stitchery from the sewing box at her side, only to realize how her hands trembled. She gave up the pretense of industry, set it on her lap, and rested her dark eyes on Linness.

And she knew in that moment she had never loved Belinda as much. Weakened still, Linness managed to sit up on the bed. She wore a rich blue robe with tiny sparrows embroidered in silver thread along the border and sleeves—'twas Paxton's gift, one he had ordered made for her last month. She looked so terribly pale, her skin almost translucent as if her life were ebbing away even now. Unshed tears shimmered in her eyes, those beautiful silvery eyes, haunted by what was happening. Clair was anxiously brushing out her hair, smoothing it neatly down her back, taking her time doing it. To prolong the moment and stretch the silence, granting Linness the time she needed to gather her strength.

After Clair finished, Linness took her hand and lovingly brought it against her hot cheek, closing her eyes a moment. The gesture, so loving, expressing without words the comfort of Clair's affection, brought tears, shining like bright pools, to Clair. Linness opened her eyes, looked to the door, and nodded.

"Are ye sure?" Clair asked in a whisper.

"Aye . . ."

Clair looked at Lady Beaumaris, who nodded as well. Clair wiped her eyes with her apron and then moved to the door and opened it.

"Mother!" Bursting with excitement, Jean Luc flew into the room.

Paxton shut the door behind him, watching as Jean Luc rushed into her arms. For one brief moment Linness held her boy against her heart, closing her eyes to savor the moment, briefly, this last embrace.

And it was so mercilessly brief.

He pulled away, kneeling before her to stare into his mother's beautiful eyes and the tenderness in her smile as words tumbled out of his mouth about the long journey, the travel plans, no inns but "tents, like real warriors," his pony's new livery, his father's parting gifts, his uncle's promises, a torrent of childhood animation and enthusiasm that covered, like dirt over a shallow grave, the pain.

The boyish enthusiasm vanished as he saw his mother's tears. The words stopped. A hand reached to her face as he said, "You're crying. . . ."

The miracle was the lightness in her tone as she said, "I will miss you, is why! 'Tis a hard thing to see my son so grown, ready for his first adventure. Jean Luc, it is . . . so very hard for me to say good-bye to you. . . ."

His blue eyes searched her face, questioningly. He would miss his mother most of all. He still did not quite understand the thing that happened to her or why she could not come with them. If only she could. "Why can you not come with me?"

She caught her lip, she shook her head, smiled sadly. "I can . . . not. I—"

He threw his arms around her neck, clinging to her. Linness closed her eyes again as she heard him say, "I will miss you most of all."

"Aye," she said, holding the small, warm body tight. "I will miss you, Jean Luc. Everything about you," she told him, and then quietly, like a sonnet or a ballad, she named these things: "I will miss scolding you for trying to sneak off with Vivian's honey cakes or your father's dagger, I will miss swimming with you in the river, getting beaten at chess every day, I will miss trying to coax you to sleep at night. I will miss all our beautiful sunsets . . . I think most of all I will miss being pounced on every morning when you come into my bed to wake me up. . . ."

The room was quiet. She held him tightly, feeling his small body shake against her. "Jean Luc," she began quietly, "you will be back to visit and you will show me all the wonderful things Paxton has taught you." She pulled his arms from her neck and kissed him tenderly, wiping a tear that slipped down his cheek. "Good-bye, my love. . . ."

Jean Luc felt his throat constricting. He could not speak. He nodded as he tried to straighten. To his credit, he made it halfway to the door before he turned and ran back to her arms. Linness clung to him, as he managed, "I love you, Mother, I love you. . . ."

Linness held him as if she would never let him go. Paxton finally stepped to the bed; his hands came over the boy's shoulders, feeling their slight shake as he cried. He gently pulled him from Linness, lifting him up to his arms. He brought him to the door. Clair stepped forward to take his hand.

"Wait for me downstairs," he said.

"Let's go see what foodstuffs Vivian packed for the trip," she said. Lady Beaumaris rose quickly, too. All the excitement of the journey had vanished now as Jean Luc understood how hard it was to go. He knew he had to leave, that part of him even wanted to, but not for leaving her.

He took one last look at his mother. She stared back, tears filling her eyes and blurring her vision. She wiped them quickly, desperate to keep this last look in her memory for the long, empty days ahead.

And then he was gone.

Paxton shut the door.

She heard his boots approach the bed. He stood over her, staring down at the wet lashes brushing her cheek. She had pulled the covers over her lap, and held them tightly, desperate for something to cling to, and as he saw this, he felt as if the weight of his life were slipping away, disappearing into some hazy fog, and all he had left was this one impossible moment to say good-bye.

"I do not know how it is possible," she said, echoing his thoughts. "I know in a moment I will feel your arms come around me. I know that as you hold me, as I feel your arms for the last time, I know that somehow you will have to pick a moment to part from me. I keep wondering at this, how you can possibly pick that moment."

His fear of this truth filled the silence. He felt the tremble start in his hands as he hesitated, wanting so desperately to touch her one last time and yet terrified that it was true, that he would not have the strength to choose that moment.

Suddenly she was in his arms, clinging to him. He closed his eyes, feeling the slim and soft and warm form against him. The scent of her sadness filling him: the taste of tears and summer lilacs and warmth.

He wondered at how much pain it was possible to endure.

"Paxton, Paxton, tell me I will survive, that somehow I will find the strength to survive you leaving me. . . ."

He wanted to give her this; more than anything

in the world, he wanted to give her this strength. But he did not think he had it himself. Sometimes he felt he did have the necessary fortitude, but then, when he projected himself into this future, he saw only the empty shell of a man left. The understanding brought the awareness of just how much of himself she had claimed. Not just his heart but his very soul . . .

He closed his eyes tighter and held her so close, he was afraid he might hurt her, and still it was not enough. "Linness, I love you, I love you. . . ."

He drew back just to touch his mouth to hers, gently, tasting the lingering trace of her tears. He knew instantly it was a mistake. Desire was felt as a warm rush of feeling, of love; it blossomed and then changed with the surge of desperation. And he was drinking from her mouth like a dying man led to the sweet well of life. . . .

He broke the kiss, his breathing changed as he stared down at the lovely features of her upturned face. "Linness," he whispered. "Help me, Linness, help me now. . . ."

She felt the tension stealing into his body. "Nay, I can't, I can't."

She remembered little after that. His hands reached over her arms to take them away. The miracle of his first step away from her, then the next. Her vision blurring as the door opened. The sound of it shutting.

The light was gone. Darkness surrounded her, penetrating physically, a darkness made of silence, emptiness, longing. The darkness that was to be for the rest of her life . . .

Chapter 12

"Wait, milady! Wait!"

Linness stopped and turned to see Morgan flagging her from the steps of the château. He raced down, taking the steps two at a time until he reached her. His arm still rested in a sling. He had lost weight since his injury and he drank much less, even though he, like all of them, felt the weight of what had happened. Like a dark cloud over all of Gaillard, there was no happiness here, and no drink could possibly cure it.

His brown eyes brushed over her. The cloak seemed to swallow her whole, leaving only her pale face and her deep, sad eyes uncovered. Hollowed rings underlined the gray eyes, making them look larger, too large for the delicate features. A basket rested on one bent arm. She was leaving again. Just as she did every afternoon. He was losing her, he knew, and he felt helpless to save her.

"Where are you going, milady?"

His voice was curiously soft and filled with his anxiety for her. "To the old quarry," she said.

"Again?"

"Aye."

"Why?"

She settled her gaze on the horizon appearing through the gate. " 'Tis a place where I find solace, is all."

He paused as he tried to think of something to say. Now even Clair, whom she loved, was gone. They had sent her to Beaumont to be with Jean Luc. The boy had become despondent, missing his mother too much, and though neither of them wanted to lose Clair now, it was all they could think to do to ease the ache in Jean Luc's heart. "I'll send Michaels with you—"

"No, please, milord," she begged. "I need to be alone. I need desperately to be alone. . . ." Then, without looking at him, as if to herself, she said, "She died last night. . . ."

He drew back with shock, thinking of Clair. "Who?"

"The lady in black. Paxton's wife."

A chilly breeze lifted the heavy circle of her winter cloak as he searched her face to guess the significance she found in this death. He saw at once it did not matter. He felt a twinge of relief, before he realized it really didn't matter. It altered nothing for her, meant nothing to her.

No one ever saw Linness cry. Ever. Yet the tears hung like mist in her eyes, shimmering like a haunting light, and conveyed the extent of her struggle as no words could. Father Thomas had begun hearing her confession, and last night the man hinted that he was afraid she was losing her will to live.

"Not suicide?!"

"Nay," the father said, " 'tis more subtle, as if life is just slipping from her."

And the words had struck him with fear, for

every night he suffered a nightmare about this very thing. Though she went about life in the same manner she had always gone about it, she was so different, so terribly changed. 'Twas indeed as the good father said, the light of her life was fading.

He hadn't wanted to believe it, that she was as much in love with Paxton as Paxton was with her. At first he had been imagining only Paxton had loved her, like everyone else; his brother had gone and fallen in love with his wife. It never occurred to him how very much she had fallen in love with Paxton as well.

The idea was a punishing one.

Because he, too, loved her. For in his mind she was like no other woman. And it was not just her miraculous sight and visions, but her extreme kindness, the intelligence and perspicacity of her understandings, the music of her laughter with his son, and its effect on his heart, the wealth of her simple and good love for people, all people. He only understood how much he had come to love Linness since he lost her. It was rather a subtle and gradual building of respect and admiration, a softening of his own rough edges. . . .

He looked away, as if it were too hard to see her now, and he thought, love—what a cursed proposition! If he didn't love her, it wouldn't matter at all. He would be able to bear the profundity of her unhappiness; her happiness would not be the treasure that it was.

Every night he dreamt of her now. Drink could not alter this dream, its vividness of emotion. In this dream he saw her, Linness, and she was fading. Just fading, becoming less and less until she was gone, and as he watched this fading, he felt a mounting desperation to save her. Paxton always appeared at his side to yell: "Keep her safe, Morgan! Keep her safe!" His desperation mounted, helplessly; he watched in fear, a growing fear of her death, and this fear dropped him to his knees, crying, wanting to save her but not knowing how.

When he woke there were real tears in his eyes.

He was going mad. His anxiety to help her mounted as her melancholy grew. If only he knew what to do . . .

Her hand emerged from the folds of her cloak. She reached to his face, to soothe the anxious lines of his brow. There was tenderness and sympathy in her touch. Then, wordlessly, she turned away.

Morgan's gaze followed her cloaked figure until she faded in the distance.

The desolate landscape loomed eerily against its solitary bleakness, this place she always came to in the afternoon. The quarry made of nothing but piles of dirt, rock, and empty holes filled with water. It was about two miles downriver from Gaillard, the place where long ago the rocks had been dug for the château and the township.

The bishop stared down from the highest ridgeline. Why did she come here to pray at such a cold and barren landscape?

The forest started just beyond the ridge where he and Father Thomas stood watching her. The bishop held out his hand, and in silence, Father Thomas gave him the spyglass. The bishop brought it to his eyes and aimed it at the spot where she knelt in prayerful supplication.

She wore a dark blue woolen cape that surrounded her in a half circle, its hood drawn over her hair. Her eyes were shut. Through the magnifying power of the glass he could see her slightly parted lips, the small breaths drawn in and out. He imagined he could see her humility at last.

A haunting serenity surrounded the woman.

He dismissed the perception; he was not to be deceived. Satan took no rest. Nothing would separate him from his purpose: to bring this depraved and wicked woman before God. At last he had sent the damning evidence—twenty pages of proof—to the Vatican, to demonstrate the necessity of an ecclesiastic trial.

He had begun reading the copy of this again last night. At first he had thought it had been altered. Somehow, by treachery, she had altered the testimony so he suddenly could not see from these carefully penned words how it was that she turned the faithful from God. Yet how could she alter the paper in which the testimony was writ? 'Twas impossible.

He read them over again, then twice more. Yet, all the anecdotes seemed suddenly innocent, unworthy of his interest even, let alone the interest of his Vatican superiors. He felt an embarrassed prick of panic at the idea.

He needed something more, something with far greater weight and profanity. He was hoping her mysterious sojourns to the quarry would provide it. Father Thomas promised he would be greatly surprised by the things that transpired here.

Father Thomas would know this, for he had begun hearing the lady's confession. "So," he said to the priest at his side, "this is where she comes every day?"

"Aye, milord."

"She is always alone?"

"Always."

"And from here you say she goes to the chapel?"

"She lights a candle at Mary's altar for vespers."

He nodded, and still looked down at her. He knew he should not ask it, but he had to know. The question pressed so heavily on his mind, the answer would be the explanation of her power, how she had . . . had changed Father Thomas. "You hear her confession now?"

Father Thomas straightened visibly, hesitating. Why should he be surprised that the bishop would approach the issue? "Aye, milord . . ."

"I would hear what was confessed."

Father Thomas stared intently at the lone figure kneeling in the distance. He wondered if the bishop would be changed, too, by hearing the lady's confession. No, probably not, he realized. His mind was fixed on the idea she was a danger to the faithful; he filtered everything through cold and hateful eyes.

He himself had not wanted to be changed, but he had, for her confession was a window to her heart. A rich and sacred place, it was, a place where he had found, much to his surprise, he could pass no judgment. He alone was witness to her struggle and suffering, and through this witnessing he found the light of his own heart changed, altered, different. The change, he had come to understand, was his own redemption.

Now he found himself desperate to save her.

He lied, of course, the lesser sin. "Nothing extraordinary, milord."

The bishop let the glass drop as he asked, "Why

does she come here?" Angrily he asked, "Do you even know?"

"Aye. I have come three times now."

He turned to see Father Thomas's face much changed by something he saw. "Why?"

"You will see," he said.

The men stood atop the ridgeline, staring down. The sun set and shadows lengthened. A sudden gust of wind blew down from the ridge, echoing through the stones of the quarry, and sent shimmering ripples over the stilled water of the desolate ponds. The bishop watched as Linness suddenly opened her eyes to stare at the cliff before her. A tremor of alarm shot up his spine as he followed her gaze.

A contorted pile of rocks stood between the woman's kneeling form and the cliff. The sun set behind it. A shadow climbed up the cliff as the winter sun blazed colors of gold and orange around it. A miracle of image formed: a tall shrouded figure holding a child. Mary and the Christ child.

The mystery of the holy image held him spellbound.

Then it was gone. The violet sky darkened. Linness genuflected and rose; head down, she turned to make her way back to Gaillard. The bishop remained in stunned silence, staring off at the place where it happened. His vision blurred and for a long moment he wondered wildly what was wrong. His hands reached up, rubbing his eyes. He let out a bewildered gasp as he felt the heat of his tears on his cold hands.

The bishop's face changed horribly; his thoughts were written there. He was thinking this was somehow a trick of magic, that she had tricked him. Father Thomas looked away, saddened by this revelation. He would not be surprised if the bishop wanted the quarry and the rock pile examined, an explanation produced, the lady damned by it.

The poor foolish man . . .

Abruptly the bishop turned away, his crimson robes flapping in the wind.

Father Thomas knew something must be done to save her. Someone, somehow, had to save her before the bishop won his hateful, misguided campaign against her.

And he began to pray. . . .

The window was always left unlatched, and except for the coldest days, open. The servants had learned never to latch the window against the incessant drafts; like a bad omen, it could bring tears or an inexplicable panic to their lady's eyes. She often sat there, too, in the alcove by the open window staring out. As if she were waiting for something.

Beaumont had sent the birds last week. Pigeons that were said to fly from one spot to the next, capable of bearing messages. With a fervent prayer Linness had released the three birds from this window ten days ago.

The window from which Paxton appeared in secret . . .

A fire blazed in the hearth. Linness sat at her window, a blanket on her lap, as she carved Jean Luc's bow for Christmas gift giving. His letters tried to assure her that he was thriving, yet she knew this was a half-truth. For she saw her boy crying alone at night for missing his mother. She knew an overwhelming desire when her sight brought her images of Jean Luc, crying with this longing. Yet she was unable to go to him. Yesterday she saw Paxton find Jean Luc on the highest turret. The wind pulled tears from Jean Luc's eyes as he watched the sunset and thought of her.

In desperation she had sent Clair off on the long journey to Beaumont. Clair would be a comfort to her boy, not the same as herself but the next best thing. Needless to say, she had not wanted to lose Clair and Clair had not wanted to go, but they agreed it would only be for a year, no more, until Jean Luc was stronger and more grown, accustomed to his new life. She had not known what else to do. . . .

She saw Paxton's dark blue eyes, too, mirrors of her own, made of longing, the terrible longing that stole her voice and silenced her laughter, that made a smile an act of will. When would it abate? When would the ache in her heart ease, the longing cease, the memories fade?

The answer was death.

Death alone would alter this life. She wondered if her own longing would lessen if she could ease their pain. If she could wipe their love from their hearts, would she? Was it better to have known their love and suffered its loss or to have never had such a gift?

She was glad she did not have that choice.

Yet hadn't she made that choice? She had, but in ignorance. Long ago she had begged Mary to let her know a man's love and a mother's love, and Mary had granted the wish. So it had come to pass.

And now only death was left. . . .

The lady in black had died. She saw her two nights ago, lying on the small cot in a strange convent, not the one she had always known. Two sisters murmured prayers, drawing the cloth over her head. John had been at her side.

"I am not long for the world," the lady in black had foretold in one of the many dreams in which she had mysteriously appeared. It was odd how sometimes she felt as if the lady talked of herself, as if she, Linness of Sauvage, were not long for the world. As if the lady and herself had been blended into one person. It scared her now, the knowledge that only death could save her.

The vision was no comfort now. It did not seem to matter anymore. Paxton would still be separated from her. Francis might even find him another wife. . . .

A bird circled in the winter blue sky. Lower and lower it flew as if searching for something. She watched its flight, not hoping, not yet. Paxton had sent the homing pigeons more than a week past, but it could not have flown its journey so fast. . . .

The bird circled just above. Her heart leaped to greet the tiny creature as it landed on the ledge outside. She leaned out the window, slowly, afraid she would scare it away. It was interested in the tiny grains she placed there every night, faithfully, before she went to sleep.

The creature approached, exercising its own caution. She focused on the tiny paper wrapped tightly around its thin leg. Paxton's letters were read by Morgan, and there was nothing intimate in the carefully scripted words. And so that tiny paper represented a small piece of Paxton for her eyes only; that tiny paper was a potion powerful enough to ease the ache in her heart.

Or so she thought . . .

She called sweetly to the creature, leaning back inside. The bird hopped onto the windowsill and let out a soft coo. She slowly reached for it; gentle and loving hands encircled the bird. She slipped the tiny loop from his leg and set the bird back to the ledge.

She unfolded the paper. Paxton's voice sounded in her mind as she read his mercilessly brief words:

Thy memory burns bright in thy absence, resounding in scorching lashes upon my soul. I am but an empty vessel without you and I dream of filling my empty flesh with the warmth of yours. I cannot go on much longer, and yet somehow I do: ghostlike, a hollow echo of my former self. I dream each night and I wonder if it is death I am seeing.

Linness, I love you. . . .

A knock sounded softly.

Linness wiped her eyes and sat up, crumpling the treasure in her hand. Morgan opened the door and stepped inside. She stared in wonder at his presence. His gaze roamed the surroundings with agitation, as if unable to settle on anything until finally they came to rest on her.

She looked so beautiful against the gray stones and the winter light shining through the window. She wore a maroon gown that made her skin seem paler.

He saw that she had been crying. A bird cooed behind her, happily pecking at grains left on the sill. One of Paxton's pigeons. He then looked for the message. His gaze came to her hand.

"Morgan, what is it?"

"You have been crying."

She turned away to the window, putting her back to him.

"Did he send you a message?"

There was no answer. Then softly she said, "Morgan, do not torment us more. . . ."

She did not say do not torment *me* but rather *us*, and the fact registered in his mind. As if she knew of his torment, too.

She asked quietly, "What do you want?"

"Only your happiness."

The answer went through her like a small shock, but after a moment, she shook her head. 'Twas impossible. " 'Tis not yours to give me." It never was; it never could be. It had been bought with her heart long ago.

"I know," he confessed. "Sometimes I think I always knew. But when he was here it did not seem to matter. I guess I thought it would just all work out, but . . . but it hasn't, has it?"

His voice held the unexpressed weight of his feelings, and it touched her heart. She shook her head again and in a whisper she said, "Morgan, I am sorry, I am so sorry. . . . I do not think you deserve this. . . ."

"I am not as sure."

She turned round to face him, looking at him questioningly. He waved his hand as if to dismiss his next words. "Paxton spent a good part of his life envying me, what was granted me by right of being the firstborn. And now as we reach this point in our lives, I find it is my turn to envy him." His voice lowered with regret. "For how deeply this cuts. Milady, I envy him your love. . . ."

Emotions shimmered in her eyes. She did not

know what to say, what she could ever say. There was no changing what had been done.

"Aye," he said. "I have this nightmare every night now. And in it I see you and you are fading; like a ghost or worse, you start to fade, to disappear before my very eyes. Then Paxton appears. The day he left he made me promise to keep you safe forever, and in this dream he says it again, over and over: Keep her safe, keep her safe." In frustration he added, "But I am helpless to stop this fading!

"Until last night. Last night Paxton said something different. Last night he did not say to keep you safe. No, he said to me: Let her go, Morgan, let her go. . . ."

A trembling hand went to her mouth. This was too painful. "Morgan, please—"

He stepped to her, shaking his head as his hands came over her arms. She stared up into his face: the dark brown hair, curling at the ends, the widely spaced brown eyes and the arch of his brows, the strong tilt of his nose. For the first time since she understood the mistake of marrying him, she saw his similarity to Paxton. 'Twas a trick of the light or the heart, the way he suddenly seemed so like Paxton: the strength in his gaze, and aye, the love there.

And he said slowly, "I want to do this. I want to let you go. . . ."

She shook her head, her eyes wild with confusion. "But you can't, Morgan, you can't. We are married. Only death can set me free!"

"Aye." He nodded. "Only death can set you free. . . ."

* * *

The bishop's deep, rich voice rose with the Latin prayer in heartfelt admonishment of man's grievous sins, lowering with the undeserved absolution God offered. The sun was fading fast. The huge stained-glass windows in the chapel depicting Mary holding the Child darkened, so the Madonna's red cloak turned crimson and then brown as her sad eyes turned from a pale blue to dark ones. The light in her eyes appeared to dim with the bishop's inflection. This was what Lady Beaumaris thought as she knelt at Morgan's side for vespers, waiting, nervous, terrified something would go wrong, terrified something had gone wrong.

Four guards had been sent out to search, including Michaels. They would be returning any moment. The announcement would be made to everyone.

Morgan comprehended the lady's anxiety as it was his own, too. He reached a hand to hers and squeezed, reassuring her.

The carved wooden doors of Gaillard's chapel burst open. Peters stood there, looking mortified as he announced, "Milord! Something terrible has happened!"

The bishop's gaze widened; he drew back with a start. Morgan rose, as did Lady Beaumaris. The roomful of people held their breaths. "Aye?! You have found the lady?"

"Nay. We found only her dress! At the edge of the river. She must have gone in! The light was fading and she was nowhere to be seen. Michaels leaped into the water to try and find her and, and *Mon Dieu*, he hath not come out, and we fear, we fear—"

Screams and startled cries broke out. No more

words were heard in the sudden pandemonium as the news was absorbed. Morgan was rushing out to join in the obviously futile search, his face pale with the shock. Lady Beaumaris clasped her hands together with a brief cry as she sunk to the pew in a crumpled pile of gold muslin.

Father Thomas felt his hands go clammy, his pulse and blood a great roar in his ears. He turned to stare at the bishop. The man stood staring at the chaos before him, staring without seeing. He didn't know how he knew, but he did; Bishop Luce was thanking God for her death.

It didn't matter, he supposed. It was over for him. He would have to accept Duprat's banishment to Florence and no doubt live out the remainder of his days in silence and anonymity. He would never know the truth. For neither the lady's nor Michaels's body would ever be found. Drownings occurred, if not with frequency, at least with sad regularity in Gaillard. The river was a fierce and swollen monster at this time of year. They rarely found the bodies of its victims. . . .

The truth was that death had indeed saved her.

He genuflected quickly. For show. For luck.

Bishop Luce turned to stare at the stained-glass window of Mary as he attempted to absorb this shock. It was over. So sudden. So easily. The woman was dead now; drowned by suicide or accident, she was dead.

His head spun with the unexpectedness of this as he grasped the startling fact: His work here was done at last; with God's help, it was done. The judgment of Linness of Sauvage rested in His hands now. Holy visions or clever ruse, pious or wicked, God alone would know in His infinite wisdom. Now he could accept Duprat's final edict that sent him to the holy order of the Franciscans in faraway Florence.

As he stared up at Mary, his mind still spinning, he felt a sudden prick up his spine. He imagined Mary called to him to find his compassion. He turned away, confused. He suspected even then he would wonder all his days: What was God's final judgment of the woman?

Paxton kept a light burning as he lay upon the huge bed, easing his frame against the soft cushions. The light helped him delay sleep as long as possible. Sleep offered the only respite from the darkness, the emptiness, the longing, but it also brought him to the very edge of madness with his dreams: erotic dreams of Linness.

She appeared to him every night. . . .

Shrouded in a tousled mass of thick, curly hair, her beautiful silver eyes darkening with passion as he laid her to the ground. His desire heightening, thickening his blood as she reached out to him and he eased his weight against her. The heat in his loins magnified as he stared down at her rounded breasts, the small curve of her narrow waist, the feminine flair of her hips, and the long line of her legs. He listened avidly to her cries as he orchestrated her passion, raising it to crescendo until, finally, mercifully, he parted her slender thighs and—

Then he'd wake.

And she would be gone.

So sleep became the cruelest tease, one that left him restless and frustrated and dark with the longing of unanswered desire, a lingering sense of the hopelessness of his life. So he fought the cruel night's play, delaying sleep in hopes that he would be too tired to suffer through his dreams of her: Linness, the only woman he would ever love.

Linness, his brother's wife.

If Jean Luc did not start adjusting better to her absence, he would have to send him back to Gaillard. Clair eased some of it, but it was still bad for him, and damn if Clair was not heartsick from missing Linness as well. Jean Luc's appetite suffered, his tutor said his mind wandered constantly, and more than anything, he showed little enthusiasm for so many things he once loved. He himself was no better off than his boy, a good deal worse. The only difference was he had a man's ability to hide emotions.

If it were any other woman, he would force the boy to pass through his loneliness, but because it was Linness, he knew it in a different light. Linness claimed so much of those who loved her. Her love was a warm and fine light in their life; now that it was gone, life was empty, colorless, meaningless.

He stared unseeing at the empty spaciousness of the room, barren except for the bed and his four trunks, the fire still blazing in the brick and stone hearth. The new furnishings, being made in Paris, had not arrived as yet. There were no carpets on the wooden floor or paintings on the wall. The stark and vacant room seemed to mirror his soul. . . .

The farming village sat twelve miles from Beaumont, in Alsace, four miles from the start of Paxton's land. An inn was nestled at the crossing point of the two main thoroughfares, and this modest establishment had been owned by the same family for two hundred years. The current generation of proprietors prided themselves on the inn's cleanliness and their hospitality. Gone were the days when they were more likely to get robbed than paid, when every man who walked through the door was viewed with suspicion. King Francis had brought peace to France at last, and now, with the region's new lordship, Lord General Paxton de Chamberlain, there would be many travelers who stopped before making the last half day's trip to the grand château.

The proprietor's wife had grown up in the Swiss Alps, and the charming little house looked more Swiss than French. It had a high thatched roof, open shutters, and windows lined with flower boxes. There were four rooms upstairs to let. Four or even more people could stay in one room on straw mattresses, but of course, when it was a person of distinction or nobility, he would take a whole room to himself.

The entrance and tiny rooms of the bottom floor—where the aging owner and his wife lived— opened onto a tavern. They were sound asleep when they were roused from bed by the cowbell outside the door. The woman rose dutifully, and hurriedly pulled on a smock and smoothed her graying hair as she made her way to the door.

The door opened and she confronted the stranger. An older man dressed in fine traveling clothes. A short, weary-looking servant stood behind him. She murmured a sleepy greeting as she opened the door, mentally assessing how much they would be willing to pay as they stepped inside.

"There is no one about to take ye horses," she told them abruptly, hospitality always a bit wanting in the middle of the night. "Ye can unhitch the horses and bring them into the stables. A bucket of oats be a half ducat. We have two rooms left, at four ducats apiece; ye can take one room or both. A pot of stew for two ducats, all the ale ye can drink for two more." Few men could drink much after midnight before they fell asleep, she knew. Like the young man in the tavern. Fell right over his first cup of ale, and never made it up to his bed, he had been so weary.

John Chamberlain had traveled over three hundred miles in three weeks, certain every mile of the long journey had stolen precious time saved for the end of his life. Never had he felt the weight of his years more. He imagined when he reached Beaumont tomorrow, it would be a very long time before he would be able to return to Gaillard. He had only one question of the good woman as he withdrew his money bag: "Are the beds feather or straw?"

"Straw," she said with a slight grin, "but once you're asleep, a body hardly knows the difference."

He supposed she was right. He handed her the money as his man left to tend to the horses. He directed the woman to present two bowls of stew and cups of ale before approaching the tavern.

It was dark there. A single lantern hung over the place where a man sat at the table, his head resting across folded arms. John eased his weary bones onto a bench across the way. He looked at the man again. The same gold hair as someone else he knew—

John's gaze dropped to the young man's spurs and then his cloak. "Michaels!"

The man did not stir. John got up and stepped over to him. "*Mon Dieu!* Michaels! Wake up, good man!"

Michaels lifted his sleepy head and opened his eyes. The familiar face came into focus. "Milord! By the heavens! What are you doing here?"

"I'm returning, at last, from Milan. I stopped on my way to Beaumont, of course. But what are you doing here? Do you have a letter for Paxton from his brother?" He imagined some kind of catastrophe. "Why would not the usual carriers do?"

Michaels froze, his gaze darting to and fro before, with a deep sigh, he vigorously rubbed his face, as if to come more awake. He would have to tell John. In the rush of all that happened, Morgan had never said whether John would be one of the few people who would be told the truth, but of course, he would have to be. John must be told the truth—not only had he come to love Linness dearly, but he would be one of the very few people to travel between Paxton's and Morgan's estates.

Indeed he was traveling there now. . . .

"Milord, I have a story to tell. . . ."

"Is anything amiss? What has happened?"

"You will not believe all that has," he began just as the old woman appeared with two bowls of stew and mugs of ale. These were set on the table. John ordered for another to be brought to his servant. The woman rushed back to fill Michaels's cup. She noticed the intense look as the younger man began a story, and she hoped the house generosity had not been a mistake after all. . . .

Two hours later, after she'd refilled their cups several times, the men were still talking. She not only knew that it was a mistake, but that even the overcharge for the oats would not cover it. She gave up waiting for them to retire and went to bed herself. . . .

The whole incredible story had been laid before the older man and he turned a thoughtful gaze up the stairs. "So she is sleeping up there now?"

"I had to force her. She kept falling over in the saddle. I promised I'd wake her in one hour, so we could reach Beaumont by midnight, but God knows she needs a full night's rest after this trip, and anyway, we are days ahead of the messenger bringing the news of her *death*. . . ."

"And Paxton knows nothing of this incredible plot?"

"Nay," Michaels said. "Nothing . . ."

John sat quietly on the edge of the bed, watching her sleep, deeply, dreamlessly. He had woken feeling surprisingly refreshed. Nothing could revive an old man like a happy ending to this love story.

She stirred in her sleep, nudging her face against the pillow. The trilling cries of birds out the window roused her senses and she dreamt briefly of glorious pigeons in flight, then of porridge, great big bowls of steaming porridge. She woke with a rumble of hunger stirring through her, and this itself was strange, for she had not had much of an appetite for some time.

Light poured through the closed shutters of the window and she opened her eyes. The man sitting on the edge of her bed made her gasp. "John . . ."

"Michaels told me."

"Everything?"

John nodded. She waited to see his condemnation but saw his smile instead. She returned a tentative smile. He said, "The magnitude of what Morgan gave you—"

She interrupted in a whisper, "Is nothing less than my life."

The emotion in which this was uttered registered through him, like a caressing sweep of warm wind; her words conveyed the profundity of the gratitude she felt. Nothing less than her life and—" 'Tis Paxton's life as well. . . ."

She nodded and then he was reaching for her. She fell into his embrace and closed her eyes, willing down her impatience to reach Beaumont, but she was so close, so terribly close. Today she would be in Paxton's arms and she would witness his joy. Today she would feel his lips, touch his smile, today she would lay her head against his heart and hear its swift, steady beat . . .

Today and every day for the rest of her life . . .

She pulled back to see into his thoughtful gaze, wise beyond his years.

"You're crying, milady. . . ."

"For happiness." She nodded, a tingling warmth suffusing her. "A happiness I never dreamt I would know."

"Let's get ready, milady. My coach is waiting."

By the time she was finally prepared, the sun reached the meridian and shone in a rare winter brightness. Michaels and John waited for Linness outside by the coach. She stepped into the sunshine in a burst of pretty violet colors. Paxton's favorite dress—the only one she took. There was no one to dress her hair, and so it fell unbound to her waist, held back by a matching purple band.

John thought Linness had never looked more beautiful. Her smile, soft and mysterious, seemed to light his soul from the inside out. Curiously, he felt as if he were delivering a daughter to her new husband, and how strange that was! How strange the entire magical circumstances of this one young woman's life!

Linness felt as if she walked in a dream.

"I've never been in a coach," she said, seeing John's two trunks secured on top.

"After what you've been through, you'll find it quite comfortable, I'm sure."

She gathered her skirts and stepped up. 'Twas like a small room suspended on four wheels. The curtains were drawn over windows. It had maroon velvet-lined seats and a wooden floor, and as she reclined, she realized it was in fact quite comfortable. Anything would be comfortable after the ten days riding a horse across France, snatching bits and pieces of sleep at small inns, and most often the forest floor. That she could still pull her knees together seemed nothing short of a miracle.

Every moment seemed suffused with the light of a miracle. Mary's miracle. The gift of Mary's love in her life.

She willed her heart to slow for what she knew would be the longest part of her very protracted journey. John took the seat across from her, while the Lady Beatrice's sole remaining servant sat on a narrow cushioned seat above, to hold the reins. Michaels rode alongside, holding the extra horse.

The coach started forward.

The area they crossed first was made of an endless stretch of flat farmland, barren now before the spring planting. Mountains rose in the farthest distance where Beaumont waited. Where her new life waited. She tried to temper the race of her thoughts with the question of what she would tell Jean Luc. Morgan begged her to tell the truth as simply as she could: that it was the only way they knew that she could be with him. . . .

She abruptly realized John was speaking to her about his own mission in Italy to oversee Paxton's estates. He didn't realize her mind could not fix on a thing so simple as a string of words. Not now.

Though John had always found in Linness an intelligent and perceptive listener. He had often counted on her help in making Morgan see reason through his impetuous and rash judgments to the better policy, and so, long denied any familiar company, he discussed the land preparations he had made, all the purchases, his worries over leaving, the two men he left to oversee the properties, what they were like, the repairs he initiated. "And, you see, if we could just get the western fields to barley by March . . ."

She nodded, smiling, while internally excitement burst through her in a heady rush; 'twas all she could do not to stop the carriage and run the rest of the way. She cast her gaze out the window, tilting her head to see the mountains rising in the far distance, much larger than any at Gaillard.

An outward calm concealed her inner turmoil and excitement. What would he do when he learned of their changed fate? Of what Morgan had given them? She kept forgetting that while she had this long time to contemplate this miracle, he was in ignorance still. . . .

She remembered the ferocity of the battles after they made love, lying entwined in each other's arms and fighting desperately against the thief stealing their last moments together. Sleep. Often the poignancy of his lovemaking would make her cry, but once she remembered waking to see the tears shimmering in his soft, dark eyes as well. . . .

"I love you, Linness, I love you. . . ."

"Michaels said you foresaw the Lady Beatrice Lucia's death? That you already told Morgan . . ."

She abruptly understood what he was saying and realized John waited for a reply. She could barely create a polite pretense of acknowledgment of his wife's death. "Aye," she added stupidly, "she was so young. . . ."

"She was such a strange creature, you know," John mused out loud as the carriage brought her closer and closer to her blessed destiny. "And it was odd, but one of the few things she said to me was that she feared she would not make the trip. I thought it was her extreme delicacy speaking; imagine that she had never once left the small convent where she grew up! The Italians are so circumspect and protective of their women. The cloistered life made her shy and withdrawn, so much so that I always had the horrible feeling my mere voice was an assault on her nerves."

The carriage hit a rivet in the road and Linness braced against the seat. "She had appeared in my dreams since the first day I met Paxton."

"Did she? Mercy, but your sight is a mysterious window to the future."

"Aye. Sometimes. She was in my dreams often after that, too. I thought of her as the lady in black. I knew somehow our lives were intertwined, but I did not know how, or even who she was until I discovered that Paxton would be marrying." She added with regret, for it had been all for naught, "Then, then I knew envy."

All for nothing, she realized now. She didn't want to imagine how hard it would be if the lady had not died and was instead brought to Beaumont as Paxton's wife. Many, if not most noblemen, kept their mistresses at their homes, often as a waiting woman to their lawful wives. Though the blessing of Paxton's love would have made such a position bearable and she would like to think she would have borne it with dignity, she was very glad things worked out otherwise.

Paxton, thankfully, would not likely have to marry again. Though if they were blessed with another child, the babe would be a bastard. She swallowed the painful reality and told herself it would not matter—it was the fate of thousands. They would have their parents' love and their father's wealth, and that was far more than so many children had. . . .

Thinking on it, she asked quietly, "How did she die? I saw her laid to rest in a convent, but somehow I knew 'twas not the convent she had always known."

"Ah, it began with a head cold right at Marseilles. She did not want to halt our journey, but she was soon feverish. We stopped at a small nunnery, part of a rectory. I stayed at an inn nearby, a lovely place by the seashore. I visited every day, but it was clear she was not getting well." He thought again of her strange last words and almost didn't mention them, but it was a curiosity—they had made no sense. "Her last words to me were so odd really. Feverish delusions, no doubt, though she had seemed unnaturally lucid in her last moments—"

"What did she say?"

"She said someone wants to step into my shoes. Aye! That's just what she said. Then she whispered, 'I hope the blessed Mary sees that they fit,' and it was strange, all last night I kept dreaming I was trying to fit a lady's large feet into small shoes. . . ."

Linness's eyes grew wide, and to his surprise, she laughed. "She meant me, do you not think? I always thought of her just like that—as the woman who had everything, the only thing I ever wanted: to be Paxton's wife. But now I am dead and I am nobody again—mercy, but I do not even have a name anymore. . . ."

"No, you do not, do you?"

Linness stopped thinking long enough to see a strange expression cross over John's face. "What is it?" she asked. " What are you thinking?"

He was thinking of shoes, of fitting a lady's large feet into small shoes, of a dying woman's last words. He was thinking how no one, but no one, of any consequence or importance had ever actually seen the Lady Beatrice Lucia, except for the one servant, a good man who could easily be paid off. His mind raced and he saw that while there were bound to be a few people going back and forth between Beaumont and Gaillard, the distance of three hundred miles would keep that number very small, and with any effort, it could be completely limited to those who knew and loved Linness. He was thinking he had the lady's death certificate in his trunk.

He was thinking she had done it once, and somehow, miraculously, she had managed to make everyone believe. He was thinking she could do it again.

Yet suddenly what John was thinking mattered not at all, for Michaels's exclamation sounded. "We must be approaching Beaumont!"

The carriage started down the main thoroughfare of a village. She looked out the window. She climbed on the seat and stuck her head out for a better view. They were quickly passing through the small, sleepy village and onto a road, divided by apple orchards, that led to Beaumont.

Forests surrounded the outlying area.

The château rose in the distance about a mile away. It was growing dark. The setting sun cast the vast park that surrounded the château in lovely hues of gold and pink, and the faintest violets. She knew this grand place. She had seen it a hundred times in her dreams. Dreams created by the many descriptions Paxton and his architects had discussed: descriptions of the magnificent forests, interrupted by huge, chaotic rocks, piling up in "the most savage landscapes. . . ."

A square acre of parkland had been forged from this. The carriage passed quickly through the lawns, and the château came closer into view. It was as beautiful as she had imagined.

She spotted riders in the distance.

"Stop!" she called breathlessly. "Stop!"

The carriage came to a halt.

The sunsets were the worst.

"Why, Jean Luc? Why do the sunsets affect you?"

They were returning from their afternoon ride back to Beaumont. Jean Luc shrugged at the question. 'Twas hard to say in words. Words could not explain how the heaviness in his heart felt like a physical pain in his chest; a pain that made him breathe too much, then not enough; that made it hard to eat and harder to sleep. Words could not explain how he feared he would never see his mother again, that was all, and if he could just see his mother, just have one look at her, he felt he would be all right. Words could not explain about the sunsets.

For whenever his mother and he could, they went to the battlements to watch the sunset over the narrow forested mountain range behind the river. She held him in front of her, her arms wrapped around him, and they'd watch the sinking sun for the two minutes exactly that it took for the rim of the sun to disappear. He remembered how once she wondered if God was part of nature or the creator of nature, and she suspected the former. It was one of the secrets they shared.

"The sunset reminds me of my mother, you see. 'Tis so beautiful and then it's gone. . . ."

Paxton drew up his horse. The horse stopped and he reached over to grab the reins of Jean Luc's pony. "Nay," he said in a fierce whisper, as much to himself as to his boy. "She's not gone. We will see her again. I promise—"

A feminine cry sounded in the distance and he turned to look across the lawns. His breath caught. A woman was running towards them, and how strange, she wore a violet dress and her hair—

Jean Luc stared, too, but unlike his uncle, he knew he was not imagining what he was seeing. He slipped off his mount and then he was running.

John and Michaels watched the tender scene

from the distance. Linness knelt down to embrace
Jean Luc and hold him tight in her arms. She was
crying and kissing his tearful face before she released him just long enough to run into Paxton's
arms.

Paxton seemed for a moment too stunned by the
miraculous sight to move, and suddenly he was
swinging her around and around. The sound of his
laughter reached across the distance and it stopped
as he lowered her to her feet and kissed her as if
he would never stop. . . .

"Come, Michaels. I believe it is necessary to interrupt this happy scene. For you see, I have a plan,
and this fantastic plot must be executed before Linness reaches Beaumont's gates. . . ."

Clair kept glancing out the window, waiting for
Jean Luc to return before she picked up her sewing
again, working quietly in the comfort of her very
own room. Beaumont was not at all like Gaillard.
First of all, there were over thirty rooms in the main
house. She had been given one of them. Not in the
whole of her life had she ever had her own room.
Like a lady.

The thought made her shake her head with wonder.

Not only that, but she had a four-poster featherbed, a rich green coverlet, an armoire for the new
gowns she was making, a table, sitting chairs. Like
a lady, all of it like a lady. At first she had been
alarmed by it, the enormity of Lord Paxton's generosity, and she had even wondered if there wasn't
a mistake. She was a servant, after all, not really a
lady in waiting as Linness had always pretended,
but a simple waiting woman. Between the two

stretched a gulf as wide as the North Channel.

Then she thought, who was she to point out mistakes?

The fact remained—Beaumont was a grand place. There was no keep nor battlements, for it was now impossible to imagine a hostile army's march into the secured borders of France. The old style of building was obsolete. Gaillard's château had been built from an old castle and had retained many of these elements: the battlements and wall walk and keep. Not so Beaumont.

It was a white structure, built of local sandstone and brick. There was the main building with four large towers built around what Lord Paxton said was a too large courtyard. The kitchen had four ovens. Linness would marvel at the glorious modern buildings, the carpeted rooms, the wide hallways, the windows everywhere, the fifty or so servants, and especially the lawns. How she would love the gardens! And the food, too. From her long-ago days as a peasant, the Lady Linness always loved her food, and even that was grander here, fit for the king himself. Instead of Gaillard's more common maslin, they had expensive wheat bread every night, the cream was as plentiful as water, and the possets, soups, and pottages were delicious. The chef had been recommended by Francis himself. Beaumont had its very own bird catcher, who put fresh fowl on the table almost every night. All the dishes seemed new and exotic.

If only Linness could see Beaumont. She wondered if she would ever get to see it. Originally they had thought she could squeeze a visit out of Morgan once a year to see Jean Luc. No more. He'd never let her go now. And so 'twas why Beaumont, even with all its modern convenience and beauty, could not keep Clair from longing to return to Gaillard. Just to tell Linness all that was here, to see her again and try to ease the sorrow of her days.

She shook her head sadly. She never did believe in happy endings. Not in real life anyway.

A trumpet sounded from the guardhouse, warning of an approaching visitor. Not just the town's butcher either. It had to be someone important, she knew.

She set down her sewing and went to the window that overlooked the enormous courtyard. Down the road through the archway she spotted a coach approaching. She knew that coach, the two weary-looking creatures pulling it. Lord John Chamberlain was arriving.

Clair stared down at it heatedly. John Chaberlain had returned from Italy and he would have with him Lord Paxton's wife. She hoped the lady had a pox-marked face, crossed eyes, and scraggly hair. She hoped her figure was as wide as a cow's or as narrow as a reed. She didn't wish the lady dead exactly but maybe just injured. A nice brick on the head ought to do it.

If only she had one.

Some of the servants gathered on the steps—the head housekeeper, the chef, a number of the maids, the dairy maid. She abruptly noticed Lord Paxton's horse and Jean Luc's pony tied to the back. They must have met on the road. But the young man riding alongside looked like Michaels—

It was Michaels!

Perhaps John Chamberlain first stopped at Gaillard! He would have news of Linness.

She started running. She raced out the door and

down the hall, flying down the steps into the entrance hall and finally into the courtyard. A fresh breeze blew her hair in her face and she pushed it aside, watching not the coach but Michaels. He was dismounting, opening the carriage door. She could hardly wait to speak to Michaels.

Lord Paxton emerged from the carriage. He looked to the people gathered, more still arriving, racing from all corners of the estate for this long-awaited event. Clair, in the back, caught sight of the lord's strange smile, the light of excitement in his eyes. He half looked like he had been crying for joy. As if he were pleased.

By his new wife?

Indignation colored her cheeks, her mouth pressed to a hard line. She didn't understand. Even less as John and Jean Luc came out beside him, both of them smiling the same kind of wicked smile. "Good people," Lord Paxton said in his deep, rich voice, "I should like you to meet my wife, the Lady Beatrice Lucia Calabria Nuovo, now Chamberlain."

He reached into the coach and took her hand to help her out. Clair held her breath. First a violet slipper appeared, then a familiar pattern of skirts.

Linness stood up.

Clair's knees went weak. She caught herself from fainting and instead stared, just stared. From the corner of her eyes, she caught Jean Luc's stare. The boy winked conspiratorially.

She knew that wink.

Lord, she was getting too old for this. . . .

Paxton was introducing Linness to the new faces. She looked beautiful, the lord's new bride, a beauty more pronounced by the giddiness, the laughter, the happiness bubbling over. She was obviously a happy bride. And the groom! He looked just as happy, more even, obviously overjoyed by the sight of the lady, his beautiful new wife. She nodded, taking hands when they were offered. The chef asked in Italian how her trip was. She laughed, "The good sisters only spoke French and Latin. I fear my own native tongue is practically forgotten."

Clair almost laughed at this. She had no idea how it happened; she could reasonably guess any number of unlikely scenarios. The fact remained. Despite all else, the girl was smooth; she had always been as smooth as the king's pudding.

Linness finally reached Clair. With eyes that shone brightly with happiness and tears, Linness said, "And you, madame, must be Jean Luc's nurse?"

Clair decided she might as well make her lady perspire, just a little. "How did you know?"

"He rode with me through the gates. He told me all about you. . . ."

"Did he? In such a short time?"

"Indeed—"

She never finished. Paxton, certain he was dreaming, still quite unable to absorb all that had happened in the last half hour, could wait no more. He reached under her and, laughing, swept her up in his arms. " 'Tis a tradition in our country for the groom to carry the bride through the doorway to the bedchambers—"

Everyone parted happily for the lord and lady, smiling at the good fortune, Lord Paxton's understandable eagerness, the bride's blushing modesty as he carried her into the entrance hall and proceeded hurriedly, without interruption, up the stairs and down the hall to his apartments.

The sound of their laughter quieted as the door shut.

Paxton set her on the bed. Her hair spread in a riot of dark color over the bedclothes. He came on top of her. For a long moment they just stared at each other.

"I'm dreaming," he finally said as his senses filled with the heaven-made sweetness of her scent and the warmth of her body beneath him. "From the moment I first saw you running to us, throughout the hasty explanations, John's mad plotting, then presenting you as my wife, all the way until now, I keep thinking I am dreaming, that it can't possibly be true. I keep thinking any moment I will wake and you will be gone. Linness." He kissed her mouth and closed his eyes to confess, "I am afraid. . . ."

Her silver eyes filled with sadness and pity.

There were no words that could ease his fear, for she felt it, too. Just seeing him, feeling his hand travel over her face and neck, over and over as if to reassure himself she really lay there, brought a surging sense of joy, but some bewilderment, too. For it was too good to be true. Their fortune had shifted too dramatically for easy comprehension; it would take time to adjust to their changed fates.

Fortunately they had the rest of their lives.

She suddenly slipped from beneath his arms and rose from the bed, and as he watched her, he thought again, it was a dream. "Linness," he murmured in this dream.

He watched as she reached her thin arms behind her back to the buttons. His favorite dress because it came off the quickest. Lord, how he loved that dress. It slipped off her shoulders and fell into a pile at her feet.

He felt another rush of heat to his loins. More as he watched her undo the laces of her undergarments, ripping the bodice laces and pulling that off, stepping out of the whole. The dream was alarming for its vividness of detail.

He stared at the naked beauty shrouded in firelight.

He still made no move, waiting for the apparition to leave, disappear, vanish into the air from which it emerged. "I must be mad now. . . ."

The words made her stop and stare as the magnitude of this point crashed through her consciousness. She had come so terribly far. She understood in sudden clarity her whole life was lived to reach this one point. She had stood on a cliff, overlooking a deep and dark death, waiting for a push over the side, but instead of falling, against all expectation and cruel turns of fate, she discovered she did in fact have wings for flight. . . .

She said, strangely, in a whisper of tears, "I am your wife now." She smiled as another tear escaped from the corner of her eyes. "I am here now and . . . forever. Forever, Paxton." In a compelling whisper still, she added, "When Morgan freed me, when he let me go, Michaels and I rushed through the days and nights to reach you here. During that whole time only one thought sustained me, and that was this moment. The moment when I told you that I am yours forever, for each blessed day of our lives, bound by our love . . . forever. . . ."

The words turned over slowly in his mind.

He didn't understand the jolt of his heart, numbing in its intensity. Not yet. He still thought he might be dreaming, that this was an even crueler trick, that this was the newest form his madness had taken. In all his life he never felt more fear than at that moment. For he was afraid if he stood up and reached for her, she would fade into the stark white walls behind her.

She was a dream too wonderful to be real. . . .

She stepped to the bed. Tension worked into every fiber of his being as she came over him. Her hands braced against his shoulders as she straddled him; he felt the shocking and real warmth where her softness touched him. The perfume of her hair penetrated his senses as he stared at the firelit features of her face, the love shining from her tear-filled eyes as her mouth lowered to touch his lips, once, lightly, before she drew back, opening her eyes to study his reaction.

"Linness, I am dreaming. . . ."

"The only dream that ever mattered, milord. I'll kiss you again to see if we wake. . . ."

Afterword

❧ ∽∼ ◯✣◯ ∼∽ ❧

This book is unlike any other I have written. As I was doing research on Mont Saint Michel, France, hoping to set my next novel there, and reading through historical books on sixteenth-century France, I came across an intriguing reference to a young girl, one of the last women condemned to die at the stake on the charge of witchery. The reference was written by a famous theologian and it included a nobleman's response to the rumors that claimed his paternal grandmother was this very same girl who was tried and condemned by the church for the practice of witchcraft. Intrigued, I began a search for more details about her extraordinary life.

The fantastic facts are mercilessly bare and brief, with only the most significant occasions marking the timetable of her life. As one of her grandsons wrote many years later in the late sixteenth century, he could not in faith deny the old rumor. He would only say that if his grandmother's life constituted a stain on his family's honor, so be it, for the subsequent generations who grew and thrived from this red mark owed its very lives to the shining light of his grandparents' extraordinary love.

The curious reader will want to know the bare facts of our heroine's life. All that is known is that she was born poor and fatherless, and like many peasants at that time, she did not have a surname. She was placed in a convent as soon as her startling powers were perceived; she was said to be a seer, and touched by miraculous visions of Mary, the very things that eventually brought the church's powerful wrath upon her and condemned her to die at the stake. The girl was rescued from this cruelest of deaths by the valiant sword of a young nobleman, who was said to have fallen deeply in love with her. The theologian had found three different priests who claimed to have witnessed her rescue. Facts leave us at this point. There is no explanation of how she—a mere peasant—came to be married to the young nobleman's older brother. Nor are there details of her years of marriage, though records of the family's vineyard harvest were scrupulously kept during these years.

Her death, too, is shrouded in mystery. She was said to have inexplicably disappeared in a river after a series of miraculous visions, but that she was actually dead was disputed by the church for many years. All we know is that within weeks after this disappearance, her lover, a man of considerable wealth and landed titles, met with his Italian bride for the first time, and this woman bore a remarkable similarity to his brother's recently deceased wife.

There are a number of historical references made to the family on which this story is based. (The name has been fictionalized and there are numerous descendants in France, the United States, and Canada who can trace their family history back to this sixteenth-century beginning.) Many of these references allude to the rumor that the lady was not of noble birth.

One reference seems particularly interesting. It was taken from a collection of letters written by the Italian ambassador to the French court. This man had returned from abroad where he stayed with numerous distinguished members of the French nobility. Most of the following letter concerned wine production, but he also said this about the lady of the manor:

> . . . I must confess, after meeting her, my suspicions mounted. She does not look Italian, though that is not damning by itself, as many northern Italians are quite fair. She has a lovely pearl complexion and indescribable pale-colored eyes; a gray color, neither blue nor metallic, somehow suffused with the sun's warmth. Despite the fact that she is well past the first blush of youth, nearing thirty-five years, I found her more beautiful than even the rumors claimed. For there is that special light about her, commonly considered an "inner beauty."
>
> The Lady has given her husband three sons. These boys were exhausting, wild boys each, like the older uncle, from whose constant rebellion both parents seemed to derive endless amusement. The Lady swore she loves nothing more than spending the better part of her day chasing them down, which she does even though she recently gave birth to a baby girl, a dark haired, blue-eyed child, who seems the very light of her parents' lives. They christened the child Joy, which seems strange to an Italian, but as you well know, there is no accounting for French tastes (with the noteworthy excep-

tion of their wines, of course). Most of my suspicions, however, arose with the astonishing discovery that she can speak no Italian. The lady claims she has been away so long, she has completely forgotten her native tongue. She only laughed at my shocked bafflement . . .

And from this humble outline of the bare facts, I invite readers to draw their own conclusions on the veracity of the story of Linness of Sauvage, a simple peasant girl who rose through the grand corridors of French nobility to at last fulfill a remarkable destiny and claim the greatest treasure of all. . . .

Avon Romantic Treasures

Unforgettable, enthralling love stories, sparkling with passion and adventure from Romance's bestselling authors

CAPTIVES OF THE NIGHT *by Loretta Chase*
76648-5/$4.99 US/$5.99 Can

CHEYENNE'S SHADOW *by Deborah Camp*
76739-2/$4.99 US/$5.99 Can

FORTUNE'S BRIDE *by Judith E. French*
76866-6/$4.99 US/$5.99 Can

GABRIEL'S BRIDE *by Samantha James*
77547-6/$4.99 US/$5.99 Can

COMANCHE FLAME *by Genell Dellin*
77524-7/ $4.99 US/ $5.99 Can

WITH ONE LOOK *by Jennifer Horsman*
77596-4/ $4.99 US/ $5.99 Can

LORD OF THUNDER *by Emma Merritt*
77290-6/ $4.99 US/ $5.99 Can

RUNAWAY BRIDE *by Deborah Gordon*
77758-4/$4.99 US/$5.99 Can

Avon Romances—
the best in exceptional authors
and unforgettable novels!